TOBY MORBY AND THE CR/

(A CHRONICLE OF ALEXANDRIA)

(Book 1)

By
R.L.Sherlock

ISBN-13: 978-1978317192

In conjunction with Ralph L Sherlock,

Published (2017) by HawkMedia

53 Stucley Road

Bideford

Devon

Ex393eq

http://www.hawkmedia.co.uk

10-03-2018

Dedication

'To Caroline for all the years of friendship and Nikki for pressing the return key at The End'.

Chapter One – The Party

The buzz was all around the house. In the garden children were running, jumping and whooping! Tracey Waltbeck tripped and fell headlong onto the ground scraping her knee and sat crying. Tracey was always tripping and falling. She was a small, plumpish figure of ten years old. She had been at St. Claire's Village Junior School in the small Village of Little Farthingworth for almost six years. She had started school at five years old during September of that year. She was rather a loner type of child with very few friends.

The only reason for her being at the party was due to her Mother being friends with the Hostess. Tracey cried and as usual, her Mother Lynn came running over to pick her up and give her a hug. Rachel was watching from the Kitchen and came out to Lynn, telling her to bring Tracey into the Kitchen to clean up her knee and put a sticking plaster upon it.

This was a Birthday Party, a kid's Birthday Party, so scrapes were just to be expected. Tracey was soon patched up, her eyes dried and she was sent back out to re-join the festivities. Inside the house, in the Dining Room, was a large, long oak table which stood at the centre of the large, long room. Upon the table was to be found a plethora of plates and bowls filled full with cakes, jelly with ice cream, sweets and other goodies. Along both sides of the table was a row of chairs, with a clear space at the centre of the table. At either end of the table was another chair. Underneath the piles of plates, bowls and food could be found the table cloth which was white with blue checks and covered the table.

In the Kitchen the Parents of the children playing out in the garden were busy rallying around preparing the feast and getting it ready including the Birthday Cake with thirteen candles upon it. Then Carl Morby gave the signal to his wife Rachel, that all was set. Rachel then walked to the Kitchen door and into the hallway. She walked out of the rear door of the house and stood in the porch, and then she called to Toby, who was sitting upon the Patio steps.

"Toby Dear, would you organise the children to come in now for the Birthday Tea please" asked Rachel

Rachel stood and smiled, as before Toby was able to hardly move, he prepared himself to speak but was instantly drowned out by the loud excited cheering and a big whoop! In their excited rush to get to into the house and tuck into the greatly awaited Birthday Tea, the kids almost mowed down poor Toby as they rushed past him cheering in a scene reminiscent of a cattle stampede!

Rachel couldn't help but laugh a little as the cloud of children flew past her into the house. Toby was left all alone standing in the falling dust cloud which surrounded him, looking somewhat bewildered!

He stood there upon the Patio for a few moments, flagging the dust cloud from his face and blinking. Then he decided to walk slowly up the steps to the porch where Rachel put her hand around his shoulder and lead him into the house. Toby was now thirteen and not a kid any longer but a teenager. He knew that he would be starting school next term at the Big School after leaving St. Claires that summer. The Big School was Toadford School, just outside of the village in an old Manor house out on top of the Moor. It was tradition of Toadford House that the Students all joined the School when they were thirteen years old.

About five feet tall, slim with Blonde hair, which was short, freckle faced, Toby walked into the house with Rachel. He had been sitting outside watching the children play in his garden. The children he would leave behind at St. Claires who, as their Parents were not able to afford the fees at Toadford, would otherwise attend St. Marks College in nearby Cranleigh.

Toby was one of the lucky ones of Little Farthingworth, his Grandfather being the Lord of the Manor, was paying his School fees for him. This at first upset Rachel, who didn't wish to accept the 'Charity' of her Father-in-law's gesture but soon Rachel came around to the idea, as she was told that the fees would be difficult to keep up on Carl's and her wage as a teacher at St. Claires, the only logical thing to do would be to let him pay the fees; after all, Toby was his Grandson and he wished to see him obtain the best education available, also it was tradition that the Morby boys attend Toadford School.

Toby was wearing his Birthday clothes consisting of the Football Strip of blue shirt and white shorts with red stockings of his favourite team, Frackston City. Like his Father Carl, Toby had been a Frackston City Fan for as long as he could remember. He would often go to the short distance into the city of Frackston to the Football stadium with his Father to watch the team play. They would try to get to see as many games as possible on Saturdays, when they were out at matches, his Mom Rachel, would have a leisurely afternoon watching soppy weepies and devouring chocolates in between household chores.

Carl had been called lucky by his friends for being able to 'pull' such a stunning 'Babe' as Rachel, as she was the most beautiful girl in Frackston and at Toadford School. Rachel had long Blonde hair and striking blue eyes. Rachel was five feet seven and slim, Carl was a lucky man indeed. That was fifteen year ago now but Rachel was just as stunning now as she was back then.

The children were standing in the large hallway outside the Dining Room while they waited for Toby to come and join them. Toby arrived with the pack of kids all fidgeting, waiting for their entry into the room and a chance to gorge on jelly, ice cream and cakes. Rachel stood by the door and ushered Toby to it. Both Carl and Rachel put their hands onto the handle of the door and smiled together. They then turned the door knob slowly, the door gradually opened and they gestured Toby through. He walked into the room with the big long table along its centre. On the walls hung paintings, pictures and photographs in frames draped with tinsel and balloons of red, white and blue of Frackston City colours. Toby's eyes lit up and shone at the sight of all the goodies upon the table. Rachel led him to the central seat nearest the wall. Down the other end of the room was a bay window filled with boxes in multi-coloured wrapping paper tied up with ribbons, the Birthday presents.

Toby took his seat all smiling and the rest of the kids were lead in and were shown to their seats along the wall side of the table either side of Toby's chair. Then the parents entered the room and walked over to their seats along the table opposite the kids. Rachel took her seat at the window end of the table and Carl took his seat at the door end of the table. There was one empty seat, which was for Toby's Grandfather, Simon, who was now walking into the room approaching the table carrying the cake. The cake was shaped as a football pitch with a goal at each end and a figure of a Soccer player standing at the centre in the colours of Frackston City. Simon carefully placed the cake in the empty space upon the table in front of Toby, making sure he didn't drop it. He took a box of matches from his pocket and struck one, placing it to the wick of one of the thirteen candles on top of the cake. The candle lit into a tall yellow flame and Simon repeated this with all of the remaining candles. Paul Joyce, who was seated two seats to Toby's left, a smallish thin boy with round rimmed glasses, watched as the flames took hold of the wicks in the candles and grew. Paul was ten years old and known to be fascinated by fire and had been luckily, caught with matches a few times before he could burn down his Parents house; Paul loved watching flames.

Toby stood and looked into the flames of the candles. He thought that he could see something within the flames, a kind of fuzzy picture. As he looked, he could see the figure moving around. Toby blinked a couple of times, the picture was gone. Toby didn't dwell upon the matter and prepared himself for the next task. The enthroned gathering sang "Happy Birthday" to Toby and then to a chorus of cheers and applause, Toby leaned forwards and took a deep breath. He then exhaled and blew upon the candles, quickly extinguishing all of the thirteen candles in front of him, remembering to make his secret wish as he did so.

Simon Morby had lived at Pegasus House in Bogart Street, Little Farthingworth for many years. In fact, for as long as anyone was able to remember, he had always lived there. He had once been married with a wife, Katherine, who sadly died three years earlier, when Toby was ten years old. A strange thing was that no one was able to remember exactly when Simon had come to own the house? Simon tells everyone that his family moved into the house before the war but never specifies which war? Most of the elderly people of the village say that as long as they can remember that Simon's family had been at the house. The House stood in its own grounds, a large Gothic looking façade betraying a large a hidden structure of part medieval and Jacobite additions. The long hallway where the children had gathered with its many off shooting rooms, as one entered through the front doors, after walking up the steps to the Portico porch; the hallway lead off in front.

Upon the walls of the hallway were more pictures and paintings. To the right of the hallway were doors which lead into the Dining Room, Lounge and Carl's Library. Between the Dining Room door and Lounge door raised up a large magnificent staircase with a minstrel's gallery at the top and then it descended again the other side of the hallway. The staircase was ornately carved from Oak and descended with the patina of age. In fact, the whole look and feel of the house was one of age. Behind the staircase to the back of the hallway was the Kitchen on the right hand side with the door leading out to the rear garden. To the left was a door of old dark Oak beneath the staircase which leads into the West Wing of the house. Up the stairs was a long landing which covered the width of the hallway. The landing curved around the wall next to the staircase against the East Wing, where there was a Bedroom, then the Bath Room and around the corner was another three Bedrooms, which all were above the study, Dining Room and Lounge.

The room to the front was the Master Bedroom, which was over the Dining Room. This was the room where Carl and Rachel slept. It was large with a double bed and bedside cabinets either side. To one side of the Bay Window, to the front of the room was Rachel's dressing table with three large mirrors. On its top were laid out her makeup, hair brushes and jewellery box, which Carl had bought for her as a tenth wedding anniversary present.

Next along this side landing was a spare guest double Bedroom, which had a wardrobe, shower cubical and double bed with bedside table and chest of drawers, this was over the study. Behind that to the rear of the side landing was yet another guest double bedroom which was furnished the same way as the other.

The Bathroom had tiled walls of marble and floor, with under floor heating and a heated towel rail. There was a Bathroom suite in white which had two sinks and a bath with a Power Shower. This was because Toby and Carl liked to take a shower but in need of some relaxation, Rachel preferred a good soak in the bath. Next to this was Toby's Bed Room, which overlooked the rear garden.

Toby's Bedroom was the typical Boy's room. He had a single bed in the centre of the wall beside the door with a bedside table next to it. On his walls were comic strip Heroes upon posters and Frackston City football players upon posters. Hanging from the ceiling was a number of model aircraft which Toby had built from model kits. He had a chest of drawers and a wardrobe in white. It was difficult to see what colour the walls were due to all the posters covering them, but the few bare patches could be seen to be of pale blue. The Duvet cover upon Toby's bed was adorned with a big badge of Frackston City to one side; under the window was a writing desk where Toby liked to draw. On one end of the desk stood a completed model kit of a NASA Space Shuttle attached to its Boosters ready for launch. Lying in a corner was a Rugby ball and a Soccer ball, among a heap of dirty clothes which Rachel tried to ask Toby to put into the washing basket. He quite obviously did not understand the request.

Rachel was now thirty nine and had matured into a stunningly beautiful woman. Rachel had looked after herself very well and was quite fit. She seemed to age quite normally, her figure she had kept quite trim and exercised regularly to stay that way. Carl was quite proud that Rachel had stayed so beautiful and trim since giving birth to Toby.

Toby was a typical teenager now, angry, awkward, freckled and some would say cute. He seemed to be growing not unlike any normal teenager. Toby had the same likes and dislikes as any other teenager. His main interest was Frackston City Football Club. Then it was the trips to Taunton Cricket ground with his Father. Carl would drive them across the border into Somerset and they would spend the day watching the Cricket and then to the park for Ice cream and feeding the Ducks. It was always apparent that Carl and his Father were slower to age than those around them.

They finished the Birthday Tea, the children were like Locusts and had practically cleared the table and left a fallout of crumbed plates and jelly stuck to the table cloth. The feeding frenzy over, all the children were called to the bay window. Here Toby stood next to the pile of coloured ribboned boxes. One by one, Carl and Rachel handed them to the excited Toby. What wondrous treasures would be received? Would they be different to the normal presents that he received? After all, this was his thirteenth Birthday and he was starting Toadford School after the holidays. Toby received each present happily and bright eyed, tearing open the wrapping paper and revealing the boxes containing the present.

A Computer! Now that he was moving up to the Big School to Toadford, he would need something to do all that home work on. It was a Desk Top Computer with a nineteen inch screen. Toby would be boarding at Toadford, but this was to do his homework upon in the holidays when he returned home. Toby was thrilled at this, the best present he had ever had! There was another present, a guitar, as Toby would be taking lessons while at School; then some clothes and a new pair of football boots. He also opened a set of Cricket pads and a new bat. The last few presents which Toby opened were model kits to add to his collection. Once the Party was over it was time for all of Toby's guests to leave. They all retrieved their coats and then said goodbye and thanked Toby and his Parents individually before walking out into the Portico porch and down the steps to their Parents cars. Some walked down the driveway towards the road with their Parents as they didn't live far down the road from Pegasus House.

Away down the drive went the Parents cars and out through the gates onto Bogart Street. Most turned to the right and drove off towards Little Farthingworth Village, others turned to the left and drove off towards the Moor. Toby felt tired after all the excitement of the day; he was also keen to set up his new computer before he went to bed. He said his goodnights to Rachel, Carl and Simon, gave them each a hug, then Toby walked up the stairs and into his Bedroom, carrying his presents.

Toby walked into the room and put down the presents onto his bed. This enabled him to sort through them, so that he could put them away in their respective places. He put the clothes away in their draws and wardrobe, then he put the Model kits away in his toy cupboard to wait for him to build them. Then it was the turn of his new Computer. He took it out of its box, putting the monitor onto the desk top under the window. He then placed the CPU under the desk and put the keyboard and mouse onto the desk top. He connected up all of the wires and put the plug into the socket beside the desk.

Toby had removed the old defunked computer from the desk top; Carl would find an appropriate place to dispose of this. Toby sat for a while starting up the computer and updating the settings to his personal preferences. Toby took out the software from a draw and began to install it onto the new computer. Once he had done this, he tried out some of the functions, just to orientate himself with any new features on this machine that were different from his old one. After he familiarised himself with some of the new functions of the computer, Toby then shut it down and turned it off. He then changed and got into bed. Once his head hit the pillow Toby was soon asleep. It wasn't long before that familiar dream came to Toby, the one which always left him unnerved. Through the haze of sleep, Toby could see the usual elements of the dream. He was running through woodland, he was alone, it was misty. Suddenly through the trees a swift Hawk appeared and swooped down upon him, and then it all went black. This dream often came to Toby and was a recurrent dream. Toby could not remember afterwards, but when it came, it was always the same dream.

Simon said his good nights to Carl and Rachel, who were sitting in the Lounge watching TV upon the sofa.

"Well, it's been a long day and I can hear my bed calling to me. I have an early start tomorrow, so I won't disturb you when I leave" Said Simon.

"Another Business trip, Dad?" Rachel asked, quizzically.

Carl looked quickly between Rachel and Simon and then said;

"Good night Father, sleep well and have a good trip tomorrow." Said Carl.

"Good night Dad" Said Rachel.

Rachel liked to call Simon Dad; it made her feel more part of his family. Since Katherine had died, Simon seemed to always be away on Business trips, what his Business was she didn't know and was too polite to stick her nose in and ask.

Rachel was a Teacher at St. Claires Junior School in Little Farthingworth. After Toadford, she had gone to Exeter University, so that she didn't have to travel far from home to return to Frackston during holidays. She then attended Teacher Training College at Tiverton. Rachel then got the job at St. Claires so that she could spend time with Carl. After Leaving University, she married Carl after a five year romance. Three years later, Toby was born. It seemed strange that Carl looked hardly any older than he did when Toby was born. Even though he was now forty years old, he only looked to be in his late twenties to early thirties. The same was true with Simon, no matter how long Rachel had known him; he always seemed to be in his mid to late Sixties and seemed to age very slowly. Rachel just simply thought that this was a family trait of all the Morby men. Simon left the Lounge and walked out into the hallway. He then turned and walked across to the door under the stairs which lead into a smaller, older West Wing. This was Simon's part of the house and only Simon entered the West Wing. Upon Marriage, Simon had agreed that with the prospect of raising a family, that Carl and Rachel would occupy the East Wing. After Katherine's death, Simon spent more time in the West Wing alone rather than with the family, Rachel, at first had been saddened by this but after Carl had told her it was Simon's way of grieving, Rachel had put the thought out of her head. She was now used to Simon 'disappearing' for a few days every so often upon his 'Business trips'.

Pegasus House had stood for a long time, in its different stages, for centuries. It had always been the house for the Lord of the Manor. Before him Simon's Father had been Lord of the Manor.

The house stood just outside the main centre of the village of Little Farthingworth. The Village stood to the south of the Manor and to the north of the town of Cranleigh. They were satellites to the small city of Frackston. Frackston was not a city for its size, but due to the Cathedral at its centre. Bogart Street led down from Pegasus House into Little Farthingworth Village. A short distance along the street was a line of small Cobb cottages. The Village had a Square at its centre with streets radiating off from here in a cross shape. Off the four main streets were a number of side streets with cottages. The streets horizontally across the village through the centre either side of the central Square were to the East, Lower High Street and to the West, Upper High Street. Here were located the small shops of the village. To the north was the Parish Church and Village Hall, which stood upon the beginning of Bogart Street. Also in Bogart Street could be found the War Memorial and a small park. Here could be found some of the oldest buildings in the village, including Pegasus House. To the South was Cranleigh Street, which led out of the village to the nearby town of Cranleigh and then continued on to Frackston and then Exeter. Most of the older inhabitants of the Village didn't like to venture the mile or so up Bogart Street on foot, they would rather avoid this part of the village. Simon had attended Toadford School when he was a boy, as had his Father before him.

Chapter Two – The School Run

This morning was the usual rush for Carl. Out of bed after leaving the alarm clock to snooze too many times. A hurried shave and shower then down stairs. Rachel had prepared breakfast for everyone and Carl had eaten his. He put on his Body Warmer and green cap and quickly pecked Rachel on her lips to bid her goodbye. Carl then walked out of the door and down the porch steps to his new Landrover Discovery parked outside. Carl had not had his new car long. He learned to drive to look more part of the Lord of The Manor image, as Simon was away on Business, Carl needed to drive for his own transport needs. The Bus service to Little Farthingworth was not very reliable, so for their need of access to the nearby towns for work and their own personal freedom, most teenagers of the village learned to drive and obtained their licences soon after they were eighteen.

Carl had bought the Landrover to help him with his job as a Park Ranger upon the nearby National Park up on the Moor and, so he thought, it made him look Cool!

Carl had a busy day ahead working with the team fixing and re-enforcing an area of the Parkland. Carl began his job with the National Park when he left Toadford. He had told Simon, his Father, that he was the Lord of The Manor and that it was important for Carl to take on a simple job and one involving the National Park meant working in an environment with the countryside and wildlife which he had always had an interest in. Carl always enjoyed the short drive into work, especially on a fine day. Once out of the Village, it was onto the Moor. Firstly past the tall hedges made up of beech trees trimmed into thick hedges, then some occasional Hazel and Oak. Here and there being allowed to grow up above the hedges like lamp posts were Ash trees. Carl would then drive out from the hedges onto the open Moor, where the Heather and Bracken Fern grew as far as the eye could see. This was Carl's domain. Carl climbed into his car and sat in the driver seat, putting his jacket and lunch box onto the passenger seat beside him, pushed the key into the slot and turned it. The engine roared into life and he drove down the driveway, turned out of the gates onto the road and drove out to the left up to his work place upon the Moor.

Rachel had spent her waking morning so far preparing the breakfasts for Carl and Toby. She stopped briefly to eat some toast herself for her own breakfast. Then Toby came into the Kitchen and sat at the breakfast table. Once she was finished with the breakfast, Rachel then would take Toby to school and then go onto her own job as a Teacher at St. Claires Junior School in the village. Toby tucked into his bowl of Shreddies with milk and savoured each mouthful. This would be his last Breakfast in the house for some time. Toby contemplated this thought as he chewed each mouthful and a little shudder ran down his spine.

While he was enjoying his breakfast, Rachel made sure that Toby had packed his Ruc-Sac with all that he needed for his first day at his new school. He had packed the Ruc-Sac with the books he needed for his lessons. He also had packed a suitcase with the clothes which he would be wearing. Each student needed to identify their personal clothing, as it was laundered at the school and then returned to them. Rachel had sown name tags into everything so that Toby would not lose any of the, hopefully. Toadford was a Boarding school, so Toby would be spending the term times here and going home for the long Holidays such as Summer and Christmas. In the suitcase were uniforms, casual clothes and sports clothes. Toby finished his Breakfast and fetched his jacket. He didn't ware his Jacket as he would be travelling to School in his Mother's car. The weather was fine at the moment so no coats or jackets would be needed to be worn just now.

Toby carried his Ruc-Sac and suitcase out to Rachel's car, a Vauxhall Corsa, turquoise, which was referred to by the garage she bought it from as 'Sapphire Silver' but Toby just thought that this was posh talk for turquoise.

Toby walked up to the car and opened the back door, put his Ruc-Sac, jacket and suitcase onto the back seat and then closed the door. He then opened the front passenger door and climbed in to sit in the front passenger seat. Toby made himself comfortable and clipped his seatbelt into place across him. He reached into the glove box on the dash board and pulled out a CD to put in the car's CD player. Toby liked to go for car rides with Rachel. She was a good driver and he liked to chat to her as they journeyed along listening to CD's as they went. He had chosen a Jessie J CD, one of his favourites.

Rachel walked to the car, opened the driver door and climbed in to sit in the seat beside Toby at the steering wheel. She pulled the seatbelt across her and clicked it into place. She was almost ready for the off. Rachel put the key into the slot and turned it; the car started and on came the CD Player. Toby pressed the switch which brought out the tray, placed the disc onto it and pressed the button again. The tray holding the disc returned into the depths of the CD Player. Rachel put her foot down onto the accelerator pedal and the car moved forwards to the sound of Jesie J.

"So ..... time to be off the Big School for my little man" said Rachel. Toby smiled back at her as she drove down the drive way. Rachel stopped at the end.

"This is it ", smiled Toby "My introduction to Farthingworth Tradition!"

Rachel remembered her first day at Toadford, spotty, smelly boys all around who she didn't have the least bit of interest in. She made friends quite easily and soon had a small following as even then at thirteen, she was quite a cute, pretty girl. Rachel had been quite popular at school excelling in class, especially in English and in sports. She was also quite musical playing the guitar, piano and flute. It was her academia that shone most, why she went to University and Teacher Training College, the staff had always thought that Rachel would make a good Teacher.

Then Rachel met the guy who would change her life and be the Father of her Child. An unassuming quiet boy, the year above her. It was usually unheard of for a Grunt to be seen as anything else other than a Grunt by the higher classes, but Rachel was no ordinary Grunt. Carl liked nature and could be seen most of his time in between classes sitting outside with one or other creepy crawly running through his fingers and over his hands. He was so gentle with the creatures that this first attracted Rachel to him. The fact that he was not like the other boys, arrogant and obnoxious, but just himself and gentle. Also, he was slim with the beginnings of a six pack and well spoken. The more she got to know Carl, the more she fell for him. She would come to see the Cricket, Rugby and Football matches which he played in for the School teams and he would watch her play the Hockey and Net ball of which Rachel represented the school. Carl was quite the Athlete, eventually holding all the school athletics records. He especially proficient in the races was also unmatched, especially in the longer more endurance races. After leaving Toadford, Carl went to College on day release after joining the National Park. He and Rachel dated for five years; then one day Carl got down on one knee and popped the question. A Wedding was held on Carl's twenty first Birthday, a tradition in the Morby family.

Tradition was that the Heir to Pegasus house would marry upon his twenty fifth Birthday. Simon was a little uneasy about this but respected his Son and allowed the ceremony to take place at St. Martins Parish Church in the Village. Many people turned out to the Wedding including the Parish Council, all were there keen to see the Wedding of the heir to the Lord of The Manor and Hargus Eldridge was keen to get to the reception for the free beer and Buffet. Two years later, Toby was born to become Heir to Carl.

The car sat between the gate posts at the entrance to the driveway of Pegasus House. Atop the post on either side of the gates were the stone figures of Dragons, the Arms of the Morby family. Rachel pulled out into Bogart Street and turned to the North. Toby smiled at her and she smiled back. His journey into his new life had begun. She drove away from the Village on the Moorland Road. Toby looked in the wing mirror and watched Pegasus House disappear behind them. The car sped on for about five miles past hedgerows and field gates. They had been rising steadily and were now atop a ridge. Toby watched as Rachel came down in gear moving her hand on the gear stick and then raising it to the steering wheel to flick on the indicator switch. The little Vauxhall turned the corner and drove along a small one track lane. The lane was lined with Poplar trees and ran for about half a mile away from the Moorland Road. Rachel smiled as she turned the curve between the large stone gate posts, in through the tall iron gates. She was somewhat excited and somewhat sad. Excited to think that Toby was beginning a new chapter to his life at Toadford and sad to see her little boy growing up and moving on with his life. The big party was not only to mark Toby's journey into his teenage years but also to mark the transition from child to Toadford. Rachel knew that once at Toadford, Toby's life would never be the same and that he would begin his tutorial into adulthood. Like her, she knew that Toby would become a different person as he grew and learned new things and had new experiences, he would become his own person. Atop the gate posts could be seen a rather grotesque pair of Gargoyles, seemingly guarding the entrance.

13

Either side of them along the top of the wall at intervals, were more Gargoyles. It was as Toby had said, tradition for wealthier family's children to attend Toadford School but also tradition for the Students of not to tell of their time at the School to their children. This was partly due the past and partly due to Toadford wishing to keep an air of mystery for the new Students who join. Toadford was a mystery to all the Students who entered it's hallowed halls at the age of thirteen. Toby was excited as although he didn't know much about the School, only that his family had apparently always attended the School, he was excited also because he was now embarking upon his part of Little Farthingworth tradition. This was the first day of Toby's career at Toadford School, the first day of the rest of his life.

Rachel turned a corner and rounded a curve then drove into an open court yard area. Circular in shape with gravel, which was around a central fountain. Around the driveway was a number of flower beds with brightly coloured flowers to welcome the visitors. The only other thing featuring in the Court yard was the high stone wall which stood across the end of the circle. The wall was about fifteen feet high which stood across the end of the Court yard and was Crenulated across the top which gave the look of a Castle Curtain wall.

These were the fortifications that Toby had heard about, although he was not aware of why the School would have fortifications. The wall was constructed of large stone blocks which were worked to make a tight fit to strengthen the wall. In the centre of the wall was a large Oak gate, eight feet tall and four feet wide, it looked dry and cracked, it looked old.

At the gate stood a tall figure about six feet dressed in a Master's Robe with a Mortar Board hat. He had grey hair, that which was not under his hat. The lines on his face showed his age. This was Cederick Thybold, Deputy Head Master of Toadford School. Rachel stopped the car close to the gate and turned off the engine. Thybold walked over to the driver's door and opened it. He gestured Rachel to get out of the car. He then walked around to the passenger door. He opened it and gestured Toby to get out of the car. Toby stood up out of this seat and Thybold closed the car door. His old face smiled, he looked at Rachel;

"Well, hello Rachel Tanery" He said with a thin voice "so very nice to see you again"

"It's Rachel Morby now Sir, I married Carl Morby" She replied.

"Ah yes" answered Thybold, "I was aware of that Rachel," His eyes turned to Toby "So this must be young Master Morby" He said "He is your only Son?"

"Yes" Said Rachel, turning her gaze to the ground, "Toby is our only Son."

Rachel was a little saddened by the fact that the year before Toby was born she suffered a Miscarriage and lost a child. Toby was her only Son. Rachel was deep in thought about who the child would have been and what the child would have achieved in life had it continued and been born. She then heard Thybold speaking again.

"I should think his Grandfather would be proud to know another Morby is beginning his Journey through Toadford. Simon would be so proud I imagine, of this day when a new generation of Morby takes his place within these hallowed walls." Said Thybold. He had a look on his face of proud arrogance, like he was announcing that Toby was joining the Royal family or something. He also had a look in his eyes of more deep rooted things, knowing eyes that only a privileged few knew about.

Rachel knew some of the traditions of Toadford School, although she was not aware of most of its secrets, especially the biggest secret. The School was old and looked it and had deep rooted old traditions and even more deeper rooted secrets. Only the privileged few knew the secrets and that was how Toadford liked it.

Thybold motioned towards Toby to walk towards the large gate. Toby turned to Rachel before he joined Thybold.

"I'll see you at the end of term Mom; it's not that far away. I'll keep in touch and phone every chance I get" Said Toby.

This was the first time he had been away from home for a period of time and it now was beginning to pull at Rachel's heart strings and she was aware that her little boy, her baby, was moving into a new stage in his life which included her not being there to watch him grow so often as she had been up until now.

"Bye bye Mom, see you soon." Waved Toby, smiling across his face.

"Bye bye Toby Darling be good. Gonna miss you." Answered Rachel, who was now able to feel the lump growing in her throat and tightness in her chest. Rachel watched as her Son took his first steps into his new life and into Toadford. She could not help thinking that a new era was beginning not only for her, Toby and her family but for Toadford School and Little Farthingworth. She somewhat dreaded this thought as it made her unnerved to think of their entire world changing and moving into a new episode. Slowly Toby walked away from Rachel who gradually finger by finger let go of his hand. She watched Toby as he walked away into his new life dressed in his new School uniform with crisp white shirt and Toadford Tie, bright blue with a golden Dragon Motif. At first the new Students who joined Toadford wore the School tie on their first day. Over this he wore a black Scholar's Gown, black trousers and black shoes, all shiny from where he had shined them up that morning. Toby crunched across the gravel and then reached the big gate together with Thybold. Standing there at the large Oak gate. Toby turned one more time to face Rachel and waved. Thybold smiled. Rachel, choking back her tears, waved back to him and smiled. This would be her last view of her Son for a few months. Thybold reached out and took hold of the big black ring which hung approximately chest height upon the gate, with his right hand and lifted it. He brought it down upon the gate twice, knocking loudly.

Chapter Three – First Day at Toadford

Toby and Thybold stood at the gate; the two knocks echoiong now dying out. The large Oak gate began to swing open and light appeared through a gap between the gate and the frame. Toby watched as it swing open to reveal a small paved court yard, where a throng of new Students were standing.

Also accompanying them could be seen Cragus T Parfinkle – Head Master of Toadford School. Accompanying Parfinkle were some of the other Staff at the School. Standing ready to greet the new students were John Cracken, Science Master; Eberneezer Finkle, English Master; Abbigail Norwall, Art Master; James Marden, Boys Games Master and Susan Olden, Girls Games Master. Cragus T Parfinkle had been head Master at Toadford School for twenty years and in normal circumstances would have been pensioned off long ago. He had been a pupil at Toadford many years ago and had taught at the School for twenty years before becoming Head Master. He had been familiar to the traditions of Toadford for most of his life. As Head Master, he was also keeper of its deepest secrets.

John Cracken taught Science at Toadford and had been a teacher there for fifteen years. Eberneezer Finkle was the English Master and had taught at the School for twenty years. As a member of the Master's Committee, who ran the School, he was also subject to some of the secrets of the School. Eberneezer was not much liked by the Students and he did not much like them either. It was during Eberneezer's class that a great deal of the Students pranks took place.

Abbigail Norwall, the Art Master, had only recently joined the School three years previously, but as she was the daughter of the previous Art Master, She was the replacement upon the Master's Committee when he had died. Abbigail did not attend the School, but it was her Father who had secured her the job with Parfinkle shortly before he died. Abbigail had been educated in Exeter and had been to University at Cambridge. She returned to the area when her Father had been taken ill five years ago and took over as Art Master when he had retired due to ill health. The circumstances of his illness were a mystery to all, save Parfinkle and the Committee.

James Marden, another of the Committee, was the Boys Games Master. He was a Toadford man and in his time there had been the Captain of the Soccer team, Cricket team and Rugby team. He was a Toadford man through and through and believed in training the boys to the highest standard. The worst case scenario to Marden was to lose out to the neighbouring High School in Cranleigh or one of the Schools in Frackston. His one dream was to win any of the sports in the Devonshire Cups and maybe to win one of the National Cups.

Susan Olden was the Girls Games Master. Like James, She was a Toadford Girl and had been with the School for most of her life. She did at one time have the opportunity to leave when she fell in love with Stuart, but he had not been enough for her to give up the School for. They had contemplated Marriage but the pull of Toadford left her a spinster. She was still young enough though, to find another. Like Abbigail, she was in her early thirties and was not in any way too old. Attractive, athletic as her games lessons with the Girls kept her and a good teacher. She was also fiercely Toadford in competing just as James was with the Boys.

Cederick Thybold had been Deputy Head Master for ten years, following on from Peter Farquinson who took over from Parfinkle when he was made up to Head Master. Peter Farquinson had disappeared suddenly and had never been seen again. One day he was at the School and then he had vanished? No One knew what fate had befallen him; at least no one was aware of any one who knew. Thybold was now in his late fifties and was looked upon as possibly the natural successor to Parfinkle when he finally handed the reins over to his next Incumbent of Head Master. Cederick was also on the Committee and being Deputy Head, was privy to the secrets of the School; well some of them.

It was necessary for only a small number of people to know the secrets, as the School held its position of class in the education system and its local reputation by means that certain things remained secret and not in the public domain. Thybold was tall, some six feet four and thin. He was going grey and had lost some hair from his forehead. He had long piano player fingers, which he liked to point at pupils when he caught them misbehaving.

Toby was last to arrive of 'The new Batch' of Students. He and Thybold joined the group walking from the gate across the court yard to where they were standing. The Collective were now complete, all the new Students for this term had arrived and were now standing in the outer court yard to the School.

Chapter Four – The Crash

The large Oak gate swung closed and the scene inside was hidden from Rachel's view. A scene she knew very well from her own first day experience upon arrival. She remembered that it was nerve racking and a little frightening to be entering such an institution as Toadford. She had gotten used to the place in her time there. Her Holidays spent back home in Frackston. Rachel had not been back to the School since leaving to go to college and then onto Exeter University. The only time she had really left Frackston was to go on Honeymoon with Carl, to Paris and to move into Pegasus House. She wasn't one for foreign Holidays and so on; Rachel believed that if you wanted Countryside, then Devon had the best to offer across Dartmoor and Exmoor. If one wanted the beach, there was plenty to choose from not far away, Woolacombe, Croyde and Westward Ho! in the North then Beer and Dawlish in the South, maybe a venture to Weymouth across the border in Dorset.

Rachel stood and looked at the gate in the wall for a long moment. Her little boy was now on the other side of that gate beginning his turn to grow up within those walls. She let out an audible sigh and turned to walk back to her car. Rachel opened the drive side door, sat in the seat behind the steering wheel and wiped a tear from her eye. Then she built up the courage to start the engine. She had to leave now and leave her Son at the School. She put her foot onto the accelerator and released the break. The car pulled forwards and she drove around the fountain the gravel crunching under the tires. Rachel turned the steering wheel and the car headed back along the Poplar lined driveway towards the main road. Through the gate posts she went and along the lane. She reached the junction of the lane and the Moorland Road and flicked on her indicator switch; she turned the car and pulled out towards Little Farthingworth Village. Rachel was thinking about leaving her Son at the School and how empty and quiet the house would be without him. She was deep in thought and failed to notice the truck looming large in her mirror. Suddenly with a thud- screech of breaks – crash, Rachel felt the car lurch forwards as though a huge hand had suddenly pushed it. She felt the pressure of the side of the car begin to press into her as the car turned sideways across the radiator grill of the truck. She felt the car being shunted sideways and when the wheels no longer turned and their sides gripped the road surface, Rachel felt the pressure upon her legs of the whole forward section collapsed and wrapped itself around them. She felt the swimming movement and heard the screeching of the tortured mental bending as the little car suddenly flipped into the air and tumbled along the road, shards of shattered windscreen flying everywhere. The truck had jack-Knifed upon impact when its driver had seen what was taking place and he jammed on his brakes. The horror before him as the little Vauxhall had tumbled down along the road, each turn denting more and more of the car.

The Scene fell silent as the car came to a stop and its tumbling halted. The little Vauxhall rocked slightly a few times until it completely came to a stop. As the dust cloud made by the tumbling of the car settled, the scene became clearer. The truck driver climbed gingerly down from his cab. He was somewhat shaken by the impact of the collision. He had sat in the cab watching the dust cloud clear to see more clearly the aftermath of the incident. The moments were agonising to him as he sat watching the small hatchback tumbling away in front of him. The truck driver walked slowly towards the car, through the debris which littered the road.

He walked through the pieces of discarded metal and glass which was strewn from the point of impact up to the car. The driver took his time carefully approaching the stricken vehicle with caution just in case there was a risk of the car exploding. He looked at his truck and saw the gash across the radiator grill with streaks of Sapphire Silver paint scraped across it. He continued along the road to where the crumpled car lay broken upon its side, the only movement from one of the front wheels which was still slowly turning. The truck driver walked slowly up to the car, wary of the possibility that the fuel tank may be ruptured.

He couldn't smell any petrol, so he thought it was relatively safe to proceed. He was on edge, not only from the collision but from the possible need to suddenly turn and run away in a hurry. He peered inside the car. Still strapped in her seat he was able to see Rachel. Her seat belt held her to her seat. She was unconscious; a head wound was visible upon her forehead and showed a streak of blood running down her face upon the right hand side. She had a broken nose which was now showing the darkened eye sockets typical of this injury, a gash across the bridge of her nose and blood visible from her nostrils. Also visible upon her face were a small number of cuts and bruises from the shattered windscreen glass and windows as the car had tumbled along the road.

The driver was able to see Rachel's top half of her body pinned to the seat, her head supported some what by the deployed air bag which was now beginning to deflate after doing its job. Rachel's lower half and legs were not visible easily to the truck driver as partially covered by the ebbing air bag, but also especially her legs, which were obscured by the crumpled front wing of the car which wrapped itself around them.

The truck driver was sure he could detect a fluttering in her closed eyelids, so he ran quickly back to his truck and climbed back into the cab. He picked up his Mobile phone out of the holder attached to the dashboard and dialled 999.

"Number 07795 374655 calling Emergency Operator" Came back upon the Mobile, "Which service do you require caller?"

"Ambulance", he stuttered out, "There's been an accident out upon the old Moorland Road, just at the junction of Poplar Lane. I think it's serious like, there's a woman in a car upon its side and she needs urgent attention! The truck driver told them.

"Were you involved in the collision caller?" The Controller asked.

"Yes, my truck hit her car and it turned over a number of times, I think the Fire and Rescue crew are needed and may have to cut her from the wreckage", added the truck driver.

"We have crews being despatched right now, Caller, they will be with you very shortly", Replied the Controller.

He clicked off the call upon his Mobile; the truck driver sat in his cab looking through the windscreen towards the shattered Vauxhall. Now at last the shock of the incident began to set in. He felt sick, his hands began to shake and he felt his head drop into his hands.

The call came through to the Control Room in Cranleigh, some ten miles away from Little Farthingworth. Cranleigh was the major town in the area closest to Little Farthingworth. It stood about thirty miles North of Exeter, going out towards the Moors. The signal was sent out to the Ambulance Station and the next available crew boarded their RT Vehicle and roared out of the Ambulance Station forecourt and onto the road out of Cranleigh towards the Village. When they had gotten started along the road, Jill Carter, lead Paramedic reached up to the panel over the windscreen of the Ambulance and flicked the switch. The claxon blared into life and announced the siren to inform all traffic ahead that the Ambulance was on an emergency call and needed a clear road. The blue lights strobing away upon the top of the vehicle, cars and vans parting in the road ahead like the parting of the Reed Sea as Moses led his people through.

The Ambulance sped on through the outer laying streets of Cranleigh and was soon out upon the Little Farthingworth Road. They turned the junction which sent one road to Farthingworth and one road to Little Farthingworth. These villages were not too far apart, but Little Farthingworth was the older of the two. The Ambulance sped upon its way into the Square of the village and manoeuvred itself into the road and drove up along Bogart Street. The vehicle roared past Pegasus House and on up the Moorland Road. Finally it reached the scene of the collision. Also already here upon the scene was a Fire Tender from the Fire and Rescue team. The Ambulance Station had alerted the Fire and Rescue that cutting equipment may be needed.

First the Fire Chief walked slowly up to the car to check for danger. He had been with the Fire and Rescue Service since 'Fire Fighters' were known as 'Firemen'. Bob Newhart joined the Fire Service as a raw recruit when he was twenty one years of age. He had fought some of the fiercest fires in the area. Bob had risen through the ranks gradually until he had reached his current position. Bob checked the car carefully for any sign of rupturing the fuel tank. He looked along the back of the vehicle and although the car was very battered, he was quite satisfied that there was no immediate risk of explosion. Bob signalled to the Paramedics, who then ran over to the car to assess the situation regarding Rachel's condition.

When they arrived at the car they checked her neck for a pulse and found a weak register. They searched for a vein and put in an I.V. line to give much needed pain relief. The Paramedics wore green overalls with fluorescent yellow over jackets with 'PARAMEDIC' written across their backs. They carefully checked Rachel's neck for any immediate signs of injury and as a precaution placed a neck brace around her neck to secure her head and neck from any further injuries. Then they slowly inch by inch, slipped a back brace down behind Rachel's back between her body and the seat.

Next it was the turn of the Fire and Rescue Crew. They fired up the generator for the Pneumatic cutters and it spluttered into life. Two of the Fire Crew came over and placed the cutters into the mangled wing of the Vauxhall. The cutters tore away chunks of the metal skin around the bolts that secured it to the Chassis. They then freed the bolts which held the windshield to the framework and it fell away with a crunch.

Then they cut away the stanchions which connected the bodywork to the roof. While this was taking place a crew were slipping the large air bag from the tender under the other side of the car, the crew with the cutters stood back away from the car. the other crew began to let air into the airbag, little by little and inch by inch the car began to rise.

Paramedics kept close eyes upon Rachel as the car began to move making certain that they maintained as little movement of her body and head as possible, as the car began to lift. Gradually, the little battered Vauxhall righted itself up onto its wheels again. Now the paramedics gave Rachel another check over and the crew, with the cutters, resumed they work. They completed cutting through the struts of the roof and it was lifted clear of the car body. Now they had clear access to Rachel.

The Crew cut away the hinges of the door and it too fell away from the car. Now Rachel was fully visible. Paramedics moved in and applied field dressings to Rachel's bloodied legs. The Cutting Crew then finally cut through the bolts which held her seat in place. They slipped another section of brace under her bottom between her and the seat, and then the Fire and Rescue Crew with assistance from the Paramedics gathered around and lifted Rachel's Seat clear out of the car and placed it onto the road next to the wreckage. Now the Paramedics lifted her legs very gently inch by inch, trying not to cause Rachel too much pain.

Rachel was still unconscious, which following the accident had now been helped by the Paramedics by medication which had been administered by them, to help her cope with the pain and also to help them extract her from the car. Once the final piece of the brace was in position under Rachel's legs, the Paramedics carefully inch by inch, released the recliner catch and switch upon her seat and began lowering Rachel backwards into a laying position. As she became horizontal, the catches of the brace snapped into locking position until finally, the brace had become a stretcher. The Paramedics then placed an inflatable splint around Rachel's legs and inflated it to protect her legs. They then lifted her onto the stretcher clear of the seat and carried her into the Ambulance where they placed her stretcher onto the waiting trolley bed and closed the Ambulance doors. One Paramedic stayed in the back with Rachel to keep observation over her for the journey to Cranleigh General Hospital. By this time the Police had arrived upon the scene. The truck driver was still sitting in his cab, shocked. PC Philip Thomas walked up to his cab, looked at the front radiator grill, covered in streaks of sapphire silver paint and then spoke to the driver.

"Good morning Sir, would you please get out of the vehicle." Said PC Thomas. The driver slowly climbed down from the cab onto the road.

"Would you blow into this please Sir, purely routine, you understand?" Asked PC Thomas, producing a digital breath meter. The driver took the machine in his trembling hand and steadied himself. He then placed his lips around the plastic tube sticking out of it.

"Please give one sustained long breath until I tell you to stop, Sir." PC Thomas said.

The driver blew into the machine for what felt like an eternity, and then PC Thomas told him to stop. The PC Checked the meter, waited for a few moments and a 'Ting' sounded. The meter showed a digital readout upon a screen and a green light flashed on. PC Thomas pressed a button upon the machine and the screen cleared, the green light went out and he returned the meter to its case.

"You will be pleased to learn, Sir that your breath test came up as negative for Alcohol". He said.

He put the meter away in his pocket and turned back to the driver.

"Would you give me your full name and date of birth please, Sir. " Asked PC Thomas.

"Paul Jenkins, fourth of tenth, sixty seven." Replied The Driver.

"Well Mr Jenkins, could you tell me what took place here this morning please?" PC Thomas asked.

"Well, you see Officer; I was driving along here from Barnstaple on my way down to Exeter for a delivery and just out of nowhere came this car. I could do nothing to avoid her. I tried to break but was simply too late, the truck just hit the car and pushed it along a short way then the car simply flipped and tumbled a number of times "'till it stopped." Replied the truck driver, shakily.

PC Thomas walked along the truck, looked at the road, where he could see rubber marks upon the tarmac showing where Paul had in deed tried to brake and the truck had jack-knifed with the momentum of it's speed. He looked down to the junction and saw the Poplar trees coming to the end, so he concluded that Paul Jenkins would have most likely been unsighted if Rachel had suddenly pulled out into the junction while Paul was passing, without warning. PC Thomas came back to Paul and gave him the news of what he thought.

"Well, Mr Jenkins, the tyre marks upon the road and situation of the junction would seem to support your version of the event. I will be seeking to talk with the other driver at the Hospital but for now, you can go. If I need to speak to you again, I'll be in touch." Said PC Thomas. He then walked back to the Fire and Rescue Crews and radioed into Control that they would need a clean-up Crew to come and pick up the wreckage of the Vauxhall to take it to the pound for any possible future need of checks. The Fire and Rescue Crew had already been clearing up the road of debris, metal and glass, away from the tarmac surface to minimise the prospect of any other vehicles having accidents due to punctures. PC Thomas waited for the tow truck to arrive and lift the wreckage onto the flat bed of the truck. The truck then drove off towards the village; PC Thomas then got back into his Police car and drove off also back towards the village.

After getting back in his cab and watching this take place, finally the road was clear and Paul felt he was able to continue. He started up the truck, backed it out of the Jack-knife to straighten up and then slowly drove off towards the village. He took it slowly at first, just to make sure he was OK for driving onto Exeter. Paul had phoned into his boss back in Barnstaple to tell him of the delay in reaching his delivery on the scheduled time due to the accident. His boss seemed more concerned about his truck rather than Paul, but then Paul was already aware that he didn't all that much exactly like his boss, but a job was a job.

Chapter Five – The Reception

Within the great Oak gate stood the Masters and the 'New Batch'. The road where the accident had taken Place was far from here out of the grounds.

The courtyard was old, squarish with the same high walls on two sides and the fourth wall completing the square, another high wall punctuated by a wooden Lynch gate. In the courtyard stood the new Students for this new term. Many of them from families of Little Farthingworth, Cranleigh and Frackston, plus others from further afield but all here for the same reason. The new Students who were the first year Students were traditionally known as 'Grunts' at the school. Some worried and frightened faces, wondering what was in store for them at their new school. Others, like Toby, excited at what lay before them. Cragus T Parfinkle addressed the crowd before him.

"Welcome to our Grand Old School, Toadford." He said in a thin old voice. "Toadford is a very old school which has its own customs, which I hope you will all learn quickly. I am Mr Parfinkle and will be your Head Master for your stay here at the School. This is my Deputy, Mr Thybold." Parfinkle said, pointing towards Mr Thybold.

"These are the Senior Masters", pointing to the other Masters with him, "Mr Cracken, Mr Finkel, Miss Norwall, Mr Marden and Miss Olden". He said.

"Please follow me to your new home". Parfinkle gestured through the Lynch Gate and the assembled group followed. Through the Lynch gate was a stone corridor which had a pillared colonnade along both sides and beamed Oak roof along the top of it. Toby Marvelled at the workmanship of the stone work and the carvings of the roof. As they walked along the corridor Toby looked to one side and through the gaps between the pillared arches, he noticed a large deep Gorge dropping away beneath them and realised that the corridor was in fact a foot bridge which took them across the Gorge to the School. Toby then thought about it and realised that all that was preventing the group from plummeting down into the depths of the Gorge was the footbridge which they were all now walking across. As the group neared the far end of the foot bridge, Toby was able to see another Lynch gate. They eventually reached this and Parfinkle opened the Lynch gate and lead the group through, making sure to secure it behind them, he didn't want any mishaps.

The group now entered an open green area which Toby saw encircled an inner wall. Parfinkle told them that this was the Outer Bailey of the School. He said that some of the older Students very often used this area for study and walks. He told the group, that on no circumstance must a Grunt be seen in this area without express permission from a member of Staff. Grunts were not permitted to leave the school during term time unless it was a family crisis and completely necessary.

On the green could be seen a series of scenes involving older Students. Some playing Chess, Soccer, painting and walking. Some were sitting reading. Parfinkle lead the group through these Students along a stone path. Parfinkle explained that all deliveries to the school were dealt with in the outer court yard where they had met and were then transported by the use of hand carts across the bridge they had crossed. He explained that there were no motorised vehicles allowed beyond that point. They now reached the wall at the far side of the green area opposite the Lynch gate. Beside them on either side, the green Outer Bailey stretched away and around the walls towards the rear of the School. There was another large Oak gate in the wall, which Parfinkle opened. The group followed him through and he made certain that Thybold closed the gate behind them. Parfinkle turned to the congregation and told them;

"This is your furthest allowance of space from now on apart from when you return home for the major Holidays, Christmas, Easter and Summer. No Grunts as previously stated, are permitted beyond this gate". Said Parfinkle, "Welcome to the Inner Bailey". He added.

Before them they were able to see the rambling Medieval Fortified House. To Toby, it looked every bit a Castle standing before them. The Granite façade stretched out on either side of a large central gate house. The gate house was edged by two large towers with two huge Oak doors between them.

A wall above the doors was crenulated. Stretching either side of this, the façade was wide, some twenty yards in either direction and cornered large tall towers tipped with tall spires. Behind the façade, Toby was able to see more buildings and more spire topped towers. He was not able to count all of the windows that he could see. Toby just stood and his jaw dropped, all Toby was able to utter in a whisper at this sight was "Wow!"

Parfinkle lead them through the two large Oak doors at the centre of the Gate House. Above the doors Toby was able to see an old stone shield embedded into the stone façade of the Gate House, its surface a embossed piece of masonary. Thybold made sure that the doors were closed.

Through the doors the group now found themselves standing in a large open hallway. The hallway had many rooms leading off and a huge stone staircase which rose up in front of them at either side of the hallway. The hallway had corridors leading off in different directions to different parts of the house to their own wings. All around the walls of the hallway were hung paintings of notable past Students and Masters of the School. Hanging from the ceiling of the hallway was a great candelabrum. Either side of this hung four pennants of red, Yellow, Green and Blue. To one side of the staircase on the left was a large glass cabinet full of a multitude of trophies of gold and silver.

Parfinkle lead them along the corridor to the right and passed some doors. At the end of the corridor was a large pair of double doors which Parfinkle opened. These lead into the Great Hall, where the rest of the school were to be found.

Seated upon forms at long Oak tables along the length of the Hall. Hanging from the ceiling over the end of two lines of tables could be seen a deep blue pennant with a Boar's head in gold, next to that over another line of tables was a Red pennant with a Griffin's head in gold, then a green pennant with a Swan's head in gold and finally a yellow pennant with a toad in gold. At the far end of the Hall was a large table across the back of the Hall where the Senior Masters and the School Secretary were sitting. In the centre of the table was a large throne like chair which was now being approached by Parfinkle, while the other Masters and Thybold took up their seats upon either side of Parfinkle. The Grunts were now shown to sit upon forms across the front of the Upper Table. Parfinkle welcomed the rest of the school to a new term and then addressed the Grunts.

"Good Morning Toadford School" He cried.

"Good Morning Sir". The school answered in chorus.

"We once again we find ourselves at the beginning of another year at Toadford. Yet another year which follows all the previous years for the time which the House has been a school. I welcome the Weeners to this year, who were our Grunts of last year. One year older and now established into the School traditions. I welcome the Toffs for this year, mid-way through your stay with us. I welcome the Cardinals, who now begin their penultimate year with us; I welcome the Seniors who will sadly be leaving us at the end of the year to move onto their adult lives. I Welcome the Grunts, our new comers who have much to learn during their stay here and many traditions to become part of. Our first task shall be to allocate you all to your respective Houses, which you will remain in throughout your stay here at Toadford." Said Parfinkle.

Parfinkle then pulled a golden chord which was hanging from the ceiling next to his throne. From the ceiling a bright blue pennant unfurled rolling down along its length. When it was fully unrolled, there was visible to the assembled school a golden Dragon motif at its centre.

"The School Colours!" Cried Parfinkle.

A huge cheer rang out throughout the Hall from the Students and Staff seated at the tables.

"Toadford School was begun five Centuries ago, founded by an eminent Scholar named Guyiume Cargal. He was a learned man of the Royal Court and was the first head Master of the School. His name is remembered in the Cargal House, which takes the green pennant with the golden crest of the Cargal family, an embossed Swan's Head. Over the years Toadford has produced many notable Scholars who have gone on to greater lives. The next house is named as a remembrance to one of the greatest Scholars to have been taught at the School and a former Master of the School, Rachel Hatchell. Her house has a yellow pennant baring her crest, a golden Toad's head.

26

Then we have a former Head Master, Bombus Farley, who is remembered by Farley House and has a red Pennant which bares his crest that of a Griffin's head. Finally we have a former deputy Head Master commemorated in the house list, that of Wilhelmina Wombat, who is remembered through the Wombat House and has a the deep blue pennant adorned with an embossed Boar's head as her crest. Each of the Grunts will be called up to the High Table in turn and presented with their House Tie and Scarf. You will be allocated the House that you will join and then will be seated at the table under your house pennant. Following breakfast, the rest of the School will go to their dorm rooms and prepare for the day's lessons. The Grunts will be taken and led to their respective House dorms by their House Masters and allocated to their dorm rooms, which they will live in for the duration of their stay here at Toadford. Let the Allocation Ceremony begin!" Parfinkle stood at the Lectern upon the High Table in front of his throne and read from it.

"Delbert Eldridge, Please approach the High Table and accept your Tie and Scarf, you have been elected to join Wombat House." Called Parfinkle. Delbert Eldridge was a largish boy, not fat but well built. He had red hair like all of the Eldridges and freckles. He lived at Tugmoor Farm, a short distance outside of Little Farthingworth on the Moorland Road to the South of the village. He walked up to the High Table and accepted his package. He then shook Parfinkle's right hand and turned to walk over to the table with a sign on top saying 'Grunts' which was underneath the deep blue banner with the golden Boar's head motif and took his seat in Wombat House.

"Victoria Kale, please approach the High Table and accept your Tie and Scarf, you have been elected to join Hatchell House. Called Parfinkle. Tory Kale was the daughter of a local activist who didn't much like the way in which the Town Council and Parish Councils ran the area; he was involved in many protests at the Frackston City Council for their recent introduction of severe cut-backs. Tory accepted her package and walked over to the table marked 'Grunts' underneath the yellow pennant with the Toad's head motif and joined Hatchell House.

"Paul Keeper, please approach the High Table and accept your Tie and Scarf, you have been elected to Farley House." Called Parfinkle. Paul keeper was average height for a teenager with short brown hair. He walked up to the High Table and accepted his package, then he turned to walk over to the 'Grunts' table under the Red pennant baring the Griffin's head to join Farley House.

"Keiron Mudley, please approach the High Table and accept your tie and scarf, you have been elected to join Cargal House." Called Parfinkle. Keiron was a tall, slim gangly boy; blonde hair with glasses. He walked up to the High Table and promptly tripped and fell over. The Hall spontaneously erupted into hysterical laughter. Parfinkle motioned with his hand and the outburst died down. Keiron picked himself up and Parfinkle handed him his package. Keiron then walked over to the 'Grunts' table underneath the green pennant with the Swan's head motif and joined Cargal House.

"Thomas Taylor, please approach the High Table and accept your Tie and Scarf, you have been elected to join Wombat House." Called Parfinkle. Tom Taylor was average height for a teenager, slim and athletic. He managed to stop laughing and picked himself up to walk up to the High Table. He shook Parfinkle's hand and accepted his package. He then turned and walked over to the 'Grunts' table under the Wombat pennant and joined Delbert Eldridge seated at the table.

"Guy Watson, please approach the High Table and accept your Tie and Scarf, you have been elected to join Hatchell House." Called Parfinkle. Guy Watson was tall for a teenager, slim and athletic with red hair. He walked up to the High Table and accepted his package. Then he walked over to the 'Grunts' table under the Hatchell pennant and joined Tory Kale sitting there.

"Tilley Parmenter, please approach the High Table and accept your Tie and Scarf. You have been elected to join Farley House." Called Parfinkle. Tilley Parmenter was a tall and slim girl with long blonde hair and a pretty face. She walked up to the High Table and accepted her package. She then turned and looked towards Toby, sat upon his form. She winked! Tilley then walked over to the 'Grunts' table under the Farley Pennant and joined Paul Keeper sitting there.

"Toby Morby, please approach the High Table and accept your Tie and Scarf. You have been elected to join Cargal House." Called Parfinkle. Toby walked up to the High Table and accepted his package. He then turned and walked over to the 'Grunts' table underneath the green Pennant of Cargal House and Joined Keiron sitting there. Tilley Parmenter watched him all the way and was a little disappointed when Toby was sent to the Cargal table rather than Farley.

"Gaynell Eldridge, please approach the High Table and accept your Tie and Scarf, you have been elected to Wombat House." Called Parfinkle. Delbert gave out a little cheer when he heard that his Brother was joining his House. Gaynell walked over to the High Table, accepted his package and walked over to the Wombat 'Grunts' table, where he joined the others and took his place in Wombat House.

"Allan Kirk, please approach the High Table and accept your Tie and Scarf, you have been elected to join Hatchell House." Called Parfinkle. Allan was rather tall for his age and slim with rather athletic build. He had short brown hair. Allan walked over to the High Table and accepted his package. He then walked over to the Hatchell 'Grunts' table and joined the others.

"Olivia Hammond, please approach the High Table and accept your Tie and Scarf, you have been elected to join Farley House." Called Parfinkle. Olivia, tall for her age, long brown hair and glasses, average build, walked up to the High Table and accepted her package, then walked over to the Farley 'Grunts' table and joined the others there.

"Stephen Logan, please approach the High Table and accept your Tie and Scarf, you have been elected to join Cargal House." Called Parfinkle. Steve Logan was tall for his age and slim with blonde hair. He walked up to the High Table, accepted his parcel and walked over to the Cargal 'Grunts' table where he joined the others.

"Dexter Eldridge, please approach the High Table and accept your Tie and Scarf, you have been elected to join Wombat House." Called Parfinkle. Delbert and Gaynell both Whooped as they heard their Brother was joining them in Wombat House. Dexter, Delbert and Gaynell were the triplet Brothers of Hargus and Hettie Eldridge, who owned and ran Tugmoor Farm. The boys were well built as a result of working upon the farm from a young age to help their Father. Dexter was red haired also, just as his Brothers were and also had freckles. He accepted his package and walked over to join his Brothers and the rest of the Wombat 'Grunts'.

"Martin Cooper, please approach the High Table and accept your Tie and Scarf, you have been elected to join Hatchell House." Called Parfinkle. Martin walked over to the High Table. Average height for his age, slim and with short black hair. He accepted his package and then walked over to the Hatchel 'Grunts' table and took his place with the others.

"Jasmine Peters, please approach the High Table and accept your Tie and Scarf, you have been elected to join Farley House." Called Parfinkle. Jasmine was small and petite and had short black hair. She walked up to the High Table and accepted her package. She then walked over to the 'Grunts' seated at the Farley table and joined them.

"Peter Cougher, please approach the High Table and accept your Tie and Scarf, you have been elected to join Cargal House." Called Parfinkle. Peter Cougher was the son of Malcolm Cougher, Chairman of Little Farthingworth Parish Council. Peter was average height for a teenager and quite athletic build. Blonde haired and freckled face. Peter walked up to the High Table and accepted his package. He then walked over to the Farley 'Grunts' table and joined the others in the House.

"Aaron Pooke, please approach the High Table and accept your Tie and Scarf, you have been elected to join Wombat House." Parfinkle said. Aaron walked up to the High Table and accepted his package then turned and walked over to the Wombat 'Grunts' table. He was average for a teenager with short black hair.

"Primrose Cook, please approach the High Table and accept your Tie and Scarf, you have been elected to join Hatchell House." Called Parfinkle. Primrose was a pretty girl with long red hair and was slim. She walked up to the High Table and accepted her package. Then Primrose walked over to the 'Grunts' table of Hatchell House and joined the others already there.

"Colin Finchley, please approach the High Table and accept your Tie and Scarf, you have been elected to join Farley House." Called Parfinkle. Colin was shortish stout boy with short black hair and glasses. He walked over to the High Table, shook the hand of Parfinkle and then accepted his package. He then walked over to the 'Grunts' table of Farley House and joined the others already seated there.

"Polly Muggard, please approach the High Table and accept your Tie and Scarf, you have been elected to join Cargal House." Called Parfinkle. Polly was a smallish young girl, petite would be how she would be seen. Her demeanour would be described as a 'Prim and Proper' young Lady. She had long straight light brown hair and was pretty. Polly walked up to the High Table and accepted her package. She then walked back to the 'Grunts' table of Cargal House and joined Toby and Keiron with the others.

"Virginia Cornett, please approach the High table and accept your Tie and Scarf, you have been elected to join Wombat House." Called Parfinkle. Virginia was an athletic girl, tall and slim with long blonde hair and pretty. She was the daughter of the Magistrate at Cranleigh Court and used this to her advantage, Virginia got what she wanted. Virginia walked up to the High Table and accepted her package. She smirked at Parfinkle then turned and walked away to join the 'Grunts' table of Wombat House.

"Chantelle Marfon, please approach the High Table and accept your Tie and Scarf, you have been elected to join Hatchell House." Parfinkle called. Chantelle was of average size for a teenage girl, pretty and had short red hair which was emphasised by her pale green eyes. She was the daughter of Thomas Marfon, Parish Councillor of Little Farthingworth Village, and Cecilia Marfon, his wife, who was the Parish Clerk for her husband's Parish Council. Chantelle lived at Hawksridge Farm to the South of Little Farthingworth Village upon the Cranleigh Road. Chantelle walked over to the High Table and accepted her package from Parfinkle. She then walked away over to the 'Grunts' table of Hatchell House and took her seat.

"John Pugworth, please approach the High Table and accept your Tie and Scarf, you have been elected to join Farley House." Called Parfinkle. John Pugworth was well built and had short blonde hair. He was well fed, being the son of the village Butcher in Little Farthingworth. His Father, Jack Pugworth was also a Parish Councillor along with Thomas Marfon. John approached the High Table, shook the hand of Parfinkle and collected his package. He then walked over to the 'Grunts' Table of Farley House and took his place with the others.

"Arrabella Snoop, please approach the High Table, you have been elected to join Cargal House." Called Parfinkle. Arrabella was a plain type of girl. She was not fat but plumper than most other of the girls and had shoulder length black hair and glasses. She approached the High Table accepted her package. Then she walked over to the 'Grunts' table of Cargal House and took her seat.

Eventually the remaining Grunts were called out and allocated to their respective Houses. Once all of the Grunts were placed in their Houses, Parfinkle then read out the notices for the New Term.

"Oh Yea to the House" Cried Parfinkle.

"Oh Yea to the Master." Echoed the entire seated school, Students and Masters.

"Firstly, I welcome you all to the new year here at Toadford School. Our year will begin, as always, as Tradition with Luncheon. Please enjoy your meal and thank you for attending this assembly," Said Parfinkle.

With this said, Parfinkle sat upon his throne and Thybold took away the Lectern, leaving the table clear to receive the plate carrying Parfinkle's Lunch. The Lunch consisted of a full Steak and Kidney Pie with Boiled Potatoes and mixed Vegetables. With the Lunch was served Ginger Beer in jugs to be poured into goblets for the Students. Second Years or 'Weeners' sat on the second batch of tables in the rows, beyond them were the Third year Students, they were known at the School as 'Toffs' and their table was in front of the fourth year students table. Who were known as 'Cardinals'. The last table in the line was occupied by the fifth year Students, the 'Seniors'.

Either side of the tables along the walls of the Great Hall was to be seen four large windows of stained glass. These depicted a crest of each of the four Houses and a central fifth window which depicted a Golden Dragon, the School crest. Above these were the roof rafters. Across the high walls of the Great Hall were huge beams of Oak which were put together as 'A' frames and rose high into the ceiling. Hangings from the beams were four candelabrums to light the Hall. At one time these would have carried candles to produce the light, but now were converted to hold electric bulbs.

"I Hope we have a Lunch like this every day, I'm starving." Said Keiron Mudley.

The Students ate their Lunch hungrily, some, like Keiron, were devouring theirs as though this was their first meal for months, but of course that was not the case, they just liked shovelling it in. Polly was daintily eating her Lunch with the decorum of a young Lady. The Eldgridge Triplets on their table, just as they did when home on the Farm, were piling their food into their mouths and scoffing it down hungrily. They were used to having large portions of food for meals, with living upon a Farm. Toby just took his time; he was in no hurry to finish his Lunch. Toby was enjoying each mouthful; Lunch was one of his favourite meals, especially a full Steak and Kidney Pie .

Chapter Six – The Dorm Rooms

After Breakfast, the higher year students left the Great Hall and went on their way to their lessons. The Grunts were left in the Great Hall still remained in their seats. They were then introduced to their House Masters. The Hatchell House Grunts were introduced to Abbeygale Norwall, the Art Master. She addressed the Hatchell Grunts and asked them to follow her out of the Great Hall. The Wombat House Grunts were introduced to their House Master, Eberneezer Finkle, the English Master. He addressed the Grunts and asked them to follow him out of the Great Hall. The Farley House Grunts were introduced to their House Master, John Cracket, the Science Master. He addressed them and asked them to follow him out of the Great Hall. The Cargal House Grunts table was approached by their House Master who introduced himself.

"Good morning again to you. I welcome you as the new Grunts for this year and formally welcome you into Cargal House. I am your House master, Mr Thybold, as you may recall, I greeted you all at the arrival gate. For Centuries, new Students in their first year of attendance at the School have been referred to as Grunts. The Second year Students are referred to as Weeners, the third year Students are referred to as Toffs and the Fourth year Students are referred to as Cardinals. Finally your last year here with us you will become Seniors before your Graduation. Our Founder was Guyiume Cargal, who was also the founder of the School in its present form. Because we carry the founder's name, the House of Cargal is much respected by its members and are fierce rivals to the more unruly Wombat House. Our Crest is the Swan's head; the family crest of Guyiume Cargal. I will be taking you to your Dormitory area and this will be where you will call home for the duration of your stay here at Toadford School. We have Traditions here which are to be kept; some of these traditions are to be adhered to exactly without fail. There is an area around the School, which is out of bounds to all Grunts and severe penalties are administered in any breach of these traditions. Here we do not tolerate fighting, unless in our approved sports such as Boxing and wrestling, again any breach of this rule will be dealt with accordingly. Mr Marden, the Boys Games Master is also a Master who runs this House, so he will give those of you any help with Sports and fitness outside of lesson time if you require it. Please ask Mr Marden about his out of hours classes if you are interested. We hope you will enjoy will enjoy your stay here at Toadford and when you reach your Dormitory room, please change your tie to the House tie for Cargal. Your School tie is only to be worn when representing the School at an event. Please would you all follow me and I shall show to you the Cargal Wing of the School. I will introduce you all to the Cargal House Common Room and show you to your Dormitory Rooms." Said Thybold. Toby, Keiron, Polly and the other assembled Cargal Grunts began shuffling to follow Thybold.

"Please walk and refrain from shuffling, we do not shuffle at Toadford." Thybold scolded.

As he led them out of the Great Hall and along the corridor towards the hallway, Toby marvelled at all of the paintings that hung upon the walls of the corridor. He saw the paintings of past pupils playing Soccer in old fashioned clothes, Cricketers in Top Hats and even Horse riding in Doublet and Hoes. When they reached the Hallway, they were surrounded by more paintings of past students and Masters. Toby was able to get a better look at the cabinet full of trophies and cups as Thybold lead them over to it to show them.

"Toadford Trophy Cabinet." Announced Thybold.

Toby was able to see large Silver cups, tall Golden trophies and smaller cups and trophies. Toby Read the engraving upon one cup, a large Golden cup.

"TOADFORD SCHOOL CUP"

Upon a tablet of wood which stood next to the cup was a brass plate with the dates and names of the Houses which had won the cup. Toby was able to see that the plate recorded only three entries for Farley House, which dated back to a hundred years ago. There were four entries for Hatchell House, but most recently of these was thirty years ago. The remaining dates were spread out between Wombat House and Cargal House. Toby frowned, a quick count up approximately showed that Wombat had the most wins, including the last two years of dates.

"They won't get three in a row if I can help it." Thought Toby.

"This is the most important trophy in the School," Said Thybold, "The School Cup. I don't wish to see a third win in a row go to Wombat House, please Cargal House" He added.

"No Sir!" All of the Grunts answered collectively.

Toby also was able to see other trophies and cups in the cabinet; there was a trophy with the figure of a Soccer player on the top of the lid kicking a ball in Silver. This trophy was engraved.

"HOUSE SCHOOL FOOTBALL CUP"

Again, Toby looked at the plaque next to the trophy and yes, again the Majority of names to winning dates were Wombat House. There was a tall Silver trophy with an engraved Cricket batsman on a face plate;

"HOUSE SCHOOL CRICKET CUP"

Engraved across the plate on the plinth, again Toby saw the same story as before upon the plaque next to the trophy in the list of winners. Another trophy had a figure holding a Rugby ball under its arm and was engraved;

"HOUSE SCHOOL RUGBY CUP"

As before, the plaque beside it told the same story, that Wombat House had the most wins.

Once the Grunts had finished looking at the trophies and cups, Thybold led them on through the Hallway until they reached the second of the two stair cases. Thybold told them to follow him up the stairs. Toby saw more paintings of past Masters and Students hanging upon the walls as they climbed the stairs. When they reached the top, they found themselves upon a large 'U' shaped landing which spanned the width of the Hallway. The Horse shoe like landing spread out on either side of the two stairs cases. Along the wall to the right of the staircase they had just ascended, Thybold showed the Grunts along that strip of landing. There was a large Oak door with a Golden Toad attached to it.

"That is the Hatchell Wing, we are further along." Said Thybold.

Next to this was a tall window which Toby looked through and saw a long thin courtyard, with taller walls heading up lined with windows. Opposite he saw single windows above each other leading up five floors. In the courtyard was a small path which encircled a small fountain. The fountain was shaped like two scallop shells above each other which were topped with a bar of gold, on one end a toad, the other a swan. There were flowers planted around the courtyard.

The group at last came to a large Oak door. Upon the door was a golden swan. Thybold opened the door and walked through, turning to face the Students.

"Welcome to Cargal House Wing" Announced Thybold.

The group of Grunts then followed Thybold through the Oak door and he closed it behind them. They waited until he took up his position at the front of them again and then they followed as Thybold led them along a long corridor.

As they walked along the corridor, Toby saw more paintings upon the walls between doors. The paintings depicted more post Students, only these were purely of Cargal House Students. Toby spotted some more recent paintings and one in particular showed a young Senior wearing the School Team Rugby Shirt, which was bright blue and had a Golden Dragon as a badge. Toby looked down at the bottom of the frame, engraved upon this was;

"CARL MORBY - CAPTAIN

TOADFORD SCHOOL

SENIOR RUGBY TEAM"

Toby's jaw dropped, Carl had not told him about this, even though as he had grown up, Carl had taught Toby to play Rugby and had coached him in not only Rugby but also Football, which he played for his Village School team and Cricket. Toby smiled as he looked at the painting.

"My dad, the School Captain." He thought.

Toby then noticed that the group had gotten further along the corridor and quickly caught up with them. Thybold took them to the end of the corridor where there was, to the left, a staircase; to the right was a short corridor which lead to a door with a plaque engraved;

"CEDERICK T THYBOLD

DEPUTY HEAD MASTER"

Thybold stopped and spoke to the group of Grunts.

"This is my study and House Master's Room. When I am not teaching in class, in the Great Hall or outside cheering on the House or School at sports events. I can usually be found in here if any of you need to see me, do not be afraid to call upon me, as your House Master, I am here to help you." Said Thybold.

"The staircase that you see to your left leads up to the upper floors of the wing where the rest of the Cargal House Students Dormitories are found for the higher year Students. The floors use rotates every five years as Seniors leave. Whichever floor housed the Seniors from the previous year is vacated and that floor becomes the Dormitory for the new arriving Grunts for that year. Your Dormitory floor is this one for this year, where you will soon choose a Dormitory Room where you will live for the next five years." Then Thybold showed them to the room to their right of his Study. Here was a door which had a brass plate with a Swan's head and was engraved;

"CARGAL HOUSE COMMON ROOM-GRUNTS"

Thybold then led them through the door and into the Common Room.

"This will be your Common Room where you can relax and sit between lessons and in the evenings and weekends. As Grunts are forbidden to leave the School or venture beyond the Inner Bailey while they are in their first year, Students will not be able to go out to the playing fields or outer recreation areas until you are in the higher years. The playing fields are accessible accompanied by Mr Marden or another member of Staff. The Inner Recreation area is for use by Grunts and the Common Room." Thybold showed the group through the door.

Inside could be seen an area of seating which was a 'U' shape of Sofas surrounding a Coffee table in front of a large open fire place. The chimney breast bore a stone shield with a Swan motif carved into it. The walls were green and had more painting of past Cargal Grunts hanging on them. There was a television opposite the Sofas and three Cupboards. A stand held a Kettle and a tea pot, also there was a Coffee pot here. Underneath this, there were shelves which housed bottles of squash and Cola. There were also large book shelves filled with books around the room. Thybold then lead them out of the room and back to the corridor.

"Here we have your Dormitory Rooms. Please choose the one you wish, all Students will share in pairs. Boys will be placed in the left side rooms and girls in the right side of the corridor." Said Thybold, "Remember, these rooms will be your home for the next five years, please get settled in and remember your lessons begin after lunch." Added Thybold.

Toby walked down the corridor to the room at the centre, not too close to the entrance door and not too close to the stairs. In the middle should be just right, he thought. Toby walked into the room and looked around. He saw a window which he had seen from the landing.

In the room were two single beds, two wardrobes, a table with two chairs, two arm chairs, two chests of drawers and two bedside cabinets with lamps upon them along with two desks.

Toby chose the bed furthest from the door for his. He put his Ruc-Sac and suit case onto the bed and opened them. Toby began to empty out the Ruc-Sac and suit case of their contents and started to put things away. He hung his spare uniform gown, shirts, and trousers in the wardrobe. Then putting his T Shirts, shorts and other casual clothes into the chest of drawers nearest his bed, along with his under clothes.

To one side of the room were a shower cubicle and a toilet Cubicle as en suites. As Toby busied himself putting his books and writing materials into his provided cupboard, the tall bespectacled blonde haired boy stood at the door.

"H-H-Hello" He stuttered, "M-My name is K-Keiron M-Muddley, most people call me 'Muddles', mainly because I'm frequently getting into one. That is when they aren't calling me other names of course". The boy said.

"Hello My name is Toby, Toby Morby; most people just call me Toby." Replied Toby, holding out his hand. The two boys shook hands.

"Would you like to share with me?" Asked Toby, with a smile.

"Would I?" Replied Keiron enthusiastically. "Do you really mean that? Most people would run a mile if I asked them to share with me. I'm a disaster area." Added Keiron." Well then, I think it's time that someone needs to be your friend, Keiron, and why not me?" Said Toby.

Toby had always found it easy to make new friends. It just seemed to come naturally, he simply just seemed to be naturally popular.

"OK but I hope you won't regret it." Said Keiron.

With that said, Keiron stepped into the room, dropped his Ruc-Sac and promptly fell head long over it, landing sprawled with a thump onto the floor at Toby's feet. Keiron looked up at Toby, smiled and said;

"See what I mean?"

Keiron soon sorted out his clothes and other things into their respective cupboards and drawers. Then the two boys sat down to talk. Toby began by trying to find common ground between them.

"I like Frackston City, I've been a Fan for as long as I can remember; My Dad takes me to all of the home matches, well, I suppose he used to take me, as I'm here now and won't be able to go for a while." Said Toby.

"I'm a Frackston Fan too, they're great aren't they. Hopefully they will win the league this season." Replied Keiron.

"Maybe they will get into the FA League Two sometime or even the Premier League?" Said Toby.

"I want to play for Frackston when I get older, maybe help them into the Premier League and win the FA Cup." Replied Keiron.

The Boys sat in the arm chairs and felt comfortable. Toby thought that he'd made a good choice of Roommate as far as could be discerned, at least they liked the same Football team, which made things a little easier, it would be hard to get on with a Room Mate who wasn't a Frackston Fan, Toby thought.

"My Dad used to coach me when I was at the Village School and played I for the School Team. I used to enjoy playing." Said Toby.

"Me too, I love Footie" Said Keiron, "I hope this will be fun, at least we have made friends, so it's off to a good start, I think.

"Indeed, I hope we can be good friends." Replied Toby and smiled.

Keiron went to his drawer where he kept his Stationary and took out a book, it was his Diary. He opened it and Toby noticed that it was new and had completely blank pages. Keiron picked up his pen and began writing in his Dairy;

"Day one, arrived at new school, Toadford.

Some Teachers are stuffy but our House

Master is nice, at least he was today.

Met a new friend called Toby, we are

Sharing a Dorm. He's nice and we are

Both Frackston Fans YIPPEE!

Next Stop, Lunch!"

Chapter Seven – Meeting Polly

Across the other side of the corridor, opposite from Toby and Keiron's Dorm Room, were the Girl's Dorm Rooms. Directly opposite to their room was a room occupied by two young girls.

Polly was smallish, Petite would be the word to describe her, with long light brown hair and a pretty face with pale blue eyes. Her demeanour would be most accurately be described as 'a prim and proper young Lady'.

Being 'prim and proper', Polly had already changed from her School tie into her House tie. She made that a priority so as not to forget. As Thybold had told them, other than upon School events or outings representing the School, they were to at all times wear their House Ties. The same was for their scarves in cold weather. They had a scarf to be worn in school, their House Scarf and a scarf to be warning outside school or at School events, their School Scarf. Toadford School prided itself upon its traditions and that was one of the most important.

Polly was sharing with a girl a little tubbier than herself, named Arrabella Snoop. She was chattering Polly into a stupor.

"Hi, my name is Arrabella, what's yours? Oh don't tell me, let me guess; is it Jane? Susan? Elizabeth? Pauline?" Said Arrabella.

"Polly", Said Polly

"Oh I like that name." Arrabella, answered. "You're like the book, 'Pollyanna', I like that book. I like lots of books, do you like books, Polly?" Asked Arrabella, chattering away.

"Some books, and yes, I know Pollyanna is a book, my name is just, Polly, not Pollyanna." Replied Polly, quite abruptly.

"Oh, I like films too; I like old flicks, the Weepies. Mom says that I'm too much older for my age, says I should be more into modern things, teen idols and such but I have my own mind and I know what I like. Mind you, it doesn't mean I don't like more modern things, more my age, of course I do like some of the films, books and T........." Chattered Arrabella.

Polly decided to go looking for some relief, before she gnawed her arms off. Polly walked out of the door, leaving Arrabella chattering away. She walked across the corridor to Toby and Keiron's door. She stood there and waited for a few moments hearing the chattering voices of the two boys from within. Polly tapped upon the door with three taps politely. The door was still slightly open, from when Keiron had entered. The boys were so engrossed in getting to know one another, that they had not paid much attention to the fact that they had left the door open. They looked up and were surprised to see Polly standing at the door. She stood there waiting, quite correcttly, for their manners to surface and for them to ask her into their Dorm Room. She decided that being boys, this was too much to expect.

"Hello boys, my name is Polly, Polly Muggard. Do you mind awfully if I join you? You see, my roommate has only just arrived and she has already bored me half to death with her incessant chattering." Announced Polly.

"Mind awfully." Tittered Keiron, mimicking Polly with a grin like a Cheshire cat across his face.

"Of course we don't mind, please join us. We were just chatting before going down for Lunch." Said Toby.

Polly walked into the boy's room and Lady like, waited for one of the boys to leave their seats for her to sit down. Polly had been brought up properly with manners, by her Mother, Eliza. Eliza Muggard rather saw herself and her family as being part of the 'Elite' and had great ambitions for Polly. Her Mother was from an old family and had met her Father in University, which was the intended destination for Polly, once she had Graduated from Toadford. She waited, Keiron blinked, Toby stood up and moved over to one of the small chairs over by the table, leaving his armchair free for Polly to sit in the seat. Polly sat and made herself comfortable, she smiled.

"Oh how lovely, a Gentleman." She said, shooting Keiron a dissatisfied look. Keiron looked at the floor. Polly had a habit of giving disapproving looks to people she considered either beneath her or irritating , it was difficult, just now, to know which of these reason were for her look towards Keiron.

"As I said, my name is Polly Muggard. I have come here to Toadford from my home town of Cranleigh, where my Father is an Accountant. When I Leave here, I will be top of the class and go to University, then become an Accountant, like my Father." Said Polly.

"That's if you can fit your head through the door when you try to leave." Giggled Keiron, quietly. It wasn't quiet enough, because Polly shot him another disapproving look.

"My name is Toby, Toby Morby, My family live in Little Farthingworth Village." Replied Toby, to which Polly appeared to look down her nose a little. "We live in my Grandfather's house, called 'Pegasus House'." Added Toby. This made Polly take notice a little more. "My Father is the Ranger upon Pokey Moor, up above Cragmoor and my Mother is a Teacher at the Village School." He continued.

"And what does your Grandfather do?" Asked Polly, seeming as though she was waiting for an answer that she already knew.

"He's a Parish Councillor for the Village and Lord of the Manor for Little Farthingworth." Replied Toby. Polly smiled; she was right in what she expected the answer to be.

"I thought that I had recognised the name of the house." Said She.

"The House is very old, Grandfather says that the family have lived there for Hundreds of years, we're just the latest in the line of the family to live there." Said Toby.

"My name is Keiron, Keiron Muddley, my Father is a Clerk in the Local Council, I'm from Topley Village. I live with my Parents and my big Brother Thomas, he's in the third year here at Toadford and my Sister, Leonie, she starts here at Toadford next year." Explained Keiron. "We aren't rich, so to say, just that my folks don't have as much as most people and they do have three of us to put through the school." Keiron added.

The three chatted for a while before they prepared to go down to the Great Hall for their Lunch. Polly gave the boys a reminder, being 'Prim and Proper' that she was.

"You boys have forgotten something." She said, pointing to her tie. The boys looked down and noticed that they were still wearing their School Ties. Toby untied his and picked up his House Tie, tying it with a Windsor knot as his Grandfather had taught him. Keiron attempted to untie his, almost strangled himself as he pulled the wrong piece and then took it off. After attempting to tie his House Tie three times without success, Polly tutted and reached out to tie it for him.

You boys are useless." She scolded, "How did you tie your tie this morning then if you can't do it now?" Asked Polly.

"Mom did it up this morning before I left home." Replied Keiron, Sheepishly, "She knows I get in a muddle with it." He Added.

"A muddle for Muddles eh Keiron?" Chuckled Toby.

Chapter Eight – The Fall of Calistria

An arrow streaked past his face, singing his beard and stuck into the wooden post behind him. Almost immediately, the house began to burn. Another flame now struck the floor and another buried itself into the straw roof.

The young Dwarf ran from the burning building to look out over the City and stood distraught and terrified at the sight which greeted him. Most of the street where his house stood was now on fire, he looked around and saw half the streets in the City were ablaze; their wooden framed and thatched structures pouring out devastating flames. Along the street, leading to the Castle, Dwarfs were running from house after house. Caleb looked around and saw a sight which chilled him to his very bones.

Entering the outskirts of the City were hoards of Orcs, about six feet tall, murky green in colour, dry scaly skin with hideous faces. Mouths filled with huge sharp teeth, all blood stained, their eyes glowed yellow in the night darkness. Armed with heavy large swords and clubs, some fired fire arrows from bows. Some Orcs were riding Crocotta, huge dog like creatures with terrifying red eyes and huge teeth, with which they tore at Dwarfs as they passed by.

The Great door of the Castle opened and out poured Dwarfs in heavy armour. About four feet in height with masses of hair and long thick beards, with huge hands. Their beards flowing back over their shoulders as they ran to meet the Orcs with their great Battle Axes.

This was Calistria, the Great City of the Dwarfs. They were miners of Gold and Jewels. The Dwarfs dug deep into their mine to find Galem Gold, which was most pure. This was most sought after and was the highest currency throughout Alexandria and the Shires. Calistria was a Shire City of Alexandria. After attacks from the forces of Thracia, Alexandria had come to the aid of the outlying City States, which had joined in allegiance with Alexandria and formed the Shires. These were semi-autonomous City States which formed the Commonwealth of Alexandria.

Thracia was a Kingdom ruled by a Dark Wizard, a Warlock, named The Marquis. The Kingdom was once a peaceful prosperous place, until a Baron became too power hungry. The Dwarfs mined a section and discovered a Black Crystal, which the Baron purchased from them, unbeknown to the Dwarfs, they had discovered and sold a Demon Gem. With this Demon Gem, the Baron was able to access terrible Dark Magic and to bewitch many creatures into his council. The Baron arose up against the King and with an army of Trolls, Orcs and Goblins, laid waste to Thracia. The King mourned his defeat and the Baron marched upon the Castle. He entered the Throne Room, where he found the King devastated by the loss of his Kingdom. Using his Dark Magic, the Baron then entranced the King to kneel at his feet and cleaved his head clean from his neck.

The Barn then took his place upon the Throne and declared himself Marquis of Thracia. The Dark Magic of the Marquis turned Thracia black. The Sun never shone again in the Evil Realm. Over time, the Marquis attempted to conquer the surrounding City Kingdoms. Alexandria formed an alliance with the other City Kingdoms nearby and by the use of White Magic and brute force, outfought the Thracian army and secured their Kingdoms.

Following the defeat of the Marquis, his successors have tried many times to conquer Alexandria and the Shires. A powerful Wizard named Marfon placed an enchanted spell upon the City of Alexandria. This formed a protective force around the city which had a Portal built into what Marfon called 'The Skin', which lead from Alexandria through time and space to our World.

The Portal appeared in this World in an old ruined Medieval Manor House, which was rebuilt by the Alexandrian Crown Prince, to be used as a possible hiding place this side of the Portal, away from the Marquis. The School was founded by a servant of the Crown Prince to educate the people nearby so to hide any young Princes as Students from the Marquis and ensure the safety of the Bloodline. The current Marquis appeared stronger than his predecessors and now the Crown Prince and the fate of our World along with Alexandria, depended upon the defeat of the Marquis yet again.

The Dwarf soldiers fought with valour but the sheer number of Orcs were too strong for them. Trolls came lumbering in to crush Dwarfs under their huge clubs. A Dwarf soldier began to charge an Orc fighting another Dwarf with swords, when his progress was halted by an Orca's arrow smashing into his chest and driving right through his breast plate. He gasped one last breath and fell. The battle raged well into the night and the Dwarfs were gradually beaten back. They fought with all their might, with swords and spears. One Dwarf, Listus, slew four Orcs with his sword. They fought valiantly until the sheer number of Orcs had overcome the Dwarfs. They retreated to the Castle as the Sun began to rise, the Orcs began to retreat and return to where they had come from. Calistria was lost; once the Orcs had left the Dwarfs were able to assess their position.

After a few hours rest, King Boranius waited until he was sure that the last of the Trolls had disappeared back into the Mountains to avoid sunlight. The Dwarf soldiers then walked out of the Castle to survey the damage. As they walked around through the remains of the streets, they were in awe and felt great sadness.

The streets of the city were devastated and most houses lay as burned out ruins. Bodies of Dwarfs lay scattered all around. Wandering around aimlessly were the survivors of the Terror. King Boranius gathered the Soldiers to him and told them to round up the surviving Dwarfs.

"Ma men, we 'ave been struck a terrible blow an' Calistria es lost te us, fer the noo. We must gather oorselves, oor Brothers an' Sisters an' find a safe place te dwell an' regroup. Sadness fills oor hearts an' we must leave oor hame; one day ma Brothers, we wull return an' Calistria wull rise agin like a Phoenix fram ye ashes." Spoke Boranius.

The soldiers, in groups, walked around the city collecting up the people and bringing them to the Castle. Caleb walked with his group; they were joined by other Dwarfs. One named Pollock, called to Caleb crying, his face drenched in tears, his beard wet.

"Oh Caleb, Sir, ma Brother, how oor beautiful City lies en ruins. Ma hoose, ye family gone!" Said Pollock.

"Pollock, ma Brother, ma house too es gone an' all I had. We must follow ye King te lead us fram thes terror an' put as much distance as necessary between us an' ye Dark Marquis." Said Caleb. The Soldiers lead the terrified City folk to the Castle. King Boranius told the People that it was too dangerous to stay in the ruined City. If the forces of the Marquis have attacked this time, staying may lead them to attack again. The only choice they had was to leave and find somewhere safer.

The Dwarfs collected as much of their Galem Gold and jewels that they were able to pack onto ponies. The Dwarfs gathered to pay one last respect to their home before moving out. There was a troop of Soldiers leading the procession with King Boranius and Queen Marion behind them. Riding with them, Princess Surignan, Princess of Calistria upon her pony. Following were the surviving Dwarfs of the City and the carts carrying the only possessions and tools which they were able to salvage, the ponies and carts carrying the Galem Gold and jewels, the wealth of Calistria, were to the rear with more Soldiers. The City folk then trailed behind with their carts and ponies. They had buried their dead and now they left to find salvation or oblivion.

They journeyed far into the Shires, across the Plains of Cara and the Mountains of Connarch. They at last were deep enough into the Shires to feel safer. Throughout their journey they were ever watchful for the Thracian Spectre. All through their journey, they felt a great and deep sadness.

Here they cut down trees, cleared land and they began to build a new home for themselves. But this was not Calistria and they felt the loss of their homeland deeply. They built a Palace for the King and his Queen and houses for the other Dwarfs. They hired themselves out as labourers, dreaming of one day returning to Calistria to regain their Homeland, burned within every Dwarf. Theirs was the first defeat against the Thracian forces since the time of the First Marquis.

"Sire, I wull journey te Alexandria an' take them tidings o' oor plight. The Crown Prince wull be sure te lend te us aid an' join us en oor quest te retrieve what wus once oors." Said Listus.

"Listus ma loyal friend an' Brother, take with ye a troop o' ma Guard an' swiftly bring us news o' the Crown Prince's werds." King Boranius answered.

"God's strength be wuth ye an' keep ye safe." Said Queen Marion.

General Listus packed his Pony with provisions and his weapons and called a small troop of Soldiers to join him in his journey to the City of Alexandria. With the cheers of the people ringing out behind them, they rode out of their new home with King Boranius and Queen Marion waving them goodbye.

"King Boranius, Queen Marion, by ye beard upon ma face, ye strength en my arms an' power en ma sword, Dwarfs shall once agin rejoice en walking ye streets o' Calistria." Called Listus. With that said, he and his troop turned upon their ponies and rode out of the new settlement to begin their journey to Alexandria.

Chapter Nine – The Discovery

Out upon the Moor, there was much activity. Carl was working upon cleaning out a drainage ditch by the roadside. The digger he was working with was smoothly cutting through years of detritus which the weather had created. Bucket full after bucket full of silted mud and grass and twigs was lifted out of the clogged ditch. Carl turned each bucketful with a leaver and dumped it into the open backed tipper lorry parked beside the ditch. Carl noticed a glint in the soil, a metallic glint.

Carl turned off the motor of the digger and climbed down from the cab. He jumped down and walked over to the ditch. He jumped down into the ditch and brushed aside some of the mud. There before him he was able to see a long metal rod. He climbed out of the ditch and went back to his digger. Taking a small spade from the cab behind his seat and an old rag, Carl returned to the ditch and began to dig the rod out of the mud. When Carl lifted the rod from the mud, he washed it off in a nearby puddle of water. It was now that he was able to see that this was not simply a metal rod, but a sword, Carl wrapped the sword in the rag that he had brought from the cab and carried it with him back to the digger cab. He placed the rag bundle behind his seat then climbed back into his cab.

The truck arrived with their delivery of wire, posts and materials for the new fencing. Carl continued to dig out the ditch. This was part of the National Park but unlike the open wild Moor, this section was fenced off as an enclosure. It was an area where the local Deer of the Moor were herded into for inspection each year. As the main tourist attraction to the area, The National Park brought in Veterinary workers to gather up as many Deer as could be found at the time, to check them and treat any illness or injuries.

Upon the Moor, there were at least sixty Deer in two herds of thirty animals. Each heard consisted of a Monarch or Alpha Male who was in charge of a Harem of up to a dozen Hinds, then there were the lesser males; juvenile Bucks and young female Does. Also each spring brought forth the new batch of Fawns. Carl knew the Monarch well and often sighted him up upon the Moor. He was old, almost ten years old and likely to only have a few years left in him until the lesser males challenged him for his position.

He was big and had an eight point Antler, huge, the largest stag that Carl had ever seen. During the Rutting Season, none of the Park Rangers or anyone with an ounce common of sense would dare to approach him. The reason why they were getting the repairs to the enclosures finished now before the rutting Season set in. Carl's Foreman, Bill Wetting, was overseeing the unloading of fencing materials and doing a rough count of the posts, rolls of wire, bags of fixings and cement etc.

Carl continued on the digger with clearing out the ditch that he was working upon. He was almost half way along the ditch, which was the last drainage ditch to be cleared before they put up the new fencing. Other workers were beginning to ready the ground around the enclosures, to take out the old weathered posts and clear away the old rusted wire.

Once the enclosures were finished, they would be able to begin the task of rounding up the Deer to get them to the enclosures. The Vet would go out with the team and track where the Harems were. They would then tranquilise them with darts, so as not to stress them then load them onto trailers and carry them back to the enclosure. The Vet would then be able to closely check the Deer for injuries or ailments. The tranquiliser was necessary as these were totally wild Deer and were very unpredictable in their behaviour.

After they were checked and cleared by the Vet, they would be transferred to the holding paddock where the Vet would give them an antidote injection to wake them up. They would be held until fully recovered and the gates to the pen opened and the Deer would be allowed to run free back out onto the open Moor. Unnoticed by Carl, behind his seat in the digger, the bundle of rags begun to glow gently with a pale blue light.

The phone call came through as Carl was working on his ditch. He didn't hear it ring to begin with, as his mobile rang he felt it's vibration in his pocket. Carl turned the engine off of the digger and took his mobile out of his breast pocket and pressed to answer the call.

"Mr Morby? Mr Carl Morby?" A voice on the other end of the call enquired.

"Speaking". Replied Carl.

"I am Dr Frost, from Cranleigh General Hospital. I'm sorry to have to tell you that your wife was involved in an accident this morning and has been brought into us here at the Hospital", continued Dr Frost.

Carl fell silent, his head spinning at the words. His mouth went suddenly dry as he answered.

"What type of accident?" Asked Carl after a few moments.

Carl leaned against the digger to support his numb body.

"I do not wish to go into details over the phone Mr Morby, so would it be possible to come into the Hospital to see her?" Asked Dr Frost.

"Y-y- Yes Doctor, I-I-I-'ll be there as s-s-soon as possible." Stuttered Carl.

Carl sat in the digger for a long time trying to take in the news that he had just been given. His elbows were upon the dash board, his head fell into his hands. Not Far away, Bill Price, The Foreman, was working upon sorting the fencing materials into their order, to make using them more efficient. Bill noticed after a while, that Carl's digger had fallen silent. He put down the piece of wire roll which he was holding and walked over to the digger.

"Hey Boss, everythin' alroit?" Asked Bill.

Carl waited silent for a moment, then answered Bill with the news.

"Just had a phone call, said something about Rachel and an accident, was a Doctor, asked me to go to the Hospital," Said Carl, shakily.

"Oh my God Carl, is you OK Mate?" Said Bill.

"Bill, I hope you don't mind, I have to go to the Hospital to find out what is going on, you'll be OK to carry on here will you, with the digging for me and keep the work upon the enclosures going, Mate?" asked Carl almost in a daze.

"Of course I can, don' ee worry 'bout that, I'll teck care o' it. You'm get agwain m'dear an' I'll teck over 'ere. I 'opes Rachel b'aint too poorly, Mate." Replied Bill, swapping places with Carl upon the digger.

"Thanks Bill, so do I Mate." Said Carl.

Carl Climbed out of the cab and turned to the rag bundle behind the seat. He picked it up and carried it to his Landrover parked nearby. Carl put the bundle onto the back seat of the Landrover and climbed into the driver's seat. He pulled the seat belt around him and clicked it into place. Carl turned the key in the ignition and the car started. He pulled away from the parking space and turned onto the road and drove off in the direction of the village.

Carl drove along the road with the hedges passing like a blur. The countryside passing by but Carl didn't notice. He sped on passing the end of the lane where the accident had taken place; only a short time earlier Rachel had been cut out of her car here, loaded into an Ambulance and driven off to the Hospital where Carl was now heading.

Carl drove on past Pegasus House; he didn't stop or call in as he knew that Simon would be 'away on one of his Business trips' and out of touch for a while. Onward he drove until he came down the hill along Bogart Street, past the row of little cottages and into the Village Square. He then drove around the Village Square and up along Cranleigh Street, leaving Little Farthingworth behind. He drove on once again along hedge lined lanes until he entered the town of Cranleigh.

Cranleigh was the nearest town to Little Farthingworth, which was a short distance from the nearest City, Frackston. Cranleigh was the Administrative Centre for this area, covering Little Farthingworth, Farthingworth, Great Farthingworth, Pausey and Topley Villages.

Great Farthingworth was a small village like Little Farthingworth, as were Pausey and Topley. They lay in a series of valleys close to the open Moor with Taunton to the North and Exeter to the South. As Carl drove around the Ring Road, he drove into the entrance to the car park for the Hospital. Carl drove around the Car Park three times, stopping when he thought that there was a space, just for a car to cheekily slip into it before Carl was able to put the Landrover into reverse. Finally he found a space and successfully managed to park. He turned off the engine and unclipped his seat belt. Carl climbed out of the Landrover and pressed his key fob to lock the car. He then walked across the

Hospital Car Park to the main entrance. Carl walked through the entrance and walked up to the enquiry desk. Sitting there was an elderly lady with blue rinse hair and her age visible in her face. She was dressed in a blue and white check dress with a white crochet cardigan.

"Excuse me please, would you tell me where I can find Doctor Frost?" Asked Carl.

"He's a Looney". Replied The Old Lady.

"I beg your pardon?" Exclaimed Carl in surprise.

"Mad as a box of frogs on Friday". She added.

Just at that moment a younger woman walked into the reception behind the counter, mid-thirties with brown hair and blue eyes, wearing a blouse, jacket and skirt in pale blue with a badge pinned to her jacket saying "Julie".

"Sorry about that", said Julie and picked up the telephone, pressed a few buttons and said, "Yes, Reception here, sorry to trouble you but Mrs Mc Kreedy has got out to us again; would you please come down and collect her, thank you."

Julie put the phone down and turned back to Carl.

"Sorry about that, she keeps 'escaping' from her ward; the Nurses have terrible trouble with her poor thing. Now, how may I help you Sir? Asked Julie.

"I was looking for Dr Frost?" Asked Carl.

"Ah yes, you'll find him on Furgus Ward, same floor, just walk down towards the lifts, up along there and the door is to your right, marked above it." Replied Julie, directing Carl, along the corridor leading away from the Reception Desk.

"Thank you, I hope Mrs Mc Kreedy gets back to her ward OK." Said Carl, as he walked away from the Reception Desk.

"Oh she'll be OK" Replied Julie, smiling.

Carl walked away and saw two Nurses walk behind the Reception Desk pushing a wheel chair. After a little struggle, they put Mrs Mc Kreedy into the wheel chair and wheeled her out of Reception. They disappeared along a corridor to the left; then Mrs Mc Kreedy appeared again, making for the lifts with the two Nurses and wheel chair hurrying alone behind her.

Carl walked along the corridor to the right and walked through a pair of double doors with a sign above marked,

'FURGUS WARD'

Inside the doors, Carl identified the Reception Desk and walked over to a young Nurse in a pale blue dress and white net hat.

"Hello, I was asked to come along to see Dr Frost." Said Carl. The Nurse looked up from her seat and smiled.

"What name is it please; I'll page him for you Sir." She said.

"Mr Carl Morby" Carl replied.

The Nurse picked up her phone and dialled a number, she then spoke into it and said,

"Mr Carl Morby for Dr Frost."

She then turned to Carl as she put down her phone,

"If you wouldn't mind taking a seat Mr Morby, Dr Frost will be along shortly." Said She.

"Thank you." Said Carl, turning to walk over to a row of seats which he had noticed against a wall opposite the Reception Desk. He also noticed a box of rather old and somewhat tatty magazines. They were mostly Women's Magazines but he did notice a Nature one so he decided to look through this while he waited.

As he read an article about the aggressive nature of the 'Sweet Robin', Carl saw over the top of the Magazine someone approaching his seat. He was tall, bespectacled with Pepper and salt greying hair. He was wearing a long white coat. As he arrived to where Carl was sitting, he put down the Magazine and prepared himself for his meeting.

"Mr Morby?" Asked Dr Frost.

"Yes, Carl." Replied Carl.

"Very pleased to meet you." Said Dr Frost holding out his right hand for Carl to shake, "Would you come into my Office please." He added, gesturing Carl to follow him into as room next to the Reception Desk. Inside, Carl saw numerous certificates all with citations baring the name,

'DR ALLAN P FROST MD BA FRCS'

The room had a number of filing cabinets around it, upon one wall was a chart showing Patients names and their whereabouts upon the Ward and in front of him was a large wooden desk with papers covering everything, piles of files, a telephone and a photograph of a family all lined up and saying cheese towards the camera. In front of the desk were two seats, which Dr Frost motioned Carl to sit upon one of them. Carl sat down and Dr Frost spoke to him; he had a 'reassuring' tone of voice.

"I called you today Mr Morby, as this morning, your wife Rachel was brought into us following an RTA; that's a Road Traffic Accident. She had apparently turned out of a side turning onto the main road and her car was hit by a truck…." Dr Frost began to explain.

"HIT BY A TRUCK?!!" Exclaimed Carl, surprised.

Terrible thoughts ran around in Carl mind, visions of the collision and the crash of her windscreen, Rachel's body like a rag doll, thrown through the splintering glass, headlong across her bonnet onto the road, his beautiful Rachel.

"Yes Mr Morby, she is stable at the moment and is in theatre. Rachel sustained a number of serious injuries to her legs, arm and hip. Her right leg is broken, also her right hip and right arm. She sustained a slight head injury but not too serious and some whiplash. I have operated and pinned her leg and hip together, she is currently having her right arm pinned back together. The driver side of the car took much of the impact and she was crushed in her seat, but luckily only these injuries were sustained." Said Dr Frost.

Carl was now able to notice his blue scrubs underneath his white coat. Dr Frost had come out of the Theatre now the worst of Rachel's operation had been completed.

"I must return to Theatre, Carl, to complete the operation. Then Rachel will then be placed upon the ward. I will then come and collect you when we have her comfortably installed upon the ward." Said Dr Frost.

"Thank you", Said Carl.

They left the office, Dr Frost shook Carl's hand and walk away back the way he had come. Carl sat down again in the waiting area and picked up the Wildlife Magazine again and begun looking through its glossy pages again.

It seemed like an eternity that Carl sat there in that seat. He had found a further three Wildlife Magazines rummaging in the box and read all of them. Above him upon a bracket fixed to the opposite wall was a smallish television. Upon the screen Carl was able to see the 'Hairy Bikers' explaining how to cook a gorgeous looking meal and enthusiastically scoffing up their handy work once it was completed. Dr Frost reappeared down the corridor approaching Carl.

"Mr Morby, I hope that you were not too put out while you were waiting; sorry it took so long, but we wanted to make sure that we did a good job for Rachel." Said Dr Frost.

"I found some Magazines to read so that helped to pass the time." Replied Carl.

"I have been able to pin Rachel's arm back together and she will be in plaster for some weeks. Then we will have to see what the Physio has to say about their assessment and her learning to walk again." Dr Frost reported.

"So Rachel is going to be out of action for some time yet?" Asked Carl.

"I'm afraid so, Rachel sustained a broken leg and hip to her right side, due to this type of trauma happening to one complete side of her lower half and the time it takes for the injuries to heal, it will require her to learn to walk again. Rachel will be confined to a wheel chair while in plaster, then she will undertake a Physio program to strengthen her arm and legs again to help her walk as best as possible.

Mr Morby, Rachel has been through an ordeal and she will simply take a bit of time to recover. One thing I can tell you, that once she get's through the next few days, she will be through the worst of it." Said Dr Frost.

"May I see Rachel." Asked Carl.

"Yes, if you are quiet. We still have her sedated for a few days, just to let her body get used to her new repairs and to help the healing process begin." Replied Dr Frost.

DR Frost led Carl along the corridor and showed him into a side ward where there were four beds. Rachel was occupying the bed to the right at the far end next to the window. Dr Frost offered his best wishes and told Carl he was needed in Theatre again for another Patient. He thanked Carl for being so understanding in his wait. Carl thanked Dr Frost for all that he had done for Rachel. Dr Frost walked out of the side ward and away down the corridor towards the Theatre.

Carl walked up to Rachel's bed and pulled up a chair. He sat down and looked at his broken wife lying in the bed asleep. Rachel had a dressing up the right side of her forehead, a cast upon her right arm and an IV drip in her hand. Carl was not able to see her legs or hips, as they were beneath the clothes and were hidden inside a type of box like structure designed to keep pressure off her legs and hip to help the healing process. Rachel had an oxygen mask covering her face to help her to breathe. There were machines beside her bed beeping away.

Carl sat for a long moment trying to take in what he was seeing. Carl just sat looking, trying to build the courage to talk.

"Hello my lovely," Said Carl to Rachel lying next to him, "The Doc says that they're keeping you asleep like, for a few days, to help you heal. You had quite a bump Darling but the Doc says that you'll be OK."

Carl sat for a long while talking to Rachel, trying to find something to say to a person who is asleep and not answering. Eventually, Carl reached the end of visiting hours and had to leave Rachel in her bed at the Hospital. He walked out of the ward and along the corridor to the main entrance, Carl was in a trance, just acting upon autopilot, oblivious to what was going on around him as he left the building and walked across the Car Park to his Landrover.

He opened the door and climbed into the driver's seat. Carl pulled the seat belt into place and started the engine. He then drove out of the Car Park and out of the Hospital grounds back onto the Cranleigh Ring Road. All along the road, Carl's mind kept drifting to Rachel laying in that bed all alone, broken. She would be there for some weeks, while her injuries healed and she began Physio Sessions to help her to walk again.

Carl turned into Cranleigh Street and drove out of the town. He drove across the Moor past the hedge rows and fields and then into the Little Farthingworth Village Square. Carl stopped the car outside the Fish and Chip shop, as he concluded that Rachel would not be home to cook his dinner. He paid the Counter

Assistant and got back into his car. He then drove around the Village Square and up onto Bogart Street. He eventually came to the driveway of Pegasus House and turned in. He parked his Landrover in the turning circle outside the main door and turned off the engine. Carl sat for a moment looking at the house. There were no lights on anywhere. The house was in total darkness, the Living Room with no Simon as he was away, the Kitchen dark as Rachel was not there cooking Dinner, no light was burning in Toby's room , as he was away at Toadford. Carl knew that he was not able to tell Simon just yet about the accident, as he was away, unreachable. Then Carl thought with a start, Toby – he needs to know about Rachel's accident.

Carl walked up to the door and opened it with his key. He switched on the light to the hallway with the switch next to the door. He then put his Body Warmer upon a hook beside the door in the hallway. Then Carl closed the door. He walked into the Kitchen and placed his Cod and Chips onto a plate. He then opened the cutlery drawer and took out a knife and fork. Carl then opened a cupboard at eye level and took out a bottle of brown sauce, he decided against Ketchup, as this put him off due to the thought of his Hospital visit. The aroma of the vinegary chips rose to meet Carl's nose. He breathed it in deeply and made him feel a little better. Carl picked up the plate and carried it into the lounge on a tray. He sat down after turning on the light, upon the sofa and switched on the TV.

There was a comedy program on, but Carl wasn't cheered up, he thought of Rachel. He sat eating his Cod and Chips; he would call Toby to tell him after he had finished his Dinner. Carl took his plate back to the Kitchen now empty and washed it. He placed it in the drying rack and returned to the lounge.

Carl sat back upon the couch and picked up the phone. He dialled the number for Toadford and heard ringing on the other end of the line.

"Good afternoon, Toadford School, Mr Parfinkle, Headmaster speaking." The reply came over the phone.

"Good afternoon Mr Parfinkle, Carl Morby here. I was wondering whether it was possible to speak to Toby please. It is an important matter and rather urgent." Said Carl.

"What is the problem Mr Morby, I hope all is fine with you." Said Parfinkle, "My Secretary has just sent for young Toby."

"It's Rachel, my wife, Toby's Mother. She was involved in an accident this morning and I need to let Toby know and what we are doing." Replied Carl.

"Ah I see. I did catch something about an accident on the news, but the report was vague and did not name any victim; so this was Rachel?" Said Parfinkle.

"Yes I'm afraid so Mr Parfinkle, that's correct." Confirmed Carl.

Just then there was a knock at the door and Parfinkle called out

"Enter,"

Through the door walked Toby accompanied by the Secretary. Parfinkle asked Toby to sit in a seat in front of his desk. Toby sat down upon the seat.

"I have your Father upon the telephone Master Morby." Explained Parfinkle, handing the phone to Toby.

"Hello," Said Toby, putting the phone to his ear.

"Hi Toby, its Dad. I have some bad news for you I'm afraid, Lad. Your Mom had an accident upon the road this morning, after she left you at the School. She's in Cranleigh General Hospital; Mom had an operation and they fixed her up, so she's going to be fine. She has a little bit of recovering to do, but the Doc says with patience and time, she will be right as rain." Said Carl.

Toby didn't answer straight away; he was speechless for a few moments. Eventually he brought himself to speak.

"Where did it happen?" Asked Toby.

"On the Moorland Road as she turned out of the Toadford Lane." Replied Carl, not going into too much detail to worry Toby, like mentioning being hit by a truck.

"She is staying in Hospital for now, until her injuries have healed enough to come home." Carl added.

"Shall I come home?" Asked Toby, trying to be of some help, offering to go home rather than being useless and stuck at School.

"No Son, you stay there. I can't pull you out on your first day at a new school now, can I? You stay there, as I said, Mom will be in Hospital for a while yet, so you coming home would just upset your school work. She is in good hands and will be back with us soon." Carl reassured.

"Are you sure you don't want me to come home?" Asked Toby, just to make sure.

"No it's OK, Toby, you enjoy yourself there and do your best with your grades, Mom would want that. Mom will be back soon and we will see you at the end of term." Replied Carl, trying to reassure Toby that all would be fine, rather reassuring himself at the same time.

"I've made some new friends and they said that they would like to visit in the Holidays and maybe I would be able to visit them also." Said Toby, enthusiastically.

"Sounds great Toby, We'll see when the Holidays are here." Said Carl, let's just see how Rachel get's on, he thought.

"OK Dad, see you soon, give my love to Mom when you visit her." Said Toby.

"Will do Son, See you soon." Replied Carl.

Carl put down the phone, half pleased that Toby was making new friends at the school, that he was settling in alright.; half worried still for Rachel, what if the Doctors and Physio couldn't help her walk again? She would maybe have to give up her job at St. Claires, which she loved and would break her heart. He thought about her having to live with little or no independence, being reliant upon others for the most simplest of things, the most intimate of things, embarrassed to ask for help.

Doctor Frost had assured Carl that the operation had gone well and it was simply just a matter of waiting for her injuries to heal and her body to adapt to Physio. He had no doubt that Rachel would fully recover. He did specify however, that Carl should not be too alarmed if Rachel were to be left with a slight limp, as her broken hip had needed particular attention.

Carl sat watching TV, wondering when he would be able to see Simon and bring him up to date with the days events. He sat and wondered what was going to happen when Rachel returned home and how they would cope. He thought of how long it would take for Rachel to recover? Carl decided that he would call Bill Price and fill him in with the news. He would have to take at least a week's compassionate leave off from his job to initially keep an eye upon Rachel's progress.

He picked up the phone and dialled Bill's Mobile number. Out upon the Moor at the enclosure area, Bill Price heard his Mobile ring. He took it out of his pocket and pressed the answer button.

"Hullo, Bill Price Speakin'", Replied Bill.

"Hi Bill, it's Carl Morby." Said Carl.

"Oh 'ullo Carl, 'ow's thangs with Rach then?" Asked Bill.

"She had a pretty bad smash; her car was hit by a truck, a write-off. They operated and she's OK at the moment. They've got her sedated for a few days to let her body heal. The Doc says she will need Physio and have to learn to walk again, but says that she'll be fine." Carl said.

"Arr, OK Carl, ooh sounds nasty does that M'dear." Said Bill.

"I'll have to take a week's Compassionate Leave Bill, will you be able to cope with things while I'm away?" Asked Carl.

"Sure will Carl. You look af'er Rach, an' I'll look af'er thangs yer. 'Ope her pulls thru OK Mate, let me know ifn you'm needs anythin', OK." Said Bill.

"OK, thanks Bill, appreciate it Mate." Replied Carl and put the phone down.

Bill went back to nailing the Stretchers to the post he was working upon to attach the first piece of fence wire to. The nails were just to hold it in place while he set up and screwed in the heavy duty bolts to take the strain of stretching the fence wire taught. Carl sat watching the TV until it was time for bed. How he would sleep with the thought of Rachel not there, the thought of Rachel alone in her Hospital bed.

Back at Toadford in Parfinkle's Office, Toby handed the phone back to the headmaster who replaced it upon the cradle. Parfinkle assured Toby that if he needed extra time, under the circumstances, to complete homework tasks, he would have a word with the masters and would put word out that any mention of the accident would be kept to the Masters. By this time, when Toby left Parfinkle's Office, it was time to go along to the first of his afternoon lessons. Toby had missed his Lunch and was rather hungry. The School Secretary walked with Toby along to his lesson of English with Ebeneezer Finkle.

Mr Finkle was a man in his sixties like many of the Masters. He had a short horse shoe of grey hair around the back of his head and to his temples with a domed forehead and bald top above the hairline. He was average height and wore a grey suit underneath his Master's Robe. The Secretary knocked upon the classroom door.

"Enter." Said Finkle in his usual officious way. The Secretary opened the door and lead Toby into the room.

"Sorry Mr Finkle, emergency I'm afraid. Mr Morby had a telephone call from home. Mr Parfinkle knows all about it and asked me to ask you for him to be excused being late for the lesson." She said.

"That is perfectly alright Miss Tatum, if the Head had business with Master Morby, that is fully acceptable." He said.

Miss Tatum left the room and Toby walked over to a desk which was kept vacant for him. He joined his new found friends Keiron and Polly next to his desk. As he sat down, Keiron passed him a note under the desk.

'Got you some grub from Lunch to have during the break between classes after this.'

Toby took the note from Keiron and holding it under the desk read it.

"Thanks Keiron, I'll need that." Toby whispered to Keiron.

Ebeneezer set the Students to work upon Verbs, learning their structure and tenses. They had to read in Dictionaries the meaning of the Verbs and where their uses were to be found. They learned their place in Language and the tenses placement in sentences. To help with this, their coursework involved some tables of spelling and exercises in word play. Then the Homework was set. Using the notes and coursework they had been working upon during the lesson, Mr Finkle asked the students to write an essay. After the English class came their break for tea.

When excused from the class, the Students walked out of the room and along the corridor. Toby, Keiron and Polly walked up the staircase to their Cargal

Common Room, where they sat upon the sofas. They had fifteen minutes before they had to leave and make their way to the Maths class. Keiron opened his Ruc-Sac and handed Toby a napkin bundle. Polly had brought a plate over to him and a bottle of Cola.

"There's what we were able to get for you Toby," Said Keiron.

"Hopefully it will see you through until Dinner tonight, I hope you like it." Said Polly, with a smile.

"Don't I get a Cola?" Keiron enquired.

"The stand is over there, I got Toby one because he had no Lunch." Stated Polly.

"Girls, who needs 'em." Grunted Keiron quietly under his breath as he walked over to the drinks stand to fetch a bottle of Cola. He returned to the sofa with his Cola and sat next to Toby, with Polly on the other side.

"So what did Parfinkle want you for, can't see it was all that serious, we've only been here this morning?" Enquired Keiron.

"Yes Toby, what was the problem? I noticed you looked quite pale when you came into the English class and seemed rather quiet. I hope there isn't anything serious?" Asked Polly, shooting Keiron another of her disapproving looks. Toby sat for a moment and took a swig of his Cola. Then he told them about the phone call from his father.

"I had a call from my Dad. He told me that after leaving me at the School this morning, Mom had been in a car accident." Said Toby.

"Ruddy Hell!" Exclaimed Keiron.

"Oh my God Toby, I hope she was alright?" Said Polly, moving beside him putting her arm around Toby's shoulder and pulling his head down onto her shoulder.

"She had an operation Dad said, and is staying in Hospital for a while to recover. Dad said that Mom should be OK, but it will take time for her to heal." Replied Toby.

"You poor Dear." Said Polly, placing a quick kiss upon his forehead.

Toby was at this moment vulnerable and Polly noticed this as did Keiron. This seemed to pull the new friends closer together, to cement a bond between them. Polly and Keiron were the only friends that Toby had at the School so far, as they had only just been to one lesson and had not had much chance to meet more Students yet. This meant that Polly and Keiron were the first to hear his news, the first to console him and Polly the first to lend him a shoulder of support. Keiron knew, like Polly, that following that type of news, that Toby would need good support from the best of friends and that between them that they had to make sure that Toby was not injured or wounded in any way while learning to cope with the news.

"Dad said that Mom will have Physio sessions before returning home, but he doesn't see it as important enough for me to go home." Said Toby, from the warmth of Polly's shoulder. He could smell her hair next to his face and slight odour of a body spray which she used. Toby liked having his head upon Polly's shoulder, he wished he could stay like it for a long time.

"Time you ate your Lunch." Said Keiron, unwrapping the napkin bundle upon the plate which Polly had placed in front of Toby. There upon the plate was a stack of four sausage and salad sandwiches.

"Sorry it's not a full meal, but it's all we could gather quickly and carry." Said Keiron.

"Oh thanks Guys, at least it's better than starving, so I appreciate this." Replied Toby as he sunk his teeth into the first sandwich and took a bite. He chewed this and swallowed, 'at last' his stomach thought, 'something to digest'.

Looking at the time, Toby finished the sandwiches and the three Pals left the Common Room and walked along and back down the staircase. Polly held Toby's hand as they walked. They walked into a corridor opposite the one which lead to the Great Hall and joined the line-up of Students outside a class room. Polly let go of Toby's hand while they stood in line. Polly knew what bad news felt like, the kind which Toby had so suddenly received. Her Grandmother had passed away the month before she had joined Toadford. This still hurt, as Polly was close to her Granny Gwenn. She felt compelled to rest Toby's head upon her shoulder and to hold his hand as they walked to class, as this is what she would have expected Toby to do if he had been her friend when her Granny Gwenn had died. She had been hugged by her Mother when she had been given the news, her Father had just told her that it was sad and kissed her forehead as she had stood in her Mother's arms.

They were greeted at the door of the class room by the Mathematics Master Leonard Sheldon. They walked into the room after each of the Students had entered and found a desk to sit at. As in the English class, Toby sat with Polly and Keiron either side of him. Mr Sheldon was one of the younger section of staff at Toadford. In his late twenties, short blonde hair and blue eyes, he was tall, over six feet. He introduced himself to the class.

"Hello Grunts, I'm Mr Sheldon. I will be taking you for your Mathematics class. I have set papers of Arithmetic for you to do so that I can gauge your level of numeracy." He said.

Mr Sheldon walked around the room handing out pieces of paper with columns of sums written on them upon each desk. Keiron, Polly and Toby picked up their pens and began to attempt the page of sums. This was Polly's forte; she whizzed through the paper and was soon asking Mr Sheldon for another. Another paper filled, Polly fairly flew through the sums and constantly asked for more papers.

"Proper little brain box you are, aren't you Polly?" Sneered Keiron.

"One must practice arithmetic often if one intends to become an Accountant." Replied Polly.

"If Polly wishes to do sums, then that's Polly's choice." Said Toby.

"I think the head on the shoulder thing has gone to your head." Said Keiron.

"You're just jealous." Replied Toby, smiling to himself.

Keiron was just finishing his first sheet of sums, when Polly was finishing her fifth. The lesson continued this way until at last, Mr Sheldon asked the Students to hand in their papers. Toby had completed fifteen pages of sums, while Keiron had managed to complete only ten, after getting in a muddle with some of them. At the time to hand in their work, Polly had eventually completed thirty pages of sums. Mr Sheldon walked around the class picking up the papers, when he arrived at Polly's desk, he was impressed.

"Well done Miss Muggard, it would appear that from this pile you would give the impression of possibly being the top of the class." Said Mr Sheldon.

"Time to see if she can get her head through the door again." Sneered Keiron. Time for another of Polly's indignant looks aimed at Keiron.

"A little disappointing Master Mudley, only ten pages, let's hope that gets better over your time here." Said Mr Sheldon.

Polly looked at Keiron and grinned.

"Shut up." Barked Keiron.

The trio left the Maths class with everyone else. They began to walk along the corridor. Keiron walked away, found his classroom map to be upside-down, turned it right side up and caught up with the others.

They walked along to two class rooms along the way from the Maths Classroom. This was the Art class with Abbeygale Norwall, the Art Master. Abbeygale was young and pretty, in her late twenties.

"Cor, not 'arf bad." Whispered Keiron to Toby, who grinned back.

"Boys." Whispered Polly and rolled her eyes into the top of her head.

Miss Norwall just handed out paper, paints and coloured pencils as this was the final lesson of the first day. She was about five feet four with slim figure and long slender legs. Blonde, with her hair in a pony tail down her back. Toby drew some Toadstools and coloured them in with bright red and white sports, as a Fly Agaric. He was able to remember these from his dream in the woods. Polly was drawing some flowers; art was something else she was good at. Keiron was drawing a castle with Knights in Armour on Horseback.

58

Toby thought about his dream, the recurring one in the Forrest and running, running for his life and the Falcon diving down upon him, then blackness. He had been having the dreams for as long as he could remember.

"Why do you suppose they call us first years 'Grunts'?" Keiron speculated.

"We'll most likely find out soon enough. I should think." Replied Polly.

"We'll probably be told that after Dinner in the Common Room." Toby added.

Their Dinners were brought into the Kitchen Staff and placed in front of them upon the table. Tonight was 'Toad in the Hole' and as a Senior chuckled from the top Cargal table.

"Grunt in the Hole." He called.

Then Parfinkle stood and cleared his throat ready to address the assembled Students and Masters in the Great Hall. He stood at the lectern and spoke out across the Hall.

"Ahem! Pray silence." Parfinkle called out and then the Great hall fell silent; the hubbub from the tables ceased and all of the Students looked to the Top Table.

"Tonight we welcome our new batch of First year Students to the School and to their first Dinner here. You first year Students will notice upon your First year tables' that there are notices inscribed 'GRUNTS'. This is because there is a Tradition at Toadford School, which each year has a 'Nick-name' and the nick-name given to new first year Students is 'GRUNTS'. The other nick-names for Second year Students are 'WEENERS'; for the Third year Students, they are called 'TOFFS'; the Fourth year Students are called 'CARDINALS' and the Fifth year Students are called 'SENIORS.'" Announced Parfinkle.

"It is also a Tradition at Toadford School to say 'Grace' before beginning our meals; Let us Pray". Added Parfinkle.

The Students and Masters all around the Great Hall at their seats bowed forwards with hands held in Prayer, eyes closed.

"May the Good Lord make us truly grateful for what we are about to receive and make the sustenance fees our bodies and souls; AMEN." Said Parfinkle. The gathered occupants of the Hall answered "AMEN." They opened their eyes and looked at their plates.

"Tuck in Lads." Cried Keiron.

"And Ladies!" Polly added.

The noise of clashing cutlery and chewing followed. Mouthful after mouthful of 'Toad in the Hole' was scooped up and emptied into hungry waiting mouths. Once the 'Toad in the Hole' had been successfully dealt with, it was the turn of the pudding. They all greeted, with glee, the sight of the Kitchen staff bringing in and placing in front of them the Treacle Pudding and Custard. This too was heartily wolfed down in no time at all. Polly was disgusted at the sight of the boys gorging themselves upon 'Toad in the Hole' and now Treacle Pudding. Keiron sat with a stream of Custard pouring down his chin, where it had leaked out of his mouth between mouthfuls.

"You eat like a JCB." Scolded Polly watching Keiron with horror.

"Growing Lad." Keiron slurped through a mouthful of Pudding and Custard.

Polly gave Keiron a very unimpressed look. Toby had enjoyed his meal and sat waiting patiently to be excused.

"If you were my Boyfriend, you would have to adopt much better and more appropriate manners than that." Scolded Polly.

"If I were your Boyfriend, I'd ruddy Top myself." Replied Keiron, gloomily.

Again Polly shot the very unimpressed look at Keiron.

"Thankfully that is one thing that you will never have to worry about, isn't it Keiron." Quipped Poly.

The tables were cleared and Parfinkle rose from his chair to address the Great Hall.

"To you one and all, this concludes our business for tonight and I dismiss you for today. Goodnight all." Said Parfinkle. With that, Parfinkle walked around the table followed by the Senior Masters. He lead them out of the Hall. Parfinkle then walked across the hallway and into the wing opposite, heading for his quarters in the Staff wing of the School.

The four House Masters stood at the doors to the Great Hall and ushered the Students through in their Houses, up the staircases and into their respective House wings. The higher classes went up the stairs at the end of the corridor and Thybold said goodnight to them as they climbed the stairs. Then he turned to the First years as they stood outside their rooms and wished them goodnight, which they returned; then he walked around the corner to his office. Thybold would work in there for a couple of hours before returning to his quarters in the staff wing. Keiron and Poly had remained silent as they walked out of the Great Hall and up the stairs to the House wing. They now stood outside their respective dormitory rooms.

"Polly, would you like to come across when you're ready and we'll all go down to the Common Room together, if you would like to?" Asked Toby.

"Very well Toby, see you soon." Polly replied, "I have a few things to sort out and then I'll be across, don't go until I call over will you?" She added enthusiastically.

"OK Polly, see you soon." Replied Toby.

"GRRRNT." Said Keiron, indignantly.

"That's probably why they call us 'Grunts'," Laughed Toby and nudged Keiron, who fell flat upon his face through the bedroom doorway.

In their Dorm Room, Keiron and Toby changed out of their Uniforms and into more casual T Shirts and Jeans. When not in lessons and dismissed for the day or at weekends, the Students were allowed to wear their own casual clothes. Toby sat upon his chair looking at his Lessons Rota for the rest of the week and studying the School map to see where he had to be for each lesson and how to move between classes. Keiron came over and compared his maps and Rota, so that they both were able to co-ordinate their lessons and to try to help Keiron from getting lost! Their first lesson next day was games, with James Marden, the Games Master. This would be one of the few lessons where the boys would not be with the girls, as most Games lessons were segregated unless it was a joint lesson like Athletics, when it was leading up to Sports Day.

Keiron began to read a book, one with lots of pictures; he liked the pictures. In the rooms they found notes to each of them which informed them that a presentation would be taking place in the Common Room that evening. There was a knock at the door and Toby thought that this must be Polly, come to see whether they were ready to go to the Common Room.

"Come in Polly." Cried Toby.

The door opened and in stepped Polly, now not in Uniform but dressed in a red T Shirt with a picture of a Rabbit upon the front and Jeans. Toby stood up from his chair and let Polly sit down while he sat upon his bed. Polly had brought a small digital camera with her.

"How about I set my camera up to 'Self Timer', and get a photo of us new friends upon our first day at Toadford together?" Asked Polly.

"That would be great, sound's cool!" Said Keiron eagerly and sat down upon the bed next to Toby.

"OK Polls, that's a good idea." Said Toby with a smile.

Polly set up her camera upon a tripod she had brought with her, pressed the shutter button and the camera whirred; a small red light flickered on and off and Polly skipped to the bed and quietly said to the boys "Budge up."

They parted and moved aside to allow Polly to sit between them. Just in time, they looked up at the camera with beaming smiles then the flash went off and the shutter fired. Polly turned to Toby and whispered into his ear.

"By the way, my name is Polly, not Polls!" She told him.

"Sorry Polly, no offence meant." Replied Toby.

"None taken." She smiled.

Keiron pretended to put his fingers into his throat to look like he was being sick. Polly gave him another unimpressed look.

"There's nothing wrong with politeness." Polly scolded Keiron.

"Sorry Miss Bossy Boots." Replied Keiron sarcastically.

Poly ignored his remark and turned to Toby.

"Are we off to the Common Room then?" Asked Polly.

The two boys nodded and they all stood up. Polly picked up her camera from the tripod.

"OK If I leave the tripod here for now?" She asked.

"That's OK." Replied Toby.

"The camera goes everywhere with me, except into lessons of course, Mommy and Daddy bought it for me last Christmas." She added. They then all three walked out of the Dorm Room into the corridor. Toby motioned to Polly to walk out first.

"Creep." Said Keiron from the corner of his mouth.

They walked down to the Common Room along the corridor admiring the pictures of past Students of Cargal House along the walls between Dorm Room doors. They entered their area of the Common Room through the door marked 'GRUNTS' and noticed a Senior boy standing in front of the stone fireplace with a number of boxes upon the Coffee table in front of him.

This was Thomas Peeling, the Cargal House Head Boy, a Prefect. Thomas called the 'GRUNTS' to him. They all gathered around, all twelve of them and waited to see what was going on. Thomas was tall, slim and had short wavy brown hair. He stood at the table and called forwards the Grunts to hand them a box each. Thomas stood before the group of Students and announced.

"It is with great pleasure that in Honour of Guyiume Cargal, our Founder and Patriarch of Cargal House, that we present to the new Grunts of Cargal House for this year, as a welcome gift, a little something."

"Hip hip Hurrah." Called Thybold, who was standing alongside Thomas. Thybold lifted a green cloth which was covering the table and the eyes of the Grunts lit up. There upon the table were twelve computer tablets with their own docking keyboards either side of the table.

"These Tablets are to help you with your Course Work through your stay here at Toadford School and for your Homework. You will keep your docking stations in your rooms to use for completing Homework. We also include with the Tablets, Memory sticks for you to keep your paperwork stored upon. When completing Homework or Course Work assignments, it is advisable to back up your DATA and to keep Hard Copies and file them away in case of any 'mishaps'." Said Thybold.

The Grunts were called forwards and each received their Tablet with glee. Thomas handed each Student their Tablet and told them;

"The School is now 'Wi-Fi', which means that you will be able to complete your Course Work and Homework research from anywhere within the School; the Library, your rooms or even the Inner Bailey. Please enjoy them and take good care of them." Said Thomas.

It would appear that although there were many strict traditions at Toadford School that they moved with the times where necessary.

"When you return to your rooms, you Grunts will notice that a printer has been placed in there for your use. When you need replacement paper or ink cartridges, please come to see me or Mr Thybold and ask us to hand them out to you." Said Thomas.

A big cheer went up from the Grunts and some patted Thomas upon his back, then they filed out of the Common Room and back to their Dorm Rooms to put away their Tablets.

"Gonna have some fun with that Tablet." Grinned Keiron.

"How wonderful," Polly squealed," that will be a great help with our Homework." Polly added, shooting Keiron another disapproving look.

Toby was thrilled with his Tablet. This would mean that in the Holidays, he would be able to take home the memory stick and work upon his assignments then tweak them finally when returning to School before handing them in. He was delighted with the opportunity to be able to produce some fine Coursework upon the Tablet towards his exams.

Upon returning to the Common Room, Keiron, Toby and Polly sat at the Coffee table upon the couches. In the Common Room the seats were covered with green leather, to match the walls and the mats which were scattered around the varnished wooden floor. Polly had brought along her School Hand Book with her to read. Keiron was lounging upon a couch while Toby sat with a book next to him. Polly walked across from the door of the room to the couches and sat opposite the boys.

"Anyone like a drink?" Asked Toby.

"Wouldn't say no to a Cola." Replied Keiron.

"May I have a cup of Tea please, Toby." Replied Polly, all prim and proper.

"Be right back." Replied Toby, getting up and walking over to the drinks stand.

Atop the stand was a tea pot and Coffee pot. Next to these was a kettle, which had a stack of tea cups, saucers and mugs beside it. Beneath these upon a lower shelf were many bottles of Cola, Lemonade and Orangeade which stood next to stacks of glasses. Toby placed two teabags into the tea pot and once it had boiled, poured the boiling water from the kettle onto them. Toby then took a bottle of Cola from the shelf and a glass. He then placed these upon a tray and then poured out two cups of tea and placed these next to the Cola upon the tray upon the tray.

Toby then carried the tray over to the Coffee table and placed it down. Keiron swung his legs around to sit upon the couch and Toby handed Polly her cup of Tea. Keiron reached out and picked up his glass and bottle of Cola.

"Cheers Pal." Said Keiron as he opened the bottle of Cola and poured it out into the glass.

"Thank you, Toby." Said Polly smiling as she took the cup of Tea from Toby.

They sat drinking their drinks; Toby had brought a bar of chocolate with him to the Common Room and offered it to Polly. She took some pieces and Toby then offered the chocolate to Keiron.

"You live in Pegasus House then, do you Toby?" Asked Polly.

Yes, with my Parents and my Grandfather." Replied Toby.

"What about your Grandmother?" Asked Keiron.

"My Grandmother died when I was ten years old." Replied Toby.

"So sorry to hear that." Keiron and Polly said, comfortingly together.

"Have you heard of Pegasus House then, Polly?" Asked Toby.

"Yes I have, but I don't know much about it really, as I don't live in the village, just heard little snippets." Replied Polly.

"Well, its rather a large house and belongs to my Grandfather. The house stands in its own grounds with our own short driveway. Said Toby.

"That's a Mansion." Said Keiron.

"Yes, a Medieval Manor House; it has an existing wing and centre piece, added later was another wing, to give the house as it is today. The house is made up of a central spinal area, where the Entrance Hall is, which leads into the main hallway. Here are the stairs and this leads back to the Kitchen. To the right as one enters, is the East wing, which is where me and my Parents live. To the left of the entrance is the West wing which is where my Grandfather lives. He comes into us occasionally for his meals and for family gatherings but mainly stays in his part of the house. He is frequently away on Business and can be gone for days. The front of the house upon the West wing is fairly plain with battlements upon the roof area, while the later added East wing has a Gothic design to it and a tower over the Entrance Hall. To the rear is a well landscaped garden with a lawned area for me to play in, a vegetable patch – for Dad and a flower garden for Mom. Behind the West wing is a separate garden which is more formal in layout." Toby said

"Wow! Sounds like some house." Said Keiron.

"Yes, sounds quite grand to me." Agreed Polly.

"I'll ask Dad when it would be OK for you to visit, so that we would be able to stay at the house for some of the Holidays." Said Toby.

"I could ask." Replied Keiron excitedly.

"Me too, I hope they agree, would be Grand." Replied Polly.

"Please ask them and let me know, it would be perfectly safe and you would each have your own room to stay in." Replied Toby.

I will give my Parents a call and ask." Said Polly.

"Me too." Added Keiron.

Then Keiron and Polly left the Common Room and went back to their respective Dorm Rooms, to fetch their Mobile Phones. The pair returned ten minutes later with big smiles upon their faces.

"My Parents are OK with it, just wanted assurance that your Parents would be there." Said Keiron.

"My Parents are OK with it too, same thing, just wanted assurance that your Parents would be there." Added Polly.

"My Mom will be there, most of the time as she is recovering from her accident and My Dad will be there in the evenings and weekends." Replied Toby.

"That's Good then, you can count me in." Replied Polly, enthusiastically.

The three then settled down in the Common Room for the evening. Toby turned on the TV and checked through the channels, while Keiron checked a cupboard next to the TV stand and found a 'Play Station' within it. He took it out and set it up. There was a note attached to the door of the cupboard with sticky tape.

'To The Students

At the end of each term or

whenever away from the School

For an extended period of time

the Play Station MUST be disconnected

and stored back into the cupboard.'

Polly noticed a stack of games in the cupboard; she was not very impressed with the titles, so she decided to give it a miss.

"You boys have a game; I'll just continue reading my book." Said Polly.

It was important that she continue to read her book, so as to stay 'Prim and Proper' and top of her class. Polly sunk back into the couch which was opposite to where the boys had been sitting. The padded seating moulded around her frame and supported her nicely.

Toby and Keiron had moved to sit upon small chairs in front of the TV stand, Play Station handsets glued to their hands, fingers a blur upon the buttons. They opted to play a football game, Keiron not too happy as Toby soon began to show him who was boss upon the football pitch. The two boys glanced over at Polly, face stuck in the book.

"Swatting already Polly and it's only our first day." Taunted Keiron.

"Just familiarising myself with the Traditions and such of the School, just so that I know what's what and where's where." Replied Polly.

"Crumbs Toby, do you play like that upon a real pitch?" Exclaimed Keiron.

"I try my best." Replied Toby.

By now, it had attracted the attention of a number of the other Grunts, who were watching as Toby thrashed Keiron upon the football game.

"Would someone like to fetch me over a glass of Cola please?" Asked Polly.

"OK." Replied Toby and between matches, walked over to the drinks stand and picked up a bottle of Cola and a glass. Then he took them over to Polly and handed them to her, who was still sitting reading.

"Thank you Sweetie." Said Polly.

She opened the bottle and poured the Cola into the glass and took a sip, then put down the glass upon the Coffee table in front of her chair and continued reading her book. Toby returned to the chair he had occupied and resumed playing the Football game with Keiron. The rest of the evening passed much like this and then it was nine o'clock, time for the Grunts to return to their Dorm Rooms for bed. Keiron turned off the TV while Toby turned off the 'Play Station' and placed the handsets neatly on top of the machine ready for another day's play. They all three then walked out of the Common Room after Polly had washed up her glass and disposed of the bottle into a recycling box and walked back along the corridor to their Dorm Rooms. They stopped outside and Toby turned to Polly, who was standing outside her Dorm Room.

"Goodnight then Polly." Said Toby.

"Yeah g'night." Keiron echoed.

"Good night then boys, sleep well and see you both tomorrow for Breakfast." Replied Polly.

Then they went into their respective Dorm Rooms. Polly changed quickly into her night dress, pale pink with a teddy bear upon the front. Toby and Keiron, as they had no Homework, this being their first day, changed into their Pyjamas and climbed into bed.

"Good night Toby." Said Keiron.

"Good night Keiron, see you in the morning." Replied Toby.

They then turned out their bedside lamps and settled down to sleep. As soon as Toby's head touched the pillow, he was asleep.

66

Chapter Ten – The Recurring Dream

Through the night Toby was running again, from the School, he seemed to be running for hours. Her dodged around the bushes as he entered the forest, hoping to avoid the roots. Toby glanced around behind him, he could hear the bushes crashing around. Toby's heart was in his mouth, his lungs were rasping for breath. He tripped, flew through the air, tumbled and came to rest upon his back, staring upwards in terror. The Falcon swooped down then black.

"Toby, Toby, Toby." Called Keiron.

Toby sat up in bed with a start, sweat pouring from his brow. His eyes were wide and in a fixed stare. Keiron was beside Toby's bed, shock was upon his face. Toby had been tossing and turning and thrashing about in his bed, he was crying out and whimpering.

"Hrrrgth! I – I – w – was having a b – b – bad dream, s – s – sorry Mate." Stuttered Toby, still staring into space.

"I heard you calling out and you were thrashing around, thought there was something wrong Mate." Replied Keiron.

"Sorry Keiron, just a recurring dream I keep having. I don't know where it comes from, but it's always the same, I'm running through woodland and then a bird swoops down and that's it." Explained Toby.

"Put on your dressing gown; let's get a drink to calm you down." Said Keiron.

Toby got out of bed, his legs a little wobbly, and then pulled on his dressing gown. Toby and Keiron quietly opened their Dorm Room door and tip-toed along the corridor until they reached the Common Room. They entered and walked to the couches. Toby sat down and Keiron walked over to the drinks stand. He took out a bottle of Cola and a glass and brought them over to Toby along with one for himself.

"How long have you been having the dreams, Toby?" Asked Keiron.

"I don't know, some time now as long as I can remember." Replied Toby.

"Have you got any idea why you have the dream?" Keiron asked him.

"I don't know what causes the dream, I've never been to a forest and been chased by a bird?" Replied Toby.

They drank their Cola drinks and then crept back to their Dorm Room. Toby assured Keiron that hopefully, there should be no more disruptions that night, as the dream usually only came once in a night. Next morning, Toby and Keiron were up and out of bed early and showered in the en-suite and then returned to the bed area of their Dorm Room to dress.

"You OK this morning, Toby." Asked Keiron, concerned.

"Yes thanks Mate, thanks for the talk and the time that you gave to me last night, I appreciate your help, the Cola was welcome too." Replied Toby.

There came a knock at the Dorm Room door and Keiron called out.

"Come in Polly."

The door opened and in trotted Polly. Toby once again got up from his seat and sat upon his bed, motioning Polly to sit in his place.

"Morning boys," Polly smiled, "Keiron, tie Dear." Added Polly.

Keiron looked down to check his tie, he was wearing the School tie rather than his House tie. He quickly removed it and replaced it with his House tie, at the second attempt, he finally achieved tying it.

"There you go, Keiron, all present and correct, ready for to face the new day." She reported.

"We'll see you at Lunch, after Breakfast, Polly; have a great morning won't you." Said Toby.

"Thank you , Toby, but we have Breakfast first though, so let's go then." Replied Polly.

Toby and Keiron picked up their Ruc-Sacs and checked inside. When they were quite happy that they had not forgotten anything for the day, they secured the Ruc-Sacs and put them onto their backs with their arms through the straps.

"All here." Said Toby, with a big smile.

"Me too." Agreed Keiron.

"OK then boys, now we're ready to make our way down to Breakfast." Said Polly.

The trio of friends left Toby and Keiron's Dorm Room and walked to the door to their wing. The rest of the Cargal Students were filing out of the door and onto the landing, heading for the stairs. Along the landings came the Students from the other three Houses to their stairs. Across the width of the Hallway, upon the opposite landing, Toby was able to see the Wombat House Students walking out of the door to their Dorm Wing, almost barging past the Farley House Students leaving their wing trying to get to their staircase first. The Wombat Students seemed to think they were the Bees Knees at Toadford, the top dogs. Maybe it was time to bring them down a peg or two, thought Toby. Due to their domination of the School Cups and records, Wombat House Students did really think they were superior to the rest of the School Students and marched around the School with according arrogance.

The Cargal House Students reached their staircase as the last of the Hatchell House Students were descending towards the hallway. Once again, Toby marvelled at the abundance of paintings around the landings and hallway. Polly was walking was a happy smile upon her face, but awkwardness in her eyes, looking forwards to the new day and what lessons they would be taking but also enduring the constant chatter from behind her as Arrabella was trailing her down the stairs and into the hallway. Inside the Great Hall the House Students all split up and went to their respective tables. They sat at their tables and waited for Breakfast to begin. Parfinkle was satisfied that all of the Students were in their correct place and ready, so he began.

"Dear Almighty Lord, make us enriched and empowered with this Breakfast and give us the sustenance to help us through until Lunch. AMEN!" Parfinkle announced.

The Students all echoed the 'AMEN' and waited for Parfinkle's address.

"Good morning to you Students and especially to the new Grunts, who's first full day at Toadford this is. We now have Breakfast and then you will all be joining your masters for your morning Classes. During your Breakfast, Mr Cracket will be attending your tables with any Postal deliveries that may have arrived for you. Please begin." Said Parfinkle.

The Students all received their Breakfasts from the Kitchen staff upon their tables. There was Full English Breakfasts for each Student, plates with Grapefruits, bowls of Cereal, jugs of orange squash and lemonade, pile so f toast. The Students tucked in enthusiastically.

"Enjoy your swill boys." Said Polly indignantly.

"Will do." Grinned Keiron.

"Oink." Said Toby, matching Keiron's grin.

"What went on last night? I heard a muffled noise coming from your Dorm Room and then heard the door open and you whispering." Asked Polly, inquisitively.

"How did you hear us?." Asked Keiron, surprised.

"When one's ears are subject to bombardment of noise regularly, one is sensitive to when it is quiet and easily disturbed." Replied Polly, glancing at Arrabella.

"Sorry that was my fault, I was having a bad dream' Said Toby.

' I suppose it's the different environment and all that, not used to being away from home." Said Polly.

"No, it's a recurring dream, which began years ago, before I came to Toadford, so it can't be due to relocation, although since I've been here, when I had the dream last night, it does seem to have intensified. Said Toby.

"We'll have to look into this, chance to sort out a mystery." Said Polly enthusiastically, with a smile.

"Could be something to do with School, its old and could be doing funny things to you?" Added Keiron.

"You may have a point there Keiron." Agreed Polly.

They continued their Breakfast, enjoying each mouthful.

"Seems strange that the dream should be amplified here, if we look into the History surrounding the School, we may find some reason for this." Said Keiron.

"Oh goody, some quality time in the Library coming up." Smiled Polly.

"Boring!" Toby and Keiron replied together.

"Well you may think that studying in the Library to find answers is boring, but how else do you expect to find answers." Said Polly gruffly.

"So at the weekend, as we can't leave, we should meet up and do some searching in the Library." Said Toby.

"Good Idea, boring or not!" Agreed Polly.

They finished their Breakfast and Parfinkle dismissed the Students from the Great Hall. They walked out into the hallway and Toby said goodbye to Polly.

"See you later Polly, have a nice time at games, see you at Lunch." Said Toby.

"Yeah, see you later." Said Keiron.

"Thank you, see you at Lunch boys." Replied Polly, skipping off with the other girl Grunts to her Games lesson.

Toby and Keiron then turned to walk through the hallway and around underneath between the staircases to a door at the back of the hallway. Through the door, the Grunts walked across a courtyard with a fountain at its centre and through another door into another corridor. They then walked into the boy's Changing Room. Mr James Marden was the boy's Games Master; stockily built with thick set shoulders and dark hair. His blue eyes lit up at the sight of the boys entering the room. Inside the room they were asked to change into their sports kits. The Grunts from the other houses were there and they were asked to wait for Mr Marden to begin the lesson. Mr Marden left the room to return a few moments later with a bag of footballs. The Grunts from Cargal House looked splendid in their green shirts with gold trimmings and a golden Swan's head emblem upon their chests; white shorts with golden trimming, green socks with golden hoops. The Grunts of Hatchel House wore yellow shirts with golden trimmings and a golden toad emblem upon their chests, white shorts with golden trimmings and yellow socks with golden hoops. The Farley House Grunts wore red shirts with golden trimmings and a golden Griffin emblem upon their chests, white shorts with golden trimmings and red socks with golden hoops. The Wombat Grunts wore deep blue shirts with golden trimming and a golden Boars head upon their chests; white shorts with golden trimmings and deep blue socks with golden hoops. The Grunts from the different Houses sat upon separate benches, then Mr Marden walked up to them and stood between them.

"Good morning boys and welcome to your Games lessons at Toadford School. What we are about to begin with will be a few laps of the playing fields out the back. I'm Mr Marden and I'll be taking you through to Lunch. Our agenda is to train you up to represent the School at the highest level in a number of sporting events. I expect you to work hard to bring glory to your House and the School and to emulate your predecessors or possibly even excel past them." Said Mr Marden. The boys listen closely.

"After the little run around the fields, we will choose which House play who and then play a bit of Football to see how you chaps fare. So now follow me out to the playing pitches to play." Said Mr Marden.

The boys from all of the House teams stood up and followed Mr Marden out of the Changing Room and out to the rear of the buildings. They walked out through the double doors onto a collection of fields. Toby was able to see across the fields to some goal posts and was able to define that there were five Football pitches, two Rugby Pitches and one Hockey pitch.

Further away, Toby was able to see a pavilion next to a Cricket pitch, a running track and other Athletics facilities; also a scaffold structure of stands. This was the official pitch used for School Team matches of Football and Rugby and for School Cup Finals. Toadford was very sports minded School. After running around the perimeter of the fields, some Grunts were out of breath, Keiron was one of them.

"Is he trying to kill us or something?" Spluttered Keiron.

"I don't think so, he was just checking out our fitness levels, I think." Replied Toby.

"Feels like it to me, I thought that I was quite fit, shows how wrong I am." Said Keiron.

"Don't worry, I think you will live." Replied Toby with a smile.

Mr Marden then gathered all of the Grunts together and separated them into their Houses. Toby and Keiron looked over towards the deep blue shirts of Wombat House and grinning back were the triplets. The triplets were the sons of Hargus and Hettie Eldgridge of Tugmoor farm; Delbert, Gaynell and Dexter. They were quite thick set, stocky with thick arms and shoulders and legs like tree trunks. On top of their heads was a thick mop of ginger hair and they had beady eyes with large noses and full mouths, the boys looked every inch the stereotypical Rugby players.

"Gulp! I hope we don't get them to play against, I haven't had chance to make a suit of armour." Said Keiron nervously.

The Eldgridge Triplets were standing cracking their knuckles as though they were preparing for a boxing match. It was decided by Mr Marden that there should be two Football matches to see how they played. He picked the House teams to play against one another, then addressed the Grunts again;

"OK Grunts, we'll be playing two matches and they will count as the first of the House Cup matches. I've picked the teams who will play one another and they will be Cargal House versus Hatchell House and Wombat House versus Farley House. The House Cup is played as a round robin league system, where each House plays the others twice. Then the teams who are first and second play in the Final for the House Cup Trophy". Announced Mr Marden.

"Sir, do we play upon the big pitch?" Asked Marcus Trippet of Wombat House.

"No Trippet, not until you reach the Final, if you do." Replied Mr Marden.

The House Captains picked by Mr Marden then sorted the teams into their positions. Toby took up his place up front as Striker and Keiron went back into defence. Then in their line ups, Mr Marden told them which pitch they would be playing upon; he introduced Mr Sheldon as the Referee of the Wombat v Farley game. He then lead the Cargal and Hatchell teams onto their pitch while Mr Sheldon lead the Wombats and Farley teams onto their pitch. Mr Marden then stood with the Captains from either side in the centre and tossed a coin allowing it to land upon the ground. As it spun in the air, Steve Logan, Cargal House Captain, called for choice.

"Heads." Called Steve Logan.

The coin landed upon the ground and was clearly showing the tails side of the coin. Hatchlel had won the toss. The teams prepared and Mr Marden blew his whistle which indicated the start of play. The Hatchlel team kicked off and the match began. Hatchlel players cautiously made their way into Cargal territory and up the Cargal end of the pitch. They reached the rear of the midfield but were then tackled and lost possession. Cargal then took their turn to push the ball up the filed into the Hatchlel half. The Cargal team passed the ball around and kept the Hatchlel players away from the ball. The Cargal team started to play with a bit of confidence and the ball was passed out to the wing to Peter Gough, who then ran the ball down the wing until he reached the 'by-line' and hoisted a cross through the air across the penalty area where Toby, running into the area was able to catch the ball perfectly upon his right foot and expertly volleyed the ball like a guided missile straight past Guy Watson in the Hatchlel goal and it crashed against the back of the net.

"GOAL." The Cargal team shouted collectively.

Toby had played for his Junior school team and had been coached by his Father Carl in Football and Rugby and had become rather an accomplished player for his age. Toby knew all too well that to get on and achieve he would need to excel here at Toadford, then maybe, he would be picked for the District Football team and possibly a scout from his beloved Frackston City would see his progress and then give him his dream, signing him up for the Club as an Apprentice Player. After regrouping, Hatchlel began another attack, this time their Striker, Allan Kirk, was fed the ball and let fly a stinging shot. The ball fizzed towards the Cargal goal directly, where Steve Logan in goal for Cargal, at full stretch, dived across the goal and parried the ball out to the feet of Keiron, who then hoofed the ball up field and out of the danger zone. Keiron's clearance fell at the feet of Peter Gough once again, who ran down the wing. This time it was covered by the Hatchlel left Back. Peter cut inside and laid off a pass to Toby, he then ran into the Penalty area and thumped a bullet shot leaving Guy Watson groping at empty air, the net bulged and the cry once again sounded.

"GOAL! TWO NIL. YAAAY!" The Cargal players cried out.

The Half Time whistle sounded and the boys all walked from their pitches to a refreshment table with cups of Orange juice and slices of Orange. After ten minutes, Mr Marden called the teams back onto their pitches for the Second Half of their matches. He blew the whistle and Toby kicked the ball over the line. It was passed backwards into the Cargal midfield and then Cargal began passing the ball around through the midfield and then Cargal began passing the ball around and keeping it from Hatchlel House. The ball was passed around through the midfield until upon the edge of the Hatchlel Penalty area, it was passed into Toby, who slipped a defender and turned to let fly another shot. This time, Guy Watson was able to get across the goal and made a spectacular Athletic save. He parried the ball out to a waiting Hatchlel defender who began to take the ball up the pitch before eventually passing it to a midfielder who twisted and turned Peter Gough aside and passed a through ball into Allan Kirk who then hit it first time, but Steve Logan was equal to the shot and caught the ball with his arms, closing his hands around it pulling it into his chest.

The match continued much in this vein of the attack, tackle and counter attack. Hatchlel eventually forced two corner kicks but sadly these came to nothing. Before long though, as they tired, the Hatchlel defence began to falter once again. It was a Hatchlel corner kick, the ball came across; the Left Back from Cargal headed the ball down once again at the feet of Keiron, who side stepped two advancing Hatchlel midfield players and then laid the ball off into the path of the advancing Peter Gough. He once again ran the ball down the wing, passed it into Philip Carrow in the midfield, who passed it back to Peter. He took the ball past the Hatchlel Left Back, cut inside and passed to Philip, who let fly a shot which flew towards Guy Watson. He was only able to parry the ball which fell invitingly at the feet of Toby as he ran into the Penalty area and slotted the ball past the stricken Hatchlel Goalkeeper who was not able to reach in time and only able to watch the ball once again hit the back of the net.

"GOAL! Hat Trick!." Shouted The Cargal players. Toby was really enjoying himself now.

After the kick off, Hatchlel House tried to push forwards, but were only able to come close, but again, more perfect keeping from Steve Logan kept them at bay. Cargal were given a corner Kick and Peter Gough placed the ball in its quadrant upon the corner. He took a couple of steps back, then swept the ball into the air and across the Penalty area. Rising full lighter than anyone in the packed area, Keiron connected with the ball with his head, glancing it to the side of him and was delighted to see the ball hit the inner side netting of the goal.

"GOAL!" Cried the Cargal team, it was now four goals to nil.

As they walked back to their positions, Peter Gough thanked Keiron for his through balls.

"That's what I'm here for." Said Keiron, modestly.

They kicked off again but before any real threat to either goal could be made, Mr Marden blew the whistle for Full Time. The players walked off the pitch, the Cargal team beaming with smiles, as were the Wombat team. Both Hatchlel and Farley looked dejected and glum.

"Well done Lads, good to get a first glimpse of what you boys are capable of. I was especially impressed by Peter Gough, Steve Logan and Toby Morby of Cargal House, Tom Taylor, the Eldgridge Triplets and Marcus Trippet from Wombat House of their displays. Some work is needed to improve in training but I think we have the makings of some good teams and maybe a contending School team for the Grunts this year. OK Boys, one last lap of the fields then back into the Changing Room and shower ready to get to your Lunch." Said Mr Marden.

Toby smiled in gratitude for his praise, then looked at Keiron and gave him a 'thumbs-up'. Keiron returned the gesture grinning across his face. They walked back to the Changing Room where they showered and then crossed the courtyard once more and made their way between the staircases and turned to walk down into the Great Hall, where a huge Lunch was laid out upon the tables by the Kitchen staff.

As they took their seats in the Great Hall at the Grunt's table, underneath the Cargal House Banner;

"You did well in the defence Keiron, is that your favoured position then?" Asked Toby.

"Yeah, I'm not too fast, like you, but Football seems all that I'm any good at. I don't seem to get into a muddle when I play, like with everything else. You played ace today, Toby, A 'Hat-Trick' upon our first time out." Replied Keiron.

"Yes, but that was just our first game, when the others get used to playing and trained up a bit more, I don't think games will be quite so easy as the year goes on. My Dad coached me in Football and Rugby in Junior School and I played for my Middle School Football team." Said Toby.

"I played for my Junior School team too, in defence." Said Keiron.

"We should train together as much as possible to help one another." Suggested Toby.

"Good idea, will enjoy that, maybe your Dad would be able to coach both of us during the Holidays when I come to stay at your House?" Said Keiron.

"Yes, I'll ask him. It would only being the evenings or weekends as I said, due to him working all week." Said Toby.

Just then Polly came skipping into the Great Hall and sat down next to Toby at the table. Then Parfinkle called them all to pay and said Grace. The Students all tucked into the magnificent spread for Lunch.

"Well boys, how did you do in your first Games lesson?" Asked Polly, as she put a fairly medium sized slice of steak and kidney pie upon her plate, followed by Vegetables and Potatoes.

"We played a trial match of football, Mr Marden wanted to see our House teams and check our potential." Said Keiron, putting a fairly large slice of pie onto his plate to a berated look from Polly.

"Did you trip over your own feet, Keiron?" Asked Polly.

"Actually, Keiron's quite good as a player; he did rather well, even scored a goal." Replied Toby, putting an equally large slice of pie upon his plate.

"How did you get on Toby?" Asked Polly.

"Oh I enjoyed the game." Replied Toby, adding a couple of heaped table spoons of Vegetables and Potatoes to his plate.

"ENJOYED THE GAME! He only went and scored three goals in our first match!" Exclaimed Keiron.

"WOW! Toby, that's good, a 'Hat-Trick', well done." Said Polly and placed a kiss upon his cheek.

Toby went red with embarrassment.

"Good? He was ruddy ace today, no one could touch him." Said Keiron.

Toby sat and turned red looking at his food, hot daring to look up at the others.

"How did you get on then Polly?" Asked Keiron.

"Oh, we had a little game of Net Ball, then a game of Volley Ball; rather an enjoyable first Games lesson." Replied Polly.

"What do we have next?" Asked Keiron, trying to read his Rota up-side down.

"Its Science after Lunch, that's 'Science which isn't Physics', which according to the Rota is a separate lesson." Polly informed them.

"That's because they split 'Theoretical Science' from 'Physical Science' here at Toadford." Said Toby.

"I can't wait for the Biology classes; we'll get to cut up a few frogs." Replied Keiron.

"Ew! Boys!" Exclaimed Polly, with a disgusted look upon her face as though a bad smell were under her nose.

They finished their Lunch and Parfinkle excused the Students to afternoon classes. They left the Great Hall and walked out of the corridor and across the main hallway to the opposite corridor. Along here they found the Science Lab. While waiting outside the Lab, a grinning Tom Taylor sneered at Toby;

"Want to watch yourself Morby, and watch this space; three goals show off in your first game? I scored two in our match and when you play against us Wombats, you won't get a chance to add to that tally."

"You'm be a nursen a broken laegs wull ee Morby!" Delbert Eldgridge laughed, cracking his knuckles.

Tom Taylor and the Eldgridge Trio burst into laughter.

"Can't wait te get 'ee 'en the Scrum in Rugger." Gaynell Eldgridge grinned, punching his fist into his other hand.

Just then, the door to the Lab opened and out walked Mr John Crocket, the Science Master.

"OK Grunts, please quietly enter the room and pick a desk, don't dawdle."

Mr Cracket was in his late thirties, slim and had blonde hair and wire rimmed glasses. He wore a tweed suit under his Master's Robes. The Grunts walked into the Lab facing the front where there was a black-board with Mr Cracket's desk in front of it. His store cupboard was beside the black-board next to the windows of the room. The windows ran the length of the Lab wall opposite the door. Along this wall were another line of benches with sinks and gas taps. At the back of the Lab, was a Vacuum Cabinet and some scientific instruments. Most equipment was kept within the store cupboard, which was a walk-in closet. Also, kept in here were the beakers and test tubes along with other equipment for experiments, some chemicals were also kept within the store cupboard.

"Firstly we will familiarise ourselves with the layout, usage and safety issues of the Science Lab. While in the Lab, all will be expected to wear white coats, this is so that not only do you protect Uniforms, but also to show up if there is any accidental spillage of chemicals upon us. While in the Lab, no unauthorised person other than me and my Assistant will enter the store cupboard at all; unless another Master is present and it is an Emergency. I have a Lab Assistant, Miss Clevane, who helps me with the lessons and she is the only person authorised to enter the store cupboard, other than myself during lessons unaccompanied.

You will notice that the benches have each a gas tap and sink, these are the main requirements we need to conduct lessons other than materials and chemicals. We shall be conducting alternate combined Science lessons with Chemistry and Biology, being taught during alternate lessons. I am the Master and most experienced, whenever in the Lab, my word is FINAL! We have lessons twice per week and one lesson will be Chemistry and the other Biology. Does anyone have any questions to begin with?" Explained Mr Cracket.

"When do we finish?" Laughed Delbert Eldgridge.

"OK Grunts, first lesson, I get it, testing the waters. You've had your little quip. In answer to your question Mr Eldgridge, when I tell you! The reason for the strict rules is simply for safety, as the Lab can possibly be a VERY dangerous place." Announced Mr Cracket. Mr Cracket went to the black-board and picked up a piece of chalk. He began writing upon the board.

"My name is Mr Cracket; I am your Combined Sciences Master. In these lessons you will be learning about the chemical make-up of your World around you and the organic make-up of the Biology of the World and how we work." Added Cracket.

"Ooooh, lovely, 'The Birds and Bees'. Sniggered Virginia Cornett.

Virginia Cornett was the daughter of the local Magistrate in Cranleigh, Milburn Cornett. He presided in the Court House at Cranleigh and was also a member of the Sacred Brotherhood. Virginia was known as being spoiled and like most children of Parents with considerable influential jobs and power, she was a Bully and in Wombat House. Delbert and his Brothers laughed at the joke along with Tom Taylor and Marcus Tippett.

"As long as it is kept to the 'Birds and Bees,' that will suffice. Replied Polly, giving Virginia one of her looks, Virginia gave her a hard look back.

"OK Grunts, enough chatter," called out Cracket, "that's all for another lesson." Virginia glared at Polly, who simply tipped her nose up and looked away.

"Today we are going to look at the basics of Chemistry. The most important elements to us Humans and to the Planet and our environment are Oxygen, Hydrogen and Carbon. Without these three elements, basically we would not exist." Said Cracket. "Please take notes, as I speak and take out your Chemistry books." He added. The Grunts all turned to their bags and took out their books and Tablets. Cracket waited for the hub-bub of movement to die down and then continued with his address.

"We are as a species and organic beings, reliant upon these elements. Oxygen, as I would think that most of you are aware, is breathed in and passed around the body to keep us alive and feed our bodies. Hydrogen is important as combined with Oxygen to create a molecule of Water, H_2O, two Oxygen atoms connected to one Hydrogen atom. Water is one of the basic necessities that most living creatures rely upon for life. The Human body is made up of seventy eight per cent Water, which keeps the cells of the body 'Hydrated' and alive. We will look more into that in our Biology lessons. Hydrogen is important also as it is the main element which produces the heat from the Sun, which keeps the Earth from freezing and all organic life from freezing to death. The other element which is essential to our lives is Carbon.

As Carbon based organic life, we are literally built from Carbon. Our bodies have cells which are based upon Carbon atoms. When combined with the Oxygen which we breath or absorb through our skins or through drinking water, this makes one atom of Carbon to two atoms of Oxygen become attracted to one another, which creates CO^2, or Carbon Dioxide; Carbon for the C and Oxygen for the O^2. There is a chemical attraction between Carbon and Oxygen, due to Organic DNA. When an element connects with Oxygen to create a new molecule, the resulting chemical structure is known as an 'Oxide'. The most common 'Oxide' which we come across in our daily lives, apart from Carbon Dioxide, is Rust, or metal which has gone bad. Iron is known as a 'Ferric Metal', meaning that it chemically reacts with Oxygen to break it down and destroy it. This process is known as Oxidation. Rust is 'Ferric Oxide', meaning that the Oxygen has fatally broken down the Iron destroying it.

When we take in Oxygen, it does a similar thing to the cells of our bodies, not only feeding them, but in time, destroying them so that we 'Rust'. In Human terms, this is known as 'Aging'. Although we need Oxygen to live, it does over time end up killing us. Carbon atoms which dissolves from our DNA and float around our bodies, connect with some of the Oxygen which we take in and forms Carbon Dioxide. The problem is, this is poisonous to our bodies, so is expelled when we exhale, or breathe out. Carbon Dioxide is absorbed by plants such as trees which use the Carbon much in the way which we use Oxygen. They then release the remaining Oxygen back into the atmosphere for us to breath. This process is known as 'photosynthesis' and is the opposite to the way in which we breathe; where we breathe in Oxygen and it combines with Carbon from our DNA to form Carbon Dioxide, vegetation absorbs the Carbon Dioxide, removes the Carbon and absorbs it into it's DNA and exhales the Oxygen, we breathe it in and the process begins all over again. Throughout these lessons we will learn the actual building blocks of life itself." Said Cracket.

"Boring!" Gaynell Eldridge called out.

"Boring it may be, Mr Eldridge, but essential to your Grades." Replied Cracket. He turned to the black-board and wrote at the top in large letters and underlined it.

'CARBON'

"Please turn to you section upon Carbon in your text books. Carbon will be the first of the elements that we will be studying." Said Cracket. The Students all turned to the appropriate section in their textbooks, where it was written all about the origins of Carbon, it's uses and the elemental compounds.

"Please take notes from the text and write an essay about Carbon" Asked Cracket. The Grunts sat for the next hour quietly reading the text and writing their essays. As they wrote, Cracket gave them more information about the subject.

"As you will see from the page, Carbon is the most important element to our lives upon the Earth, as it makes up our basic genetic existence. The cells which make up our DNA are Carbon based. The purest form of Carbon we can see...? Can anyone answer that question, what that might be?" Said Cracket, looking across the desk where Toby, Keiron and Polly were sitting. Polly thrust up her hand as though she was trying to reach the ceiling;

"Miss Muggard." Cried Cracket.

"That would be Diamond, Sir." Replied Polly, smiling.

That would be correct, very good Miss Muggard, it is indeed Diamonds." Agreed Cracket. Virginia Cornett shot Polly another look hard look, which Polly simply ignored.

"Diamonds are the hardest element currently known to us as they are created by pure Carbon, which is super-heated by the Earth's Magma and then compressed by the weight of the Earth's crust to make concentrated Carbon 'stones'." Explained Cracket. He surveyed the Students to make sure that they were listening.

"Carbon also has other uses which are less concentrated than Diamonds. Mr Morby please?" Said Cracket, seeing Toby's hand up.

"Graphite, Sir and Coal." Replied Toby.

"Correct, Mr Moby. Graphite is what we use to make pencil lead, which we write or draw with. We leave a layer of Carbon upon the paper when we write or draw. Also Charcoal can be used this way. Coal is fossilised wood, from Millions of years ago, which is dug up from mines, from underground or scraped up from Open Cast Mines to put into boilers and power stations. We also put Coal onto open fires to burn and produce warmth and energy for us. Be sure to save your work safely to be part of your Course Work Assignments." Said Cracket.

Cracket continued his lesson in Carbon and how it was used and why it was so important to all Biological life upon the Earth. Toby and Polly meticulously wrote down notes which formed their Homework. In their Dorm Rooms they would be copying out the notes upon their Tablets. They would then save the work onto their Memory Sticks and print off hard copies for their files. As part of this work, Toby used the Wi-Fi link to his Tablet to look up some websites and noted their addresses, with information and pictures along with diagrams of atoms to go with his notes. Toby saved the information onto his Memory Stick to recall it that evening to complete his Homework. Keiron was a little slower and Toby ensured him that he would help him back at the Dorm Room with his Homework.

Chapter Eleven – The Other Side

Simon Morby arose from his bed and surveyed his surroundings. He was always more comfortable when back in his half of the house, unaware of the events which followed Toby's departure to his new school as that all took place in the 'Other World'. Simon began his day by washing from his jug and bowl upon it's stand in his Bed Chamber. A tall thin man with long black hair and a thin beard and moustache stood holding a shirt for Simon to place his arms into. Once he had done so, he fastened the shirt with ties in front. He then made sure the Ruff at his neck was straight. Simon then pulled on his Britches and buttoned them. Now he felt better, dressed for the part. Hastily, Simon put his arms into the sleeves of a jacket of Purple with Gold braiding being held by the thin man. He then fastened the front of the jacket. Now he truly looked the part. The thin man combed Simon's hair and opened the Bed Chamber door. Simon then walked out of the room and turned along a wood panelled corridor to his left. He walked along the corridor until he came to a large wooden Oak door. He smiled as he took hold of the door handle and turned it. At home at last, he thought to himself.

Simon walked through the door and into a large room with a tall ceiling. Upon the walls hung tapestries of hunting and battle scenes. The ceiling was high above the room, with exposed wooden beams which led up to the roof. The Hall was lit by oil lamps hanging upon the walls as this part of the house had no electricity. This was the Great Hall of Pegasus House. The furniture of the Hall was fairly sparse. At the head of the Great Hall was a wooden Medieval looking chair, more like a throne; with seats of a similar style but smaller all around the edge of the Great Hall. Behind this throne hung a tapestry with a Coat of Arms. This depicted a red shield halved with gold, with a fleur de leis counter changed upon each half. Next to the throne was another, but this was draped with a purple cloth.

Simon walked into the room through a doorway, there was a quiet that suddenly filled the Great Hall. He turned and closed the door behind him locking it. The tall thin man stood to one side of the door.

Simon then walked up the centre of the Hall past a multitude of people, music began to play and Simon reached the throne, turned and sat.

The Great Hall was filled with people, some standing, some seated, some dancing to the music which was being played by a group of Minstrels standing upon a Minstrel's Gallery which was above the throne area. Simon turned and looked at the throne beside him draped in the purple cloth. This had been his Wife's throne but Queen Stephanie had died three years before. It was with some sadness that Simon now ruled alone. This was Alexandria, Simon's Kingdom. His proper title was Prince Royal Simon de Morteby – King of Alexandria, while he was in this World. Carl was the Crown Prince, but upon marrying Rachel, had elected to live upon the other side of the Portal, the other side of Pegasus House, where Toby was born. Carl had rarely ventured into this World since leaving and

Toby had never seen it. Carl lived now in our World as his love for Rachel was too strong for him to remain in Alexandria. Stephanie had been Queen of Alexandria and was Toby's Grandmother. She had visited the 'other World' upon occasion to see Toby and spend some time with him and his parents. When Simon told Rachel and Toby that he was going away on Business, he was actually returning to his Kingdom.

Due to a great war many years before, the Kingdom had been attacked by an Evil ruler of a faraway land named 'The Marquis'. Since this war, the Wizard Lord of Alexandria had cast a Spell to place around the City of Alexandria a cloak to protect it from the Magic used by the Marquis. Kingdoms around Alexandria had fallen to the Marquis and had been laid waste. With the help of Alexandria, a number of smaller Kingdoms surrounding the City Kingdom had been aided in fighting off the Marquis and had formed an alliance after the war, to be defended by Alexandria in time of need if they were attacked again. These Kingdoms became known as the 'Shires' and the Wizard Lord appointed Wizards to watch over them. As he Marquis used powerful Magic with Dark Wizards or Warlocks, there was a need to defend The Shires and Alexandria with equal Magic. To keep the Crown Prince safe from attack while young, the Wizard Lord cast a spell into the shield around the city and created a Portal, which brought into being a link between Alexandria and this World. Alexandria lay in another time and space to us, cut off by 'The Skin', as the shield was known. This meant that events in the Kingdom continued separately in time and space to our World. The Portal was a secret link to this World created to be covered by powerful Magic to make it undetectable by The Marquis. Because of the Portal and it's powerful Magic, if an Alexandrian passed through it, their life force was renewed, so they would appear not to age each time they crossed from Alexandria into our World.

The part of Pegasus House in this world was created as the place for the Crown Prince to live while he was here upon this side of the Portal. Toadford School was founded as a means to hide the Crown Prince and bring him up in this World safe from The Marquis and out of his reach. The local children were admitted to the School to hide the connection to Alexandria.

Because of his Alexandrian blood, each time Simon passed through the Portal, he was strengthened and appeared to live longer. But Simon was getting old now, much older than he looked and the actions of the Portal could only keep working for a period of time. Eventually, Simon would die as everyone else does. As Stephanie had passed through the portal much less times than Simon, she had died before him. Soon Simon thought it would be time for the Kingdom to pass to the Crown Prince, to Carl.

When in Battle, Alexandrians wore enchanted armour and this was only breeched by a magical weapon or Killing Curse. If an Alexandrian were to come into this World through the Portal, as Simon and Carl had, then because of the action of the charmed Portal upon their Alexandrian blood, they appeared for a while, to be immortal and impervious to harm unless attacked by an Alexandrian weapon or powerful Dark magic.

But the longer they remained in this World, their immortality drained and they became gradually mortal. As Toby had never been through the Portal, he was mortal and as Rachel was not an Alexandrian, she was also mortal; the reason she was able to be severley injured in her car accident. No one at the School was aware of the identity of the Crown Prince other than the Protectors. When courting, the Crown Prince would normally take a wife from Alexandria or one of the Shires. Rarely, especially up until Simon's Father David, did the Crown Prince take a mortal wife or spend much time this side of the Portal. In fact, Carl was the first Crown Prince to take a wife this side of the Portal and stay permanently here in this World. In this World, the Prince Royal had traditionally taken the title of Lord of The Manor.

The villages around Little Farthingworth had grown up knowing nothing of the Pegasus secret. The only people who knew were the Protectors and they were all connected to the School or to Alexandria. Due to the continued use of Dark Magic by the Marquis, the Wizard Lord of Alexandria had taught his magic to apprentices, who had included the Wizards of the Shires. They and other Wizard Apprentices formed the Wizard's army to fight alongside the Alexandrian Army against the forces of The Dark Lord. the Marquis ruled a Kingdom named Thracia and employed many fiercesome creatures into his army and also employed his own Dark Wizard Army, known as the 'Shambols'. The war against Thracia was not lightly mentioned by those of Alexandria and the Shires; they would like to think it forgotten. This magic was powerful magic, this magic was old magic.

In the Great Hall a feast had begun in honour of Toby joining Toadford School. This occasion was being celebrated as Toby's new journey had begun as all other Crown Princes of Alexandria had received a Toadford education. The feast consisted of all kinds of meat, poultry and pies. Seated around the feasting tables members of the Royal Court, who were devouring everything in sight. Simon was seated at the head of the feasting table, enjoying the feast as much as everyone else in the Hall. The Minstrels were playing upon the gallery and a Fool was trying to juggle with sticks and dance at the same time. Next to Simon sat a tall thin man dressed in bright clothes.

"Lucius, what befalls us this day?" Asked Simon.

"Your Majesty, we of Alexandria send great greetings to Prince Toby. I am aware of the choice which Crown Prince Carl made so many years ago, but he is still of our blood and perhaps one day will join us here in his Homeland." Replied Lucius.

"Aye Lucius, as Alexandrian tradition beholds, next year Prince Toby should begin his Apprenticeship with Lord Barnabus, to learn the magic as all other Crown Princes have done so since the troubles all those years ago." Said Simon.

Lucius was Lord Chancellor of Alexandria and Regent of the Kingdom while Simon was away in 'Our World'. Alexandria was a Kingdom which had not altered for centuries, due to the time capsule which it existed in. The time capsule was formed by the cloaking spell which was cast by the Ancient Wizard Lord, who cast the spell to attempt to hide Alexandria from all sight from outside, in an attempt to protect the Kingdom from the Marquis. Time had passed for us but not so much in Alexandria. There was no electricity to be found here only that from the spell casting and the Army still uses hand weapons, except for the Wizard Army. Magic was still the most powerful weapon in Battle, it was only used sparingly as it drained it's user with too many spells being cast at one time.

At the borders of the Shires, there too was a spell cast to warn off the Shambols trying to enter the land. But, being old magic, the spells were now running thin and small cracks appeared in them, as was demonstrated at Calistria and the invasion of Orcs. The old spells had done their job for centuries but more recently, due to cracks appearing in the spells, some influence was felt in Little Farthingworth from the Thracian influence; the 'last time', which had been much forgotten, but revered by the older inhabitants of Little Farthingworth Village.

The 'last time' was the 'thing' which blighted the elderly citizens of the Village so much, the mumblings about the 'Old House'. Upon 'Our side', the village, not many were left to remember the 'last time', which was passed off by the 'Protectors' as a mass case of Hysteria. This was why many of the older inhabitants did not venture far up Bogart Street, unless in a vehicle and avoided Pegasus House and the School. This was one reason for some of the more secret Traditions of Toadford School and the reason for the foundation of 'The Protectors'. If another war were to break out and there should be any risk of it spilling out over to 'Our World', Barnabus would have to seal off the Portal forever, meaning that who so ever was upon either side of the Portal at that moment in time, would be trapped in that World forever. Due to the apparent increase in strength of the current Marquis, they could not risk another 'leak' like the 'last time' of his Dark magic into 'our World. Lucius then turned to Simon, he hesitated for a moment, and then with a worrying look crossing his face, he told Simon of the concerns about the Kingdom and the Marquis.

"Majesty, while you have been away, Barnabus has been monitoring the 'Skin' with help from the Shire Wizards. They have found, he tells me, more cracks in the charm protecting the Shires and he fears that anytime now, the Thracian Army may find a way through one or more of these cracks and mount insurgencies into the Shires. He believes that these cracks may even facilitate the path for Thracian Armies to mount full scale invasions of the Shire Kingdoms." Said Lucius.

the Marquis for centuries, had the habit of using magical creatures to mount attacks against Alexandria in great numbers. This was another reason for forming the Wizard Army, to help and fight alongside the Alexandrian Army if they were badly outnumbered. Also for the same reason as the Marquis, the use of the Wizard Army in Battle was a last resort, for fear of losing valuable Wizards. Plus also, the death of a Wizard was a fearful thing, as it weakens the magic of the remaining Wizards. The Apprenticeship was a long and hard one and so to lose a Wizard was very much avoided whenever necessary. The Marquis mainly used enchanted Orcs, Trolls and Goblins as his 'cannon fodder' in Battle, attempt to bash through the enemies army by means of sheer wait in numbers. As a means to properly defend themselves in times of ambush or Battle, the Prince Royal and his Crown Prince were taught as Apprentices to become Wizards. So far the only Crown Prince to not have received his Apprenticeship was Toby, because he was not yet fourteen years old, the age to begin an Apprenticeship and because he had spent all of his life in 'Our World' and knew nothing of Alexandria and the 'Other World' or it's magic. Carl of course, being born in Alexandria was a trained Wizard, he had not told his wife or child this due to wishing to live a normal life with Rachel in this 'Other Side'.

Simon and Carl knew that someday there would come a time when Toby may have to be told of his Heritage and Carl would have to choose whether or not to take up his Birth right. Sitting next to Simon upon his other side was a stocky middle aged man in a breast plate and cloak with broad shoulders, as a warrior would be. With his helmet off, which sat beside him upon a table his black short hair was visible, as was the deep scar down his left cheek.

"General Thomas, I have word that the Marquis is planning an action to overthrow the Kingdom of Alexandria. It would seem that his Grandfather's last attempt has not ended their desire to conquer." Said Simon.

"Indeed, your Majesty, we will need to be at our alerts along our borders." Replied General Thomas.

Simon looked over intently, now becoming more interested.

"Barnabus is constantly seeking guidance and prophesy through his Divinity and has informed us that Thracian incursions have been noted close to our borders. the Marquis and his Wizard Caithius, are aware that Barnabus was alerted, through their Dark Arts, this gives them limited views into our Kingdom, but only very limited." Said General Thomas.

"Yes indeed, General, The Skin is old now and may be faltering, so we must be on our guard constantly. Caithius must have been able to sense the 'chink in our Armour' and is searching out any breaches, if any, there are any in the Skin." Said Lucius.

Simon looked back and forth between the two men either side of him thoughtfully; at last he spoke.

"We must consult with Barnabus and find his news of what is afoot, I trust he has been searching every inch of the Skin and repairing it if possible, any trace of a breach" Asked Simon.

"Indeed your Majesty, Barnabus constantly searches, but he has said that his efforts, as it be old magic, possibly can be detected by Caithius upon the other side in his Kingdom, so we must be cautious as to his use of the searching spell, lest it highlight the cracks not only to Barnabus, but also to Caithius." Replied General Thomas.

Chapter Twelve – The Messenger

The huge Oak doors of the Great Hall burst open and a short stocky man ran into the Great Hall to where Simon, Lucius and General Thomas were sitting. He was as short as he was broad and had rather large hands for such a small man. His face was that of an aged man with thick black hair and beard. He wore heavy Armour and a thick breast plate. He dropped to his knees in front of the Head Table and directly addressed Simon;

"Yoor Majesty, I em General Listus, Commander o' the Calistrian Armies. I brang grave tidings fram Calistria. The City Kingdom es en turmoil, some days past, we weer attacked wuth a force most vicious an' terrible. Most o' ye hooses en ye town weer destroyed, set ablaze by ye stenking murdering Orcs. Descending upon us wus hoord after hoord o' ye vile creatures, riding theer Crocottas ente Battle. Many, many Dwarfs weer slaughtered. The soil ran red wuth blood. Theer weer Goblins too among the enemy, dispatched the wounded and stealing whatever they were able to salvage of any value from the ruined homes. We packed our rescued belongings and all that we weer able te fiend an' salvage as much Galem Gold an' stones ente packs upon oor Ponies backs as possible an' gathered ye surviving Dwarfs te King Boranius. Then sadly an' wuth much pain en oor hearts, we abandoned Calistria. We walked ente ye Shires ooer moontains, built a new hame, te settle an' begin oor lives agin." Said General Listus.

Simon looked down at the small figure before him. Calistria was a fair distance from Alexandria and the Dwarf had travelled long to reach the Great Hall, here in the Kingdom's Capital. The City of Calistria was once a great City Kingdom, like Alexandria. Many years before, the Dwarfs who lived there thrived. They worked hard and earned great riches. As Dwarfs are Traditionally Miners and such, they also had hoards of wealth. The Currency of Calistria was Galem Gold pieces. Galem Gold was of the purest form and most sought after. Dwarfs mined the Gold for Moniers, who then struck their coins from it. The Dwarfs were paid handsomely for their efforts and all continued well until the Marquis 'Decided' that the Golden hoards of Calistria would be better suited to being more appropriately placed within his Kingdom of Thracia.

Alexandria came to their rescue and offered an alliance with the Dwarfs to become part of the Shires of the Kingdom and continue as an Autonomous Kingdom within a Commonwealth of Alexandria. Calistria had a King, Boranius, King of the Dwarfs, Grandson of Kaleb, who was slaughtered by the Marquis. King Boranius of Calistria had a wife, Queen Marion of Calistria; their daughter, Princess Surignam of Calistria and their son and Heir, Crown Prince Tyranus of Calistria, a fearsome warrior.

The Dwarfs were not only great miners and hoarders, but also great and fearless warriors. Only this time, they were over ran and defeated, which took away their pride. They were forced, many of them, to move around the Shires finding work where they were able. It was mostly labouring jobs and Farm hands work that they found most suited their employment.

"Arise General and pray tell me more." Said Simon.

General Listus raised himself from his knees and stood before Simon. In the time of Prince David de Morteby, Simon's Grandfather, with his help, the Dwarfs of Calistria were reconciled with their Homeland and King Farlan, who was the Son of Kaleb (Slaughtered during the Battle of Calistria), began much construction and aid was supplied from Alexandria by Prince Royal Olav. It was David who founded the Commonwealth and The Shires. David in accepting Calistria into The Kingdom made a treaty with Kaleb's Son Farlan that Alexandria would continue to allow Calistria to function as an Autonomous Kingdom with their own King. The inclusion of Calistria into the Shires was important to the economy of Alexandria and the Shires as it was the source of their economy and coinage. Gem stones and crystals for the wands used by the Wizard Army came from here too. Different crystals or stones found within the mines of Calistria were used to make wands with certain crystals or stones amplifying certain charms or spells. To allow this part of the Shires to fall into the hands of the Marquis would seriously damage and weaken the economies of The Shires and give the Shambols untold access to the powerful crystals and stones to strengthen their Dark Magic. It was the Son of King Farlan, Boranius, who had now to put the pieces of yet another defeat of Calistria by the Marquis, back together and it was now Boranius, who with Simon's help, would somehow need to rebuild what was left of Calistria. General Listus asked Simon formerly for the help and assistance which was so badly needed at this time by the remnants of the great Calistrian Kingdom, speaking with what we may regard as a somewhat Scottish type accent.

"Yoor Majesty, I must Humbly request o' yeh, ef yeh wud lend assistance te ye Calistrian people an' te King Boranius, te recapture an' rebuild Calistria once moor so that we poor Dwarfs are once agin able te return te oor Hameland an' reclaim oor lives an' oor own Birthright." Said General Listus.

"Aye General, I should be very happy to lend you assistance for this quest and would very much wish to see Calistria returned to that which is nothing more than what it should be, the City Kingdom of Dwarfs." Replied Simon, with some sadness in his voice. Simon was all too aware of the history of the Kingdoms and of his Grandfather's Treaty with the Dwarfs.

"We shall rejoice tonight General Listus and celebrate the allegiance of Alexandria and The Shires; we shall toast and mourn those who suffered so terribly at the hands of the Murderous Marquis. Tomorrow we shall rise and then make our journey to speak with Barnabus, Wizard Lord of Alexandria. We have much to discuss with him." Said Simon. Simon looked thoughtfully at the Dwarf, eyeing him inquisitively.

"Why did the Calistrian Wizard Army not defend you General Listus?" Asked Simon.

"We weer taken sae much by surprise yoor Majesty, ye attack wuz so ferocious an' swift that ye Wizard, Toridius the Gold, wuz unable te bring help afore we suffered ye fatal blow." Replied Listus.

"Do not worry Listus my friend, when we return to Calistria and retake your Homleand, you will have the assistance you require to make it happen and to win the day." Assured Simon.

"I bid Thee thanks yoor Majesty, ye Calistrian people wull be forever en yoor debt." Replied Listus.

"Listus, pray be seated and rest your tired body, you look weary after your journey, please stay and fill your belly; call in your companions for them to join the feast also. I shall have a bed made up for you and quarters for your men prepared for tonight." Said Simon, inviting General Listus to join them.

The feast continued into the night and Listus along with his group of Dwarfs made sure that they got their fill and enjoyed fulfilling their ravenous Dwarf appetites. There were maids dancing to the Lutes and Flutes of the Minstrels. The fool with his quartered red and yellow costume and red hat was trying now to struggle with three pewter plates while balancing upon a chair upon one foot. This grin was soon wiped from his face as he accidentally threw a plate too far ahead of his other hand. Stretched out to catch it and slipped from the chair. Legs and arms thrown into the air as with a terrible clatter the Fool fell into the floor in a heap and in turn each Pewter plate fell with a 'Clang' onto his head. A huge roar of laughter rang out through the Great Hall, a pewter plate rolled across the floor and suddenly the legs of the dancing maid were up into the air and she was flat upon her back on the floor. Another roar of laughter rang out.

"Thou dost put en a great show, Majesty." Laughed Listus, joining in the laughing from Simon and his Ministers. "Yeh too also put en a much lavish feast Majesty, we are already en yoor debt fer yoor welcome an' reception of us." General Listus added.

"I thank you General, t'was a feast already swinging when you arrived and you needed filling for Our journey tomorrow to your King at your new dwelling place. We shall need to call upon the Wizard Lord Barnabus for council. We leave in the morning, so have a good feast tonight." Said Simon.

Chapter Thirteen – The Cricket Match

Toby and Keiron walked out onto the pitch in their Flannelette Whites and green caps for Cargal House. Upon their white shirts, they wore a badge, a swans head. They carried their bats under their arms as they pulled on their batting gloves and shuffled along in their Batting Pads.

"Good luck Toby, let's give those Toads Hell!" Replied Keiron with a big grin.

Toby walked up to the far wicket and took up his position. He motioned to the Umpire for 'Middle'. He held out his bat and moved it inch by inch until the Umpire held up his finger. Toby then placed his feet and put the bat into his legs into the guard position, tapped the ground a few times to make the mark and looked up towards the far wicket. He was ready for the first bowl. Toby and Keiron had shown promise in their games lessons, in batting and bowling and Thybold had been quick to place them both as openers in the House team.

The Umpire signalled to the Square Leg, he signalled in return and the Umpire signalled to the Score Board, the game was started. Guy Watson came thundering up to the wicket and a flurry of arms and legs spinning, saw the red ball shoot towards Toby. He waited for it to bounce and pitch up in front of him and swung his bat, which connected with a Crack of Willow and sent the ball hurtling away across Mid-on. Allan Kirk ran after it and stopped it first, just before the boundary rope. Toby motioned to Keiron and they both ran down the wicket. Allan picked up the ball and threw it back towards Guy at his wicket. Just as Guy was about to catch the ball Keiron placed the tip of his bat into his crease. The openers had scored their first two runs and the first two runs of the season for Cargal House. Guy walked away from the wicket, rubbing the ball upon his trousers to shine it upon one side, to give it swerve in the air. He wore a white shirt, as toby and Keiron, but his had a badge that was a Toad for Hatchell House. He trotted forwards and then begun a short run up to the bowling crease. His arm spun like a Catherine Wheel and he hurled the ball towards Toby at his wicket. Toby watched the ball approach and bounce in front of him, placed his left foot forwards and swinging his bat. It connected with the ball with a whack and sent it flying away.

The ball flew out across the mid-on and was chased by the outfielder towards the boundary rope. It crossed the rope with a bounce and the Umpire waved his hands across the front of his waist to signal four runs. Cheers rang out again from the Cargal supporters. A few more Overs passed and the Cargal score had risen to seventy three with Toby on fifty runs and Keiron on twenty three. Guy Watson came again to the wicket and delivered a bowl to Keiron. He swung his bat and clipped it behind his wicket. Allan Kirk dived to his right and stretched out a gloved hand. The ball whizzed to his finger tip and bounced off narrowly avoiding a diving slip and ran down to the boundary for another four runs. In the Pavilion, Steve Logan, the Cargal Captain jumped from his seat and cheered loudly.

This play continued until looking up at the scoreboard as they took up their stance at the crease, Toby and Keiron saw that Cargal were a hundred and thirty three runs, with Toby on ninety six runs and Keiron on thirty seven. Toby stood at the crease, the ball hurtled down the wicket, he slammed the bat into the ball and hooked it over his shoulder and high over the field. The long leg fielder was stopped by the safety net beyond the boundary rope. The Umpire raised both hands above his head and signalled for six runs! The cheer from the Cargal Students was deafening and Keiron whooped at his crease. As the ball was retrieved and then thrown back to Guy Watson, walking out to his starting point to run up; an announcement sounded over the PA System.

"Six Runs to Cargal House and that's the Century up for Toby Morby."

Another loud cheer went up from the Cargal end of the crowd. All the while, Tom Taylor watched angrily as Toby played. He was the 'best in the School', so he thought 'who did this Morby fellow think he was, performing like this in all the sports and other lessons?' He turned to his 'Mob', the Eldridge Trio, Marcus Tippett and Virginia Cornett and sneered;

"Look at that Morby showing off again, just wait 'till we Wombats get him on the field, I'll bowl his ruddy head off." Laughed Tom. He looked around for acknowledgement and support from the others who all laughed with him.

This was the first of the six Play Off matches in the Cricket Cup, which were played between the House teams. The games were played as a 'Round Robin' system, playing each other twice, then the top two teams played a final for the House Cricket Cup. Wombat House had already beaten Farley House in their first match. Cargal and Wombat would meet in the next of the Play Offs, which was why the 'Wombat Crew,' as they called themselves, were watching closely.

"You'll make mincemeat of those Swans, won't you Tom?" Sneered Virginia; Tom smiled to her and she winked back. The game continued this way for some while until Keiron sliced a bowl straight into the hands of the third slip.

"HOWZAT!" Cried the Hatchell team and the Hatchell students in the crowd were jumping up and down and whooping. Slowly, Keiron tucked his bat under his arm and started the 'Slow Walk' down to the Pavilion.

"Unlucky Buddy, better luck next time against the Wombats; see you back at the at the Pavilion." Said Toby.

"Kill 'em Mate." Replied Keiron as he walked towards the Pavilion. He was passed by Steve Logan, walking out putting on his gloves.

"Give 'em Hell, Mate." Said Keiron as he passed Steve, who nodded and grinned. Steve took up his position upon the crease, in place of Keiron and the game recommenced. Toby and Steve played steadily until Toby attempted another 'Hook Shot' and was caught at Long Leg.

"HOWZAT!" Again rang out around the pitch. Cargal House were now two hundred and seventeen runs for two wickets. The game continued until all of the wickets had fallen for a total of two hundred and eighty six runs all out. Then it was time for Lunch. They all retired to the Pavilion where there was a Lunch set out for the players of both Houses.

"Good game so far." Said Keiron, tucking into a sandwich.

"That's just your Innings, we have to bat yet." Replied Allan Kirk of Hatchell House. They exchanged banter like this for a while then the Umpire came into the Lunch Hall and told them it was time to get back to the game. These matches were played on a day basis, with one Innings. The teams then left the Lunch Hall and went back to the pitch from the Pavilion. This time the Cargal House were the fielding team and Hatchell were in bat. Toby walked ten steps back from his crease, trotted forwards and brought his arm up over his shoulder. His wrist twisted with his fingers and he hurled the ball down the wicket. The ball bounced in front of Allan Kirk and suddenly veered off past his legs and crashed into the leg stump of his wicket.

"HOWZAT!!" Was the cry from the Cargal team, accompanied by a huge cheer from the Cargal Students.

"He's only gone for a Golden Duck! YAAAY for Toby!" Polly called out, jumping up and down. A loud cheer once again rang out from the Cargal House Students and the fielders all huddled around Toby to congratulate him.

"Makes you sick, doesn't it Guys?" Snapped Tom Taylor, who was still watching.

"'Bout time that that Morby wuz teken down a stump or two." Replied Delbert Eldridge.

The Wombats were jealous because Toby studied hard and worked hard. He was popular with the other Students and teachers alike. Tom Taylor found this totally unacceptable as he thought that he should be the most popular Grunt in the School; reality was, that he was only popular with Wombat House. Tom was beginning to make it his 'mission' to create a vicious vendetta against Toby. Bullies are different to Thugs, As with a Thug, namely the Eldridge Triplets, they would generally attack or persecute anyone who got in their way or were told to; whereas, a Bully would more often than not, take out a vendetta against one person and look for support from other likeminded people to feel justified in their persecution of the one person. Mainly Bullies picked upon people less capable, weaker or more intelligent than themselves, preferring Braun over Brains. A Thug would generally react to a situation and prefer to settle it with their fist, a Bully would very often actually go out of their way to cause a dispute and then turn to the Thugs who supported him to help him to carry out his Bullying.

Unknown to the Wombats and anyone else at the School, Toby had inherited his Alexandrian strength and abilities from Carl, his Father. Even though he had never crossed the Portal in his life, his blood still carried traits of the Alexandrians. Unknown to Toby, the vision in the flames of his Birthday candles and the recurring dream were to do with his inherited traits, his Alexandrian Genes and his Blood. These were genes which would serve him well and which he would need to learn to harness and train in the future. The match progressed steadily with more wickets for Toby, seven in all and three for Timothy Calin for Cargal House. Hatchell House eventually squeezed out a score of an hundred and seventy eight runs, being beaten by an hundred and eight runs. This score line placed Cargal House top of the table as Wombat had only scored two hundred and sixteen runs in their match against Farley House.

This was another reason for the Wombat Crew being so jealous as the teams left the Cricket filed, Toby was congratulated for his performance. The House Master, Mr Thybold, congratulated Toby upon his Century. The Cricket House Cup was the first Cup contested during the School year. There were cups for each of the School sports. Winning the House Cups for the different sports was how the teams accumulated credits towards winning the School Cup at the end of the Year in the Summer. As they walked from the field, Toby found himself being eyed by the 'Wombat Crew', who gave him a look of daggers.

"We'll see how you cope with a Cricket ball shattering against your nose, won't that be fun?!" Sneered Tom Taylor, as Toby reached the Pavilion steps and passed Tom to mount them. Peter Gough ran up to Toby and Keiron and gave Toby a 'High Five'.

"You were great Toby, we slaughtered them." Cried Peter, with a huge grin upon his face. He grabbed Keiron's hand and shook it so violently, he almost pulled it off.

Also watching the proceedings was a young Farley House Student. She watched as the teams walked from the Pavilion and back into the School. About five feet four, with long blonde hair and blue eyes, she was Tilly Parmenter and had been watching Toby all term. She was developing somewhat of a crush upon Toby, but school etiquette dictated that Students from opposing Houses did not mix too much with one another. The School Houses rather kept their own selves to themselves. Tilley was holding back her feelings for Toby for this reason, but hey, where was the harm in looking?! After the teams had showered and changed in the wash room, they then went back to their rooms to change out of their School clothes having finished their dinner. When Toby and Keiron walked into the Common Room and the other Cargal Grunts gave out a loud cheer. Polly ran to the boys and hugged them both.

"Well done chaps, you certainly showed them Toads how to play." She said gleefully. They were congratulated by the rest of the Cargal Students and sat upon the couch watching Television.

"The Weeners also beat Hatchell yesterday." Said Peter Gough, "Tomorrow the Toffs Play and then the Cardinals. The Seniors play later in the week."

"When is our next match against Wombat?" Asked Keiron.

"Two weeks' time." Replied Steve Logan.

"Next week the Rugby play offs begin, I've already had some proposals from the Wombats in regards to that." Said Toby. The Grunts chatted for a while and were then joined by Arrabella Snoop, Polly's Room Mate. She stood in front of the couches.

"What're you lot doing then? Can I join in?" Asked Arrabella.

"It's most likely that it will be too complicated for you." Polly Replied, tilting her nose up.

"We haven't decided yet, we may just sit here for a while." Said Toby.

"I'll sit with you then." Chirped Arrabella, sitting down upon a chair opposite the couch.

"If you really must." Quipped Polly.

The group watched a film on TV and then after chatting it was time to head back to their rooms. All the while, Polly had kept Arrabella in check by giving her looks if she was nattering too much. They walked along the corridor until they reached their rooms. Arrabella opened their room door and stepped inside. Polly stopped at the door and said goodnight to Toby and Keiron. They entered their room and went to bed, the exertions of the day's Cricket ensuring they dropped off almost immediately. In the room opposite, Arrabella was lying in bed. Polly came in and changed into her night dress.

"You fancy him don't you? You know, Toby?" Asked Arrabella. Polly turned to her rather irritated.

"Don't be ridiculous, they are just House Mates; Well at least I can get an intelligent conversation out of them." Polly replied. Arrabella looked at the ceiling a small tear in the corner of her eyes.

"You're such a snob." Sniffed Arrabella.

"And you're such a snoop." Replied Polly.

"I just wanted to make some friends that's all," Said Arrabella, "but no one is interested, it seems no one wants to be friends with the 'Fat Girl', just thought that as we were Room Mates for our time here, that we could be friends?"

"You're not fat, just cuddly." Replied Polly, smiling at Arrabella. Arrabella smiled at this, Polly continued;

"It's just you do go on a bit." Said She.

"Sorry, I'm just a Chatter Box, always have been," Arrabella answered, "Anyway, as we're Room Mates, you can call me 'Bella." Said She.

"OK, I'm still Polly." Replied Polly. In the morning it was breakfast again. They sat in the Great Hall eating their porridge.

"What do we have today, Keiron?" Asked Toby.

"We've got Art Class in the morning and then it's the House Football match after Lunch." Replied Keiron.

"I'm looking forwards to the Art Class, I love painting and sketching." Said Polly.

"I like to stretch too," Said Keiron, "but mine usually don't come out as what I plan them to be."

Then finished their breakfast and were met by Arrabella as they walked from their table and towards the big double doors of the Great Hall.

"Hey Guys, mind if I tag along?" Asked Arrabella.

"That's OK, 'Bella, you're welcome." Replied Polly.

Keiron and Toby looked at each other and then at Arrabella and Polly.

"You two friends now?" Asked Keiron.

"Yes, we thought that as we were Room Mates, it would be better to get to know each other and get along, after all, we will be sharing the room for our entire stay here." Replied Polly.

"We were lucky in that respect." Said Toby.

"Yeah, we hit it off from the start. I'm gonna enjoy our time here." Said Keiron, smiling over to Toby.

Arrabella smiled and joined the group, tagging into the end of the line next to Polly. The four of them walked out of the Great Hall. They walked across the Hallway and past the Trophy Cabinet and then into a corridor behind the stairway. They walked along the corridor and stopped at the third classroom along. Here they waited for the Master to arrive for their Art lesson.

Chapter Fourteen – The Departure and The Company

In the morning, Simon arose early in his Bed Chamber. His Valet helped him to dress and then he made his way to the Great Hall. He was joined there by Lucius Thamley. The First Minister of Alexandria. Simon sat with Lucius and waited for their guest to join them. The door to the Great Hall opened and in walked General Listus, who bowed deeply in front of Simon and took his seat with them at the breakfast table.

"Great Morrow General Listus, how Well do you fare today?" Asked Simon.

"I fare Well, Majesty an' I am ready fer ye journey back te ma people." Replied General Listus enthusiastically.

"We must firstly call upon Lord Barnabus beforehand, to gain his Council about this problem and find out from him his discoveries regarding the Kingdom." Said Lucius.

"We shall accompany you to Barnabus at his place and then you will take the road back to your people to prepare for Our word." Said Simon.

"Aye, Majesty, I look forwards te meetin' wuv Laird Barnabus an' returning te ma people, per chance perhaps, wuv some glad tidings." Said General Listus.

"We shall rally with you General and the Darkness which has befallen Calistria, shall be lifted." Said Lucius.

"The journey to Lord Barnabus shall take days to fulfil, we must travel incognito and not be recognised, The Marquis will have Spies abroad. It may be too dangerous for His Majesty to travel this road, but you will have company in the guise of Myself and General Thomas along with a company of Guards?" Said Lucius.

"Aye, ma Laird Lucius, most acceptable. Ma King an' ma people wull be much uplifted by ye tidings once I return." Said General Listus with a broad smile which was only just visible through his thick black beard.

"Alas General, I will not be able to Journey to your people, I have pressing Business to be done here in Alexandria. Please convey my apologies to His Majesty and your people. Lord Lucius shall be my Man, receive him as you would receive Me, General." Said Simon.

"Aye I wull tell King Boranius an' bring him yer good cheer, Lord Lucius shall be received Royally yer Majesty." Said General Listus.

"Tailforth, bring Lord Lucius' steed around and mount it with the finest tack." Said Simon.

A tall thin man with short gingery hair walked forwards to the table and bowed low. This was Marcus Tailforth, the Prince Royal's head Groom, who looked after and trained all of the Royal Horses.

"Well Gentlemen, I bid thee fare Well and safe journey." Said Simon as they arose from the breakfast table.

"Aye, our bellies are full as are our heeds, with gud thangs. I thank thee fer yer hospitality yer Majesty an' I shull convey yer werds an' deeds te His Majesty King Boranius. Said General Listus.

With that said Simon, Lucius, General Thomas and General Listus arose from the table and walked the length of the Great Hall to the huge Oak doors. Guards beside the doors pulled them open and the four walked through into the Grand Hallway. There was a Grand Hallway, decked in suits of Armour, tapestries and paintings of Simon's Ancestors and Battle scenes festooned the walls. From the ceiling hung a golden Candelabrum. They walked to the main doors and out into the courtyard. Here they found their three horses waiting for them, the two horses of Lucius and General Thomas and the Pony of General Listus with it's armour shining resplendent in the morning light. The three travellers mounted their steeds and turned towards the Barbican Gate House. General Listus mounted upon his Pony and they were joined by a small company of eight Alexandrian soldiers and the six soldiers of General Listus, who had accompanied the General across the Shires to Alexandria.

"Fare thee well Majesty, we shall inform thee of ye things we discover upon oor journey." Said General Listus.

"Fare thee Well Sire, until my return. Replied General Thomas.

With these goodbyes spoken, they all pulled their mounts to face the gate House and kicked their heels. Then Simon watched them disappear through the Gate House and out of the Castle. As they rode away out of the Barbican, they rode along the main street of the town with its market stools of food, cloth, clothes and other provisions. They reached the far end of the Main Street and arrived at the Black Smith's Forge. Here they gave him the news that many swords and pieces of armour would be needed shortly.

They then continued their ride out of the City. They left by means of the Water Gate to the south of the City walls. They crossed the Gate Bridge over the River Alexus and began their passage through the 'Skin' and out of the protection of Alexandria City. Now they would fare alone. It was most important that they raise as little attention upon their journey as possible. This was due to the fact that The Marquis sent out spies to the places outside of the City of Alexandria, who reported back to their Dark Master to let him prepare his strategy of invasion. They stopped outside the City Gate and looked back. There stood Alexandria City, home and safety; they looked out in front of them and could see the expanse before them of open scrubland and a distant forest of trees.

"We first journey across Ilkley Moor to the Village of Neem, to check for any more needed supplies. Then we journey through the Forest of Knivsey, where we make our first stop overnight. In the Forest is danger from animals and possibly Agents of the Marquis. His influence reaches far but cannot penetrate the Great Skin of Alexandria City. We must be aware at all times, especially in the hours of night, when all is darkness; we must be aware of the dangers that we face upon our journey, to stay one step ahead of the Marquis." Said Lucius.

"Then let us away, My Laird, ma courage an' strength wull no' be tainted thus night." Replied General Listus.

"My Lord, my sword and our company will keep us safe." Replied General Thomas.

They began their journey riding the road out across the open Moorland. As they rode, further out in the distance they were able to see thin pools of smoke rising upwards to the sky, gradually houses appeared which were timber framed and clad in wattle and daub as Cobb walls. They rode into the collection of houses along the road down from the Moor. There must have been at least thirty houses along this Main Street, with many more behind on either side. To the left side of the road was a small stone Church with a tower which held bells. Atop the tower pointing to the sky was a tall cross. Around the Church behind a wooden stockade fence were a number of graves marked by wooden crosses.

Beyond the Church, to the right of the road could be seen a small but Well stocked Market. Next to the Market was a Tavern, 'The Boars Teeth.' This was the Village of Neem and they thought it a good place to stop for a rest and stock up, especially as there was a handy Tavern. They pulled up their horses and Ponies and tied them to the posts outside of the Tavern. Led by Lucius, they entered the place. It seemed old and not Well decorated. It was dim inside with candles glowing from empty bottles among the tables. Much chatter, was about the place and in a corner was a small band of Musicians playing a merry tune. The group found a number of tables to occupy as three soldiers guarded the horses while two more kept watch at the door. Lucius, General Thomas and General Listus sat at one table, with two Dwarf guards, while the other four Dwarfs and remaining soldiers sat at other tables nearby. The Inn keeper, Ballidor, approached the table with the Trio of leaders while Maids served the soldiers.

"Good morrow My Lords," Said Ballidor, "I trust ye have journeyed Well an' now are in need of good sustenance to bid ye upon thy way or mayhap ye shall be a stayin' a while?"

"Good Morrow Inn Keeper," Replied Lucius, "we shall but tally shortly, we shall need a meal to see us upon our way and some of your fine ale Sir."

Lucius took hold of the Inn Keeper's wrist and spoke low to him.

"Tell me, Inn keeper, if you have had any unnerving travellers through here recently?" Said Lucius and placed two large Gold pieces into the Inn Keeper's hand.

"My Lord, such generosity to a lowly man such as I. I have no word to tell Thee, but shall give council if I should hear of such goings on. My Maidservants shall fulfil your needs and bring Thee Thy vitals forthwith and jugs of our finest ale." Said The Inn Keeper, "Ballidor of Neem at Thy humble service, my Lord." He added.

"We thank Thee deeply, Ballidor, for Thy service." Replied General Thomas.

"I should need two jugs o' Ale te begin, Ballidor, ef thee could, ma Dear fellow." Added General Listus.

"Aye My Lord, I shall endeavour to bring this to you." Replied Ballidor.

The three sat and watched around the tavern, serving maids were walking around, carrying frothing jugs to tables and carrying empty jugs back to the bar for Ballidor to refill and then be given out again. Balidor of Neem wore an open necked shirt and britches held up with braces. He was an average sized man with a bald scalp and red hair in tufts either side of his ears, He had a long face with a broad chin, full mouth and piercing blue eyes. The Dwarf soldiers appeared to be enjoying their jugs of ale, as were the Alexandrian soldiers. Sat at the opposite end of the bar could be seen a huddled figure enjoying a jug of ale, but his features could not be clearly seen as he wore a long green cape which had a hood that was covering his head. He sat watching the group at the far end of the Tavern. A cheer went up from the soldiers as two Maids came out from the bar carrying trays which held platters of steaming stew. Ballidor walked across to the table with a tray and handed out plates to Lucius, General Thomas and General Listus.

"There ye go my Lords, three plates of our finest Mutton stew to help Thee upon Thy way." Said Ballidor. A Maid then came over with a plate each for the two Dwarfs sitting at the table with the Trio.

"We thank three Ballidor." Lucius, handing out another handful of coins into Ballidor's hand. They sat and ate their Mutton Stew and supped their ale. Still the figure in green sat watching, now also enjoying a plate of stew.

"Gentlemen, what be oor destiny thus afternoon?" Asked General Listus.

"We shall travel down through yonder forest across the barren Moor stones to the Village of Cragmoor. Our night camp shall be at the forest to continue to the Village next day." Explained General Thomas.

"But ma Laird, ye forest be a dangerous place by night, an' no' fer ye faint o' heart. Said General Listus, with a worrying tone in his voice.

"Do not vex so much, Listus, we have a good stout company about us; we shall be safe enough." Said General Thomas.

"Aye we have gud company, but should stull be aware, there are many untold dangers te be had in ye forest that we must beware of." Replied General Listus.

"Caution does not kill a man, we will be cautious. We cannot trust that outside of Alexander City and far from the safety of the skin, that we should not encounter agents of the Marquis, especially if he senses our journey to Barnabus. We take this road so as to attempt to disguise our travelling to Barnabus. It is a longer journey than the direct road but necessary to throw off and followers to unearth the where abouts of Barnabus' abode and so invite Dark Forces to tamper with our mission." Said Lucius.

"It is important that we reach Barnabus to gain his council and set in motion the recovery of Calistria." Said General Thomas.

"Aye, t'would be grand te be back upon our native soil an' back aboot oor business o' mining." Replied General Listus nostalgistically, looking down into his beaker of Ale.

"We must hope that God walks beside us upon our journey and shields us from the Darkness." Said Lucius.

They sat for a while after finishing their Mutton stew and lit up a clay pipe each, resting drawing upon the tobacco within.

"T'was a terrible sight ma Laird, we fought valiantly but were simply overcome by sheer weight o' numbers, but wuth ye aid o' Alexandria an' Laird Barnabus' army, we should rejoice en returning Calistria te oor blood." Said General Listus.

Palls of smoke arose from their pipes which matched many more around the Tavern, including a pipe which protruded from the cowl of a green hood, still sat beyond the bar from their table. Their meal over and pipes smoked, they bade Balliodor goodnight and their serving Maids farewell and walked out of the Tavern to meet the soldiers and Dwarfs outside. They remounted their horses and Ponies, then began their journey once more out of the Village and back onto the Moorland. Distantly they were able to see the forest as it drew nearer upon the horizon. Unseen by the company a short distance behind them was a figure in a green cape and hood, riding upon a black horse, trailing them.

As the company rode across the Moorland the distant forest drew closer. Each hour that passed they moved further across the Moor and drew closer to the forest, until at last they entered the forest of Knivsey. Slowly they rode along the track through the forest, until they saw the dusk falling and decided it was time to camp for the night. They tied up their horses and Ponies, a soldier made a fire in some stones and then took out from their saddle bags a pan and some food; then they set this over the fire upon a stick frame. The company made themselves comfortable, here they rested for the night.

During the night, Lucius was woken by a pulling at his cape. He stirred and was surprised to see a small figure crouched by his legs pulling upon his cape, which he was using as a blanket. Lucius kicked his leg upwards and knocked a small bluish figure from his legs. It squealed and this woke up the rest of the camp. General Thomas stretched out his hand and grabbed at the creature and they all looked closer at it. It was about six inches in height, vaguely humanoid with bluish skin; thin bony arms and legs with a small wide head, with large ears and large eyes.

"What do we have here pray?" General Thomas said, looking down with a frown at the small creature in his hand.

"It would appear to be an Imp, general," Replied Lucius, "be sure to handle it with caution." Too late, General Thomas let out a cry and shook his hand; the Imp had bitten him and momentarily hung on.

Then the creature released its grip and let out another squeal, this time louder, higher pitched and longer. As the group watched with wide eyes, there came a swarm of the bluish creatures out of the bushes around their camp. They tried to untie their horses and Ponies. The soldiers and Dwarfs pulled out their swords and tried to fend them off, swishing away furiously at the little mischief makers. More and more they came and tipped over their food dishes, emptied their water bottles, one even slapped Listus across his nose. This infuriated Listus, who began striking out at them with his sword. It was tiring work and they did kill a few of the trouble makers, but sheer numbers were now becoming overpowering. Suddenly one after another of the small creatures began hitting the ground, prone and the company now looked at them and noticed that their small bodies were pierced with tiny arrows. They looked around the camp but could see nothing other than the bluish creatures suddenly stopping their mischief and fleeing from the camp back into the forest. Then from behind a tree, a figure became visible, dressed in leather britches, boots and a waistcoat of emerald green. He was wearing a green cloak which concealed his face beneath a hood. He sat upon a black horse and swung his leg over the saddle and almost floated to the ground. He stood before them, still with their weapons in their hands.

"Who are you and why have you been following us?" Demanded Lucius.

General Listus stood still with his hand still holding his sword. The figure stood and glanced at the hand which General Listus had upon his sword. He lifted up his right hand and pulled back the hood which covered his head to reveal his face. He had a long thin face; his skin was white, almost translucent with slanted eyes which had vivid purple irises. His hair was gingery red and brushed back off his forehead, straight and long down the back of his neck. This revealed his ears which were slightly tall and pointed at the top. The figure had strapped to his back a long quiver made from leather and a long thin bow carved with workmanship which the group had never seen before. The figure eyed the company carefully and silently then eventually spoke with a soft voice.

"My Lords, I am Frecilly, Scout Royal of the Forest Kingdom of Deene." He announced.

The company watched him as he found a rock and sat upon it cross legged.

"What happened?" Asked Lucius, unnerved.

"You were subject to an attempted rading party of Imps. They were trying to steal away anything and everything of any value, especially your weapons. The one which you dislodged and caught was attempting to steal away your sword." Replied Frecilly.

"Why dud they suddenly flee when ye appeared?" Asked General Listus, still with his sword in his hand.

Frecilly paused, looked around and then answered.

"Gentlemen, there are many mysteries in the forest, which I know all too Well. I shall take you to my home where you will be safe from further attacks. Please mount up your steeds and follow me, it would be better and much more comfortable for you to lay upon a bed tonight rather than laying out upon the hard ground, would it not? There you would not be troubled by Imps all night." Replied Frecilly.

They all stood and eyed Frecilly suspiciously but then General Thomas and Listus agreed.

"T'would be mere comfortable indeed, we shoud be honoured to join Thee to Thy home, as long as it does not delay us much beyond our destination." Said Lucius.

"Aye my Laird Scoot, I should be grateful te thee should I 'ave a fine comfortable beed opposed te ye hard forest floor an' rid o' those infernal Imps." Agreed General Listus.

The group all remounted their horses and Ponies and followed Frecilly out of the camp. Frecilly once again pulled his hood up to cover his head and began to lead them through the Forest. They rode on for what must have been miles along an ancient looking path through the trees.

"This be the Forest of Knivsey, 'tis but a small Forest, unlike our Kingdom Capital at the other end of the Shire of Deene Forest. I have Governance of this Forest, a Scout for our Gracious Majesty, Prince Rupid of Deene Shire. I control who enters here and where they go. We are a secretive people and do not much care to see strangers in our Shire but I notice the Alexandrian Royal Coat upon your soldiers and know that you are upon business for his Majesty Prince Royal Simon, so I shall offer you safe passage while you transverse our Shire." Said Frecilly.

"We thank you for your hospitality Lord Frecilly, we are indeed upon important business and should only tally with your Shire but a short time whilst upon our way." Replied Lucius.

After about three hours of riding, Frecilly lead them into a small clearing in the Forest. Here they were able to see many others like Frecilly milling about and busy. Then Frecilly looked up and gestured.

"Gentlemen, your slumber awaits." He said.

They all looked up and were in awe at what their eyes beheld them. Above them, across the clearing were large structures built into the trees, some covered as many as a dozen trees and were high above the ground. They were lit with lights which twinkled like stars.

"How on earth do we reach them?" Enquired General Thomas, bemused. Then suddenly, to their surprise other figures walked into the clearing, one for each of the company; Generals Listus and Thomas, Lucius and the soldiers and Dwarfs. Frecilly then took off his cloak. Each of the figures stood behind their counterparts and gripped them around their waist tightly. Then to the astonishment of the company, from their backs they unfolded large thin wings which shone like starlight with white light. Next they felt themselves lifted up to the dwellings in the trees and the flyers landed them softly and safely upon their platforms. The soldiers were in buildings next to where Lucius, General Thomas and General Listus had been taken.

"By Christ Almighty, they be Fairies!" Exclaimed General Thomas.

They found themselves standing in a huge wooden Hall in the trees. It had a high roof and around the Hall there were tables of Fairies sitting feasting. At The centre of the Hall were Fairies dancing and musicians playing music. At the head of the Hall was a large table with an empty seat at its centre, which Frecilly walked to. He motioned to the three visitors to sit either side of him and introduced the Fairy next to him.

"Be seated My Lords, join our feast. I introduce you to my wife, Gentlemen, the Lady Velea." Said Frecilly as he sat in his seat.

The three introduced themselves in turn to the Lady Velea.

"My Lady, I am Lucius Thamley, First Minister of the Kingdom of Alexandria." Said Lucius.

"My Lady, I am General Thomas of Alexandria." Said General Thomas.

"Ma Lady, I am General Listus of Calistria." Said General Listus.

The three bowed low and sat in their seats.

"It is a pleasure to meet you My Lords, pray what brings you to this part of the realm and to our Shire." Replied Lady Velea.

Lady Velea eyed them suspiciously but smiled. Her whitish translucent skin almost glowed and her bright purple eyes sparked beneath red hair. She wore a long dress which was of pale blue and had perched in her hair a crystal tiara. They were not able to see her wings as they were sheaved and hidden.

"Where be oor company?" Asked General Listus, searching around with his eyes.

"Why they are quite safe General, they are feasting in yonder house." Said Frecilly, pointing towards the house next to the Hall in which they sat.

"After their feast and a little merriment, they shall be bedded down within that house, to rest for your continued onward journey." Continued Frecilly.

"You, my Lords, when you are satisfied with feasting and merriment will be bedded down as our guests in this Hall." Said Lady Velea.

"Where be your journey to end and go forth from this Shire?" Asked Frecilly.

"We journey long and do not wish to stay long in your Shire. We have important business elsewhere." Answered Lucius.

Lucius was aware that the Fairies were fishing for information about their journey and was deliberately being evasive with his answers to their searching questions. Frecilly and Lady Velea were trying to ascertain the risk of brining these strangers into their Hall after finding them upon the road. They understood that they appeared to be who they claimed, especially General Listus, as even if he were not a General there was no mistaking him as a Dwarf and therefore no denying that he was of Calistria.

There had been much loose talk around the Shire of Deene, many strangers passing through just lately and some unexpected and strange occurrences had been taking place. Only a week before, there had been found in the Forest a slaughtered hog with its throat cut and drained of blood. This was something which the Fairies would never have done, as they ate no meat. The three were enjoying their feast and did notice that there was indeed a lack of meat upon the table. They made no mention of this and respected the hospitality of their Hosts. They talked some more avoiding the answer of their business to more questions, until quite full from their meal and weary from their travelling; they graciously bade their Hosts goodnight and were then shown to their rooms and soon were asleep in comfortable beds.

"I Must warn ye Gentlemen afore ye goes te yer slumber. Try as ye might not te dream. The Fairy Folk wull read yer dreams an' if they be ye spyin' fer ye Marquis, wull know our Quest an' be able te warn ye Marquise, wull know our journeying. So remember ma Lairds, try no' te guv them anythin' te read." Said General Listus to Lucius and General Thomas as they went into their respective rooms.

Chapter Fifteen – Departure From The Forest

Early next morning the three arose from their beds to find Fairy Valets bringing them fresh water for their wash bowls and helping them into their clothes. Lucius tied the laces of his jacket and slipped on his riding boots below his britches. He picked up a bone comb and began to pull it through his short black hair. He checked himself in the full length mirror which stood in his room next to his bed He was satisfied with the work which the valet had offered him and walked to the door of the chamber, led by the Fairy valet. Once out of the chamber, Lucius found himself in a long gallery type corridor which was adorned with many paintings, which hung upon the other side of the gallery. The door next to Lucius opened and out stepped General Thomas, followed by General Listus from the next door further along beside General Thomas. The Fairies were not very tolerant of 'Outside' people who did not belong in their Forest Shire. Under the leadership of the Alexandrian Kingdom, they were a little tolerant towards officials of the Prince Royal; whereas some lower Fairies who did not belong to the Ruling Clan did not like any intruders into their Forest. Dwarfs were aware of this and were not all together completely trusting towards Fairies, believing they could possibly have no reason not to spy for the Marquis. Either this Fairy, Frecilly and his Lady Wife were exceptional in their manner compared to other Fairies in the way they received strangers or they were covering an underlying deception, a reason for receiving the travellers as easily as they had. It was possible that being of Prince Royal Simon's Court that the scout Lord of Knivsey Forest was respectful of them. He had overheard their talk, all be it as they thought, quite with his exceptional hearing and had heard them whisper about their journey next to Cragmoor Shire. Careful not to mention the name of Barnabus, he had not heard the full extent of their planned journey; the reason for the questioning at the feast the previous night.

"Lucius, did you allow yourself to dream last night?" Asked General Thomas, with a worrying look upon his face.

"Nay General, I was quite anxious to keep from giving the Fairies the answers to their searching questions. How about yourself Thomas?" Replied Lucius.

"I fear not my Lord, as long as I remember, I was not aware of any dream." Replied General Thomas with a look of hope in his eyes.

"Afore ye ask o' me. M'Lairds, I did dream but knowing o' ye ability te read a mon's dreams, an' bore inte hus thoughts tha yon Feiries are gifted wuv. I forced ma sel' te dream o' ye feest we shull 'ave upon oour return, thus one wull 'ave meat!" Said General Listus. Looking from the corner of his eyes up at the other two companions and allowed a dry grin to cross his face under his bushy black beard. The Trio, led by their Fairy Valets walked along the gallery and turned into a large Oaken door. They found that they entered the feasting Hall which they had been in the night before. There laid out upon the tables was a large breakfast, again General Listus noticed with a grimace, the lack of meat at the tables.

"My Lords, please, be seated and breakfast with us before you depart upon your journey once more." Said Frecilly, seated at the top table with the Lady Velea beside him.

They approached the table and took their seats. Lady Velea looked at Lucius with her bright purple eyes, which Lucius now noticed, had a starry twinkle at the centre. He watched as the twinkling seemed to fill his head and he felt his mind begin to swim around as in haze. The twinkling seemed to draw him further into her eyes.

"We thank thee once again for your hospitality and for the grand beds which we slept in, that were indeed more gracious and comfortable than the hard ground of the Forest and not an Imp was noticed." Said General Thomas, smiling broadly, taking a mouthful of Mushrooms. This speech appeared to break the trance which Lucius had seemed to have fallen into, which had been noticed by General Listus.

"Aye M'Laird, M'Lady, I tank Thee fer a fine breakfast which wull aide us 'pon oor journey." Said General Listus, trying not make direct eye contact with the Lady Velea or Lord Frecilly.

"We do not need thanks my Lords, as it is our custom to honour the Court of the Prince Royal. I am glad that you had a comfortable night and would be grateful for if you would allow me and some of my Court to accompany you across our Shire to ensure you have a safe journey until you reach our borders." Said Frecilly, all the while, Lady Velea watching the three closely.

"We shall be honoured, my Lord Scout, for you to accompany us, maybe you shall be needed to ward off more Imps for us as we pass through the Forest." Replied General Thomas.

"It is not so much the Imps which would vex you rather other more fearsome creatures who may be your peril, and the spies of The Marquis who may be abroad." Said Lady Velea.

She looked at them to gage their reaction to her answer to see if they were aware of her meaning.

"We should be grateful of your service and company, my Lord Scout and thank you my Lady, for your concern." Replied Lucius.

All the while General Listus was chewing through his mushroom breakfast, watching closely the interaction between the holders of the conversation. He had observed the manner in which Lord Frecilly and Lady Velea had spoken and had sensed that they were fishing once more for answers.

"How fares the Prince these days, my Lord? I hope he is Well and does not concern himself too readily with problems outside of the Shires." Said Lady Velea again, watching with serious purple eyes.

"He fares Well, my Lady and concerns himself with anything which attaches itself to his Kingdom's notice." Replied Lucius.

During their breakfast, General Listus had noticed that the Hall had filled upon the other tables with many more Fairies, who chatted in their own language. The language of the Fairies was ancient and magical. Spoken in a musical way, if heard by a mortal man, could render them helpless but to stay and listen. General Listus sat and tried to concentrate upon the talk from his own table, lest he be entranced by the hall filled with chattering Fairy Folk. This he was becoming uneasy with, as he was sure that the chattering was a trick used by the Fairies to entrance a man to enable them to look into his mind or dreams, to find out their secrets. It was usually impossible for any length of time, for a mortal man to resist this ploy for long, without detection within the Shire of Deene. The Fairies very much all of the time were able to break a spy and then Hex them to not know what had happened. General Thomas and Lucius were not so aware of this chattering as they had been deep in conversation with Lord Frecilly and Lady Velea.

After their breakfast, Lucius, General Thomas and General Listus thanked Lady Velea for her hospitality and then walked out onto the platform with Lord Frecilly. They see their company of soldiers across upon the next platform. They were joined by a number of Fairies who once again grasped them around their waists and unfurled their wings. They lifted off the platforms and softly floated down to the Forest floor below. Once back upon the ground, Lord Frecilly called for his black horse and the horses and ponies of the travellers.

"We thank you for your pleasant conveyance to the ground." Said Lucius to the Fairies, who had flown them down from the Hall. The Fairies bowed to them and spread their wings and flew back into the trees.

"I shall accompany you, Dear friends, unto the border of my Shire, as you will not be familiar with many of the creatures and other trifles which dwell within the Forest. One, the Imps, which you have already suffered, but rest assured my Lords, while I am by your side, the Imps shall not trouble us again but others I cannot be so certain of." Said Lord Frecilly.

"We thank you for your offer, Lord Frecilly, we are grateful for your council and company." Replied Lucius.

"Speak fer yoursel'." Said General Listus, under his breath and rolled his eyes to the top of his head. The company looked around them as they rode away from the base of the tall tree in which they had experienced that wondrous Hall and the feasting. All around them were trees of Oak, Ash, Sycamore and Pine. Bushes grew between the trees with bright flowers, around them grew many brightly coloured flowers of many types. As they watched they came into sight, a little way off their path, a deer which stopped beneath a tree and began to eat the grass around where it stood. General Listus rode along upon his Pony continuously looking around himself vigilant, looking for any sign of danger or betrayal from Fairies. Fairies could not always be trusted. Following the dark Wars with the First Marquis, when most other City Kingdoms openly accepted the help from Alexandria to rebuild and become part of the Commonwealth, Deene Shire had not been readily forthcoming to join the Commonwealth, but reluctantly agreed due to being surrounded by other Shires and experiencing the wrath of the Marquis for themselves first hand. Many Fairies were slain in that time and without joining the Commonwealth forces of the City Kingdoms, which became the Shires, Deene would have been swallowed up by the Dark cloud which encompassed all of the Kingdom of Thracia and all that the Marquis conquered. Since this time, many spies of Thracia had been captured and dealt with by the Fairies, so they were not trusting of most strangers who enter their Shire.

General Listus became distracted by a Butterfly which flittered around his head and then settled briefly upon his large bulbous nose. He swiped a large hand across his face but missed the Butterfly as it's reflex to lift back into the air was much quicker than the General's. The Butterfly then turned to face the Dwarf at close quarters to his face and it was then that he noticed that it was not a Butterfly at all, but a perfectly miniaturised humanoid figure with large brightly coloured wings which buzzed as it hovered in front of his nose. His eyes widened as the bite felt like a sting and a small red mark appeared upon his nose which rapidly swelled into a purple pimple.

"Och, ye wee beastie, get away wi' thee." General Listus cried out. This drew the attention of the others and Lord Frecilly laughed.

"My Lord, it is not advisable to go around upsetting Piskies, they just might bite you or worse, Hex you and turn you into a toad stool." Chuckled Lord Frecilly, rocking upon his black horse.

"Ah wull, ma wee fellow, I wus no' aware that ye wus a wee Piskie, I thought ye wus a wee bug, Please accept ma sincere apologies." Said General Listus to the angry looking tiny figure, still hovering in front of his face looking him in the eye.

"That should fare thee well little man, all that Piskies ask is respect and to be treated as any other being of the Forest. I rather think you recovered yourself rather well after calling her a 'bug' though?" Laughed Lord Frecilly as the Piskie bowed to General Listus and then flew over to Frecilly's shoulder. She landed upon his right shoulder and whispered into his ear.

"Thorax here, would like to offer the Piskies services to your Lordship's company, if need be upon your journey. She tells me that if you encounter unwanted company that her flock are able to keep them occupied while you draw away and escape. You are privileged, my Dear Lords, it is not usual for Piskies to offer their services to men, they usually prefer to bite them!" Said Lord Frecilly laughing as he looked towards General Listus, who sat upon his Pony and frowned.

As they rode on, suddenly from out of the undergrowth, small arrows flew and hit the shields of the soldiers. One soldier received an arrow in his neck, but being so small it just felt like a large splinter, although the initial sting of it did knock him from his horse. Their mail suits and breast plates stopped the tiny arrows from piercing their skin to their arms and bodies, their helmets helped to protect their heads and eyes. The felled soldier jumped up to his feet and drew his sword from his saddle upon his horse. The other riders were finding it difficult to keep their horses and Ponies under control due to the many stings from the tiny arrows. The soldier on foot ran into the bushes swishing his sword around into the direction from which the attack was emanating. From the undergrowth ran a large number of tiny little men who were only about two feet tall, running upon their small legs. They were dressed in leather britches and boots with coloured jackets. They had tiny dark eyes and bushy beards of different colours. They stopped when they spotted Lord Frecilly sitting upon his horse and lowered their bows.

"What is the meaning of this?" Cried Lord Frecilly, angrily, "Why do you attack me and my company?"

The tiny figures dropped to their knees and the one at the front of the group looked up at Lord Frecilly as the rest kept their heads bowed.

"Well, answer me wretch, why have you attacked your Lord as he rides through his Forest" Lord Frecilly asked again, looking at the small bearded man with his purple eyes blazing, his soft voice now harsher.

"Please Sir, my Lord," Began the little man, "We didst not know t'was Thee that rode through the Forest, we saw soldiers riding through and thought that the Shire was under attack, being invaded. Forgive us, my Lord, we would never have attacked if we knew you were among their number."

"No harm done, but be more vigilant in future before you break out an ambush,; you gave away your position far too easily. If I were an invading force, you would have metered out your own capture and defeat. Said Lord Frecilly. With that, the little man and his followers turned and ran back into the undergrowth and disappeared once more into the Forest.

"Who were they?" Asked Lucius, still with the look of surprise upon his face.

"They are Gnomes, my Lord. We allow them to dwell in the Forest and they repay us by warding off unwanted visitors. Their leader, who we addressed, is named Karlox and is a little impetuous, but Well meaning." Replied Lord Frecilly.

"Well meaning, my Lord?" Said Carlos, the soldier who was now holding his neck where the arrow had stung him.

The company then rode on through the Forest until they reached the edge and Lord Frecilly bade them farewell.

"Farewell and good journey back to your Hall, we thank you most sincerely for your council and hospitality and for our beds away from the Imps, Piskies and Gnomes arrows." Replied Lucius. General Listus and Carlos looking around with frowns upon their faces.

"Farewell my friends, I bid Thee luck upon Thy journey into the Shires. Safe road to you before you return to your Alexandria." Replied Lord Frecilly. With that said he gave one last wave, kicked his heels and his black horse galloped away baring him back into the Forest, his green cloak disappearing into the undergrowth and trees as he went.

"Time to make Luncheon me thinks, afore we leaves the cover of the trees and ventures out across yonder open moor." Said General Thomas.

"Aye my Lord, should be a good time indeed to fill our bellies before we venture across the open Moor ahead of us." Replied Lucius, looking out across the landscape which stretched out before them.

After they had eaten and rested for a while, the company remounted their horses and Ponies and then continued upon their journey and rode away from the Forest and out onto the open Moor. Here the land could be seen in places into the distance towards the horizon, to rise. Some higher areas were seen to have large rocky outcrops at their summit.

"Gentlemen, we venture across Cragmoor, our next Shire. We shall bed tonight in Cragmoor Village, out yonder past the great heights that are atop the Shire." Said Lucius.

They surveyed the view ahead. In the distance to their north they were able to make out a tall rocky outcrop and also far distant ahead of them they were able to see another even taller.

"My Lords, see yonder northwards is the Tor known as Opal Crag. This is a known place for Dwarfs, a place which a small mine is located in which the Dwarfs who journeyed to this Shire now work it, it is known for the Opal gems which are hewn from its depths under the Crag. Out yonder distant is the largest of the Tors in the Shire, here be Palace Crag, which in its shadow houses the Palace of The Overlord of the Moor. Try as we must to stay unnoticed as we stay at the Village, soldiers, we must ask ye to camp outside the Village, for to save our notice of a large travelling company. We shall rejoin you upon the Morrow and continue our journey." Said General Thomas.

The company took the road through the Moor passing first the Opal Crag, where a small plume of smoke was seen rising above it, General Listus pointing out that this was the mine workings. Onward they rode into the late afternoon and further on through the Moor. In the distance across the grassy heather covered ground which stretched away from them they could see wild Ponies grazing the heath land. There was the occasional tree to be seen and thickets of bushes were visible. Scattered around were a small number of farms in which they saw sheep grazing out upon the Moor next to the farms. Ever present across the miles upon the horizon was visible the Palace Crag. As the light dimmed into dusk, the travellers stopped within a small coppice of trees. Upon a slight rise in the landscape about a mile along the road, they were able to see the lights from houses which showed them their way to the Village of Cragmoor and the three officer's overnight stay.

"Carlos, if you have any trouble or see anyone approaching at speed, send a messenger to us and we shall hasten to rejoin you. Otherwise we wish you goodnight and shall join you tomorrow for our onward journey." Said Lucius.

"Stay your ground men, keep the name of Alexandria true." General Thomas said.

"Aye my Lord, we shall keep a vigil here. I shall send a scout tonight in secret to keep thee company and to ride to us if ye have trouble for to warn us and bring thee help." Replied Carlos.

The three, Lucius, General Thomas and General Listus rode away from the soldiers as they made camp in the small thicket. Above them in an old Oak tree sat a large Owl watching with its large orange eyes. They talked for a while before Carlos called over his Scout and sent him upon his way.

"Manos, come hither, you are in plain clothing not armour?" Asked Carlos.

"Aye Captain, that I am. I have my sword concealed, my Lord. Any hint of danger to our Lordships and I will leave the place and fly like the wind upon my steed back to you to bring you back to aid our Lordships." Said Manos.

He mounted his horse and rode away towards the Village lights. Lucius, general Thomas and General Listus began to ride between houses. They were of Cobb wall and thatched with two storeys and had small windows which the light streamed out illuminated them as they rode past. They could smell turf as smoke climbed high out of the chimneys of the houses. The people of Cragmoor obviously used turf fires from the Moorland peat. They rode through the street moving deeper into the Village. Being evening, there were not many people around. They passed small houses which they saw were shops with their fronts closed up to lock away their wares inside. The sound of the music and voices could be heard and they turned a corner into the Village Square, and across the green they could see a tall house of two storeys and many windows which had a sign hanging from a bracket outside. Painted upon the sign was a bed with words painted underneath;

'Ye Travellers Rest'

This they understood as to be the Village Inn. They rode up to the Inn and saw a wooden bar frame next to the building with a horse trough beside it. Beside the Inn they could see a barn, which they assumed was a livery stable. They walked into the Inn, opening the door and being met by a strong smell of tobacco and ale, the sound of the music and voices suddenly becoming louder. They walked into the Tavern and General Thomas found a table at which General Listus joined him. Lucius then walked up to the bar of the establishment and spoke to the Inn Keeper.

"Good evening my dear Inn Keeper. We three weary travellers would like a room for the night to rest our tired heads and sleep, to continue our journey onwards tomorrow." Said Lucius.

"Thirty Marks." Replied The Innkeeper, "That includes a meal tonight of Mutton Broth and a porridge breakfast upon the Morrow, my Lord. Would Thee have horses to tend, Sir?"

Aye Inn Keeper, we have them tied up outside, two horses and a Pony. We should like them stabled for the night also." Said Lucius.

"T'will be done ,My Lord." Replied The Inn Keeper.

"We shall have three jugs of your finest ale please Inn Keeper and three hearty bowls of your good Mutton Broth, if you please." Said Lucius.

"Aye my Lord, it will come to you directly." Replied The Inn Keeper. With that, he called over a serving girl and poured out three large jugs of Ale which she carried over to their table after Lucius had re-joined the two Generals at their table.

"There Thee are Sirs, Thy jugs, here are Tankards for Thee to sup from and Thy Broth shall be along directly, my Lords." She said smiling broadly. She had a roundish face but not big. She was average in size with a tight bodice and leather waistcoat tied with laces across her chest. She wore a full length skirt which reached her ankles and upon her head a small white bonnet, which showed some of her blonde hair underneath.

"We thank Thee, Miss and will enjoy our Broth after our tiring journey today." Said General Thomas, licking his lips.

"They call me by the name of Anhild, if Thee Gentlemen will be needin' anythin' else, just call me?" She said, smiling and giving a wink to General Listus, which brought a smile to his face and a gleam to his eye.

She walked away from the table and returned to the bar, where the Inn Keeper passed her a tray over the bar baring three large bowls of steaming Broth. She carried this to the table and placed down a bowl in front of each traveller sitting waiting, their noses twitching with delight as the aroma wafted up to their nostrils and they breathed in deep.

"Och Aye ma Lairds, thus es what makes a journey wuth makin', sittin' wi' gud music, gud company an' a gudly bowl o' steaming Mutton Broth." Said General Listus.

"Well Gentlemen, if the bed is as good as the service in this Inn, then I'm sure that I will be fast asleep as soon as my head hits the pillow tonight, filled with fine Ale and Mutton Broth, what more could a Traveller want?" Said General Thomas.

General Listus was watching Anhild walk away from the table back to the bar, where the Inn Keeper sent her out again around the tables with more jugs of Ale and bowls of Broth. The door opened and a figure walked in dressed in a brown cloak and britches. He sat at a small table next to the bar across the room from the three, glanced towards their table and sat down. Anhild walked over and asked him his pleasure.

"Good evenin' my Lord, shall I bring Thee a nice jug o' Ale an' a fine bowl o' Mutton Broth?" She asked smiling.

"Aye my girl, that would suit me fine." Replied Manos. He sat at his small table discreetly keeping watch over the Tavern room. He was enjoying the music and took out a pipe and then lit it. He sat puffing upon his pipe and then Anhild returned with his Ale and Mutton Broth. In a far corner, Manos noticed a figure sitting in the shadows, clad in a pale brown cloak with a hood, which covered his head. He seemed to just be sitting there and supping his Ale.

All around the Tavern, the Village people sat at tables eating Broth and drinking Ale; laughing and talking, some were dancing to the music being played by the small band of musicians, who were standing at the far end of the bar to where Manos was seated at his table. As the jugs emptied, Anhild moved from table to table with fresh jugs of Ale. Everyone seemed joyous in the Tavern. Everyone seemed joyous in the Tavern, all but a figure seated in the shadows, not talking with anyone, not singing, not dancing, just simply sitting there. Manos kept his eye upon the figure, he was Well aware that the Marquis employed spies both human and beast . Manos was not sure which he was as his head was covered by his hood.

"Gentlemen," Said Lucius, "Me thinks that there are strange goings on afoot in this Shire?"

"Aye my Lord," Replied General Thomas, "I felt that while we dwelt within the Forest with Lord Frecilly."

"Aye no seein' the manner en whuch hus Lairdship an' hus Lady questioned us at yon feast? The chatterin' o' yon Fairies en yon Hall, attemptin' te bewuch us inte talkin'?" Said General Listus.

"I did notice the speed and urgency in which the Gnomes acted their ambush through the Forest path; they appeared to be most wary indeed of the presence of strangers moving through the Forrest." Said General Thomas.

All the while that they were talking, Manos kept watch over the Tavern and especially over the stranger in the hooded cape across the room.

"We must be vigilant for any strange appearances around and unusual happenstance which may befall us." Said Lucius.

Once they had finished their Broth and supped their jug of Ale; the three decided to call it a night with the entertainment. Manos watched them rise from their seats and leave their table; Lucius slightly tipping him a nod of his head, Manos nodded discreetly in understanding. The three walked to the bar where Anhild met them.

"All ready for bed now Sirs, are we?" She asked, "I shall show Thee up to Thy rooms, my Lords."

They followed her through the door to the side of the bar where the musicians were playing and they walked out into a hallway where they saw a corridor which lead off to the back of the bar area, to the Kitchen and cellars; in front of them, facing frontwards, there was a staircase to the left side of the corridor and a door beyond this which lead out once more to the road outside. The corridor was lined with panelling as was the bar area and they could see a number of boxes and small barrels tucked under the stairs for storage. Also, as in the bar area, the corridor was lit by candelabrum hanging from a beam of the ceiling lit with six candles above their heads. She led them along the corridor and they climbed the stairs for Anhild to show them into a room at the front of the landing which spanned the width of the building and from where they stood, they were able to see four doors. Anhild showed each to a door and opened it. Inside they saw a bed which looked Well kept and comfortable with sheets and blankets topped at the head with pillows, also within each room were tables with a chair to sit upon and a more comfortable chair beside the bed; in a corner stood a basin upon a stand for them to wash and a small cupboard for them to place anything into overnight. Anhild showed them into a fourth room, which was a sitting room; also panelled as the rest of the rooms and had a number of plush chairs around it with a small table between them. In a grate, the fireplace housed a small fire, the flames breathing heat into the room and adding some light to the candles which burned in brackets around the walls.

"I hope Thee will be comfortable here, my Lords, If thou shouldst need anything, Sirs, just call I, with the bell pull yonder and I'll be happy to serve." Said Anhild, smiling and giving Listus a wink.

"Aye Lassie, me thinks we shall be cosy en here fer ye night." Said General Listus with a twinkle in his eye.

They put down their bags and Lucius turned to Anhild and placed a couple of coins into her hand.

"'Oh thank ee' my Lord, much appreciated." Said Anhild with an even bigger smile, she curtseyed and then left the room to return to the bar. Lucius closed the door to the sitting room. They each sat in a chair allowing their tired bodies to sink into it and the weight leave their feet.

"I find it strange, the Fairies were eager to welcome us into their fold when usually Fairies are secretive and not prone to receiving strangers. It was noticeable too, that the Gnomes were so eager to attack and repell us from the Forest, that they actually failed to notice Lord Frecilly riding among us?" Said General Thomas.

"Aye my Lairds, T'would seem tha' theer wus much tension wuthin yon Forest durin' oor visit; I cud tell frum ye moment tha' we left ye 'Boor's Teeth' Tavern un yon Village o' Neem. How Laird Frecilly watched us at yon Tavern an' agin wuthin yon Forest." Said General Listus.

"It would seem that Lord Frecilly was pre-informed about our journey and knew of our break at the Tavern and had shadowed us in to the Forest." Said General Thomas.

"I think that our journey is not as secret as we would like it to be, we must therefore be much more vigilant upon the remainder of our journey. I feel that it is important now, owing to these new developments, that we should change our plan to journey Eastwards towards Meerlandse but to travel Northwards by way of the Village of Marlan." Said Lucius.

The two Generals turned to one another to see each other's reaction. It was clear by the look in General Thomas' eyes that he was in agreement with Lucius, so General Listus smiled and looked back at Lucius.

"Aye ma Laird, I am totally en agreement along wi' Thee, ye journey Nerth wud be thy best remedy, te draw ye eyes which follow us te ye wrong path." Said General Listus.

"I too am in agreement, North to Marlan Village it will be upon the Morrow." Agreed General Thomas.

"Time we were to bed, Gentlemen, we have some testing country to transverse tomorrow; so as not to cause notice to the change in our path to eagerly." Said Lucius.

"Neither te yon Overlaird o' yon Moor, too readily my Laird, lest we find oorselves spending oor days en yon Opal Mines." Added General Listus.

The two men and Dwarf walked from the sitting room and went into their respective bed Chambers; outside upon the landing, in a corner, sat the cloaked figure of Manos upon a chair. Once the other two had entered their rooms and closed their doors, Lucius stopped and spoke to Manos in his seat.

"Lieutenant, I should tell Thee that upon the Morrow we change our Path from Eastwards to Northwards, to arrive at Marlan Village; Thou must leave before upon the Morrow and ride back to the others and meet us along ye road going North from here." Said Lucius.

"Fare Thee good night, my Lord, I shall ride in the morning and we shall meet Thee upon ye North Road. I will keep watch here this night, I did feel unease towards a shadowy figure I spied in the Tavern this evening and would keep vigil upon thy rooms." Said Manos. Lucius turned and walked into this Bed Chamber and closed the door. There sounded a light tap at the door to his room and General Listus opened the door. There at the door stood Anhild.

"Evenin' My Lord, is there anythin' I could be agettin' for Thee?" She asked with a beaming smile and a wink in her eye.

"Cum en ma Deer, I'm sure I cud find somethin' fer Thee te be getting' on wi, Lassie." Said General Listus, smiling, the twinkle in his eyes once more. He moved aside and Anhild walked into his Bed Chamber, closing the door behind her. Outside the Tavern, upon a tall Oak tree, sat a large Owl with its large orange eyes watching as the lights went out in each of the three windows at the front of the Inn upon the upper floor.

Upon the landing, outside the rooms, Manos sat in his chair. He looked out of the window and out across the Moor towards the forest, which they had left behind only that morning. The Moon was high in the sky and Manos thought about the rest of his company and the Dwarf soldiers, who were camped outside of the village. He thought about the nice comfortable bed in which he had slept last night in the Hall at the Fairy Village in the Forest, rather than the uncomfortable chair in which he found himself tonight. As he thought about this he did not notice Anhild arriving at the door to General Listus' Bed Chamber, he did not notice her enter and close the door behind her.

It seems like hours that Manos sat upon the landing in his chair, he had brought up to the landing with him a jug of Ale and some bread. Manos felt alone away from the rest of his company, here upon the landing of the Tavern. He felt uneasy away from the security of Alexandria City and the protection of the Skin. The protection only covered those who were within the City walls. Once outside of the city, one was beyond the Skin and beyond its protection. He felt like the further across the Shires that they travelled, the more dangerous their mission was becoming. He felt that at every turn they were being watched and wondered when any attack would take place and if they would be ready for it when it arrived. Without realising, Manos slipped into sleep.

Chapter Sixteen – Return to Pegasus

Simon walked from his Bed Chamber, this time towards the door at the far end of the room. He opened the door and stepped through into another smaller room, square in shape and measuring eight feet by six feet. He walked over to a wide wardrobe and chest of drawers. He then took out some clothing and put them on, making sure that he was wearing the clothing which is worn in the 'Other World'!

Satisfied he fitted this requirement, he stepped across the room. It was rather as though the air at the centre of the room felt a slight resistance, as though it were denser at this point. A bright green light shone out and with a soft 'plop' sound, Simon found himself at the other end of the room facing another door. The space the other side of the room from where he had just stepped, seemed to be faded and out of focus. He turned the door handle and walked through into the Entrance Hallway of Pegasus House. He closed the door behind him and took out of his pocket a large length of carved wood about fourteen inches in length and resembling a long chop stick or the Baton used by the Conductor of an Orchestra. Upon the tip a Crystal which gave it its power and strength. He held up the wand and tapped it upon the door handle.

"Escutio!"

Said Simon firmly and he heard the door click as it sealed itself. This type of lock was an Alexandrian lock, and Magical. No one in this World would be able to pick such a lock and a door sealed in this way would be impossible to open unless using a counter spell, not even a sledge hammer would make the slightest mark if it had been locked using this method. The reason why Simon locked the door in this way to this part of the house was so that no one would be able to 'accidentally' wander into his area of the house and stumble across the portal and slip into the 'Other World' of Alexandria. Once into Pegasus House, Simon walked across the entrance hallway to the sitting room at the back of the house next to the Kitchen. He walked in through the door and crossed over to an armchair at the window side of the room. Sitting upon the sofa was Carl, watching TV and drinking from a can of Lager.

Carl was watching England loosing yet another Test Match against Australia. The Australian Batsmen had powered their way to an impressive Four Hundred and Thirty Five runs for their first Innings. Now it was up to England to score as many runs for this Innings as possible to avoid the 'Follow on'. So far, they were upon the second day of the Test and England were now in bat, but like so many other matches, they seemed to have lost their way somewhat and were currently One Hundred and Fifty Three runs for three wickets and loosing slightly off schedule to outscore the Australian Innings. Carl acknowledged Simon joining him and offered to bring Simon a can of Lager from the fridge.

"Evening Father, I trust all goes Well in Alexandria? Shall I fetch you a beer from the fridge?" Asked Carl and began to stand from his seat in anticipation of Simon's answer.

"Thank you Carl, I need a drink after the last few days." Replied Simon,; Carl looked at his Father and apart from the obvious age showing upon his face, Carl noticed something else showing upon his face.

"Is there something wrong in Alexandria, Father?" Asked Carl. He felt freeer speaking openly about 'The Kingdom' while Rachel was at the Hospital and Toby was away at school. Inwardly he chided himself for thinking things were easier without them, he didn't want that thought, that feeling getting a grip while he was alone in the house brooding.

"Aye my Son, there is. We have received word that following a few skirmishes, a few days ago a Dwarf Soldier entered the Castle at my feet and begged us for help. He told us that shortly before his arrival, after journeying across six Shires to reach us that the Marquis has attacked and taken Calistria and its Shire and has inflicted a most severe injury to the Dwarf people. It would seem that a Darkness is now descending upon the Shires once more and we are but not enough prepared for its coming. We must train our soldiers more vigorously and train new Wizard Apprentices in order to build up the Army to full strength and have enough ability to defend our great commonwealth against the might of The Dark Lord.

We must be ready for what so ever the Marquis throws at us. I think that the best strategy that we can hope for would be to bolster the Prince Royal soldiers and Kalhron with recruits and Apprentices. So far we only have word from Calistria falling to the Dark One, but there are three Shires which share a border with the Kingdom of Thracia, unless they have already been taken by the Dark Lord; it may not be very long until he crushes the Shires and takes them all. So Far we have heard no word from the Shires of Petros and Parlemann, this maybe that they are not part of this and have no knowledge of the collapse of the Shire of Calistria, but it may also indicate that no word has come out forth from these Shires because they are unable to send forth any word to us from out of these Shires." Said Simon. Carl stood looking at Simon with a look of surprise, concern and disbelief all mingling across his face at once. There had not been any attacks upon the Shires since the Marquis last attempted to invade.

"My Lord, I am surprised by what you say, it has been so many years since I chose to exile myself in this house for safety of myself, my Wife and my Son. It sickens me to hear that such Evil has once again come to our lands and that the Dark Lord again craves our blood. It is unbelievable that after so long a time, The Dark One wishes to shatter to peace throughout our Kingdom and the Shires in his greed to conquer all that is not his." Replied Carl. Carl could not truly comprehend that which Simon was telling him, that Alexandria and the Shires would be existing in a state of war and that the peace and tranquillity enjoyed by the peoples of the Shires would be shattered by the call to arms and the prospect

116

of the first War to be fought since the Grandfather of the present Marquis sat upon the Throne of Thracia.

Carl sat for a while, a long few minutes thinking about the consequences that this prospective War may metre out upon the peoples of the Shires and for the first time really understanding the risks involved for his family and for him to be Crown Prince of Alexandria. Now it was dawning upon Carl, that if Alexandria should fall into all-out War with Thracia, that there was a very real and true prospect that he may be Crowned Prince Royal of a Kingdom he barely remembered and had not entered for almost twenty years.

"Father' I expect that ALL Alexandrians are to be called to do their duty for the Kingdom and her Shires, including the Crown Princes?" Said Carl. In his face lived the growing realisation of the position that this now left him in.

"Carl, my Son, I am aware that this is ill timed and difficult for you, but yes, if it comes to all-out War with Thracia then Alexandria will need all the soldiers we can muster to fight the Marquis and his forces; and that sadly would include you........., and Toby. If I should be slain during defence of My Realm you would become the next Prince Royal to follow me. It is also important to that end, that Toby also is informed of his Heritage, as you Well know, that if you are exalted to Prince Royal in my place, that Rachel will become the new Queen and Toby would become the new Crown Prince. Rachel and Toby must be properly made aware of their positions and Toby must be properly trained to defend the Realm with sword and wand." Said Simon.

These last words hit home hard to Carl. He reeled at the thought of breaking this news to Rachel and Toby. Next year, Toby would be Fourteen years old, the age at which Apprenticeships begin for Wizards and being a Royal Prince and the prospective future Crown Prince and Prince Royal, he would need to be trained to ward off Curses and assassination attempts both from men, beasts, Wizards and maybe even expected to face the Shambols personally and be properly versed in the Magical Arts to defend himself and the Kingdom.

"Are you aware, Father, that I have been with Rachel for twenty years; been her Husband for sixteen years and been a family with Toby and Rachel for over thirteen years, without them knowing anything about who we truly are and about Alexandria or any part of 'that World'?" Cried Carl.

"I know this, Carl, but soon it may be vital to bring them into our World for them to know their true lives and for Toby to know his true destiny. We are hopefully looking to that with a full force, including the Kalhron, that we will be fruitful in recapturing Calistria, but if anymore Shires fall, then our task will be more difficult or even a dismal hope unless we know that the Kingdom is secure in it's future Government and that the Throne is occupied by it's rightful successor. If Alexandria falls, it may be necessary to seal off the Portal forever, to protect this World from the Evil horrors which the Marquis would unleash upon it. No Army in this World would stand a chance against the Power of The

Shambols and if they should capture the Oracle Stone and couple it with the Demon Stone, which powers the Dark One in his Evil escapades, they will become invincible, the barrier between the Worlds will be shattered and the Marquis would rule all the Worlds in Darkness and this World would also be destroyed, would join with the other Kingdoms and Shires in eternal desolation," Replied Simon, "if the Marquis should conquer the Opal Mines of Cragmoor Shire, he would be able to feed Dragons that he would summon against us with the Fire Opals which are to be found there.

Their power would then be more devastating, even more than an ordinary Dragon; even with Alexandrian Armour, we would not stand a chance against their empowered searing breath. If we are able to win back Calistria from the Darkness and hold off the Marquis for long enough that the Apprenticeships to be completed, as far as combat is due, then we would have a much stronger force with which to defend Alexandria, but I fear in this time, a good many Shires will fall 'till we are ready at this point in time." Said Simon. Carl walked out to the Kitchen and opened the fridge, he took out a can of Lager for each of them and returned to the couch sitting once again and handed a can to Simon.

Carl sat and looked blankly in front of him for a long while, he was contemplating the seriousness of the situation which befell Alexandria and the Shire of Calistria, but the thing weighing mostly upon his mind was due to the circumstances, he was now most definitely going to have to find some way to gently break the news of all of this to Rachel and Toby. He was going to have to change their lives forever. How was a loving Husband expected to tell his Wife of sixteen years, 'By the way Darling, while you were in Hospital, I had news from another World in a parallel dimension to this one, that my Kingdom, of which I am Heir, is in trouble and this may result in me being pronounced King and you ……. being pronounced Queen and our Son would become Heir to a Kingdom far off in time and space; how does one break THAT kind of news to one's Wife?' He thought, 'what about Toby? Oh by the way Son, I must tell you that Daddy doesn't belong in this World, but is King of a World in another dimension and you are my Heir and will be King some day after me? How do you tell your thirteen year old Son something like that?' He thought.

"Father, how do I approach this with my Wife and Son? How do I tell them that we have been living a lie for eighteen years and that I am Alien to this World? If Rachel had been killed in that car crash, God forbid, the task may have been easier upon Toby's part but how do I tell my Wife of eighteen years that Myslef and my Father have been deceiving her all our time together, right from when we met at Toadford?" Asked Carl. His head was spinning, running scenarios through his mind of the gigantic row which would ensue and Rachel telling him that he could keep his 'Other World' and hoping he would be happy with his 'ET' Father. He thought of her argument asking him 'How did you hear about the trouble in 'Your World?' did you 'phone home' or something' and laughing. Carl sat frozen in thought, frozen with fear at his family falling apart, when he revealed the truth to Rachel and Toby.

"Carl, this is a grave undertaking which I am giving to you. I shall be here for you, supporting you all the way through this, my Son. I am so dearly sorry but this must be done, as with the fall of Calistria, The Dark One has begun his latest campaign of invasion by hitting us hardest at the source of our currency, the Galem Gold Mines. In seizing Calistria, we are cut off from this and if our currency fails, we shall not survive. No Armourer will make an Army of armour and weapons, no Farrier will shoe horses for an Army, no Army will march and fight without pay or food. For the sake of the Shires and for the Dwarf people of Calistria, if more than Calistria falls, then we may have to think of an attacking force out in the Field of Battle and a defending force which guards Alexandria from all-out attack should the forces of the Dark Lord reach our Alexandrian Shire Borders.

The prospect of this terrifies me, knowing what the consequences may be for this World and ours, the prospect of losing our link to this World forever if the Portal should need to be sealed, if Alexandria falls. The consequences for this world if the forces of the Marquis find some way to breach the Portal or find some way to create a Portal of their own to gain entry into this World, would be disastrous to say the least. The People of this World would be totally unprepared for what would be unleashed upon them and would suffer incredibly horrific deaths under the control of the Dark Lord. You should remember, my Son, that I had to confront your Mother to know and accept that Alexandria and your future subjects would not see their future Prince Royal growing up, would not see him bring his Princess into 'Our World' for them to rejoice. While I was through to Alexandria for my last visit, there was a feast to celebrate Toby's enrolment in Toadford School, the next generation of Prince to begin his way through the School and prepare him for his future position as Ruler of The Shires and Commonwealth of Alexandria. This feast went well, save the absence of the Guest of Honour, The Prince himself, whom the feast was honouring, very noticeably missing!" Said Simon. Carl sat in thought again, looking blankly in front of him again.

"Carl, I did not take lightly the decision to grant you Exile from your World, from your people. I knew at that time to fight you upon the matter would have led to a danger of our World being uncovered. I knew that someday, this hour would be upon us, or that an even greater need for your return to Alexandria and the truth being told would arrive. I know that there is now a time that Toby needs to take up his daily duty as the next Crown Prince and his training for this must begin sooner rather than later." Said Simon.

Carl turned to Simon, the distant look upon his face turning to one of fear. He stood up and crossed the room to a cupboard upon which the TV stood. He opened the cupboard door and took out a cloth roll tied with string at its middle and brought it over to Simon. Carl untied the string and unfolded the cloth away from its centre. Simon looked down at Carl's hands, in front of him he was able to see the long slender blade of a silvery metal, gleaming in the light from the ceiling. It was some three feet from the hilt to the tip of the blade. The top edge was straight, whereas the lower edge bulged outwards from the tip and ran slightly narrowing as it went along to narrow into the hilt. The Hilt was of Gold, at the pummel was a globe cut white crystal and the hand grip was of tightly wound leather. Simon's eyes both lit up and showed concern at what he saw held in front of him in Carl's hands. Carl looked at Simon, holding the sword out in front of him. Along the length of the blade was carved in Elfin Script; Simon looked in astonishment at the blade, he read the script out loud.

"It says 'Mae Beit Klemor Bladen Elfin' and is written in the Elfin script. This sword is an Alexandrian sword! Carl, why on Earth do you have an Alexandrian sword? Where did you find it, for it was not forged for you! An Alexandrian may only weald the sword which has been made for him, as we who are magically trained can only weald the wand which was made for us! Carl, you do still possess your wand, please tell me that is so?" Exclaimed Simon. He looked deep into Carl's eyes, hoping that this answer would be positive.

"What do the words say, Father?" Asked Carl.

"'This is 'Klemor,' a blade forged by Elfin hands.'"

"May I weald the sword as I claimed it, obviously it's owner was either defeated or lost it." Asked Carl.

"There is but one way in which you could connect your spirit to the sword, you must carry it through the Portal, then when charged with the Power of the Portal, Lord Barnabus must quickly perform the sealing charm while the crystal is newly charged, he must join the sword to your wand in spirit; now, do you still have your wand as without it, the sword would never be yours and where did you get the sword!?" Replied Simon.

"Yes Father, I do still have my Wand," Replied Carl, who then walked from the room, still holding the sword. He went into the front room of the house, walked over to the fire place and turned an ornamental rose clockwise upon the fire surround. Immediately, a small panel in the surround dropped forwards underneath the ornamental Rose. Carl placed his hand inside the hole left by the panel and pulled out a rather old looking box, about fifteen inches long and three inches wide. It appeared to be made of deep lavender cardboard or Papier-mâché and h ad a faded golden label upon its lid, which read;

"Thadius P Karlovisky Royal Wand Makers"

'MARKALORE'

Carl put down the sword upon a chair to his left and opened the box. Inside was lined with the purest soft pale lilac silk, cushioning a length of pale wood with a darker twist at the end. The handle had a small bauble of crystal embedded at it's end and the tip showed a small point of crystal emerging from it by about a quarter of an inch. Along the length of the wand, were the words;

"MARKALORE - Treat me Well"

"Aye yes, 'Markalore', you still have him , my Son, a fine wand' which you became quite skilful with, if I remember." Said Simon.

"I may be in Exile, Father, but I don't forget my roots in our World. I would be more than a bit rusty with 'Markalore' these days; he hasn't seen much use these past years." Said Carl.

"It is time to brush up your Wandlore and bring 'Markalore' back to life. You would also need to bring him back through the Portal to recharge his crystal." Simon said.

"I still find this hard to think about, that I have to break the news to my wife of sixteen years and my Son, that I am not of 'this World', 'we are not of this World,' and that I am a Crown Prince and a Wizard!" Carl said, the fear once more crossing his face.

"Where did you get Klemor?" Simon asked again.

"I found him up upon the Moor, near to the enclosure which we were working upon. I was clearing an old drainage ditch and found him in the water." Replied Carl.

"You must show me?" Asked Simon, the look of concern returning to his face.

Carl led the way out of the Living Room and paused in the Entrance Hall. He and Simon took jackets from the hooks upon the wall and Carl picked up a set of keys from a hook next to the jackets. They hurriedly walked out of the front door and closed it behind them. Simon walked over to the Landrover and went around to the passenger side of the Vehicle. Carl walked to the Driver side, opened the door and lifted the latch upon the opposite door, Simon climbed in and sat in the passenger seat. They both pulled their seat belts across themselves and fastened them in their catches with a 'Click'. Carl wasted no time and started the engine. He turned the Landrover to face out of the driveway and drove along to the outer gates. He turned left and drove out onto the Moorland Road towards the Moor, leaving Pegasus House and the Village behind. They drove out across the Moor, leaving the hedge bordered land behind and finding themselves with open Moorland either side of the road. As they drove towards the place where Carl had found Klemor, they were in discussion about the meaning of this.

"It would appear that as we approach yet another Century since the Skin was put in place, it may be beginning to fail, the spell is old and may be worn out. I have sent a delegation to Lord Barnabus, to hear his words upon the subject, to find out how much he has discovered upon the matter and gain his Council about what to do and how we should need his help to protect the Shires and Alexandria." Said Simon the Landrover bumping slightly upon some small pot holes in the road as they went along.

"It would be interesting to hear what Lord Barnabus has to say upon the matter, Father. This foul deed deserves the full force of the Commonwealth to fight back and wrench the Shire of Calistria back from the clutches of the Marquis. I know I have been away from the Shires for many years. I never thought that this day would come when I would be forced to cut short my Exile. It still fills me with dread and fear to need to explain to Rachel and Toby about our true identities and risk losing them.

Rachel knew some of the Traditions of Toadford School, having been a Student there, she knew that there were forbidden parts of the School to certain Students, but unlike me, she was not aware of the reasons for these areas of the School to be secret. Rachel was oblivious to the secret of our being banned in the First year until we were fourteen, from entering the Second Bailey and other areas because these areas formed the Wizarding School. She was totally unaware that the Wizarding School was hidden here at Toadford to keep it hidden and safe out of reach of the Marquis upon this side of the Portal. Of Course, I have kept this from her since we left the School, since we married and since we watched Toby growing up. Now, as he is at Toadford, as you say, sooner rather than later, he would have been told this next year and enrolled into the Wizarding School to begin his Wizardry Apprenticeship and to learn our Alexandrian Customs and weaponry. With his abilities awakened by the Portal, he will be Alexandrian and so will face the prospect of becoming Prince Royal someday. I agree, however awkward it may be to me, it is vital that he be made aware of his Heritage to help him to progress at Toadford. There is one problem though, Father, which concerns me a little in this matter; Toby has made two friends, who he feels close to. They have asked to come to Pegasus House to stay during the Summer Holiday from Toadford. It may be awkward to turn them away and upset Toby, but how do we condition Toby to his duties with his Alexandrian blood activated and with his two friends looking on?" Carl said, Simon thought for a moment then answered;

"We must let him have his visitors; do not give Toby a reason to reject what we must tell him. If we can possibly swear his friends to upmost secrecy and security, maybe a word with Lord Barnabus may allow them to join Toby in his quest." Replied Simon.

"But Father, no Outlander has ever been permitted to Wizarding School? It would be very dangerous. Said Carl.

"You do not see my Son, for you have been away for many years from Alexandria and the Oracle. Toby has befriended these companions; to take him away from them would be counterproductive to the Governing of Alexandria. If he becomes too accustomed to life in 'this World' and has too many ties to 'his World', then he would never wish to believe that one day he will be Prince Royal of Alexandria and he would likely reject any form of Tutoring in Alexandria life or joining Barnabus in Apprenticeship. If we permit his friends to follow him, this bond may be the strengthening of the Skin which we need." Said Simon.

Carl slowed the car down as they approached the area where Carl had been working. The workmen had made great progress with the absence of Carl. The ditch was now cleared out and ran the length of the enclosure, ending in a small puddle of a stream which ran through a very small tunnel under a very small bridge. The stream emerged the other side of the road, then trickling down through stones and Heather off into the distance out across the Moor and out of sight. Carl stopped at a spot along the drainage ditch channel and pointed out to Simon where he had been working when he uncovered the sword.

"It was just about here, Father, I was cleaning out the drainage ditch with my small digger and I saw it in the water. I recognised it as something interesting and only when I got it back to the House and cleaned it up did I realise what it was." Said Carl.

"This is grave tidings, Carl, to find an Alexandrian sword here in 'this World' and one which is not a remnant of the last Battles, but shines with new power, this means only one of three answers, One – that Lord Barnabus, some reason or another, which he has neglected to inform me of, has opened a secret Portal to this World; two – that some other Wizard has opened a secret Portal for himself and for his own ends, it would need a Wizard of who is of at least equal ability to Lord Barnabus to achieve this; or three – our worst fear and nightmare has become true, that the Marquis or one of his Shambols Wizards has found a way through to create a Portal to 'this World'. Whichever is the true answer, this has changed everything and we now have no choice but to bring forth our plans and prepare for the war to end all wars and simply hope that the Marquis can be stopped before he turns this World into ash along with Alexandria, as he has done with his own Kingdom." Said Simon.

Carl suddenly had a look of increased concern across his face and the fear in his eyes intensified. He looked around the place where they stood, at the ditch, the enclosure which had been completed and the second which was nearing completion, he then spoke to Simon.

"Father, this seems like a nightmare, I keep thinking of waking up and then realise the reality of all this. It is tearing me apart inside to comprehend the Omens that this may lead to , to think of after so long to have to tell both Rachel and Toby of all this and expect them to take me seriously and to understand that their lives. Everyone's lives across two Worlds may be in peril and that Toby and his friends may be the only solution that we have to combine the two Worlds and to fight back as one. To tell Toby that he must attend Wizarding School and somehow expect Rachel to go along with all of this, and actually bring into all of this Toby's new friends and expect them to take all of this into their heads also; and ally with Toby in joining us in our battle with the Marquis and saving both our Worlds." Said Carl incredulously.

Carl sat upon a rock near to the drainage ditch trying to take all of this in, the meaning of finding the sword out here upon the barren Moor, Simon's tale about the fall of Calistria, the exile of the Dwarfs, the mission of Lucius and his companions to meet with Lord Barnabus for his council, The thought that as Crown Prince of Alexandria, he would now, especially under the current climate, have to involve them, to tell them that he is really a Crown Prince of a Kingdom trapped in time and space and that she is not just a Primary School teacher, but a Princess and possibly future Queen of this far away Kingdom, that Toby is his Heir as next Prince Royal after him and oh yes, the little matter of an Evil Tyrannical Wizard who is Hell bent upon destroying not only his own World but also our World along with it."

All this time that Carl sat upon the rock, Simon was standing beside the drainage ditch. He faced along the ditch and put his right hand into his pocket. He pulled it out and held up his wand. Simon began to move inch by inch along the edge of the drainage ditch and uttered a command flicking his wand; "Revelo!"

At once, his wand began to glow with a pale blue light in the crystal at the wand's tip. Carl watched as what looked like a thick silvery Mist seemed to leak out from the wand's tip, in a cloud. Simon moved the wand around as he inched his way along the ditch. Simon walked along to the small bridge which was about fifty yards away from the enclosure. Carl now stood up from his rock and walked after his Father along the ditch towards the small bridge. When Simon reached the bridge, he waved his wand out across the bridge and sent a cloud of the thick Mist across the road, this soon dissipated and Simon satisfied, then turned with his back to the bridge and road. Simon then waved his wand and sent out another cloud of Mist, which moved away from him and spread out as it moved.

Then it happened! About thirty yards away from where Simon and Carl, who had now joined him at the bridge, the Mist appeared to have struck something. There standing in thin air, the Mist touched a rectangular shape in the air which touched the ground and stood like a door. Around the perimeter of the shape, the Mist had turned bright red, tracing the edges of the 'door'. Simon frowned and stared at the shape.

"Father, the Portal, there really is one." Said Carl, struck by the sight which now befell his eyes. Simon eyed the shape carefully. He walked over to the shape.

"This was a portal, which is now locked closed tight. Whosoever created this Portal, sealed it again shortly afterwards. Once we return to the house, I must cross back over to Alexandria and send word to Lord Barnabus to tell him that a General Council of the Cenet and the Wizard Decree must take place. What we have found here could be the difference between both our Worlds surviving, only one or both being destroyed and becoming absorbed into the limbo which is Thracia and fall subject to the rule of The Dark One". Said Simon.

For two hours Simon and Carl continued to search for any more Portals around the area. Simon was satisfied that this was the only Portal and they both returned to the car. Very soon they were back at Pegasus House.

"Carl, I must ask you this, will you accompany me back into Alexandria. I know that you haven't crossed the portal for so many years, but believe me Son, I would not ask unnecessarily and with Lucius away from Court just now, it would be better to be accompanied by the Crown Prince to hold Parliament." Said Simon.

"It doesn't look like I have much of a choice, does it Father? This is so grave a matter and with so much at stake, I can't refuse can I, not with the thought that this may seal the fate of two Worlds, one of which contains my wife and Son." Replied Carl.

"Oh my Son, I am so happy to hear you say that. With your return and rejuvenation along with that of Toby, we may have a formidable force to battle back and hopefully stop the Marquis forever this time." Said Simon.

"I will need to eat Lunch first I'm afraid, Father, just to quell this uneasy feeling in my stomach about all of this. I will need to be able to keep in touch with the Hospital to follow Rachel's progress and keep her company and to keep in touch with Toby." Replied Carl.

"Of course Carl, we shall have Lunch and then we shall be ready for our crossing into Alexandria. The people of the Realm have been kept up to date with your life and I have also kept those that need to know informed of the developments of Toby as a boy and a Prince." Said Simon.

"It is so long since I passed through the Portal, I've forgotten how it feels?" Said Carl.

"You'll find out when you step through the Portal this afternoon, be prepared, you will feel an almighty rush of energy, how much so I can't think, as it has been eighteen years since your last visit and last rejuvenation from the Portal." Said Simon.

Simon and Carl walked into the Kitchen; Carl began to prepare a Lunch for them both. He placed some sliced ham and salad onto plates and took two cans of Lager out of the fridge. They sat down in the Kitchen at the Kitchen table and ate their Lunch. After their Lunch, Simon turned to Carl and made absolutely certain he was sure.

"It is time Carl, we must do this, once upon the other side of the Portal, you will soon begin to understand the importance of the plight in which we find oursleves." Said Simon.

"Yes Father, it is hard to take in but better to get some idea of where we are in this before I have to tell all this to Rachel and Toby." Replied Carl.

Carl sat and contemplated the thought that he was about to re-enter Alexandria, a land which was now Alien to him, even though it was the land of his Birth. He thought about the sudden change in their lives since Toby had celebrated his thirteenth Birthday and entered Toadford School. He thought about what he would say to Rachel, how he would tell her that he had kept this big secret all of their lives, all through their marriage, all through Toby growing up. He was trying hard to psych himself into the courage to bring himself to cross through the Portal, to rejuvenate himself, to return to his Alexandrian self. Even with his workouts, through his hard work as a Ranger upon the Moor, he still had slight love handles, his stomach was not entirely altogether a 'Six Pack'. He had begun to notice recently just a few grey hairs appearing here and there. It would seem that since Toby had joined Toadford, it had in some way triggered a kind of beginning to age to Carl. One thing that Simon had omitted to tell Carl was, when Toby became of Age, the shield protecting their blood began to fail, and that once of Age, Simon would appear to grow older and loose his protection of his blood, he would become mortal in this World and as vulnerable as Toby or Rachel were presently. It was an unknown entity for Carl, as no other Alexandrian Prince had stayed this side of the Portal for as long as Carl had. The effects of returning through the Portal were entirely a new concept. Carl's head was swimming with all these thoughts and he was momentarily caught off guard as he sat staring at the floor.

"Carl, Carl, are you ready, it's time to go back. If we don't go now, it may be too late for you to return tonight and we may have to spend the night in Alexandria." Said Simon. Simon was gently shaking Carl by the shoulder to awaken him from the trance he appeared to be in.

"Yes, Yes Father, Er…. yes, I'm ready. Just thinking about everything and trying to prepare myslef for the crossing." Replied Carl.

They stood up from the table, Carl took their plates over to the sink and washed them, he then threw the two cans into the Kitchen bin and they walked out of the Kitchen. They walked across the Entrance Hallway and stopped outside the door which Simon had entered his Pegasus House through. Simon pulled out his wand from his pocket and pointed it at the door.

"Entrée." Announced Simon clearly. The door rattled slightly, a dim green light shone around the frame and Carl heard a 'click' sound. Simon then entered the door and found himself upon the far side of the small room which had the wardrobe and chest of drawers upon the other side of the room. Simon turned to Carl and put his hand upon his shoulder.

"Carl my Son, my Prince, it is time for Alexandria to rejoice, her lost Son returns, Alexandria once more has a Crown Prince." Said Simon. He then turned and Carl watched as Simon stepped forwards to the centre of the room. Carl saw at the centre a thin greenish mist appear, then a bright green light momentarily shone around Simon and with a 'plop' sound, Simon disappeared. Carl stepped forwards, he felt as though he was pushing against a sheet of cling film, then he saw the faint green mist rise and then suddenly he felt as though an electric shock had shot through his entire body. He collapsed and a bright green light shone momentarily, then Carl closed his eyes and fell forwards – 'Plop'.

Chapter Seventeen – Rachel's Physio

Ever since her accident, Rachel had been lying in bed in the Hospital, now it was time for her to try to walk again. The nurse helped Rachel out of bed and into a wheel chair which she had placed beside Rachel's bed. Rachel put on her dressing gown before sitting in the wheel chair and the nurse wheeled her away from her bed and out of the ward. They went along the corridor and turned left into a wide corridor where they found a pair of elevators. The nurse pushed the call button to the elevators.

"Won't be long now Rachel, we'll soon have you at Physio." Said the Nurse.

Just then a bell sounded and with a 'clunk' the doors to the elevator upon their right opened. Out walked three people who turned to the right and headed out towards the ward. The nurse wheeled Rachel into the lift and pressed the button to take them to the third floor. The doors of the elevator slid closed with a 'clunk' and then with a slight jolt, they felt the elevator move smoothly down the two floors to Level Three. The elevator stopped with a jolt and the doors slid open. The nurse wheeled Rachel out of the elevator and turned to the right. They went along a corridor and turned left. Rachel saw a sign hanging from the ceiling above them with an arrow pointing in the direction in which they were travelling saying;

'PHYSIOPHERAPY DEPARTMENT →'

A short distance past the sign, Rachel saw that they were entering a wider Reception area with rows of seats around the outside walls and a counter where two nurses were sitting behind a computer each and a telephone beside them. The nurse wheeled Rachel up to the counter and spoke to the nurse upon her left.

"Rachel Morby, for Martyn." She said.

"Just a moment, " Said the Physio nurse, "Hello Martyn, Paula here from reception. Lydia has arrived with Rachel Morby for her session." She said into the telephone, and then put the hand set down.

"You can go along to Room two, Martyn is waiting for you." She added.

"Thank you Paula." Said Nurse Lydia.

She wheeled Rachel away from the counter and out to a corridor off to the right. Along the corridor was a series of doors which had plaques upon them with a room number above a sliding bar with 'Occupied' or 'vacant' written upon them. They walked along the corridor until they reached Room two, which had a piece of plastic within the slider under the room number blacking out the word 'Vacant' so that only the word 'Occupied' was visible. Nurse Lydia stopped the wheelchair outside the door and began to quickly preen herself. She quickly checked that her long black hair was presentable and that her 'scrubs' top was not rucked up or anything, then knocked firmly upon the door. There came a slightly muffled reply from within.

"Come in." Said the voice.

Nurse Lydia opened the door and wheeled Rachel's wheelchair through and into Room two. She closed the door behind them and looked across the room, her green eyes lighting up when she spoke.

"Hi Martyn, I've bought Rachel Morby for you from 'Moulton Ward'. It's her first visit." Smiled Nurse Lydia, with her perfect white teeth. Standing at about five feet five inches tall, slim with her raven hair and green eyes, she was quite pretty. Then Rachel noticed why she had stopped to check that her appearance was ok. She was twenty six years old and spoke with a soft high cheerful voice. In front of them sat at a desk with a computer upon it and a telephone and a pile of files with his back to them was Rachel's Physiotherapist.

Martyn stood up from his chair and turned to greet them. He stood about five feet ten inches tall with bright blue eyes and dark brown hair. His fit muscular build showing through his 'scrubs'. 'Hmm' thought Rachel, 'this was the reason for the preening'. Everyone who came to Physio wanted a chance to see Martyn, all the Nurses, the young ones fancied him and too did some of the older ones, secretly. He spoke with a Northern accent, 'Manchester', thought Rachel.

"Hi Rachel, I'm Martyn, your new Physio. I want to have a little chat and go through your injuries with you and work out a plan of how we are going to get you up and about again. It's not easy when you have broken your hip and leg, sometimes it can be painstakingly slow progress as you heal fully and your body becomes used to walking again. First I want to ask you to get onto the couch for me, Nurse Lydia will help you." Said Martyn. Nurse Lydia wheeled Rachel over to the examining couch next to the desk. She noticed around the room were a cupboard and some exercise equipment stacked beside it. This was obviously only an examination room, not the Physio Room. Nurse Lydia helped Rachel out of the wheelchair and to lay upon the couch.

"OK Rachel, would you take off your dressing gown for me please, to let me see better your legs and hip." Said Martyn. Rachel took off her dressing gown and laid it unto the wheelchair. She then lay flat upon the couch. Martyn gently and discreetly lifted her night dress upon the right hand side to just above her hip, trying not to embarrass Rachel. He checked her hip and leg, taking note of the healing which had already taken place since her operation to put her hip and right leg back together after they had been broken in the crash.

Martyn placed his hand under Rachel's right heel and asked her to gently and slowly lift her right leg and try as best as she could to keep her leg straight as she did so. Rachel began to slowly lift her leg off the couch with the help of Martyn's hand supporting it. She winced slightly, because this was the first time since her operation that she had needed to lift her leg in this way. Martyn took note of how her leg lifted, the muscle tone and how her scars reacted to the exercise. He asked her to lower her leg back down and placed it back upon the couch. Martyn removed his hand when she reached the couch with her heel. Martyn stood for a moment looking at Rachel's leg, Nurse Lydia thought for a moment how she would like him to look at her legs in this way. Martyn then walked back to his desk and picked up Rachel's file. He pulled out a series of X Rays from the file and looked at them. He then walked back over to Rachel, laying upon the couch, and held up the X Rays and checked them with her hip and leg.

"I can see where the damage was, it won't be too difficult to lean to walk again, but will take a little time for us to work upon this." Said Martyn.

He put the X Rays down back upon the desk and looked at the notes in Rachel's file.

"You can come down from the couch again now Rachel." Said Martyn. Nurse Lydia helped Rachel to sit up and swing her legs over then helped her back into the wheelchair.

"Hopefully after a few sessions we will be able to leave this behind us." Said Nurse Lydia, motioning towards the wheelchair.

"OK Rachel, I want you to try some light exercises before I see you next; nothing major mind, just lifting your legs straight while laying upon your bed a few times to start with, so that we can get the muscles in your legs working again." Said Martyn.

"OK I'll give that a try." Agreed Rachel.

"OK, see you on Wednesday at 10 am." Said Martyn.

"OK, see you later." Replied Rachel with a brighter tone to her voice. It was good to know that finally she would be getting out of that bed after being there for six weeks.

"See you later." Smiled Nurse Lydia and winked at Martyn. She then pushed Rachel's wheelchair out of the room and back along the corridor into the Reception area. She stopped at the desk and Nurse Lydia told the receptionist of Rachel's next visit with Martyn. Nurse Lydia then pushed Rachel back to the elevators and into the left hand elevator. She pushed the button for their floor and the lift moved smoothly.

"He seems nice, Martyn, I hope I can walk again soon." Said Rachel.

"Yes, he is nice," Said Nurse Lydia, dreamily, "Martyn will soon have you up and about, healing hands that one."

They returned to Rachel's bed; Rachel asked for the telephone and dialled the number for Toby's mobile, after noting that it was Lunch time.

"Hello." Came Toby's voice.

"Hi Sweetie, it's Mom, I've just got back to my bed after my first Physio session. The Physio Guy seems nice and he says that I shouldn't have much trouble learning to walk again. How are things going your end?" Said Rachel.

"Oh we're going Well here Mom; I have been playing in the House teams at Football, Cricket and Rugby. At the moment it looks like it will be us against Wombat House in all the House Cup Finals." Replied Toby.

"Yeah, that sounds about right, it usually was between Cargal House and Wombat House for the House Cups, it was usually between Cargal House and Wombat House for everything." Replied Rachel.

"Dad says that Keiron and Poly can come to stay for a while during the Summer, to work on our Summer Homework and spend some of the Holidays together. Their Parents have agreed so long as someone is there with us." said Toby.

"That sounds great Toby, I'm so happy that you are making friends there, hopefully I will be back then and your Dad will be there for evenings and weekends. Hopefully I'll be up and about properly by the Summer. Half Term next week Dear, are you going back home or staying at Toadford?" Said Rachel.

"Keiron has asked me back to his house for the Holidays, Dad said that he didn't mind and hopefully Polly will join us for a couple of days, if her Parents don't mind; Keiron's Parents have already OK'd it, so it's looking like fun." said Toby.

"OK Dear, if Dad agreed, have fun. I'll give you a call again soon; have a good week and stay safe. Replied Rachel.

"Bye Mom, love you." Said Toby.

"Bye Dear, love you too." Replied Rachel and cancelled the call. Toby put his Mobile back into his pocket after turning it off.

"That your Mom was it?" Asked Keiron.

"Yeah, it was Mom; she just had her first Physio session. She's OK about coming to you for the Holidays also, but with Mom in Hospital still for some more weeks, me coming to stay with you for the Holidays means Dad doesn't have to take time off work to be with me for the week, works out just fine." Said Toby. Just then Polly came tripping along into the Hall and sat down beside Toby, just as Keiron stuffed another large roast Potato into his mouth.

"Hi Folly, wherfubinm yorlate?" Mumbled Keiron through a mouthful of roast Potato. Polly gave him one of her unimpressed looks and tilted up her nose.

"Were you speaking to me JCB mouth? Pray why do you have to eat like you are shovelling it in like a Bulldozer?" Asked Polly, watching a rather large piece of roast Lamb follow the roast Potato and meet part of it. Keiron chewed quickly and noticeably then gave a great swallow.

"I said, 'Hi Polly, where have you been, you're late'." Said Keiron, this time with no food getting in the way.

"Thank you Keiron, I can understand you now, there doesn't seem to be half the Lunch table getting in the way." Replied Polly.

130

"Yes Polly, where have you been, it's not like you to be late for Lunch, it's Sunday and we don't have any lessons?" Toby asked.

"I've been brushing up upon a few things, practising." Said Polly.

"I thought we hadn't seen you all morning." Said Keiron and stuffed his mouth with more Lamb. Polly turned up the corner of her lip as she answered.

"Well that's obvious, as we weren't together were we?" Said Polly, wincing as she watched Keiron swallow another mouthful.

"What were you brushing up on?" Asked Toby.

"Oh just a bit of Net Ball practice." Replied Polly.

Toby was now watching as Keiron pushed aside his empty Dinner plate and pulled a bowl towards him which had just been put in front of him by a member of Kitchen staff, full of Treacle Pudding and Custard. Both Toby and Polly watched as Keiron stuck in his spoon and lifted it up to his face. Keiron stopped what he was doing with a spoonful of Treacle Pudding and Custard at his open mouth and looked beyond the spoon at Toby and Polly, a drip of Custard dropped back into his bowl.

"What's this, a ruddy goldfish bowl or something?" Said Keiron, noticing them watching.

"We're just wondering how many seconds that bowl of Treacle Pudding and Custard was going to last before you shovelled it all down your throat." Said Toby.

"Verifunni." Said Keiron through a mouthful of Treacle Pudding and Custard, a drip of Custard ran down his chin.

"What have we got on today then Guys?" Asked Polly, taking small bites of Treacle Pudding.

"We're going out into the grounds to have a look around, we finished all of our Homework this morning so this afternoon is free." Said Toby.

"We're going searching'" Said Keiron, who had now swallowed his mouthful of Treacle Pudding and Custard, in fact, he had almost completley swallowed all of the Treacle Pudding and Custard, having only a couple of spoons left.

"Searching for what?" Asked Polly.

"Searching for anything interesting." Replied Keiron, now wiping the custard off his chin with a serviette.

"So good that you know what they are for." Said Polly pointing to the crumpled serviette in Keiron's hand. Just then Arrabella Snoop came walking into the Hall and sat down next to Polly. She was handed a plate of roast Lamb and Potatoes by a member of the Kitchen staff and began to eat slowly.

"Hi Guys, doing anything interesting this afternoon?" Said Arrabella between mouthfuls of Lamb.

"Just looking around the grounds." Replied Toby.

"Oh, I would love to come along, may I?" Asked Arrabella.

"Of course you can join us, Arrabella." Said Poly.

"Just call me 'Bella." Said Arrabella.

"OK 'Bella." Replied Polly.

Gradually they all finished their Lunches and then waited for the Students to be dismissed from the Great Hall. They walked out through the double doors at the entrance and out into the corridor leading away from the Great Hall. As they walked, they passed the Girls Shower Rooms and Toilet, then the Head Master's Office and past numerous paintings and photographs upon the walls of the corridor. They passed the Hospital and Secretary's Office then the Matron's Office and finally emerged out into the Entrance Hallway. They turned to their left and walked out of the large double doors onto the Entrance Porch. From here they were able to see the area in front of the building leading out to a curtain wall, this was the 'Grunt's' Recreation Area.

"Don't forget Guys, as we are Grunts, we don't leave this area." Said Polly, reminding them about what Parfinkle had told them when they arrived at the School.

"We know Polly." Said Keiron, reproachfully.

"I was just reminding you as you had mentioned something about 'searching for something interesting.'" Said Polly.

"We were just aiming at getting to know the place a little better, we know about staying in the Inner Bailey, Polly." Said Toby.

"Just being upon the safe side, boys." Replied Polly.

"Let's go in a clockwise direction, good as any and walk around the Bailey and just see what we find." Suggested Toby.

"Good idea Mate might as well start somewhere." Replied Keiron.

"Tally Ho!" Shouted 'Bella as they all descended the Porch steps into the Inner Bailey; Toby, Polly and Keiron paused to give 'Bella a look of surprise.

"Oops, Sorry Guys." Said 'Bella.

The small group began their walk away from the Porch and out around the Bailey. They walked parallel with the face of the main building. Polly felt the cool breeze blow through her long light brown hair. They passed The Great Hall where they could see the huge windows from the outside set within the Gable end of the Hall. Looking across the Bailey towards the entrance Gate House, they were able to see that the Curtain wall of the Bailey was slightly angled away from the entrance Gate House. This angled wall then came to a small round tower within the wall. The tower appeared to have no door upon this side, so they assumed that the entrance to the tower was within the Second Bailey, which was beyond their curtain wall. The Grunts were not allowed into this area without a member of staff. They continued their walk around the outer edge of the Great Hall and turned it's corner. They were momentarily hit by a small gust of fresh air as they began to walk along the length of the long wall of the Great Hall and see the large windows of which were depicted in stained glass the School crest and all the crests of the four Houses in the windows along this wall. Along the walls they could see the Buttresses which lined the outer wall of the Great Hall between the windows. Along the wall there was a long flower bed filled with many coloured flowers. The flowers were now starting to fade as the year was heading on. A glance over at the curtain wall revealed that it now continued to another angle than before. They reached the end of the Great Hall and found the outside of the Chapel behind it. Here they could see the large stained glass window in the side wall and they looked again at the curtain wall.

"Seems the wall is turning everywhere we turn, must be following us." Said Keiron.

"Don't be stupid, it's Pentagonal around the Inner Keep or School building." Replied Polly.

Keiron gave Polly one of her looks; Polly continued to educate them as they rounded the end of the Chapel and approached the building which housed the changing rooms and games Master's Office.

"The Gate House over there," Said Polly, pointing towards two small towers with double wooden gates between them; "That is, as you should remember, the entrance to the Second Bailey and the Sports area. You will notice that beyond the second tower of the Gate House, the wall continues at an angle once more. This leads around to another small tower and then the Inner Bailey Gate House to the front of the School building, thus completing the Pentagon."

"And the emergency exits are here, here and here." Replied Keiron, pointing his arms and hands out, imitating an Air Stewardess. This time Polly gave him one of her very disapproving looks.

"It's all in the book about the History of the School which I read in the Library." Said Polly.

"You spend too much time in the Library." Said Keiron.

"It's the only way to learn everything, Replied Polly.

By now, they had walked around the corner of the Chapel and were walking along the side of the Changing Rooms towards the Kitchen, from where a delicious aroma of roast meat was wafting towards them, leading them on by their noses. Around the Bailey were seated other Students upon benches, by tables and around a number of small trees; there were Students playing catch with balls, some of the Wombats were having a kick about with a football over by the Kitchen building. They looked up and spotted the group walking their way. Virginia Cornett whispered in Tom Taylor's ear and he 'accidentally' kicked the football towards the group as they walked.

133

"Maybe if you do some reading, Keiron, you may get to know these things ………. OUCH! OH MY GOD! AGHHH!" Said Polly and ended with screaming and crying when the football suddenly slammed into her face. Tom Taylor and Virginia Cornett, the Eldridge Trio and Aaron Pooke all collapsed laughing. Polly threw her hands up to her face, there was blood everywhere and Polly was still screaming and crying.

"Oh my God, her nose!" Cried Arrabella in shock. Polly ran towards the rear entrance with Arrabella accompanying her, while Toby and Keiron rounded upon the Wombats.

"You Ruddy sawdust head, you watch where you're kicking that thing, no wonder we're leading the House Cup Table." Shouted Keiron, Toby holding him back.

"Want to make something of it 'Muddles'?" Said Tom Taylor, beginning to walk towards them followed by the Eldridge Trio, cracking the knuckles and Virginia Cornett laughing out loud.

"I'll ruddy kill you Taylor, you've broken her nose!!" Shouted Keiron and moved towards Tom Taylor with his fists clenched. Just then the door to the Games Master's Office opened and James Marden, the Boys Games Master came striding out.

"What on Earth is going on out here? He demanded, just as the two warring factions came close.

"He deliberately kicked a football into Polly Muggard's face Sir; I think he's broken her nose." Said Keiron.

"Is that true Taylor? Demanded Mr Marden.

"It was an accident, Sir," Grinned Tom Taylor, Virginia grinning with him, while Toby and Aaron Pooke were staring each other out.

"Grasses." Sneered Aaron Pooke through gritted teeth, the Eldridge Trio mimicking their throats being cut by pulling their pointed index fingers across their throats and grinning.

"Where is Miss Muggard?" Asked Mr Marden.

"Arrabella Snoop took her to the Hospital Wing, Sir." Replied Toby, still staring out Aaron Pooke.

"Right then OK; Toby Morby, Keiron Muddley, you go off back to your Dorm Room. Don't any of you come out until Dinner Time. Taylor, You come with me to the Head Master's Office; Cornett, Pooke and the ELdridges, back to your Dorm Wing and don't any of you come out until Dinner Time." Mr Marden said.

The Wombats, except Tom Taylor all shuffled away into the entrance, Mr Marden kept back Keiron and Toby to keep the peace and let the Wombats go back to the stairs first. Then Mr Marden, having hold of Tom Taylor's arm and leading him through the building to the base of the stairs, then indicated to Toby and Keiron to go up. He then led Tom Taylor down to the corridor to the Head Master's Office.

Mr Marden knocked upon the door and a thin elderly voice answered;

"Come in." Said Parfinkle.

Mr Marden opened the door and walked in, still leading Tom Taylor by the Arm. He stood Tom in front of Parfinkle desk and sat down in a seat to the side of him.

"What seems to be the problem Mr Marden?" Asked Parfinkle peering at Tom over the top of his reading glasses.

The Office was square in shape and lined with book shelves full of old books. Between the book shelves were paintings of former Head Masters and a large painting of Cragus T Parfinkle, the current Head Master standing resplendent in his Master's Robes, the painting of the man now sitting behind the desk, now looking up from his paperwork in front of him.

"Mr Taylor, here Sir, kicked a football into a girl's face, Polly Muggard, Sir, seems her nose was broken." Said Mr Marden.

Parfinkle eyed Tom Taylor closely, and then he addressed him with a wary tone to his voice.

"Well Mr Taylor, what do you have to say to yourself, this time?" Said Parfinkle.

"Nothing' Sir, it was an accident." Grinned Tom.

"You accidently kicked a ball into a girl's face hard enough to break her nose? Was she playing Football against you in a defensive position when you were taking a shot on goal, Mr Taylor?" Asked Parfinkle.

"No Sir, she just walked past at the wrong time." Said Tom, still grinning.

"From what I saw from my Office, Head Master, was that Miss Muggard and three of her friends were innocently walking past when the Wombat Students, Tom Taylor, Aaron Pooke, the Eldridge Trio and Virginia Cornett were a short distance away with their backs to the Cargal Group. Taylor here turned to face them and then kicked the ball straight at Miss Muggard." Said Mr Marden.

"So you would say that this was a dleiberate attack Mr Marden?" Asked Parfinkle.

"Yes Sir, I would; there seems no reason for Taylor to turn around and kick a ball towards the Cargal Group of Students other than to deliberately hit them with the ball." Replied Mr Marden.

"But Sir, it was an accident," pleaded Tom, "And Mr Marden is only sticking up for them because he's their House Master."

"Mr Taylor!!" Shouted Parfinkle, "I will not accept language and accusations such as that from a Student towards a member of Staff! Mr Marden was informing

135

me of his eye witness account. My Staff are completley neutral concerning this type of incident. It is evident to me, that this was a cruelly calculated attack deliberately upon Students belonging to a rival House and Toadford takes this form of attack very seriously; you will receive two weeks detentions and you are suspended from ALL Wombat team events for eight weeks." Said Parfinkle.

"Sir! You can't do that! It was an accident!" Tom shouted at Parfinkle.

"Taylor, please refrain from shouting at your Head Master and do not presume to tell me what I can and cannot do in my School! You will serve your detentions and suspension or would you like the punishment to be raised to a School Suspension or even Expulsion? Now Mr Marden will see you back to your Dorm Wing." Said Parfinkle firmly, his eyes blazing with anger. Mr Marden stood from his chair and took hold of Tom's arm again and led him out of the Office. He marched him down the corridor away from the Office and across the Entrance Hall to the staircase against the opposite side of the Hallway. He took Tom up the stairs and along the landing to the door of the Wombat Wing.

"In you go, Taylor." Said Mr Marden.

Tom Taylor walked through the door and into the Wombat Wing; he turned and stared at Mr Marden as he slowly closed the door. Mr Marden then walked around the Horse Shoe like landing, past the Hatchell Wing, until he reached the door to the Cargal Wing. He opened the door and walked in. He glanced at the door to his right, but found it to be closed. He knocked but received no answer. Then he tried the door opposite to his left and received the same reply. He then walked along the corridor and turned to the Office marked with the Brass plate which announced that this was the Chief House Master's Office. Mr Marden knocked.

"Come in." Said a voice from within, behind the door.

"Cederick, I have terrible news; Polly Muggard was attacked by Tom Taylor of Wombat House, he kicked a football into her face, I'm not sure what she has suffered, but the boys with her say they think she may have a broken nose." Said Mr Marden.

"James Dear Chap, this is terrible news! Where is she now?" Asked Mr Thybold.

"She's in the Hospital Wing, I haven't been to see how she is yet, I delivered Taylor to Head Master Parfinkle and then came to see you after escorting Taylor back to the Wombat Dorm Wing." Said Mr Marden.

"Was anyone else involved?" Asked Thybold.

"Miss Muggard was with Toby Morby, Keiron Muddley and Arrabella Snoop when it happened. I sent them back to here to stay out of the Wombat's way for now. I expect they are in their Common Room." Said Marden.

136

"We must speak to them and see how Miss Muggard is getting on, Come James and let us go." Said Thybold and stood from his chair then walked out of his Office with Mr Marden.

They turned to their right and walked through the door to the Grunts Common Room. There sitting in front of the fireplace was Toby and Keiron upon the couches. Near to them sat a number of other Grunts. Mr Marden and Thybold walked up to their couch.

"Mr Morby, Mr Muddley," Said Thybold, "I understand that you have through quite an ordeal?"

"Yes Sir," Replied Toby and Keiron in unison.

"Shall we go together and check to see how Miss Muggard is getting on?" Asked Thybold.

"Yes Sir, if you don't mind." Replied Toby.

"Then let us away." Said Thybold.

The two boys stood up and followed Thybold and Mr Marden out of the Common Room and along the corridor. They left the Cargal Dorm Wing and walked out along the landing to the staircase which was upon that side of the hallway. They walked down the stairs looking at the paintings and photographs which hung upon the wall. They finally reached the bottom and turned into the corridor to their left. Thybold knocked upon the Matron's Office door and the door opened; Nurse Pauline came to the door way.

"Yes Gentlemen, may I help you?" Asked Nurse Pauline. She was tall; about five feet seven with black hair tied in a bun, which was covered by a Nurse's hat. She wore a uniform of blue with a white apron pinned to the front.

"We are here to see Miss Muggard." Said Mr Marden.

"Oh yes, please follow me, but don't tax her too much, had rather a nasty shock, she has poor thing." Said Nurse Pauline. Nurse Pauline walked out of the Office, turning to lock the door and led the group across the corridor to the Hospital door. She opened the door to the Hospital and they followed her into the Waiting Room. Inside was a squarish room with one window opposite the door. Around the walls were a number of seats and there was a Coffee table in the centre with magazines in a rack beside it.

Upon the walls were posters warning of different nasty diseases and treatments. A pair of double doors led into the ward area which was lined with beds upon either side with a table at the end where Nurse Pauline sat, keeping an eye upon the Students unlucky enough to find themselves in the Hospital. Nurse Pauline led the group through the double doors and walked over to a bed along to the right of the Ward. Polly was lying in the bed with the covers held up over her head, only her light brown hair and eyes were showing over the top of the covers, showing her black eyes.

"Good afternoon Miss Muggard, I understand that you were involved in a rather unfortunate altercation this afternoon?" Asked Thybold surveying the top of her head with his thoughtful eyes. Polly nodded her head slowly.

"Ah yes, so would you please be able to tell me what took place?" Asked Thybold.

Polly slowly pulled down the bed covers from her face. Thybold looked more concerned, an angry expression seemed to pass across Mr Marden's face and Toby, Arrabella and Keiron gasped at the sight. Polly was now lying before them fully revealed. The blood had been cleaned away from her face by Nurse Pauline but there was a strip plaster across the bridge of her nose with dressings under it and her nose was terribly swollen. Around her nose was now deep purple and red where she had developed bruising and both her eyes were swollen and black.

"Well Sir," Began Polly as best that she could under the circumstances, "We, that is Toby, Keiron and 'Bella with Myslef, went for a walk in the grounds, to explore our recreation area. As we walked along the back wall to the building, suddenly I felt an enormous thud in my face and terrible pain, then blood everywhere." Replied Polly.

"And what may I ask caused this" Asked Parfinkle.

"I think it was a football, Sir, we did see some Wombat Students kicking a ball around nearby, next to the Kitchen block. Said Polly.

"So you walked into their path and was accidentally hit by the football then Miss Muggard?" Said Parfinkle.

"No Sir, I can't see that it was accidental," Polly said and began to cry again, "you see before the ball hit me, the Wombat Students were facing away from us and would have needed to completely turn around for the ball to be kicked towards us." Replied Polly, tears now running down her face and wincing each time she tried to sniff.

"Yes I do understand from your words and what I have been told already by others that this was a dleiberate act of wanton attack. I shall therefore be writing to Me Taylor's Parents outlining to them the seriousness of this incident and the Punishment which has been metered out upon him. I shall also be writing to the Parents of the other Students involved with a stern warning against their children being involved in any repeat incidents of this nature. Thank you for your time Miss Muggard and I hope that you recover soon." Said Parfinkle. He then walked away from the bed and out of the Ward to return to his Office.

"My Dear girl, you did well, thank you. I hope that you get well and are able to rejoin the Cargal Net Ball Team soon and are available for the Athletics soon? Have a good rest, I'll arrange for your School work as Homework to be brought along for you until you are ready to leave the Hospital Wing." Said Mr Marden.

"Thank you Sir." Replied Polly, wiping her tears upon her bed sheet.

"Don't keep her too long the rest of you, she needs to rest." Said Mr Marden.

"We won't Sir." Replied Toby, 'Bella and Keiron in unison.

Mr Marden then turned and walked out of the Ward. Toby, Keiron and 'Bella pulled over three chairs for themselves to sit next to Polly's bed. Polly tried to raise herself to sit up and 'Bella propped her back with pillows.

"Ruddy Hell Polly? You look a right sight." Said Keiron.

"And you look positively lovely too, Keiron!" Replied Polly.

"Glad to see you talking already, Polly, you really took a whack out there from Taylor." Said Toby.

"The Toe rag wants a good kicking. Said Keiron.

"And you're going to give it to him are you Keiron and get the same reward that he has?" Said Toby.

"What 'Reward' did he get?" Asked Polly.

"He was given two weeks detentions and banned from playing any sport for any Wombat or School team for eight weeks, which means that the will miss out matches for the Wombats in Cricket, football and rugby. This could give us our advantage of the opportunity to beat the Wombats and go clear at the top of the House League in all events. Said Toby.

"So getting my nose bashed in was worth it then?" Said Polly.

"We wish that you didn't get your nose bashed in at all, but now it's happened, you can't surely blame us for taking advantage of the opportunity to beat the Wombats in everything, can you Polly?" Without Taylor, that gives the Wombats a huge set back, as their reserves are really not up to his standard and the rest of the Wombat teams will be disorientated in their tactics without their star player. Said Keiron.

"The Cricket Cup falls within the planned period, so if we play our top game, that should be one cup for Cargal House to start with. Our next football match against the Wombats will be a little easier without Taylor and should guarantee us a place in the Football House Cup Final. If the other teams can possibly beat the Wombats without Taylor leading them, then it is possible that a heavy enough defeat against us may even knock them out of second place and out of the Football House Cup Final completley. The rugby won't be too much effected mind you, as they still have the Eldridge things, who flatten everyone who touches the ball. This could be our chance to put oursleves in prime position to win the House Cup this year." Said Toby.

Better watch out for reprisals though, the other Wombat team members will do you any injury they can to try to even the odds." Said Polly.

"Yes, you had better watch out for that." Agreed 'Bella.

Just then Nurse Pauline entered the Ward accompanied by Sister Ruth. Sister Ruth was slim, average height with blonde hair tied neatly in a bun and half

139

hidden under her cap. She was approximately in her late thirties and was wearing a deep blue dress with a white apron pinned to the front. Sister Ruth surveyed the scene in front of her with her pale blue eyes as she walked over to Polly's bed.

"Och ma poor Miss Muggard, we have been en tha wars haven't we? I am Sister Ruth an' I wull be making sure ye wull be comfortable en ma Hospital" Said Sister Ruth.

The group looked up as Sister Ruth and Nurse Pauline stopped at the foot of Polly's bed and checked her chart. Polly was being cared for at the School Hospital as she only had a minor injury, only more serious cases were taken out of the School to the Hospital in Cranleigh. Although Polly would have been nearer he family in Cranleigh Hospital, as she lived there.

"Dinna worry, ma Dear, yu'll be up an' aboot soon, afore ye know it, we'll 'ave ye back te lessons en nay time at all." Said Sister Ruth.

"How long do you think Polly will need to be here?" Asked 'Bella.

"Oh a couple of days until the swelling come down and the bruises show. Then it's just a matter of how long the bruises take to disappear. The break should heal within a couple of weeks, hopefully. We will need to keep a check upon this but I should think that Miss Muggard should be able to return to School lessons by then, may be a week if all goes well. Expect of course, games lessons or Sports team training, at least for a few weeks." Said Nurse Pauline.

"Thank you." Said Polly.

"I'll leave ye te chat for a wee while, dinna over tax Miss Muggard now wull ye laddies and lassie." Said Sister Ruth, who turned away from the bed and walked out of the Ward back across to her Office opposite.

"If you need anything at all Miss Muggard, please call me." Said Nurse Pauline.

"Oh yes, I will, thank you." Replied Polly.

Nurse Pauline turned away from the bed with a smile and walked down the Ward and sat at the table at the end and began to go through some paperwork.

"My God Polly, you're going to be here for a while, it'll be lonely up in our Dorm Room without you." Said 'Bella.

"Yes and at meal times in the Great Hall and in the Common Room, it will be strange not having you around for a while. We'll come and visit you every day when we have time, between reams of Homework, that is." Said Toby.

"Yeah gonna miss you around some." Said Keiron.

"Thank you Guys, that is so sweet of you and yes, I will Miss you around 'Bella, but I'll out of here soon and then that will be OK. You three had better get back now; I'll be OK now that I've seen you all." Said Polly.

"If you're sure." Said Toby.

"Yes. I could do with a nap actually, the pain killers which they gave me are cutting in, and I just can't keep my eyes open for long sorry Guys. See you tomorrow if you get time." Replied Polly with a smile.

Bella leaned across Polly's bed and kissed her upon her head, followed by Toby and then Keiron.

"We'll see you tomorrow then Polly, rest well." Said Toby.

"Bye Polly." Said 'Bella.

"Er - yeah, bye Poly." Added Keiron.

The three of them stood up from their chairs and took them back over to where they were stacked. Then they turned and waved to Polly, who slightly smiled and waved back. As soon as they were through the Ward doors, Polly laid back down in her bed and tears begun to run down her cheeks from her eyes. Toby, Keiron and 'Bella walked out of the Hospital and walked out of the Corridor into the main hallway. They climbed the stairs to the right of the Entrance Hallway towards their landing.

"Poor Polly, she looked terrible." Said 'Bella.

They reached the landing and turned to the right to walk along their landing.

"Yeah, poor Polly." Agreed Toby.

"I can't believe I did that?" Said Keiron, looking at the floor.

"You can't believe you did what?" Replied Toby.

"Kissed Polly, she's a girl!" Said Keiron.

"You mean you'd rather kiss a boy!?" Exclaimed Toby.

"No I didn't mean that, I meant I don't believe I let Myslef do that, I don't kiss girls, they find me repulsive." Replied Keiron.

"Well it is at times like these that we find our true friends and you kissing Polly's head in gesture of caring was God's way to tell you that you care about Polly as your friend, that's why you did it without thinking!" Said 'Bella.

They stopped outside the door to Cargal House Dorm Wing. Toby reached out and opened the door. They walked through.

"See you later boys if you're going along to the Common Room before Dinner." Said 'Bella.

"OK, see you later 'Bella." Replied Toby.

Then 'Bella turned and opened the door to her Dorm Room and went in. She closed the door and Toby opened their Dorm Room door and he with Keiron, walked in. Just as Keiron closed the door they heard a muffled sobbing coming from across the Hallway.

"Sounds like 'Bella's blubbing." Said Keiron.

"Right quick shower and then down to the Common Room, OK Keiron. We'll take our Homework; get a bit done before Dinner." Said Toby.

OK Toby, sounds like a plan to me," Replied Keiron.

About half an hour later, Keiron and Toby set off from their Dorm Room to the Common Room with a bag of books and their Tablets. As they entered the Common Room, they walked over to the couches in front of the fireplace and got out their Homework books. Just then, Steve Logan and Peter Cougher walked over to the table, Steve Logan was a very tall boy and thin, he was Cargal House Goal Keeper for the First Years. Peter Cougher was Right Wing for Cargal House and was average height, a bit stocky and had short Blonde hair and blue eyes. Steve sat down next to Toby upon the couch opposite Keiron, he had black collar length hair, slightly scruffy and Peter sat down upon the couch next to Keiron.

"We heard a rumour that Taylor is out of the whole of the House teams for Wombat, for two months? Do you know anything about it?" Steve asked Toby.

"Yeah, Taylor kicked a football into Polly Muggard's face this Lunch time and broke her nose, so he got two weeks of Detentions and eight weeks suspension from playing for any of the Wombat House teams." Replied Toby.

"Ruddy nutter, when I get my hands on him I'll throttle him." Said Keiron, with an angry look in his eyes, holding out his hands in front of him, mimicking strangling someone.

"Don't be stupid Keiron, you do that and you'll get suspended too. We need to keep our team together so that we can use this advantage to take the House Cups. Wombat aren't the same team without Taylor." Replied Toby.

"Yeah that's right Muddley, we need our team complete if any of the others can hold back Wombat, we may not even need to play them in any final until Taylor is re-instated." Said Peter.

"Too true." Replied Steve.

"Alright, alright, for the sake of the team then, I won't throttle Taylor." Replied Keiron.

"Good Lad." Said Peter.

"But he does deserve a good kicking though, Ruddy Psycho!" Said Keiron.

Chapter Eighteen – Through The Veil

After a few minutes of convulsions had passed, Simon bent down to help Carl up from the floor. He was a little weak but able to stand. The sword he was carrying glowed with a more intense blue than it had when Carl had found it. The sword lay upon the floor beside Carl where he had dropped it as he had fallen.

"It glows more brightly now that the Portal has revived it, as you will soon, my Son." Simon said as he helped Carl to his feet.

"That was powerful." Said Carl.

"Yes, that is because you have not been through the Portal for so long. We must wait for a short time as I have Envoys who are abroad in the Shires to meet with Lord Barnabus. They are taking news to him from Calistria, so we must await their return with the word of Lord Barnabus. We will abide here in the Fortress until the Company return; this will give you fair time to see much of Pegasus House in this side of the Portal. Said Simon.

"I have not seen this side for many years; it will be strange to me at first Father. I much like the other side without much thought of the Dark One's menace, my family in a safe place. As you say Father, as Crown Prince, I should take more noticed of our peril at this time, but I can't help wincing at the thought of Rachel feeling hurt or even betrayed that I had not confided this with her. She will be most upset at this." Said Carl as he took off his clothes from the 'Other side' and placed them in a cabinet next to the wall. He then pulled on a shirt and britches, took out a sword belt from the cabinet and fastened it around his waist. He then picked up Klemor. He also noticed the wand box lying upon the floor next to where he had fallen. He picked the box up also, and putting on the tunic of red, placed the box into a pocket, upon the tunic was a small loop of material and a tiny pocket like piece at the left side of the tunic. This was a wand port; where Wizards who were carrying Wands would keep them until they had reason to draw them. The tunic also had Golden trimming along the seams and around the cuffs. He wore britches of pale brown and black riding boots. Carl fastened a red and gold cloak around his shoulders. Simon had changed into a pale blue tunic over a similar shirt to Carl's, and white britches. Simon's tunic was also trimmed in gold and to finish with, Simon also pinned upon this a pale blue and gold cloak. Simon then opened the door before them which led into his Bed Chamber, followed by Carl, who made his first steps into Alexandria for eighteen years; they walked through and crossed into Alexandria.

The room which they had just left was built as an anti-room and was not known to the General Populous of the Court of The Prince Royal. Not even Simon's Valet was aware of what lay beyond that door, which was always locked when Simon was not within his Bed Chamber. They sat in richly covered chairs and Simon picked up a decanter of Wine and poured it into two Silver goblets, which Simon had asked the Valet to bring to his Bed Chamber last night. Carl picked up the wine and took a sip. He immediately felt the blood in his veins leap as though with joy and smiled to Simon.

"That is quite a wine; I had forgotten the taste of Alexandrian wine." Said Carl.

"You have forgotten much Carl, since your long exile over there, such as you do not carry your wand in your pocket in its box, it is always placed in the want loop in case of attack where it can be reached quickly enough and retrieved. You will also need to brush up upon a little Wandlore having been away from it for so long." Said Simon.

"Yes I hear you Father, eighteen years is a long time to be away from the Wand. I could not keep practice up on that side as you know, because this would have given the game away to Toby and Rachel and they would not have been ready to hear all about Alexandria and our Wizarding ways over here at the time." Said Carl.

Carl put his hand into his pocket and pulled out the box, which appeared a little old now. He opened it and inside Markalore lay upon its soft silk lining, the small crystal at its handle end and tip glowing bright blue, pulsating. Carl took Markalore out of the box and felt its weight in his right hand. At once he felt like a small electric shock which made him jump slightly.

"Don't heed that Carl; it is simply your wand bonding with you again after so long, joining its Elfin Crystal to your heart. If you remember, Carl, a wand becomes part of you and adheres to your soul and Aura. Your wand, with a little retuning and rewinding will act upon your very thoughts. You forget how it feels to weald such a powerful weapon, even more powerful than a Sherman Tank." Said Simon.

"I will need to take that 'refresher course', Father, sixteen years away from Markalore has left me more than a little rusty, but with the Crystal's help, it shouldn't take too long to put it right." Said Carl.

"Tomorrow we will begin your retraining, today we feast and introduce you back into Alexandria." Said Simon.

Simon picked up Markalore's box and replaced its lid, then put the box into a drawer of the cabinet by his bed.

"I'll look after the box here while we are upon this side, you can replace Markalore in to the box when we return to the other side in a few days' time." Said Simon. Simon pushed the drawer closed then turned to another door and walked through, Carl followed Simon into the corridor beyond and they turned to walk along the corridor.

"Feast time Carl, in your Honour of returning Home!" Said Simon. Simon closed the door to the bed chamber and they walked away towards another door.

They reached the door and Simon opened it. There rang out a loud fanfare of trumpets and as they walked through the door, Carl saw the throng of people in the hall all dressed with multi coloured tunics and dresses and the double line of trumpeters along the centre of the Great Hall, leading to the two thrones, one of which had been uncovered of the purple cloth, which had previously covered it. A voice broke out and a cheer rang around the Great Hall as Simon and Carl stepped from the door and walked up the Isle of the Great Hall and stood in front of their Thrones.

"Pray heed and Reverence for the Prince Royal Simon and Crown Prince Carl." Said an announcer.

Simon walked with Carl close behind along the Isle and they stopped at the Thrones. After acknowledging the people in the Great Hall, they sat down, the feast began! Simon had also carried his sword, Marroc, at his side safely sheaved in its scabbard and Carl noticed that Caradrile, Simon's wand was safely housed at his side within its wand loop. Carl looked at the panelling of the Hall, the great stained glass windows and the high vaulted ceiling. They reached the Dias where the two Thrones stood and walked up three steps onto the carpeted platform. Simon turned to face the congregated Court. He then signalled to Carl and they sat down upon one Throne each, the Throne which Carl sat upon was now devoid of its purple cloth covering and had now been fitted with the Crown Prince's Coronet above the Throne. Simon reached up and turned to Carl taking the Coronet from the Throne and placed it upon Carl's head. It looked resplendent, a golden rim lined with Ermine and a series of pearls around it and a Burgundy Cap within the rim. It was the first time since Simon was Crown Prince, that the Prince Royal and Crown Prince had sat Crowned upon their Thrones together in the Great Hall of Pegasus House.

Simon felt the most proud that he had ever been since the birth of his Grandson Toby. He was sitting next to his Son upon the Throne of Alexandria for the first time in sixteen years, since Carl had married Rachel at the Parish Church of Little Farthingworth; the first time since Carl had exiled himself to the 'Other World', to be a humble National Park Ranger, married to a Primary School Teacher. Carl looked out from his Throne across the Great Hall over the faces of the members of the Court. Faces he did not recognise. People were standing upon either side of the Great Hall in brightly coloured clothes, tunics over their linen shirts and britches. This, as Carl now recalled, was a totally different side to Pegasus Hose and totally different from the 'Other World'. Without warning, Carl actually began to think that he rather had missed this side of the Portal. He originally left to attend Toadford School as many Crown Princes before him, then he had fallen in love in two ways; firstly with the Moor and secondly with Rachel. He could not bear to be away from either for any length of time. Then sadness began to seep into his heart as he remembered the reason why he found himself back in Alexandria after so long a time away. The importance to both Worlds, to the people of Alexandria that he resumes his seat upon the Throne and to help his Father Govern through this crisis.

Carl glanced to his right to see Simon. The Prince Royal, his Father seated upon his throne and it crossed his mind that with the succession, one day it would be he who sat upon Simon's Throne with Rachel beside him as his Queen and that Toby would then be seated with them as the new Crown Prince of Alexandria. Simon called a Herald over to his Throne and asked him to call a member of the Court. The Herald walked out into the crowded Court and spoke to a rather tall man, who looked about twenty five years old and had short blonde hair and wore a mail shirt with a tunic emblazoned with his Crest, a Knight upon horseback slaying a Dragon. The man listened to what the Herald was telling him, then looked up to Simon and Carl upon their Thrones. The man then walked forwards from near to the far end of the Great Hall and Proceeded to approach the Thrones. The Herald lifted his long golden trumpet to his lips and blew a loud fanfare; he then spoke loudly and clearly once the hubbub had calmed down.

"Pray Silence! Sir Vincent de Molde." Announced the Herald as all the other quests applauded loudly. Sir Vincent arose to a standing position once more.

"Your Majesty, you wished for my Counsel?" Asked Sir Vincent.

"Sir Vincent, I have great need of your services at the return of Sir Lucius and General Thomas, to take a message to Restoratette and recruit the Lords therein to join our cause and to warn them of the renewed danger now mounting from the Marquis in Thracia. You will put together a Company of men and take them with you. I will warn you, Sir Vincent, that Calistria has fallen to the Marquis and the Dwarfs need our help to liberate their Shire. I have not received a Council from the other Shires as yet, so as we speak, there may be other Shires which will fall before we are able to be best prepared to remedy the situation." Simon said.

"Sire, my troth is to serve you as best that I may in any order or quest in which you wish me to undertake; I shall be happy to take your order." Replied Sir Vincent.

"I would ask you Sir Vincent that you take a capable Company, as due to the grave news that Calistria is lost to the enemy, I do not know if any or how many Spies or Scout's have been dispatched throughout the Shires to report back to their Dark Lord and aid him with his quest to envelope Alexandria with the Darkness which engulfs the Kingdom of Thracia and others which have fallen under the Bewitchment of his terrible hand." Said Simon.

"Aye, my Lord, I hear your Counsel and will dispatch a rider with news at each Shire's accomplice. Once agreement to join our forces to Liberate all that the Marquis has Hexed and laid waste to, I shall send your news back to you and will drive on unto the next with an ever growing army." Replied Sir Vincent.

"Good man, I shall join you later in the quest, as I have much to prepare for the coming Battles here first. I thank you sincerely, my brave Knight for your service to me and the Kingdom. It will not be easy for you and many shall not return to their homes or families. I will join you before you face the full might of Thracia with the Alexandrian Army. I must await here for news from Lord Thamley and General Thomas, I will then march upon Calistria and join you in the fight to free the Shires." Said Simon.

With that said, Sir Vincent de Molde bowed low to Simon and Carl, and then walked backwards away, until he reached the crowd, then turned and walked swiftly from the Great Hall. Simon sat for a few moments in deep thought. He then turned to Carl;

"Carl, would you like to see some of your Great House before we return to the 'Other Side?' I should think that you do not remember much since you have been away for so long, let me show you around." Said Simon.

"I should like that very much Father, yes it is some time since I saw the real Pegasus House." Replied Carl.

Then smiling, Simon stood from his Throne and was then followed by Carl. Simon then walked from the Great Hall, Carl followed closely behind, Courtiers spread apart to make a pathway and bowed low as Simon and Carl passed by. They walked out through the double doors of the Great Hall where Carl found themselves to be walking into a huge hallway lined with panelling of Oak around the walls and with a number of doors leading off into other parts of the building. Within the Great Hallway, stood a huge marble staircase, which led up to another floor. Above the staircase, Carl was able to see the huge painted ceiling with 'A' frame roof beams. At the centre of the hallway was hanging a large crystal Candelabra which scattered light right across the paintings upon the ceiling of the hallway. Along the walls hung large and small paintings and Tapestries. The paintings, some with hunting scenes, Battle scenes and old family members from the long history of the house. Around the hallway, stood suits of Armour and beside the huge entrance doors, stood two Guards, dressed in similar suits of Armour. Simon gestured to Carl to follow him along the hallway to a room which was towards the back of the building. When they had reached the door, Simon took hold of the door handle and turned it, opening the door; then walked through into the room.

As Carl followed Simon through the door into the room, he was able to see that the room was large and circular in shape and lined around the walls with huge shelving units from floor to ceiling full of books and scrolls of Parchment. Si8mon walked over to a huge desk at the centre of the room. He sat in a chair behind the desk of carved walnut, with ivy leaves entwined throughout the frame; which held aloft a carved crown at the top of a headrest. The chair was upholstered with a well faded leather seat. Around the room stood many objects upon small tables, some if this realm and some of the 'Other World'. A tall window was in the wall behind the desk; narrow and was glazed with leaded panes of coloured glass. In front of the window, stood a brass stand, which held a brass telescope trained to a view out of the window. Upon the desk, in front of Simon as he sat, was a roll of Parchment.

147

Upon it was a message which had been brought to Simon. To The right of the desk was a wooden calendar, which bore titles marked with the dates and days of the year. To the left was a portrait upon a small stand, the size of a photograph, of the late Queen, Stephanie, Carl's Mother.

"I have word here from Tyler, Lord of the Marches of the Shires Petros; and Caleb, of the Shire of Parlemann. They tell me that their people have needed to flee from their Shires, just as the Dwarfs of Calistria, after sudden attack from Orcs and Goblins. It would seem that Zenos the Grey of Parlemann and Talakos the Honourable of Petros are to journey to Alexandria for Sanctuary. I have welcomed Toridius the Gold of Calistria into our Sanctuary. They are all of the Marches and fear without our wall that they would be vulnerable to mind attack from the Marquis or his Chief Warlock, Lord Caithius. Here within the 'Skin', we can offer them protection for a time; to be turned in mind to Evil is a terrible thing, to experience by someone who has a good and kindly being. The curse placed upon such a person withers and darkens their heart until such point that they willingly entrust their duty to the Dark Lord or they become engulfed into the Darkness and destroyed." Said Simon. Carl looked upon Simon and shuddered visibly. He then answered;

"Father, this is graver news than I thought. To have now lost the entire Marches, the Shires at our borders, this means a devastating blow. This would bring the dark cloud of Thracia much nearer to our borders, and only within two days ride of Lord Barnabus' cave, where our Lord Regent and his company are now headed. If Quensborough and Woodcarm fall, then the Shire of Moorhampton, this would mean that the Commonwealth would lose half the Shires within it to the Evil of The Dark Lord. They would then be within reach of Alexandria itself!" Replied Carl.

"Yes, my Son, now do you see the importance of brining Toby under our training and teaching him of the Wizardry? He needs now to begin his Apprenticeship and hopefully we can hold out against Thracia until he's ready to defend his Kingdom and secure his safe line to become Prince Royal someday." Said Simon. Carl looked down at the floor; he rocked slightly in the chair where he sat in front of the desk.

"Father it is a difficult decision to make. I could lose everything, my family, my life, everything, if Rachel reacts the wrong way. Hopefully if I can be persuasive enough, she will understand the need there has been for keeping this all away from her for so long, it will be difficult to do this." Replied Carl.

"I know this may be the hardest decision you have ever had to make Carl, just like the decision to return to Alexandria after so many years away and immediately be confronted with escalating news from around the Commonwealth. I know this will be difficult for Rachel to take in at first, but we must do this for Toby to take up his rightful position and fulfil his duties for the job which he was born to do. These are but small ripples in the Great Purpose, my Son, we must all be prepared to take risks and make decisions which may be

148

painful to us from time to time, this you will learn when you sit here upon my Throne." Said Simon.

"Yes Father, I understand my position, my duty, but it doesn't change the task ahead of me any easier." Replied Carl.

"Let me show you around the Castle, you haven't seen much of it for so many years." Suggested Simon.

With that, Simon stood from his seat and walked out from behind the desk. Carl too, stood from his chair and followed Simon to the door of the Library. They walked out into the hallway and turned to their right. They walked through a pair of double doors at the centre of the wall and were in a short passage with a door either side, which led out to another door. Simon opened the door and they both walked out into a porch made of stone with fluted columns; four in number, holding up an exquisitely carved stone capping. Steps from the porch led down into a courtyard and Carl was able to see that this was gravelled. To either side of this courtyard, stood two stout buildings, a chimney upon their roves each billowing out smoke. The building to the left was showing steam emerging from a vent in a side wall. The building was of stone and rectangular in shape. The roof was covered in slate clinkers with the chimneys at its centre. Around the walls were a small number of small windows, from which a few were issuing clouds of steam. The building to the right was in two halves; the first was also rectangular in shape, of stone, with a clinker roof, there were again a number of windows around the walls. The other half of the building was circular, attached to the first by a short corridor. This part of the building also had a circular roof, which was conical in shape and tapered up to a point which was open to the sky using a wooden slatted shutter. Emanating from this building however, was just not steam, but a very sweet aroma mingled with a very bitter afterthought. The first building to the left was the Cook House and Refectory, where the meals were cooked for the Courtiers and Princes and the Refectory was the eating house for the Staff, The other Building to the right was the Ale House, where Ale was brewed for the Prince's table and Refectory.

Simon and Carl walked past these buildings to the far side of the Courtyard, where they approached a tall gate in the wall which surrounded the Courtyard. From here, Carl Momentarily looked back at the House. It was a little like the House upon the 'Other side' of the Portal, save for the addition of towers and battlements. Where 'his' living quarters were situated in the Pegasus House upon the 'Other side'. Carl was able to see The Great Hall standing there and the Prince's Apartments. Above this he was able to see the upper chambers of the House and the stone Buttresses. The roof was also of slate clinkers and was tall with Gargoyles along the eaves. Some of the towers were large and broad in diameter to form part of the main structure of the Central Keep buildings, where as some of the towers were narrow and topped with spires, most of which bore flag poles to fly standards.

They walked through the gate and found themselves in an almighty formal garden. Stone paths led off in all directions planted generously either side with a multitude of flowers. They began to walk along a pathway deeper into the garden underneath an arbour which was hanging with long fragrant Wisteria flowers. Carl caught the scent in his nostrils which reminded him of his childhood spent in these gardens before being sent away to Toadford for his education. That was the beginning of his desire to remain in the 'Other Side', since once he had met, married and began a family upon that side of the Portal. It would have been difficult to tell a young impressionable girl that when they were courting and became engaged, that she would become a Princess of a secret Kingdom and possibly the future Queen. He was reluctant to break the news when Toby was born to Rachel that she had given birth to not only a Son but the future Crown Prince of that secret Kingdom, but also the future Ruler. Carl had wrestled with his thoughts, hoping that he was never going to have to tell them this story.

Simon and Carl walked around the garden until they reached their starting point. They walked back through the gate and back through the corridor into the Hallway. Then they entered back into the Great Hall and crossed over to the door from which they had originally entered. They walked along the corridor until they reached the Royal Apartment of Simon. Simon opened the door then he and Carl entered. They walked across the bed chamber and Simon drew out Caradrile; with a flick of his wrist, a blue flash of light shone around the door and they heard a 'Click'. Simon then opened the door and then he and Carl walked through into the room with the wardrobes against the walls. They stopped just inside the room and retrieved their 'Other World' clothes out of the wardrobe next to the door. Simon and Carl changed their clothes and then prepared to walk across the room to the door opposite.

"Time to return to your World, Carl, but don't forget how important your next task will be." Said Simon.

"Ready Farther, will I fall this time, only I'd Like to prepare for that?" Said Carl.

"You won't feel it as severe as before, Carl, as you have already recharged your Alexandrian Blood, by your first crossing. You will find a slight shock, but nothing really noticeable." Replied Simon. Carl smiled across at Simon and they walked across the room. As they crossed the centre of the room, they felt that the air was thickening and creating some resistance to their movement. A flash of green light and Carl felt a slight tingle, like an electric shock run through his body. Carl stood up and turned to Simon;

"Not as bad as the first time, Father, we forgot the box for Markalore." Said Carl.

"Don't worry Carl, I'll bring the box back with me on my next visit, just be careful with Markalore while you have him out of his box. After all, there should come a time soon when you will need him by your side at all times and will not need to put him in his box." Said Simon.

Chapter Nineteen – The Semi-Final

The terms had passed gradually, the football matches all resulted in wins for Cargal House and defeats for Hatchell and Farley Houses; Wombat House had drawn a match against Farley House and there was the return fixture to be played. All the wins for Cargal House had already placed them into the Final of the House cup. If Hatchell House were able to hold Wombat House to a draw, then they would be meeting Cargal in the Final, as Wombat House had been beaten by Cargal and had also drawn one of their matches against Farley House.

Most of the Cargal students were inside the School at their Common Rooms studying; but Keiron, Toby and 'Bella were outside at the football pitch watching to see who it would be that Cargal would be facing in the Final. Polly had stayed inside to study and also to avoid the Wombat Crowd. Following his Suspension, Tom Taylor had returned to the School and had been bragging to everyone in Wombat who would listen, how Polly's nose had gone 'Splat', when the ball and smacked her in the face.

Toby was livid at what he was saying, he thought it just as well that Polly had stayed out of the crowd, he didn't want her to see the steam rising in his face as Taylor once again, was bragging to the Wombats of his 'Cargal Slaying'. Tom Taylor flashed his hands across his face and pretended it to be his nose shattering and sending blood over everyone, then as Toby's blood finally boiled, Tom Taylor mimicked Polly crying back into the School and to the Hospital Wing. Toby had heard enough, he stepped forwards, his face red with anger and before he could utter a word, both Keiron and 'Bella grabbed his shoulders and pulled him back.

"Don't be so stupid Toby, crikey Mate, if you go and throttle that ruddy looser, you'll get what he got and then you'll be out of the Final team line up and we won't win the Cup. Said Keiron hurriedly.

"That's right, Polly will be grateful that you stood up for her Honour, but she would have felt terrible if that had led to you missing the House Cup Final." Said 'Bella. Toby reluctantly relaxed and took a step back. He decided to watch the match to take his mind off the antics of Tom Taylor.

"He's just trying to show off because he can't play. His Suspension lasts until the match after the Final, so that would be next Term before he can play for his House or the School again. He's just trying to get support from his crowd because he knows that they can't give him any upon the pitch. Let's just watch and learn, whoever gets through to the Final, we must be aware of their strengths and disadvantages. Toby Mate, just don't let Taylor ruddy well wind you up and ruin it for us. If you get chucked out of the Final, he'll be laughing all the rest of the Term; what Hell do you think that would be like?" Said Keiron.

Toby sat staring at the Football pitch, watching the Hatchell and Wombat teams running around. There didn't seem all that much difference between them without Tom Taylor to lead the Wombat team. After a very few chances in the goal areas, they reached Half Time with no score. The two teams walked off the pitch to the groans from both sets of House supporters. Tom Taylor had stopped showing off and bragging about attacking Polly and was shouting very animatedly at the players as they trudged off the pitch, telling the Wombats how much better their performance would have been with him playing. Toby, Keiron and 'Bella were highly delighted with the First Half, at this rate, the Wombats would not be playing in the Final. The Half Time break was soon over and the players returned to the pitch for the Second Half. As the Hatchell players trotted back onto the pitch, Toby, Keiron and 'Bella jumped up and down applauding and cheering, which did not please Tom Taylor one little bit. Primrose Cool gave them an extremely filthy stare and then shouted repeatedly;

"Come on Wombats, Kick their backsides."

The Eldridge Triplets heard her calls and turned to grin at her. The players ran back onto the pitch and the whistle blew for the start of the Second Half to begin. The Second Half began much as the First Half had finished. The Wombats did not have the fire power up front without their star striker playing and Hatchell House were finding it difficult to get past the Human Brick Wall of the three Eldridge Triplets in their way. Suddenly Martin Cooper for Hatchell House slipped forwards a through ball into the Wombat Penalty Area and Allan Kirk latched onto it. Just as he drew back his right leg, his standing left leg was sliced from under him. Allan let out a cry and tumbled to the ground, rolling over a number of times. The Referee, Mr Marden, blew his whistle with a shrill blast and pointed straight to the Penalty spot. Amid loud protests from the Wombat players, Mr Marden walked directly up to Delbert Eldridge and whipped out his Red Card, brandishing it in his face and pointed straight towards the changing rooms. More protests could be heard from the Wombat team and now Tom Taylor was shouting from the side of the pitch in protest, saying that if he were playing there would never have been a through ball. After much argument and what looked like threats towards Mr Marden from the Eldridge Trio, eventually, Delbert was led off the pitch by Leonard Sheldon, their Head of Wombat House. Tom Taylor was now shouting that Mr Marden was fixing the result for Wombats to loose.

Allan Kirk, after the delay in the game had recovered from his trip enough to walk up to the ball, now sitting upon the Penalty Spot and stood to face Aaron Pooke in the Wombat Goal. Allan Kirk took four steps back and stood waiting for the signal. Aaron Pooke stood upon his Goal line swaying slightly to and fro. Mr Marden put his whistle to his lips and blew. Allan Kirk skipped once, then took four steps forwards and blasted the ball to the right of Aaron Pooke. Aaron dived and then realised he was moving to his left rather than his right. He landed upon the ground in a heap and was then able to watch as his Goal net bulge as it was struck by the traveling ball.

Aaron Pooke was powerless to stop it as the ball fell to the ground wrapped in the Goal net. A huge cheer went up from the Hatchell Students and from Toby, Keiron and 'Bella. Hatchell House were now leading Wombat House one goal to nil. There was only five minutes left of the match, which passed without incident; the sending off of Delbert Eldridge had ended any chance of a comeback from ten man Wombat House and the Hatchell team had pulled back for the last five minutes, plus the injury time of two minutes by instigating an eleven man defence. The Final Score to the dleight of the Hatchell Students and to Toby, Keiron and 'Bella, was Hatchell House one – Wombat House Nil. The Wombats silently trudged off the pitch, the Eldridges heatedly informing many Hatchell players and Students in the crowd of their impending punishment to be metered out in the coming weeks in repayment for daring to beat Wombat House and deprive them of their place in the Football House Cup Final.

"What the HELL were you doing!? What the HELL was THAT!" shouted Tom Taylor over the noise of the Hatchell Students celebrating their team reaching the Final. "If I were playing we would have won, what were you Morons doing out there?" Added Tom.

The players didn't answer as they walked past him and simply walked away towards the changing rooms, staring at the ground. Meanwhile, the Students from Hatchell House were applauding their team and cheering as they walked from the pitch.

"Well done lads, we'll see you in the Final." Said Toby as they walked past him.

"Well done lads for getting rid of that Ruddy Wombat team for us." Added Keiron.

"I've never been to a Football match," 'Said Bella, jumping up and down excitedly, "I like them now."

"Well you'll love our next one 'Bella, it's the House Cup Final and you'll get to enjoy watching us thrash Hatchell and lift the House Cup." Said Toby.

"Yeah, we'll Ruddy thrash them, we'll do it for Polly." Said Keiron.

Once all of the players were off the pitch and being accompanied back towards the changing Rooms, Toby, Keiron and 'Bella decided to make their way back to the School building to see Polly and tell her the result. They walked through the gates of the second Bailey, away from the Sports Grounds and into the Inner Bailey, past the Kitchen building and changing rooms, where they were able to hear Tom Taylor still trying to tell the Wombat Team how he would have made them win if he'd been playing. They entered the Entrance Porch past the fountain and walked through the doors into the back of the main hallway. Toby, Keiron and 'Bella hurriedly walked along the main fallway and found Polly walking out from the corridor to their left at the front of the Staircases, which led to the Great Hall.

"Hi Polly, you missed a great match." Called 'Bella, as they greeted her.

"Yeah, Ruddy brilliant." Said Keiron.

"Oh good, glad you all enjoyed yourselves." Said Polly in reply.

"The Wombats are out and we will be playing Hatchell House in the Cup Final, so best result we could hope for." Said Toby.

"That's good." Replied Polly.

"Where've you been?" Asked Keiron.

"Oh just been to see Sister Ruth, she put some make up onto my eyes and gave me some to take with me. The bruises are nearly gone now, but the redness is still upon my nose and my eyes still have pale grey rings around them. Sister Ruth says that this should clear up in about a week, so if I use the make up till then, it won't be so noticeable at meal times and in classes." Said Polly.

"Tom Taylor was bragging about what he did to you, Toby wanted to rip his head off, but we stopped him just in time, me and 'Bella. We need him for the Final against Hatchell; we don't want him suspended or anything like that ruddy looser Taylor!" Said Keiron.

"Thank you for guarding my Honour, Toby, but Keiron and 'Bella are quite correct. It would not have been fair upon you to throw away all the hard work which you put into the Final, just to miss out on it for that Evil little boy!" Replied Polly.

"Should've ripped his head off myslef instead, filthy Wombat half-breed, doing that to you, Polly." Said Keiron.

"Oh, so gallant, Keiron," Polly replied. "But don't they need you also for the team in the Final?" She added.

Keiron chuckled slightly and looked at the floor before he replied.

"'S'pose so." Replied Keiron, as Toby tried to change the subject of the conversation.

"Now let's go and get some Dinner, I'm starving, don't know about you three. Hungry work watching Tom Taylor humiliate himself, might need to drop into the Hospital Wing to put my sides back together again where they're splitting at the thought of Taylor going onto the rest of the House, about how he would have won them the match and the House Cup, even though he won't be playing until next Term." Grinned Toby.

"I think it makes up for his attack upon poor Polly, to see him made to look a complete fool, in some way, I suppose, seems like justice for him to be responsible for getting Wombat House knocked out of the Football Cup." Said 'Bella.

"Thank you 'Bella, but I don't think it will be much comfort to me at the moment while I have to use make up to cover up the damage that he left behind." Said Polly.

The group then turned and walked along the corridor to the end and entered through the large tall Oak double doors into the Great Hall and took up their places at the Grunt's end of the Cargal House tables. As they walked to their seats, Toby noticed over at the Wombat Tables, Tom Taylor, who was once again bragging and demonstrated the 'Splat' of Polly's nose once more for the Wombat students next to his table. They all looked over towards Toby, Keiron, 'Bella and Polly as they sat down in their seats, Toby and Keiron gave them very serious stares for a few moments and Polly simply turned up her nose at them and ignored them. It was fast approaching Christmas and Toby was looking forwards to staying with Keiron for the second week of the Holidays. First though, was a little case of Guy Fawkes, This year the Wombat House had been given the task of building the Bonfire. Tom Taylor and his crew of followers had made a Guy and stolen a Cargal jumper to put upon it. Toby and Keiron shot looks of Daggers at him as he climbed a step ladder and placed the Guy on top of the Bonfire, Poly and 'Bella noticed the look upon the boy's faces, still angry now they were in the Great Hall and eating their Dinners.

"Don't even think about what that slime ball Taylor is doing with the Bonfire. He's going to try to get you wound up every day leading up to the Football Final just so that he can get you Suspended. Boys, he is jealous that you are playing and he is not, he's jealous because he can't show off how were going to beat Cargal, because Wombat won't be playing. Just listen to myslef and 'Bella, we'll help you to resist any urge you may have to flatten Taylor." Said Polly.

"Yeah, we don't want to miss out for that Looser." Said Keiron.

"Thanks Polly, 'Bella, we hope that you won't need to do much persuading." Said Toby, with an attempted smile. Meanwhile, Keiron was tucking into his Potatoes and Sausages like it was his last meal, Polly glanced at him and tucked up her nose with disgust. Keiron stopped with a half sausage impaled upon his fork, with a blob of mashed Potato on top;

"WOT?" Spluttered Keiron.

Upon the Wombat table, Tom Taylor was still bragging, this time about all the spare time he was getting now that he was not playing in any of the sports teams and how many exam passes that he would be getting because of the revision time, Toby, Keiron, Polly and 'Bella left their seats at the Cargal table and walked out of the Great Hall. They walked along the corridor past the Hospital Wing, then out into the hallway and turned to climb their staircase up to their landing.

"I need to get a couple of books to check out some things in my Homework." Said Polly, indicating along the landing to the Library at the front of the building. The four friends walked along the landing past the Cargal wing door and entered the Library door. Toby, Keiron and 'Bella walked to a table and sat down while

155

Polly walked to the book racks which were filled with books, rows of Shelving full of almost any type of book imaginable.

They looked from where he was sitting at the table and watched through the tall large windows which spanned the central Wing above the entrance Porch. He could see across the courtyard and grassed area with the gardens to the Gate House of the School Pentagon Courtyard. From where he was sitting, he was able to see along the footpath which led out from the Porch way to continue across another Bailey, the Central Bailey which housed the stable building for the horses which some of the Staff members rode and some of the more privileged Students, for leisure. The other side of the Bailey, Toby could see a number of small cottages with small walls around them forming small gardens. These were the homes of Senior Staff Members. Other Staff either lived off site in one of the nearby villages or they were, if available, able to occupy one of the many towers of the Building. Toby then noted a very much larger Gate House with its own small Courtyard, but as this outer curtain wall to the Central Bailey was taller than the Inner walls nearer to the Main Buildings, this was about as far as he was able to see.

"……. and of course, when we beat Hatchell House and lift the Trophy, it will be our first mark upon this School, one of many yet to come. Stuck there in the Trophy Cabinet to be viewed by all the future Grunts and other Students with awe and for Tom Taylor to cry over." Keiron was saying through Toby's day dream.

"Sorry Keiron, I was miles away." Replied Toby to Keiron, apologising. Just then, Polly came to the table carrying about nine books precariously, being only just held in her arms.

"I thought you said that you just wanted a couple of books to help you with your Homework, not the entire ruddy Library!" Exclaimed Keiron with a surprised expression upon his face.

"Well, it is just enough for me to check through, to find some really good stuff for the Homework." Replied Polly.

"I'll give you a hand to carry them back your Dorm Room if you like, Polly." Said Toby.

"I'll help too, if you don't mind and will give me some to carry for you." Said 'Bella.

"Would you carry a few for me also please Keiron, I would be so grateful as I have my bag to carry and there are another three books in it and it is rather heavy," Asked Polly Politely.

"S'pose so, can't have you straining yourself, can we?" Replied Keiron.

"Oh, you're all heart, aren't you." Said Polly.

156

The four walked from the Library looking like they were helping to move it's contents to a new home and stopped at the door to the Cargal Wing. Toby pressed the correct combination into the numbered lock and the door opened with a 'Click'. Once through, they turned and walked into 'Bella and Polly's Dorm Room after Bella had unlocked the door. Inside it was laid out much like all the other Dorm Rooms, except for the abundance of pink everywhere. 'Bella had a bed cover of pink, pink pillow cases and pink night dress; paler than the rest with a deeper pink kitten upon it. Pink fluffy slippery by her bed and a pink shaded bedside lamp. Polly's was similar but with Paler much softer pink and with other colours too. Keiron noticed there was a white night dress hanging upon a clothes hanger next to her bed and just as Polly realised it. Keiron's eyes were drawn to the white bra which was hanging from the bedpost of Polly's bed. Polly noticed Keiron's gaze, realised and snatched it up and hurriedly stuffed it under her pale pink pillow.

"Whoops!" Said Keiron, smirking. Toby stood trying to look away and cover up that he was smirking too.

"Oh shut up Keiron!" Said Polly forcefully, as she steadily went redder in the face. "Well, after your little thrill, shall we head off to the common Room and start our Homework?" Suggested Polly, now looking a little cross with Keiron.

"That's a good idea, Polly, we will get our books from our Dorm Room, we may be able to help each other with our Homework if we work together." Said Toby.

"Hmmm….. white lace, very classy." Smirked Keiron dreamily.

"Oh shut up Keiron, anyone would think that you'd never seen a girl's bra before!" Snapped Polly.

"He hasn't." Giggled Toby.

"You mean that you'll watch while Polly looks up it all in the books, then you'll copy what she finds, that's what you call working together is it?" Said 'Bella.

"Yeah, something like that." Grinned Keiron.

"Maybe if we all look something up in the books and compare notes it will take your minds off lacy bras." Said Toby to Keiron with a giggle.

"Well let's all take a book or two and go along to the Common Room." Suggested Polly.

First they went across the corridor to Toby and Keiron's Dorm Room to collect their books and then walked along the corridor. They walked past all the paintings of past Cargal Students until they came to the Common Room door for Grunts. They walked over to the sofas next to the fireplace and put all the books onto the coffee table in front in front of them.

"Drinks anyone?" Asked Toby.

"Just a Cola for me, please." Asked Polly.

"Can I have a Coffee, Please?" Replied 'Bella.

"And I'll have a Cola too Mate, please." Replied Keiron.

Toby walked over to the drinks table and took three glasses and a cup with a saucer. He then picked out three bottles of Cola and placed them all upon a tray. The kettle clicked off and he poured out the Coffee into the cup. Toby then carried the tray of drinks over to the others who were looking at the books. Owing to a large pile of books upon the coffee table, Toby was only able to place the cup and Cola's down and then take the tray back to the drinks table.

"Thank you." Said Polly, unscrewing the bottle cap and carefully poured out the Cola into her glass.

"Cheers Mate." Said Keiron, as he poured out his Cola.

"Thank you." Said 'Bella, taking her cup of Coffee from Toby. Toby then sat down upon the couch next to Keiron, opening his own bottle of Cola and pouring it out. Polly, meanwhile, had found the text book for Biology and had turned to the section about the Heart and Lungs. Keiron had gotten out his Biology book and was comparing the texts. He was trying to think about what to write in his essay about the Respiratory System apart from his name at the top of the paper.

"It is easy to write an essay, Keiron, One simply reads the text book and then writes down one's own interpretation of the text. I'm quite sure that you would be marked down for Plagiarism." Said Polly.

"Can't I just copy what is there?" Asked Keiron.

Don't be silly, the Master would most likley notice know the book and be able to tell you simply copied it. Why do you boys always try to get out of doing Coursework and just try to copy everything?." Asked 'Bella.

"Guess we're just made that way?" Shrugged Keiron.

"Speak for yourself." Said Toby, as he was reading through the text and taking notes.

They sat upon their couches in the Common Room in front of the fireplace for about two hours and then decided it was time to retire to their Dorm Rooms. As Keiron was last to pack away his Homework books and papers, Toby sat looking at the flames of the fire, which was burning within the fireplace between their couches.

Toby was sure that he was looking at some shapes within the flames, at figures upon horseback riding across a wide moor. He suddenly thought to himself that it was just his tired brain, working overtime after all the concentration he had been using to take notes and write an essay. All packed up and ready to go, they arose from their Couches and carrying their papers and books, walked out of the

Common Room, They walked along the corridor until they reached their opening rooms facing each across the corridor.

"Well I think I did my best with the essay for Biology and hope the one for English is OK too." Said Toby.

"Out of the two of you, I think your work ethic was more productive, Toby; Keiron was a little lax in research skills. I would be pleased to help with extra lessons Keiron, to make your skills improve and to help you to improve your chances of gaining a reputable mark for essays in the future." Said Polly, with a slight smile.

"What's it gonna cost me?" Replied Keiron, suspiciously.

"Just being nice to me for a change, I wished to show you my gratitude for defending me the way that you did." Replied Polly.

"But I didn't do anything?" Said Keiron incredulously.

"I know, but the thought was there and although I don't think that hitting Tom Taylor was a good idea, I do appreciate your wanting to protect me in your own way and you of course, Toby." Said Polly, turning from Keiron to Toby.

"I was of help too!" Said 'Bella cheerfully.

"Oh yes, I am glad now that we decided to be more friendly as we are sharing a Dorm Room. You helped me no end, 'Bella, getting me to the Nurse as quickly as you did. I would have had a hideous nose if I hadn't got me there in time for Nurse Pauline to re-set my nose for me. You were there when I needed you and I won't forget that." Polly said. 'Bella started to cry a little and turned to enter their Dorm Room. They said their good nights to Toby and Keiron and then entered their Dorm Room and closed the door.

"Are you OK?" Called Polly.

"It's OK, I'm just not used to being thanked for anything or praised; just caught me off guard a little." 'Bella said, sniffing her tears back and went to their sink basin to wash her face. The two girls changed into their night dresses and got into their beds.

"G'night, Polly." Called 'Bella.

"Good night 'Bella." Replied Polly.

"You fancy Keiron, don't you Polly, I mean, offering him extra lessons and all that?" Asked 'Bella.

"Oh dear, sorry to disappoint you, 'Bella, but I don't fancy any boys, I have too much study to do to achieve my Grades. I only offered the extra tuition to Keiron to help him concentrate upon the notes to put together better essays and achieve higher marks. I just thought that it was a small way to replay him for his gesture, as a friend." Polly explained,

159

"Oh, right then; so ….. you don't fancy Keiron then?" Said 'Bella. Polly didn't answer; she simply turned over and went to sleep. 'Bella lay there for a little while longer, smiling to herself at the thought of Keiron being Polly's Boyfriend, because, as she imagined, that would leave the way open for her to be Toby's Girlfriend, to make up the foursome; where all four friends had closer ties with each other. With this thought, 'Bella snuggled down and went to sleep.

The Guy Fawkes Celebrations went by, Tom Taylor burned the Effigy of the Cargal Guy upon the Bonfire to the sound of much geering and booing from the Cargal; House Students and the Whooping and cheering from the Wombat House Students.

Then it was into December and soon came the end of the Autumn Term. The parents of Students arrived and parked their cars in the Car Park. Students having had their breakfast in the Great Hall and being sent off with a cheering speech from Mr Parfinkle, then all scrambled to their Dorm Rooms to collect their bags and filed down to the Entrance Hallway. There the heads of House led them across the Courtyard and out through the gate to the main Gate House past the Outer Bailey. The tall walls either side of the pathway through the Gate House obscured any sign of what lay behind them and what was concealed within the Outer Bailey, where Grunts were forbidden. Either side of the path way at the middle of the walls there were gates either side which were locked. Through the Main Gate they walked onto the covered bridge across the deep Gorge which led them through the Litch Gate into the Car Park. Keiron spotted the silver BMW with his Mother standing by it and said good bye to his new friends.

"That's Mom over there, good bye Polly, have a great Christmas and see you next Term." Said Keiron cheerfully.

"Thanks Keiron, although I still may be able to make it over to your house for next week if it's still OK?" Said Polly.

"Yeah, no worries, that'll be great. I can show you the village, my old school, our park and loads more." Said Keiron.

"See you next week, Keiron, have a Great Christmas Mate." Said Toby.

"Thanks, you too Mate." Replied Keiron.

"Merry Christmas everyone, see you next year." Called 'Bella, as she walked away across the Car Park to a short plumpish woman with long dark hair standing by a Ford Focus. Toby looked up and noticed the Landrover parked up.

"Best be off, there's dad, see you both next week." Toby said and walked away smiling and waving. Keiron was waving back as he walked over to the BMW. Polly, smiling and waving, walked over to a Mercedes and got into the front passenger seat.

"Those your new friends who're coming to stay next Summer?" Asked Carl as Toby walked up to him.

"Yeah, Keiron's the boy, he's my Roommate that I share my Dorm Room with and the girl with long brown hair is Polly; she's in Cargal House too." Replied Toby.

"It's Keiron that you're staying with next week, isn't it? You'll be taking your stuff for School with you then, and leaving for the new Term from Keiron's house then?" Asked Carl.

Yeah, that's right. He lives in Topley Village, The Thatches, next to the Old Manor. Polly lives in Cranleigh." Replied Toby, They got in to the Landrover, as Toby was fastening his seat belt, he saw the silver BMW, carrying Keiron drive around the fountain at the centre of the Car Park and head off up along the driveway and out of sight; then a couple of cars later, the blue Mercedes, carrying Polly, drove out along the driveway.

"There they go, 'till next week," Said Toby.

"So Polly's going to be at Keiron's house next week too?" Asked Carl.

"Yeah, she's coming too." Replied Toby.

With that, Carl started the engine and drove around the Central fountain and out up along the driveway, lined with Poplar trees, which Toby remembered from his first day. Carl turned out onto the Moorland Road and they began their journey the short distance past the high hedges and then to the last house of the street in the Village. Toby saw a sign go past which said;

'WELCOME TO LITTLE FARTHINGWORTH'

Toby knew their next turn would be into the driveway of Pegasus House; and so it was.

161

Chapter Twenty – The Gathering

The morning after their stay at the Travellers Rest Tavern in Cragmoor Village, the three awoke, so too did Captain Manos. They all walked from their Bed Chambers, refreshed from their sleep. Manos awaited them upon the landing of the Inn, still sitting upon the chair where he had been all night. Lucius Thamely and General Thomas walked out of their Bed Chambers and were greeted by Manos. General Listus opened his door and emerged much more cheerfully than usual. They went down stairs into the Bar area and were greeted by the serving girl, Anhild. She brought them over four jugs of Ale, once they had sat at a table.

"I hope you'm all 'ad a gud noit, my Lords?" Asked Anhild politely.

"We did, very much." Replied Lucius.

"Most enjoyable." Said General Listus, winking at Anhild.

"Do 'ee 'ave a long journey 'afore ye , my Lords?" Asked Anhild.

"Not too far, by my reckoning, maybe another three days or so." Replied General Thomas.

"I 'ope you'm 'as a very noice journey, my Lords, an' don' 'ee be a forgetting' t'call in 'pon us agin' wen you'm this way again'." Said Anhild. Anhild then walked away from their table and returned to the Kitchen. Shortly after, she returned carrying a tray with four bowls upon it.

"That y'are Milord's, four lovely bowls o' my own Mutton Broth an' some bread for 'ee 'pon thy way Sirs." Said Anhild, as she handed out the bowls around the table with the bread. Lucius took out his money bag and paid her for their meal, the previous evening, the suite of rooms, which they slept in and for the breakfast she had supplied them that morning; adding a generous tip for her troubles in looking after them, aided by General Listus.

The four travellers continued their breakfast in silence, each contemplating their next part of the journey. From the reaction of the Fairies as they had passed through the Forest Shire, the vigil by Lord Frecilly and his careful watch over the party, the ambush from Piskies and Gnomes. All seemed to be watching for something. Since they left Alexandria, the Company had been finding it relatively easy going this far, but as General Listus had pointed out, as they crossed the Moor watching Opal Crag in the distance, that there were maybe dangers abroad for which they should be well prepared. The Marquis had quite obviously sent out spies and small raiding parties to report back with information about the movements within the Shires. They knew that following the fall of Calistria Shire and Petros Shire and now unknown to them, the Shire of Parlemann at the point of being overrun by the Orcs of Thracia.

This they were aware meant that almost half of the Shires had fallen to the Marquis and each footstep that they walk forwards took them closer to the boarders with Thracia and nearer to the Orcs now occupying three of the Shires. At risk was Quensborough Shire, which was the most logical next move to make. The Group bade their farewells to Anhild and her Father, the Landlord of the Travellers' Rest Inn and their horses and General Listus' Pony were brought around from their stables by the Landlord.

"Gud boye my Lords, an' 'ave a safe journey t'ye, 'ope t'see 'ee back at our 'umble tavern some time." Said The Landlord.

"Thank you, kindly, for your service, Landlord, we hope that someday soon we may be back to visit once more." Said Lucius.

The four then climbed upon their horses and Pony, then saluting the Landlord, they rode off away from the Tavern back along the road from which they entered Cragmoor Village. The four rode out of the Village and out across the Moor along the road to meet up with the rest of the Company, who were camped waiting for them. They rode up to the camp and Captain Manos rode forwards to herald their arrival.

"My Lords, how goes it at the Tavern?" The Master cried out as they rode into the Camp.

"'Tis not as safe as I would like." Replied Lucius. They dismounted from their steeds, which were led away by soldiers to be stabled and joined The Master in his tent. They walked towards the tent, which stood like a small Marquee of pale green with Gold Runic decoration. They entered and four chairs were placed at the table at which stood the Master's Chair. The General then walked around to take the chair of the Master and he in turn chose a chair among the visitors. Lucius, General Listus, The Master and Captain Manos then sat upon their chairs, followed by General Thomas upon his, The Master sat unhlemed, with a coat of Mail covered by a tunic depicting the Arms of Alexandria. He surveyed his companions through his piercing blue eyes set within a long face and topped by long blonde hair. He wore a number of long plaits in his hair, his 'Warrior Braids'. The Master placed his helm upon the table in front of him, as did General Thomas, General Listus, captain Manos and Lucius Thamley.

"I bid return Thy tent to Thee General at your return." Said The Master.

"I bid Thee thanks for your safe keeping of it." Replied General Thomas.

"I wasn't exactly comfortable in that Inn." Said General Listus.

"No Listus my friend, not until you retired to your bed Chamber," Lucius smirked. General Listus reddened slightly at the words.

"Nay Ma Laird, I speak o' sum observations, whuch a' made aroond yon Tavern Bar whilst we sat suppin' oor Ale an' talkin'." Added General Listus.

Then a Steward walked in carrying a flagon of Ale and five goblets. He placed the goblets upon the table in front of the company then filled them before placing the flagon containing the remaining Ale upon the table at its centre. He then left the tent after bowing low to the occupants.

"Arr Ale, 'tis a goodly camp." Said General Listus.

"I too noticed some people among the drinkers who were observant towards us." Said General Thomas.

The only person who came near last night was the General's friend from across the Bar, although I did hear a slight amount of movement from downstairs. After checking I was satisfied it was merely the Tavern cat walking around. Handsome fellow, with white belly fur and light and dark grey stripes with blue eyes." Said Captain Manos.

"Aye, ma Lairds, oor mark ;ad surely been noted en that Tavern an' thus wus a mark, no' only o' suspicious strangers, but also o' recognition an' plotting." Said General Listus.

The Steward once more returned to their table, now carrying bowls which held small loaves of bread. He placed these before each of the occupants, bowed and walked out of the Tent.

They broke their bread into the bowls and ate small pieces along with alternative swigs of Ale from their goblets.

"Where do we go from here?!" Asked The Master.

"With the fall of other Shires possible, we must make for the bridge at Millslade, our enemy spies

may think that we move Eastward towards the Mandrake Bridge, but this maybe being keenly watched as it would be the obvious route to take to the Shire of Moorhampton at its southernmost.

The Marquis and his spies and Minions would expect us to follow this course as our most direct route to the Enchanted valley; we shall then take the road north to Millslade, to possibly and hopefully, achieve our Mission to reach Lord Barnabus. As it is possible that other Shires have fallen, the number we cannot know while we have been upon the road; it is to be safety conscious not to allow the Marquis an easy task to follow us. The Enchanted Valley is, as was for the extent of Curses wrought there Barnabus, to keep out The Marquis and his Minions. If we change our original route unexpectedly, we may buy some time and avoidance of The Marquis' spies and Minions, and reach Barnabus through evasive manoeuvres. The way north then across Millslade Bridge and then Southwards to meet the Enchanted Valley, every precaution open to us to reach Barnabus." Said Lucius.

"Taking that road would place us in grave danger if the Thracian forces have already taken The Shire of Parlemann; t'would place them merely just beyond the Mountains of Connarch between us and may be full of spies." Said General Listus.

"Aye General, but hopefully, we will take them by surprise and not as they would predict, which stand us in good stead." Replied General Thomas.

"Ye do realise that there may be great danger wi yon Millslade Bridge satndin' upon yon foothills o' yon Mountains o' Connach, do ye no'?" Said General Listus.

"This whole journey is wrought with great dangers, possibly around many corners, waiting to prevent our meeting with Barnabus." Said Lucius.

"An' don' ye f'get yon wee Marsh o' Gorr, that ye'll have te' cross when approachin' from the North." Said General Listus.

"We forget nothing General Listus, which is why my men are trained to observe and to wiled their craft if needs be to arise." Said The Master.

"And we shall be ready." Added Captain Manos.

For the next three days, the Company moved across the Moor, camping for two nights and the usual group of Lucius, Generals Thomas and Listus, staying at the Inn at Marlan Village. Again there were small observations made within the Inn, but no incident occurred. The Company passed out of the Shire of Cragmoor, crossing the Boundary markers at the border and entered the Shire of Oxshott. From this point it was just one day's ride to reach the Millslade Bridge, where once across they would be able to stop overnight in the village of Millslade, which lay across the bridge.

The Company rode to the crossroads, which led to the road which crossed the Millslade Bridge. They turned to the East along the road and came to the slight rise in the terrain, just before the Bridge. Before them, stood the stone pillars which announced the entrance to the Bridge, carved with Runic symbols. Beyond these was the approach to the Bridge itself. The high stone sides like walls running for its length upon either side of the Bridge. These walls were the height of a horse's back and were punctuated along their length by a series of small arches.

The Bridge stood upon a plinth at either bank of the Meerlandse River, which were cut and slotted into rock cliffs, which bordered the river at this point, to form a short gorge, which was about fifty feet deep down to the river flowing underneath, southwards. Unseen by the Company at this time, was a cave entrance, some thirty feet down the cliff face, under the Bridge. The lead soldiers began to ride forwards and approach the entrance to the Bridge. Just then, there cane from over the cliff edge the sound of falling stones clattering against the side of the cliff, as they fell into the river. Then the soldiers halted in their advance, when upon the cliff edge, next to the Bridge to its right hand side, the Company saw first one, then a second huge hand appear and grab the cliff edge. Then gradually a large bald head began to appear above the edge, then huge bushy eyebrows of black wiry hair. The skin upon the head was greyish in colour and seemed as though almost leathery.

As the head rose, there then came huge brown eyes, followed by a large bulbous nose with wide nostrils. Then a large mouth, with darker grey lips and horribly yellowed teeth followed. Then suddenly the mouth gave out a huge low roar and the rest of the body, immediatley swung up onto the cliff edge next to the Bridge. There standing before them, the whole creature which was about nine feet tall and broad of shoulder and chest. He had huge muscular arms and hands which were holding a huge wooden club, which had an Iron cladding around its upper end. The club was about a foot and a half wide and some three to four feet in length. Upon his huge feet he wore a pair of leather boots and he was dressed in a rather ragged tunic and britches of grey, which somewhat resembled his skin.

"By the Lard Christ, ma Lairds. I tried te waren ye aboot thus path, 'is a Moontain Troll we find oorsleves facin' ye noo, whuch gives us a wee problem wuth crossing yon Brudge." Cried General Listus.

"Aye General, 'tis a Troll we face and must master. It would seem that the Marquis' spies did indeed foresee our traveling this road, or that each road to the east is well watched and guarded by the Dark Lord's Minions." Replied Lucius. The Company sat and watched the Troll, as he moved and walked across the stand in front of the Runic Pillars, to block their way across the Bridge. The Troll was holding up his club and was slowly lifting it, waiting for the first soldier to attempt crossing the Bridge.

To test the Troll, two Alexandrian soldiers rode forwards and galloped, one pulled forwards to ride directly at the Troll before him. He drew his fighting Lance from his saddle strap and tucked it under his left arm. At arm's length of the Troll, he lifted his great Iron shod club and swung it across his body. The Troll's turning was exact, the club met the oncoming Lance and crashed into it a short way along it's length from the sharpened steel tip. The Lance was almost ripped from the grasp of the soldier which shattered and many shards and splinters of wood flew into the air. The impact finally took its toll of vibrations through the length of the Lance and then the soldier found himself lifted from his horse and flying through the air to land a short distance, away to the left of the Troll.

The horse of the soldier continued towards the Troll for a short distance and all too quickly, the club of the Troll came once more swinging through the air and connected with the side of the horse's body. Shattered armour came flying through the air and with a loud neighing; the horse rose into the air and disappeared over the cliff top to fall the fifty feet down to the gorge. As it fell, helplessly, the last strength in its shattered and broken body feebly kicked it's legs once more before, with a loud terrible crash, the horse slammed into rocks, just into the river from the bank. Parts of armour once again flew through the air and fell with splashes into the running river water and what was not shattered by the club now was as the broken body of the horse. Which came to a halt across some rocks at the water's edge and lay broken across the rocks, it's blood ran down the rocks and was wasted away into the river current.

Almost immediately, the Troll turned its attention to the rider which it had just been unseated from the horse. With speed which may not usually be attributed to such a large creature as was now before him, before the soldier was able to move away, the Troll lifted his club above his head and with a slight bend in his knees, the great club came swishing down and a great loud and terrible scream issued from the soldier as the iron clad end of the club crashed down upon him, he momentarily felt the breast plate of the suit of Armour bend and collapse into his chest. Excruciating pain shot through his body as his arms and legs spread eagled either side of him from the impact. Because the protection from the Armour, it did not shatter, but he could not be afforded protection for his body and the flesh and bone beneath, from such a huge terrifying impact of such force. Blood issued in spurts from under his arms as the impact forced it from his body. To make certain, the club rose again and with no lungs left to inflate for a breath, no cry this time, the soldier with his last second of conscious sight, saw the club swing down again and all went black for him as the next blow from the club smashed down upon his helmeted head and a crack of bone and a spurt in both directions from under the club of blood and brain tissue; the skull of the soldier caved in and was pressed some inches into the soil of the ground upon which his broken body lay. The Troll looked up at the Company, which faced him, the second soldier turned and rode back to his rank as the Troll opened his mouth and roared at the soldiers and officials who sat upon their horses and ponies in front of him, a sense of Victory momentarily in his demeanour.

Then General Thomas raised his right hand and bellowed;

"CHARGE!"

The remaining soldiers of the Alexandrian troop drew their lances from their saddles and charged at full gallop towards the Troll. He once again raised his club preparing to sweep them aside when just as he was about to bring the club across in its deadly swing, the Troll was interrupted by six arrows crashing into his chest, It was seconds later before he was able to collect himself to his senses; another six arrows crashed into his chest. The Troll reeled and staggered slightly as the galloping soldiers reached him with their lances drawn under their arms. The horses hooves thundering, the lances made contact with the Troll's abdomen, before he was able to swing his club once more. The force of the impact from seven lances at full gallop pushed the Troll backwards upon his feet a step and the Troll staggered, lost his footing and fell backwards over the cliff edge to fall fifty feet down to the river bowl. With a loud 'Splash'; the Troll's body fell into the river and floated away downstream, passing the body of the horse as it went; it's brown eyes staring blankly and it's long purple tongue lolled out of its mouth.

The Company of soldiers turned from, the cliff edge and rode back three Officers behind them and re-joined the Dwarf soldiers, who were just repacking bows and arrows back into their saddles upon their ponies.

"The way is clear now my Lords, but at the cost of one brave soldier. Said Captain Manos.

"Aye Captain, we shall bury his body and say some reverend words for his Soul; then we must be away from here before any more of the Marquis' Minions or spies show themselves to prevent us from reaching Millslade Village." Replied General Thomas. The Alexandrian soldiers walked out after dismounting from their horses and collected the body of Alkan Throthorpe, their fallen comrade. The six Dwarf soldiers, meanwhile, busied themselves with digging the poor man's grave.

Before long, the grave was prepared and the expert stone carvers of Dwarfs had prepared a marker stone carved with a legend of Runic symbols to record the falling of Alkan, the first Alexandrian casualty in the new war against the Marquis of Thracia. The body of Alkan was wrapped in a standard which was being carried within one of the soldier's saddle bags. They were unable to retrieve any of his weapons from his saddle as they had fallen into the gorge and been swallowed up by the river as his horse Gideo, fell to his death. All that they were able to put into his grave for him was his battered and splintered lance and shield. The carved stone was placed the head of the grave.

This was the inscription carved into the stone which read in the common tongue.

"Here Lies Alkan Throthorpe

Warrior of Alexandria"

Around the grave the remaining Alexandrian soldiers gathered, left hand at their side, right held across their chest. The Dwarf soldiers gathered upon the opposite side of the grave with Lucius and the Generals at its foot facing the carved stone. The company bowed their heads and a low singing began from the soldiers of Alexandria:

"The brave ride out to meet a foe,

Across the land they ride to go,

Their swords they hold'

And match their steel,

Their fight is bold,

The enemy they Quest to kill."

Then joining them in song, The Dwarfs, Lucius and the Generals;

"Their fate is sealed unto the day,

The Battle rages, to the Victor glee,

A Comrade falls their fight to weigh,

The vanquished kneel 'pon bended knee.

We sing this song his soul to save,

168

As he journeys on into his grave,

The fellow men shall shed a tear,

For loss and love and hunting fear,

We say good bye to our friend so long,

And must now end our soldier's song."

Then for a short few moments the Company stood in silence still with their heads bowed.

"Lord, we pray to thee to take the Soul of our dear friend and Comrade Alkan Throthorpe into Thy loving care to rise him up when need is great to once again defend his Realm. Lord we commit him to Thy safe keeping until we all can meet again" Said Lucius.

"AMEN"

Was the collective cry from the standing company. Then as Lucius and the Generals walked back to their steeds, the soldier's, Alexandrian and Dwarf, all filled in the grave. They too then mounted their horses and ponies and once more stood for some moments in silence in reverence to the grave, then they rode away and through the carved pillars and across the Bridge. Once upon the other side, they slowly rode along and watched the marker stone upon the other bank as they passed, saluting to their fallen friend. Once past the marker stone, they galloped off along the road.

Before long they found themselves riding into a line of small cottages with smoke issuing from out of their chimneys upon their roves. The Cottages looked rather old and rickety, wooden framed with different outlines and upper stories jutting out from above the lower. The plaster between the beams of the upper stories of some of them white washed, while some had bricks laid in a Herringbone pattern between the beams of lower portions. Dotted here and there throughout the Cottages were small windows with diagonal leaded frames, the roofs covered in badly fitting tiles, some missing holes visible. Behind them the Company were able to make out already the snow-capped mountains of Connarch in the distance.

"We were lucky there my Lords, alas poor Alkan was not so, because there was only one Troll to guard the Bridge and road. We are close to the Mountains of Connarch, where there would seem that the Dark Lord may have possibly sent more Mountain Trolls. We will have to be vigilant when we return this way to journey to my new Village." Said General Listus.

"Aye General, it will be most dangerous now that we know that The Marquis has sent troops into The Shires already." Replied Lucius.

"So we must journey once more over the Bridge, may there be another Troll or more stationed there by the time we return" Said Captain Manos.

169

"Aye Captain, there may Well be, but we cannot think at this evidence to allow the Dwarf soldiers to journey alone back through this perilous place so soon after slaying the Troll. It is possible indeed that we must be prepared for a revenge attack or another to take the first Troll's station in order to prevent our returning with Council to the Prince Royal and King Boranius of The Dwarfs." Said General Thomas.

"We thank Thee General, Regent, fer Ye aid te us poor Dwarfs, we can feel mere stout o' heart wuth Thy hand behind us te steady oor hand an' offer us support again' oor enemy". Said General Listus.

The Company now rode through more streets of small cottages as before. Now that they were one less in number and he had tasted first hand an example of the things they may have to face in their Quest to Liberate the fallen Shires and reunify the Commonwealth. For these reasons, it was decided that the full Company should stay together as much as possible. They decided that the Company with the Master at its head, should not stay outside of the town but they found a field within the town within sight of the Tavern to pitch their tents and stay for the night. Meanwhile, once again Lucius, Generals Thomas and Listus along with Captain Manos continued their journey into the heart of the Town. They rode along a small street and passed a stone Chapel with slate tiles upon its roof, a single large window upon the east gable and a smaller one upon the west. Half way along the longer walls of the building, upon the either side were single Oak doors. A top the roof at the eastern end was a bell loop housing one bell.

Beyond the Chapel they reached a shabby looking building similar to the Cottages but slightly larger. Light spilled out from its many windows and the sound of merriment, singing and music playing could be heard. Outside the front door, just under the eaves of the roof hung a faded sign;

"YE MIGHTY CRACKEN

Tavern and Inn of Millslade"

Next to the Tavern was a barn, which they supposed was the stable house and so took their horses and Pony to it for to bed them down for the night. They found they had guessed correctly, there was a young man dressed in leather britches and tunic with a white shirt and riding boots,

"Hey young Sir, we wish to house our steeds for this night." Called Lucius.

"I be Jan Scape, my Lord. For a few pennies your steeds shall be safe yere wi' me." Replied The man.

"Thank you master Jan, we shall need the best of care for them, rested, fed and watered, we have a long journey ahead 'pon the Morrow." Said General Thomas.

"An' make sure ye look after ma Pony wee Jan." Said General Listus.

170

"Aye my Lords, your steeds will be will fed and rested for the morrow and your Pony Master Dwarf shall also be well kept." Replied Jan.

Jan stood some five feet seven, medium build about twenty years old. He had longish blonde hair and striking blue eyes.

"I have a way with horses my Lords, I feel them and them feels me I suppose, spirit like. I loves horse I does." Said Jan.

"Then we shall leave them in your very capable hands Master Jan. Until the morrow then." Said Lucius and handed Jan some silver Pennies. Then the horses were led into the stable with Jan and closed up for the night after he had brushed them down, fed the finest hay and watered them. The four travellers walked through the door of the Tavern. The music and singing grew louder as they opened the door and walked through into the Bar room. The Bar was rather large compared to what they gauged the room of the Cottage may be. To one side of the Bar area was a small room, the Private Lounge, then the Public Bar area, where the noisy revellers were sitting at numerous tables standing in front of a wide bar behind which stood the Landlord. A sturdy man in his fifties with thinning grey hair and a large receding forehead. He wore a white shirt with black britches and boots, covered by a leather apron hung around his neck and tied around his waist.

The Landlord surveyed the four as they entered and walked over to the only empty table in the bar area. It was a longish wooden table with benches either side upon which they sat, two each side. In the centre of the table stood a candle stick with one small lit candle whose tall thin flame illuminated the four faces. They were joined shortly after being seated by a youngish, about eighteen to twenty year old woman. She wore a fairly faded dress of blue and a white bonnet. Her long black hair trailed out of the bonnet down her back to her shoulder blades.

"What'll you'm Gentlemen be a wantin' then in our 'umble little house?" She asked with a beaming smile.

"We will have a Flagon each of your finest Ale and four cups. Then we should like some Mutton for our dinner, we have been traveling for a long while and would like rooms if they be available, four in number please Miss." Replied Lucius.

"My name is Mary, I shall attend to yer needs directly my Lords, 'afore you'm knows it, I shall be back with Thy sustenance and four fine flagons of Ale." Said Mary, the barmaid. Mary walked back to the Bar where she gave the order to the Landlord, who disappeared through a door behind the bar, followed by Mary. A few minutes later, Mary came out from the door behind the bar carrying a large jug hand and walked over to the table and put the jugs down. Mary was followed by another young woman about the table. This other girl was slim, blonde haired and pretty. She smiled and her blue eyes twinkled as she poured out a goblet of Ale for each of the Travellers.

"There ye are my Lords, our finest of Ales for 'ee. This be Alice, my Lords, she also serves here in the Cracken." Said Mary.

"We thank Thee Mary, and Alice, I am sure we will enjoy our Ale." General Thomas replied.

The Barmaids smiled and returned through the door behind the Bar. About five minutes later, the two Barmaids once again emerged from behind the Bar, this time carrying a large tray each which held two plates roasted sliced Mutton with greens and vegetables upon each of the trays. The faces of the Travellers lit up at this sight and the plates were placed upon the table for them. The Barmaids bowed to them and then Mary showed them to their Chambers.

"My Father has prepared chambers for you Sirs, and when you'm are ready, we will let you know when we are ready to retire for the night." Said General Thomas. Lucius handed Mary some coins, two Galem Gold coins. She smiled much broader and hurried back to the Bar to give the coins to the Landlord. A few moments later, they were joined at the table by the Landlord, who thanked them for their generosity.

"My Lords, I bid 'ee welcome to my 'umble Tavern. I have prepared rooms for you'm all an' a sittin' room fer your use. I 'ope you'm enjoys your stay with us, I would ask how lang you'm be a stayin'?" Said The Landlord.

"Thank you Landlord, we shall be staying but two nights. We have a long journey ahead of us." Said Lucius.

"Very gud Sir, The gold pieces will surface for your stay and more, an' if'n you'm be needin' anythin' at all Sirs, you'm only need ask ol' Tamas, my Lords and t'will be thine!" Replied The Landlord.

"Thank you Thomas, we will bare that in mind." Replied Lucius.

The merriment and singing continued for a long while all though the Travellers eating their dinners and drinking their Ale. The door of the Tavern then opened and a man walked in. He was about five feet seven tall, stockily built with brown britches and boots, with a green tunic over a white shirt. He had a short black beard and longish black untidy hair, which rather hung down into his eyes, which were the palest blue almost silver. Over his tunic, he wore a sage green cape fastened with a silver broach at its shoulder. The man walked to the Bar and took a stool to sit upon. He glanced around the Bar and noted the table where the Travellers were seated. He turned to a man at the Bar seated upon a stool next to him.

"Well Garge, seems a chill night this night, 'ad te put on my cloak te keep out the wind which 'as blown up in the last couple o' hours." Said The Man.

"Well, 'ee'll 'ave te wrap up then when I leaves fer 'ome then Pickert." Replied George.

I notices we 'as some new Comers en ye night, Tamas?" Said Pickert.

"Oh thame, they're just travellers a passin' thru'." Said Thomas the Landlord, "I baint made enquiries that far yet Pickert, 'been servin' thame their vitals an' Ale."

"Yeah, well, you'm know thares been some shifty characters 'angin' around the village latley, some folk are prapper afeared; we've never 'ad so many strangers prowlin' around the place." Pickert said.

He placed his hand absent mindedly upon the hilt of his sword in its scabbard, momentarily. General Thomas and Captain Manos both noticed this and noted it.

"I tell 'ee, Tamas, it's best we finds out their business in the village, just in case, you'm know what I means." Said Pickert.

"I wouldn' vex thame too 'ard Pickert, me thinks they'm Official like, paid me in gold coins, so they did." Said Thomas.

"Gold coins?" Said George, "Aint that Nobles money?"

"Aye Garge, 'tis Nobles money, this makes thangs a little more interestin'." Replied Pickert.

With that Pickert stood from his stool and slowly walked over to the traveller's table. He stood and addressed them.

"Gud Evenin' Sirs, I trust you'm enjoying yer stay yere en our 'umble Tavern. I just was wonderin' like, what brings ye fine Gentlemen te Millslade this time o'yer?" We don' usually see new comers now 'till Spring time." Asked Pickert, all the while Generals Thomas and Listus eying the man along with Captain Manos.

"We are simply travellers just passing through." Replied Lucius.

"I 'eered that 'ee paid wit' Noble Monies, would 'ee be Lords o' some sort?" Asked Pickert, letting his right hand move towards his sword hilt. General Thomas and Captain Manos watched intently and moved their hands around towards the hilts of their own swords. Lucius placed his hand around the hilt of his sword 'Talos' and began to slowly pull it slightly out of its scabbard. Visible upon the pommel of the sword was the Eagle's claw clutching a large Garnet stone, the claw in gold. As it was drawn, Pickert gasped and could now see the Emeralds encrusted into the hilt and blade, engraved with Elfish writing. Pickert stooped to bow and dropped to one knee;

"Forgive me Lord Regent, I did not recognise ye." Said Pickert, recognising the Royal Sword 'Talos'. Lucius spoke quietly.

"My Dear man, you are forgiven, we travel under cover so I did not make my true identity known widely. I would ask of you Sir, please not to reveal us to the Tavern in general. We are passing through upon a Royal Mission." Said Lucius.

"Aye my Lords, I shan't reveal 'ee, Sirs." Said Pickert and returned to his stool at the Bar.

"So, what're thame d'wain en these yere parts then Pickert?" Asked George as he sat once more upon his stool. Thomas listening closely from behind the Bar.

"Just travellers passin' thru', that's all." Said Pickert, taking a swig of his Ale from the goblet which Thomas had placed in front of him upon the Bar.

"Seems a bit vague that Pickert?" Said George.

"Well, I's satisfied thame means no 'arm." Said Pickert.

"'Well, I'd just keep alert an' watchful, Pickert, seein' as thame travellers be wit' a Dwarf." Said George.

"Dang Garge, you'm worries too much. I's sure thame be solid as a rock." Replied Pickert.

Before long, gradually, bit by bit, the revellers, singers and musicians all filed out of the Tavern door into the cool night air. All that were left in the Tavern Bar were the Travellers seated at their table. They decided time was passing and elected to leave the Bar and find their suite of rooms for the night. Thomas walked out from behind the Bar and over to the traveller's table, accompanied by Mary.

"I sees you'm about ready fer yer Chambers then, my Lords?" Said Thomas.

"Aye, that we are Tamas." Replied General Listus.

"If'n it pleases yer Lairdships, wud 'ee permit me te speak with 'ee en Thy room briefly, a'fore 'ee beds down fer the night?" Asked Thomas.

"I think that would be acceptable." Replied Lucius.

Then Thomas went back to the Bar and picked up five jugs accompanied by Alice the Barmaid.

"I'll fill these fer us, my Lords, an' bring thame up fer us." Said Thomas, as he and Alice began to fill the jugs with Ale.

I'll show 'ee te Thy Chambers, if'n it pleases 'ee my Lords." Said Mary.

"Lead on Lassie." Replied General Listus, and they followed Mary out of the Bar and into a hallway with a door at the end and a staircase to one side opposite to the door, which they had all just walked through.

A short distance in time later, Mary had led them up the stairs and onto a long landing area, where there was a number of doors. Mary showed them each into a door where they found Bed Chambers with a bowl upon a stand, for washing and a bed and a wardrobe. She then showed them into the lounge Room. It was fully panelled all around the walls and there were rather important portraits of people who the travellers did not know. There was a rather large window opposite the door. In front of the window was a wooden table and around it were five empty chairs around a small circle of the table. The four travellers entered the Room, General Thomas handed a couple of silver pennies to Mary and thanked her for her hospitality and for showing them to their Rooms. They then walked over to the table and each of them took a seat and sat down.

Moments later, a knock wrapped upon the Lounge Room door and Thomas entered with Alice carrying a tray each. Alice's tray had two jugs of Ale upon it and two goblets, while Thomas' tray had three jugs and goblets upon it. Each of the travellers looked up with a smile upon their faces. Thomas carried his tray over to the table and transferred the jugs and goblets onto the table, then Alice also did the same. She bowed to the travellers and they smiled back to her; then she left the room to take the trays back to the bar and then left the bar to go to her room and so to bed. Once Alice had left the room, Thomas made certain that the door to the room was closed and then returned to the table and sat down onto the empty seat between General Thomas and Captain Manos.

"Well my Lords, a prapper welcome te my 'umble 'ome is called fer, I dare say. Sorry an' all that about Pickert abotherin' 'ee earlier in the evenin', but we've been getting' some shifty strangers 'angin' about yon village latley an' folks is real rattled somewhat. Pickert an' Garge was rattled good like, an' thayme was made suspicious like, when thayme sees you'm en yon Tavern bar asittin' drinkin' Ale an' eatin' you'm Vittels, like." Said Thomas.

"We are traveling far upon our Royal Business. The strangers which you mention are the reason for staying as inconspicuous as possible, to not stand out to the strangers. Much is abound for the strangers to gleam and we must ask this, Thomas, to keep us as travellers passing through so as not to alert the strangers to our presence." Said Lucius. He once again partly drew his sword 'Talos', to show Thomas and handed to him another three Gold pieces.

This payment is for your help Thomas, to keep us as unnoticeable as possible and keep as best, any fightsome looking strangers from approaching us. We are upon The Prince Royal's errand and must be ever vigilant for the Dark Warriors." Added Lucius.

"Aye my Lord, I shall do my best as to help 'ee, I see what Pickert seed, your sword Sir, 'tis the Commonwealth Regents Sword. In the name of Prince Royal Simon, I do declare I shall endeavour te keep 'ees Kingdom safe as best I can; an' I will make yer stay yere more pleasurable an' avoids unwanted attention vrom other parties." Said Thomas.

"We thank Thee Thomas, for your friendship and service, alas time draws on and we have much to do upon the Morrow." Said General Thomas.

"Aye my Lords, it be time fer you'm te get yer beeds an' beed down fer the night. I shall 'ave breakfast ready fer you'm Sirs at eight of the Clock if'n that suffices yer Lordships, an' I'll be atlelin' Pickert an' Garge te button their lips an' not te go broadcastin' yer presence in yon village; as far as anyone will know from us thray, you'm be just a'passin' through as travellers like, who are known to us an' that's we'll be a'tellin' folk." Said Thomas.

"We bid Thee good night Master Thomas and shall see you again upon the Morrow." Said General Thomas. Thomas the Landlord Bowed to them and left the room. The travellers left some Ale in their jugs for the morning then all left the Lounge Room and went into their Bed Chambers.

Unseen by the Travellers, moving around outside of their tents, The Master was at rest with his Company and the Dwarf Soldiers. Then suddenly the perimeter Guards raised the alarm as a number of Goblins attacked from out of the darkness. The Goblins wore rough armour, thick chest plates with leg and arm plates strapped over their suits of chain mail. Upon their wide heads were heavy helms marked with symbols depicting their Clann. Rage showed upon their pointed small faces sharp yellowish teeth, brandishing at the soldiers. They had stout chests but with thin arms and legs, bony hands with long fingers and claw like finger nails. Their eyes, slit like and black, like pools of ink. The Goblins charged towards the encamped Company, who formed a forward Guard of Alexandrian soldiers, supported from the rear by the Dwarfs who drew their bows as they had against the Mountain Troll.

The Goblins clashed into the perimeter Guards who took out a small number of them before retreating to join the forward line. Then the Goblins ran forwards towards the forward line. The Dwarf Archers drew their bow strings and let fly their arrows. Their arrows flew over the heads of the forward line and crashed with shrieks of pain into the attacking Goblins, some Goblins being struck in their chests, another gurgled to the ground, eyes bulging with an arrow head protruding from one side of his neck and the fletched shaft from the other side.

The still standing Goblins then clashed into the forward line of Alexandrian soldiers. The seven men and The Master engaged the enemy upon foot as they had not enough time to mount their horses. The Goblins swung their heavy swords and axes and they were parried by the Alexandrian blades. Swish – block, swish – block, The Master blocked yet another swipe by a Goblin's sword and then turned upon the spot and swung his sword as he turned. A sickening thud and a shriek, the Goblin fell lifeless to the ground, his green blood splattered over the Tunic of the Master. Bang – clash, more swords upon swords and another Goblin fell. Swish – twang, the Dwarf bows once more sang as more arrows over flew and bore down upon the advancing Goblins. After a number of minutes passing, but hours so it felt to the Company, eventually the piles of Goblin bodies were discouraging to their remaining Clannsmen and they decided their attack was futile. As soon as the attack had begun, it was finished, the Goblins retreated from the camp and disappeared back into the darkness from where they had come from. The soldiers and the Dwarfs regrouped and cleared away the piles of Goblin bodies. Then they once again set up a perimeter Guard to the camp. The rest of the night would see no further attacks from the Goblins. It would appear that the Goblins had endured quite enough for one night and suffered far too many losses to wish to try another attack.

Chapter Twenty One – The Parish Council

In the Church Hall of Little Farthingworth, sat a number of figures around a large table, made up with many smaller tables, of the stage hung some spot lights which stood at the centre of the hall. At the top of the hall, opposite the entrance doors, was a stage which ran almost the full width of that end of the bottom of the hall was another wall which h ad a door to its left; the Entrance/Exit to the toilets. The door to the left of the stage led out of the hall to a small office, used by the Chairman of the Church Hall Committee, a Cleaner's cupboard stocked with cleaning products, buckets, brooms, and mops; also through this door was the small kitchen which was used for parties and other functions.

Along either side were walls which had four large windows in them. The ceiling had beams which made up the roof and strip lighting. In front of the stage hung some spot lights. The windows had blue curtains and the doors were painted blue as were the window frames and window sills.

Around the table sat a group of people. They were Parish Council Chairman Simon Morby, Lord of the Manor; Malcolm Cougher, District Councillor; Hargus Eldridge, Farmer at Tugmoor Farm; Cragus Parfinkle, Head Master of Toadford School; The Reverend Greenaway, Vicar of St. Martin's Parish Church of Little Farthingworth; Thomas Marfan and his wife Ceilia, who took the Minutes of the Meetings as the Parish Clerk; Jack Pugworth, Local Butcher; Pennie Slowcher, Headmistress of St.Claire's Junior School and Colin Sharpe, Landlord of The Farthingworth Arms, the only pub in the Village. Malcolm Cougher sat with his gavel in his hand, which he handed to Simon as the new Chairman. A rather serious looking man in his forties with a touch of grey hair here and there upon his head, dressed in a tweed suit with a white shirt and green tie.

"Present Tonight, Councillor Morby – Chair; Councillor Marfan, Mrs – Clerk; Councillor Marfan, Mr; Councillor Ledridge; Councillor Parfinkle; Councillor Greenaway; Councillor Pugworth; Councillor Slowcher; and Councillor Shape. Apologies from Councillors Thomas, Pike and Slarry, who were unable to attend." Called Malcolm and Simon lifted his Gavle.

"I declare the Meeting of Little Farthingworth Parish Council for 28 July, Open." Called Simon, bringing the gavel down with a whack upon the table. Ceilia began to write down that the meeting had opened at 6.30 pm sharp.

"First item upon the agenda is – Road Sweeping. I've had a talk with the Council in Cranleigh, they say that funding is tight but assure me that the Road Sweeper will be continuing to visit Little Farthingworth twice per week. I know this is a cut of one day per week, but in the present climate we should be grateful that we have a Road Sweeper at all, seeing that we are a somewhat small Parish." Began Simon. Ceilia was quickly jotting down the Minutes in her best standard shorthand, ready to type them up when she got home after the Meeting. "Next item, Extension to cattle barn at Tugmoor Farm, granted."

177

"Much obliged." Replied Hargus, with a grin.

"Next, New Garage at Fox Street, Number four. Rejected; it is the view of the Parish Council that it is not in keeping with existing buildings and would review the application if a revised plan were resubmitted. Next Item, Bus Service to Cranleigh. It has been suggested by Cranleigh Council that the No. 6 Service bus serving Little Farthingworth and Cranleigh, be cut back to every two hours. Who is with me when I say that this is unacceptable and we ask that this plan be scrapped and the No.6 Service be kept as it is at an hourly rate?" Said Simon.

A show of hands made the application unanimous for the Service to remain at an hourly service.

"Can't see why folk can't get a Tractor an' get themsel' te town meslef? I've been a'doin' that fer nigh on forty yeres, meslef." Said Hargus.

"The point is Hargus, not all of the population of Little Farthingworth possesses a Tractor or indeed drive any vehicle, so the Bus Service is an important link for those people to get to town for shopping and for Dental and Hospital appointments." Stated Reverend Greenaway.

"And the children have to get to school in Cranleigh for there are no more High School Busses, because of budget cuts, they now rely upon the Service Bus to get them to school on time." Added Pennie Slowcher.

"OK, next item – Graffiti upon the walls of the Park Pavilion; we have been subject to this far too long just lately, and the Police agree that it has to stop. Police will be upping patrols in the area in a bid to end this mindless vandalism and save the Parish Council the cost of repeatedly repainting the Pavilion." Said Simon, glancing towards Hargus.

Hargus glanced back at Simon, then shifted his weight in his seat and let out a huge fart! Everyone coughed and Hargus grinned. He was fully aware that Simon was referring to his Triplet Sons, Delbert Gaynell and Dexter, who were attending Toadford School. The Pavilion was one of their favourite places to hang out and many times they had left their mark upon the Pavilion walls; Hargus didn't care, he just thought that 'Boys would be boys' and that a little horse play was just part of their growing up. His wife Hettie, would hear of no wrong doing from her boys, no matter what anyone reported. Hargus was a stubby, stocky sort of a man, broader than he was tall with a rather flattish head. The hairs that remained upon his head were a greying red colour. His eyes heavily creased with age and buried under thick red eye brows were of a piercing green and stared straight ahead. His jowelled cheeks hung either side of his bulbous nose which was a crimson red with a full lipped mouth and a full set of yellowish uneven teeth. His chin was covered with greying red stubble. He wore a yellowish green tweed suit with a dirty greyish shirt, which had once, long ago, been white. Around his thick neck, he wore a blue cravat.

"Any help needed on that score please don't hesitate to ask." Replied Cragus. He was the headmaster of Toadford School and even though it was only Half

178

Term of the first year of having the Eldridge Triplets at the School, he was already starting to build up a dossier of their antics around the School. Hargus just grinned again.

"Next item – problems with people dinking away from the Village Pub." Said Simon.

"I Know it's illegal to drink in the streets of Little Farthingworth away from my Car Park, but I can't stop this. I have tried to help by not serving take out bottles to people I think are inebriated enough to flout the law and continue drinking away from the Pub; but there is little I can do to help. I can't stop selling take out take out cans and bottles without harming my profit level." Said Colin.

"The Chair acknowledges your efforts, Colin and is grateful for your contribution to the cause, what we really need is bodies upon the ground, more patrols but the Police say they have Budget constraints." Replied Simon.

All the white, Cecilia was scribbling this all down in the Minutes. She was a woman in her fifties, married to Thomas Marfin and helped him run the Moorcroft Farm. The Farm stood on top of a ridge of land which was circled by a meander of the River Exe. The River came down from the Moor to the north and went away southwards past Little Farthingworth and Cranleigh towards Exeter. Little Farthingworth was recorded in the Domesday Book as a small Village. It had been thought that the name derived from an impression that it was of little value to its Lord. The House of Pegasus was originally thought to have been built during the early Thirteenth Century but no one really knew exactly when . Over the years the House grew with differing styles being added to as time went on.

The Portal had, it was thought, existed for many years, no one was quite sure when it was first created. The time frame of the Kingdom of Alexandria seemed Medieval so it is possible that Skin and the Portal were cast at the same time, originally.

The House, due to the spell which maintained the Portal and the Skin, was only visible in this World as it appeared. There was nothing of Alexandria visible in this World as it was, to the people; also nothing of this World visible to the people of Alexandria.

The Kingdom of Alexandria, the Shires of The Commonwealth and Thracia were locked in time and space from our World and appeared to be had in fact interfered with the Fabric of the Space Time Continuum, which has resulted in the whole of this World including Alexandria being torn away from the Natural Course of time and space and forming a pocket in the Matrix of its own.

If the forces of Thracia were to learn of The Portal and indeed leak into this World, then they would be tempted to destroy the Portal to attempt joining this World to their conquest but to do this would sever the Time Space Continuum and render both Worlds to be torn apart as the rift tried to right itself. As he was a product of both Worlds and was more of our World than that of Alexandria. Toby was the Key to the survival of our World and that of the other World. The

179

members of the Parish Council dismissed more mundane trivial matters and then the Chairman, Simon, brought down his gavel and declared the meeting over.

Hargus sat and saw the others pouring out Coffee. They sat drinking and chatting. Hargus reached under his seat and brought up an old duffle bag. He put his right hand into the bag and pulled out a Thermos Flask. He opened the lid and poured out a thick brown liquid which the others assumed was some form of tea, Hargus always brought his own flask with him to meetings. He would never partake of the beverages provided at the Meetings.

"How is Mrs Eldridge then Hargus?" Asked Pennie.

"Much same as always 'spose. Workin' 'ard, bakin' an' like." Replied Hargus.

"How are things at the School these days Cragus?" Asked Pennie.

"Oh much as they always are…….. we at Toadford do not differ much, School Traditions you see my Dear. How is your place of Education coming along" Replied Cragus.

"We try to get by. Funding is getting a bit of a problem, but we are finding ways around that." Replied Pennie. The Funding of St. Claire's was not like Toadford. Toadford was run from Annual Fees paid by Parents of the Students who attended, where St. Claire's was run from funding raised from Cranleigh Council along with Fetes and sponsored events. Funding had seemed to be becoming more and more reduced, it appeared each year as the Cranleigh Council Budget became more and more cut by the Frackston City Council.

The usual excuse was that the County Council in Exeter was having cut after cut from the Government in its funding. So individual Councils were being forced to find funding from alternative sources. As Lord of the Manor, Simon Morby made some donations to St. Claire's each year and other funding came from charitable organisations. Pennie Slowcher found it increasingly difficult to balance the books with the Curriculum and income sometimes out of weighing one against the other. Pennie had been Headmistress for only five years, after Miss Paver had retired to her small cottage upon Bogart Street.

She had been a Principle Teacher at St.Claire's for over ten years before that. Pennie lived alone in her flat near to the Village Square at Little Farthingworth, opposite St. Martin's Parish Church and Church Yard. Pennie was sure that upon occasions after dark, that she had half seen figures moving around in the Church yard in the early hours of the morning, She hadn't told anyone else they think of her to be a crazy woman, with being head Mistress and all!

Pennie hadn't so much chosen Spinsterhood, as she just hadn't found 'Mr Right' as yet. She didn't do that much looking for him though, so her prospects were rather slim. This didn't really worry her that turning forty either, as that was a mile stone which She was not afraid of. Pennie considered that her lack of giving Birth to her own children was irrelevant, as to her, in her own opinion, she could just give them back to their Parents at the end of the day. Being the head at St. Claire's meant that she had had hundreds of children to look after and teach, also being Head meant that she was usually too busy running the School and raising funds to worry about 'Mr Right'. Jack Pugworth had, upon some occasions made a few advances towards Pennie, but being fifteen years her senior and the size of one of the cows which had graced his Butchery slab, he wasn't exactly ticking all the boxes to be her 'Mr Right'. Soon, she felt that she would need to put all thoughts out of her mind of finding 'Mr Right' and resign herself to endless days of being upon the shlef.

Pennie drained the last of her Coffee and walked over to the table with the kettle upon it and poured out another cup of Coffee; she then returned to the main table to sit down. Her knee length straight blue skirt moving with her hips as she walked. She was wearing a knitted cardigan in blue wool and a white blouse. Her long pointed face had a small pointed chin and then came a wide mouth with thin lips, a long and shapely nose and her eyes of Emerald green; all which was topped with long red hair which was usually put up when she was teaching at St.Claire's. Pennie sat opposite Hargus Eldridge. For a couple of hundred years, Tugmoor Farm had been in the Eldridge family. The Farm stood to the south west of Little Farthingworth, some three miles away from the Village.

It was upon the Moor and had a Long House of Cobb which had many rooms and was finished off with a barn attached at the right hand side when viewed from the front. The house stood within a farm yard in which there was a row of three small barns opposite the front of the House. Around the farm yard and house stood a number of small outhouses and larger barns. The farm stood at the end f a Lane which ran for about half a mile from the road which passed the farm. Horses, Cows and Sheep populated the many fields around the farm, as did old rusted farm machinery which had fallen out of use, superseded by more modern equipment. The roof of the house, were the barns and other outhouses, made from slate tiles.

Missing from the barn which was used as a garage for Hargus' car and Tractors, along with other farm machinery, was indeed the Jaguar Mark Two, the Navy blue one with chrome trimmings and grey leather seats. This was currently parked in the car park of the Village Hall. Also parked in the car park were Pennie Slowcher's little pale blue Renault Clio, Simon Morby's BMW Seven Series, looking immaculate in its pearly white paintwork. There was also the Ford Mondeo which had brought Malcolm Cougher to the Meeting; the Transit van belonging to Colin Sharpe, white and emblazoned along its side panels with 'Farthingworth Arms'.

Parked furthest from the door to the Hall was the Landrover belonging to Thomas and Ceilia Marfon and eventually the green Vauxhall Corsa, belonging to Reverend Greenaway, who rather enjoyed the joke among the Parishioners about his car being green and being driven by a 'Greenaway'. The Reverend Peter Greenaway had been Vicar at St. Martin's Parish Church in Little Farthingworth for ten years and had been a Member of the Parish Council for that length of time also, replacing the previous Vicar when he arrived in the village. Revered Greenaway was a native of Somerset. So had not travelled too far to take over the Parish from where he was previously Curate in Quantocks.

Reverend Greenaway enjoyed his time at Quantocks, having been placed there after qualifying as a Priest. Born at Wheddon Cross, it was not very far to travel for him to take up his first Calling after returning home from Birmingham University. He spent some twelve years here and during that time he had been taught by his Mentor, the Reverend Marlowe, Vicar of the Parish. While serving at Quantocks, Reverend Greenaway got to know the people of surrounding villages, hamlets and farms.

Evident all around his Study and occasionally around the rest of the Vicarage, was to be found a multitude of glass cabinets and plinths which either housed or were stood upon by numerous fossils which Reverend Greenaway, as a Curate, had collected while walking along the cliffs of East Quantocks beach. The prize of his collection was a large Ammonite, perfectly preserved which was about the size of a Mini's steering wheel and was attached to a metal stand and then stood upon a plinth and was standing just inside his Study, in the Vicarage.

This Fossil he had struggled a little with to carry it up the long and precarious steps up from the beach, back to the footpath and his car parked next to the Duck Pond, near to Ford House. Reverend Greenaway paid many visits to that particular beach finding many Fossils and also paid visits to Lyme Regis, to scour the beach there at the base of Fenn Cliff for more examples.

Cragus Parfinkle had parked his old Ford Focus in the Car Park after driving down from Toadford School. Next to this was the Transit Van with the logo upon its side panels displaying the legend 'J Pugsworth & Son – Butcher', along with his telephone number. There had been a Pugsworth Butchers in the village since about 1900. The 'Son' written upon the van referred to John Pugsworth Jr, Jack's only Son. He was currently attending Toadford School along with Toby and was in Farley House. He was a good Student academically but lacked slightly, upon the sports filed. He was not quite in the same class as the players and athletes of the two leading Houses of Cargal and Wombat.

Malcolm Cougher sat enjoying his cup of tea. He didn't like Hargus much, thought that he was rude and scruffy. He always smelled of some farm yard odour or other, each time he attended the Parish Council Meetings. Malcolm was not only Parish Councillor for Little Farthingworth, but also a District Councillor for nearby Frackston City Council. Malcolm was the outgoing Chairman, he had been Chairman for ten years but now wished to have less responsibilities within the Parish Council to enable himself to concentrate more upon his District Council work. He was a little resentful that Simon was taking over as Chairman, and he was taking a back seat because he felt that he was handing over a little of his power to Simon and as Lord of the Manor, Malcolm flet that Simon had quite enough power already.

Malcolm was nearing Retirement and so wished to cut down his workload. He lived in a town house near the Church, not far from Pennie's flat. He was wearing his usual pale grey suit and red shirt with red tie.

Colin Sharpe was getting ready to leave. Tall, well-built, ex-soldier, who was Landlord of the Farthingworth Arms. The Pub had been in Little Farthingworth for at least four hundred years, originally a Coaching Inn. Colin had been there for about ten years and for much of that time had been gradually restoring much of the building so that the bar and Restaurant area and some of the Bedrooms were panelled as they were originally and the Bedrooms had four poster beds. Colin was quite proud of his renovations so far. The large Function Room behind the Bar was also panelled, where it was hired out for Parties, Wedding receptions and Private functions. Also held in this room each year was the Pool and Darts Annual Tournaments to find the League Singles and Pairs Winners and Team Trophy Winners from the Cranleigh Leagues.

Thomas Marfon was just finishing his cup of tea while his wife Ceilia, was straightening out and putting away into her bag the Minutes to the Meeting, which she had been taking throughout the Parish Council Meeting. The Marfons lived at Blackmoor, which stood a short way in the distance to the North West of Little Farthingworth towards South Molton. They lived there with their two children, twins Chantelle and Thomas Jr. Thomas Jr and Chantelle were Students at Toadford School with Toby and were members of Hatchell House. Thomas Jr played in Midfield for the Hatchell House football team and also played Ruby and Cricket for Hatchell House. Both Twins were members of the Hatchell House Athletics team. When everyone was just about ready to leave, Simon indicated to Parfinkle, Hargus and Colin to have a quick word before they left.

"OK now that I have got you three away from the others, we need to set up a meeting of the Guildsmen. I have some very important news to discuss with ALL Members." Said Simon, quietly, so that the rest of the occupants of the Village Hall were unable to hear them or what they were planning.

"Righty Ho then, I'll be there m'Dear." Replied Hargus, with a rather worried look upon his face." Jus' let me know when it be that you'm be 'avin' yer meeten', an' I'll be thar' no mistakin' like."

"Same with me, Simon." Said Colin.

"I will, of course inform my Colleagues of the time and date of the meeting and arrange for the hall to be ready for use." Replied Parfinkle. The three men appeared slightly uneasy at what Simon had said. The last time that a meeting of the Guildsmen was convened, with expected important news was for the birth of Toby. As Toby was still only thirteen and not yet at Apprenticeship age, they were wondering why the meeting was being arranged.

"I will inform you in the usual manner." Simon told the three of them. They then, all four left the hall and got into their cars and drove away out of the Village Hall car park.

183

Chapter Twenty Two – Mount Vondor

The air was thick, all around the sight and smell of decay. An ancient woodland strewn with the carcasses of long dead bodies of animals lay skeletons where they had fallen upon the ground. The knarled and dead trees forming a thick barrier save for the pathway between them. A muddy Pathway which headed out of the forest into the hills. Atop the highest of these hills, a Mountain, high with craggy faces, stood silhouetted against the ever grey sky. It was a tall towered and spired Castle with many towers topped by tall spires. At the exit to the forest stood either side of the muddy track, Totems baring skeletal parts and skulls but these were not parts of animals, but were Human skulls and bones.

The Pathway led up to the Castle, to a huge Gate House, with a massive drawbridge and Portcullis. The Drawbridge spanned an exceptionally nasty stinking section of the moat which lay around the Castle, stagnant and filled with bodies of Inferi. Inferi were the undead, killed by The Marquis by use of his Killing Curse or his sword and their rotting carcasses enchanted too remain as guardians of the moat in case of an attempted enemy assault across it. The Inferi would drag any attacker who tried to swim the moat or fall into it, under the stagnant water and devour them alive. The bite of the Inferi would itself render an attacker's body to reanimate and to become an Inferi themselves. The Inferi would mostly simply devour any good meat which happened into their moat, but would often create more Inferi also. At times of war, if attacked, the moat would writhe with bloated half rotten bodies ready to attack and kill any stray soldier who ventured into the moat either by design or by accident.

The arms of the drawbridge which stretched across the perilous moat, were richly carved and were spanned by Oaken planks which provided the passage across. Once across the drawbridge, the first part the Gate Houses with in the Barbican arose tall and housed a great iron Portcullis, who's great iron spikes which protruded from the bottom, still could be seen clung to by impaled skeletons of attacking soldiers who had received the misfortune of never reaching past the first iron gate into the Castle. Upon entering this gate, above were visible a multitude of holes in the ceiling of the passageway through the Gate House. These holes were used by the Minions of the Marquis to pour down boiling oil and fire cross bow bolts upon enemy soldiers who had made a success of penetrating through the first Portcullis. Then beyond these 'Death Holes', as they were named, was a second great iron Portcullis. This too was solid and housed its own compliment of impaled remains along its base.

Beyond the Barbican and outer Curtain wall was the Inner Bailey, which was peppered with buildings of barracks for the Marquis' Personal soldiers, his Bodyguards. Also here were the vast Kitchens to prepare the feasts of which he was very fond. Standing centrally within the Inner Bailey was the vast Keep of the Marquis' Palace. Tall, with many towers and deep dungeons. Within the Keep was the Private chamber and Court Chambers of the Marquis. In the Great Hall, part of the Court Chambers, the Marquis sat in his fine robes of Gold and Black, which he wore over his armour. This armour was of the finest steel and carved exquisitely with figures of Mythical Beasts which were gilded. A huge Brest plate contoured his chest and his powerful arms covered by plates of steel, figures and gilded, worn over a dense coat of steel mail. Within a mail hood was the head of the Marquis, a steel gilded face mask covered with his features was upon him, covering the upper part of his face, his eyes and nose, leaving the lower portion, his mouth and lower jaw visible. His jaw was heavily scarred both from battle with defeated conquered armies and with Evil. Only visible above his lower face, were his deep golden eyes, bloodshot, visible through the eye slits of the mask. Upon his head he wore a golden crown of a single band of gold heavily jewelled with Garnets and Emeralds and the Crown was ringed with points tipped with Silver.

Thracia had at an ancient time been a thriving Kingdom ruled by a good and just Ruler, King Reuben. The Kingdom was prosperous and traded happily with many Kingdoms including Alexandria and the surrounding Kingdoms. As the Kingdom became prosperous, so the Wife of a Warlord, The Duke Almonde, became increasingly ill. Then one day, Fortuna died and Almonde was greatly aggrieved.

He sought out a pair of twin Sisters, Hags who had stolen magic from the Court Wizard. He journeyed deep into the forbidden valley of Kartorak, where the cackling Sisters lived in a cave. Here for a price, the Sisters taught Almonde the ways of Magic, powerful Magic and he learned the art of Necromancy. Though afraid of this, the Sisters of Kartorak taught the Duke all they knew of Necromancy. He saw the Books which they taught from, the exquisite pages filled with Rites and Incantations, some to be used for raising the dead. So it was that once learned in Magic and Pronounced a Wizard by the Sisters, and being deeply versed in the diabolical Art of Necromancy, Almonde made his move. First he slayed the Twin Sisters of Kartorak and stole their putrid Book of Necromancy, which taught of raising the dead. Written within the Necronomicon, that to achieve the raising of the dead, a Wizard must be strong in Magic and Lore and powerful enough to achieve the combining of Dark and Light. For years, Almonde searched the books which he had stolen from the Sisters for the answer to this instruction, but without success. The more he delved into the Dark side, deeply it drew him in. The Dark Magic began to affect him, body and Soul and to possess him. He knew of the wealth of Alexandria and thought that combining that with Thracia, it would create and opportunity to possess everything in his search for the 'Dark and Light'. He tried to advise King Reuben, King of Thracia, to invade Alexandria with a view to capturing enough of its wealth to fund for himself his search. King Reuben refused to allow his Council, stating that he enjoyed good relations with Alexandria and had no reason to wish to invade.

This angered Almonde tremendously and within weeks, the Duke Wizard formed an army. With Evil driving him on, at last a force was prepared and

185

Almonde gave to himself the title of 'Wizard Lord' and called himself 'Althere'. Then at the head of his Army, he rode upon the Castle of King Reuben, along the journey, he used his Dark Magic to enchant Magical Creatures to bring them under his control and force them to join his ranks. He used a charm of slavery to bind their service to him and anyone who attempted to break this charm died in a most unpleasant manner. The Army with the Dark Wizard Lord Althere at its head, marched upon Thracia and a great Battle raged for over a week, with heavy losses upon both sides, but with the Wizard Lord's swarm of enchanted Creatures, such as Orcs and Goblins within his ranks, purely the weight in numbers became too great for King Reuben's army to hold back and Thracia fell to the Wizard Lord.

Althere entered the Castle triumphant and then threw King Reuben into his own dungeon. King Reuben was devastated at losing his Kingdom and now finding himself imprisoned. Althere then went about to gather Wizards from throughout the Kingdom and trained them in the 'Dark Arts'. He was then able to build himself a Wizard Army. He then gave orders that Reuben was to be brought before him. Althere then asked one more time of Reuben, that he would support him in conquest of Alexandria. He informed him that with the Dark powers of his Wizard Army, he would be invincible and would be assured of a victory. Once again Reuben refused, again making plain his support for Alexandria. Reuben was much astonished by Althere's words concerning the training of Dark Wizards, as until this time, Wizards were mainly used simply as Soothsayers and Fortune tellers.

Althere forced Reuben to his knees and ordered two soldiers to hold him there kneeling in front of him. He forced Rueben to renounce the Throne of Thracia, then with a cry which echoed around the Great Hall, he swung his great sword, Nagil, and with one swift blow, he sent the head of King Reuben clean from his body. The head struck the ground and the Crown rolled along the tiled floor to the feet of Althere. He picked it up and handed it to one of his soldiers as they let go of the headless body of Reuben and let it fall to the floor to lay in a huge puddle of blood. Althere sent for the Priest and Bishop, who were reluctantly brought into the Great Hall by soldiers. Then under the Slavery Charm, which Althere had passed over them by a wave of his hand, the Bishop took the Crown from the soldier and Althere sat upon the Throne of Thracia. The Bishop said an Incantation and under the Charm, placed the Crown upon Althere's head.

The Bishop then, with the soldiers and Priest as witnesses, announced the declaration that Althere was crowned 'Marquis of Thracia'. The Bishop and the Priest then bowed low to the Marquis and were allowed to leave the Great Hall to bring tidings to all that the Monarchy of Thracia had changed hands. The Marquis ordered the head of Reuben to be taken around the Kingdom; Throughout the streets of the towns and Villages and then returned to the Castle where it would be set upon a spike at the gates, so that everyone approaching the Castle would see that the Monarchy had officially been replaced. Word reached the City Kingdoms, Calistria, Restoratet and Alexandria, all independent Kingdoms at this time.

The Marquis then proceeded to use Dark Magic to strengthen himself and build the Kingdom of Thracia into an Empire. First he took all of the nearby Kingdoms within striking distance, all the way to the Mountains of Melokan. All that separated Thracia from the City Kingdoms of Calistria and Petros were these Mountains, the Mire of Calek, the Forest of Karnack and the Opal Mountains.

In time, Kletar, Wizard of Alexandria, sealed the air surrounding the borders of Alexandria with a 'Skin', a Magical Charm impenetrable by only the very strongest Dark Magic. The more Evil deeds which the Marquis partook of, the more Evil ate away at him. He was cursed and eventually died leaving the Kingdom in the hands of his Son; and so he continued to rule the Kingdom with increasing Evil and more and more Dark Magic. The Son continued his Reign of Terror, treating the people of the Kingdom with complete malice. They were tortured the most horrible ways and eventually the Kingdom became a wasteland of the rotting corpses it is today. The evil within the Kingdom did not allow anything to live but a half-life. The Rivers were contaminated and did not allow anything to live in them other than Evil creatures. Anyone or anything other than the most Evil of creatures to drink from the rivers died a most painful and horrendous death. The Marquis continued to enchant more and more Magical Creatures to join his Armies. All who resisted were impaled upon stakes and their bodies displayed as a warning to others. Only the Unicorns, because they were so pure and the Elfs, because their Magic was much stronger, were able to resist.

Eighty years before, Oman, Son of Althere exacted a reign of terror across the Kingdom of Thracia. Many of his subjects were brutally tortured and put to death for any opposition to his power. The Evil which drove him on, like his Father, consumed him and disfigured him. Calistria was the first to be attacked. The Dwarfs withdrew to lands further from the Thracian borders. Ragged and forlorn refugees littered the lands in great groups, surviving where they were able. Olav de Morteby gathered an Army and rode from Alexandria at its head, flanked by his Son, David. They fought valiantly and long. Many fell upon each side. Joined by the Dwarfs of Calistria and Elfs of Restoratet, they eventually won the day. After many weeks of Battles, the Thracian Army lay depleted too far to continue and Oman retreated to his Kingdom. Then the great cost of the War was realised as Prince Royal Olav was found upon the Battle field mortally wounded. He had fought off and killed twenty four Orcs but succumbed to eight arrows which penetrated from his chest to his legs. He was carried to his campaign tent, where he betrothed his Kingdom to his son David, who was Simon's Father. Olav died in his tent and David was proclaimed Prince Royal of Alexandria. His first great task and feat was to agree a truce and treaty with the surrounding City Kingdoms, to allow them to become Semi-Autonomous but to operate as provinces of Alexandria, with David as their High King.

This was the formation of the 'Commonwealth of Alexandria', the City States became known under the treaty as 'Shires' of Alexandria, which made up the Commonwealth.

From this time, it was also noted that due to the dangerous use of Dark Magic by the Thracian Wizard and the Marquis, meant that it was necessary to create a Wizard Army to defend against the Dark Magic of Oman. So the Wizards became more than just mere Sooth Sayers and Fortune Tellers, but became 'Warriors for the Light'. The Power used by the Wizards of Alexandria and the Commonwealth of its Shires was derived from a Crystal which was hidden for its safety. This white Crystal was the source of the Magical power of the 'Skin' and the weaponry and Armour used by the people and wizards of Alexandria. When the first Marquis, Althere, had attempted to overthrow Alexandria, his Armies were engaged elsewhere building his Kingdom. It fell to his Son to mount the first War against Alexandria. The Evil which consumed them gave them longer life and it was not until his three hundredth year that Althere finally succumbed to the Evil and it ate away at his Soul so much that he died. Then one hundred years ago, his Son, Oman, mounted the Great War which raged across his World and ours. Many hundred years before, the Wizard Lord of Alexandria had cast a spell to create a Portal through to this World, where he built a Manor House, Pegasus House. Then The Prince Royal was elected to be the Lord of the Manor to enable the use of the Portal to be secured as a means to allow the Crown Prince to 'hide' in this World at time of Peril for the Royal Family.

This was when a disused and derelict Manor House upon the Moor was rebuilt by the Lord of the Manor and created Toadford School. The School was created to educate the Crown Prince and other important Alexandrian offspring in a safe place away from the dangers of Alexandria and Thracia. The power which was born into the Alexandrian Prince's blood came from the Crystal known as 'The Oracle'. The swords and Armour of the Alexandrians were manufactured by Elfs and were set with Crystals to magically shield them and make their swords stronger and more powerful. But to counter this, when Oman invaded Calistria the first time, he captured a Dark Crystal, known as the Dark Gem, which had been mined by the Dwarfs. The Marquis soon discovered that the Dark Gem gave his Wizards similar powers to which the Oracle gave to the Alexandrians. This was powerful Dark Arts, difficult to defend against unless a powerful Wizard was able to counter it.

The Marquis sat upon his Throne in his Great Hall, when entered a thin wiry figure dressed in a ragged grey cloak and robes. Caithius the Vengeful approached the Throne almost as though he were walking upon eggshells, fear raging through his mind. Caithius bowed low at the Throne and trembled upon the spot. The Marquis leaned forwards and stared at Caithius, his elbow upon his knee and his hand upon his heavily scarred chin. His eyes burned through the mask slits and bore into the Wizard.

"Sire, the Thracian forces have captured Calistria, Petros and Parlemann Shires; they are gradually working into the Commonwealth and will hopefully reach Alexandria soon. There is a need for more weapons and Orcs, as many have been lost in the Battles." Said Caithius, in a trembling voice.

"Good, the Orcs are proving valuable in my conquering. They shall have their re-enforcements and weapons. The Orcs and Goblins are but as Cannon fodder, so numbers are the only tactic to their fighting; they are too imbecilic to use as anything else. My enchantment of them is working well." Replied the Marquis.

"Sire, we fight hard but Lord Barnabus The Enlightened has noticed that we were able to enter the Commonwealth unawares and conquer Calistria, he has realised that some failures in the warning spells surrounding the Kingdom of Alexandria are becoming useful to us. We will continue to detect these failures and exploit them My Lord." Said Caithius.

"Failure is not an option, Wizard, we must not allow the Kalhron to strengthen their defences and the Land Troops to gather and build up strength. We must keep pushing on until we reach Alexandria and Capture the Oracle." Replied The Marquis.

"Sire, this shall be done but we need more time to build a full force to attack Alexandria all out and capture the Oracle. With the Council of Lord Barnabus, The Prince Royal will be raising his own armies and will be preparing his forces with Armour and weapons. There are many Shires and many fighters to be recruited from them, we shall push on with Conquering more Shires. By doing this, we shall eventually reach Alexandria with no intact Commonwealth and no allies to help them. We shall capture the Oracle My Lord, without the Oracle, their Armies will be weaker and their Wizards will be powerless." Said Caithius.

"Be gone Wizard, bring me Alexandria." Said The Marquis.

Caithius waved his right hand and a blinding red light momentarily shone in the Great Hall, then Caithius was gone, leaving The Marquis sitting upon his throne.

Wizards were able to travel in a number of ways; Evaporation, which was what Caithius, had just done, using a charm meant that the Wizard's body was broken down into atoms and then converted to light, so that they were able to travel at light speed to where ever they wished close by. Owing to the way Evaporation worked, it was highly dangerous to mess about with, with Evaporation not used unless by an extremely experienced Wizard. This took many years to perfect and if got wrong, could result in serious injury to the Wizard, if not death.

Other forms of transport were used by the Wizards, such as Dragon Powder; this was obtained by the Dragon burning a Maiden for his food and as a sacrifice to appease the Dragon with the hope that the village where the Maiden was from would be safe from the Dragon. These were the largest Dragons, the Dracos.

They were mostly impregnable, only by the strongest Magic and were only vulnerable to a blow from an Alexandrian sword or spear to their underside, to where their heart was inside a hole in their chest, which was used as an air intake to ignite their ferocious and deadly fire breathing.

If a sword or spear were to enter this hole and pierce his heart and the Dragon would be slayed. Only an Elfen Bowman would be of any use for this, as the reflexes of the Draco would be too fast for any other Bowman. Against the Dracos skin of tough scales, only the most powerful spells from the most powerful of Wizards would be effective. The only other most vulnerable area to strike the Draco would be in its eye, but as his head is where it is located, it would be most dangerous to strike in this area and avoid being eaten or incinerated.

Keystones, where the Wizard would wish to travel a long distance undetected or by Broomstick. Also, in times of Battle, Wizards may ride Dwarf Dragons as Cavalry, striking against the enemy Troops upon the ground from the air and also striking against Wizards from the enemy Wizarding Army in the air.

When Evaporating, the colour bestowed upon the Wizard at graduation from apprentice is the light of his Aurora, which he uses to Evaporate. This form of transport is most dangerous to the Wizard so is only used when the Wizard Lord summonses the rest of the Kalhron to Council or for short distances; most Witches and Wizards use broomsticks for this, as Evaporation also drains the Wizard of energy if used frequently; Witches prefer to use Broomsticks as standard. All this was what had to be explained to Rachel and Toby before the attacks because more perilous to the Kingdom or to this World. The Wizards of Alexandria used only White magic to defend against the Dark Arts of the Marquis and The Shambols. Also the White Magic could be used against the enchanted Magical Creatures which were employed by the Marquis in times of War.

Once again Caithius ordered the Generals and Captains of the Thracian Armies to gather in more Magical Creatures to be enchanted and to join the ranks with the rest of their kinds in the Thracian Armies. Dark Arts were used for War and torture, Killing Curses were used in single combat of Wizards or against ground troops, as did Kalhron Wizards, but Killing Curses were only used by Kalhron Wizards in defence, not to be used for gratification, whereas the Wizards of The Shambols enjoyed nothing more than to be given an opportunity to use a Killing Curse. The Marquis, driven on by the Evil in his veins, arteries and in his Soul, relished any excuse to use the Killing Curse to fuel his Evil Soul and prolong his life. When The Marquis used a Killing Curse, his life force was boosted by the life force captured from the dying victim, to avoid his agony of this Curse is to cast an Obliteration Spell to destroy them and therefore relieve them of their suffering eternally.

Chapter Twenty Three – Christmas Arrives

Christmas that year was a little different than usual, as the little family spent Christmas Day at the Hospital in Cranleigh. Decked out in all the Christmas Cheer in the sitting room for Patients, was a huge Christmas tree. Rachel sat in her wheel chair, which she was still using. The Physiotherapy was coming along fine and soon the Physio would be trying Rachel to see whether she was able to walk without the Bars. Of course, to begin with this would only be a short distance, so her wheel chair would be valuable to her for a little while longer. When she had been taken for Hydrotherapy in the Pool, wearing her swimming costume, Rachel had noticed the prominent scar which ran the length of her thigh and ended just above her right hip. This was from the operation to fix her hip fracture and leg fracture. Below her right knee was also a prominent scar from the damage to her Tibia and Fibula. The Surgeons needed to screw plates into her Femur to knit it back together; also she had plates in her Pelvis and Right arm.

In the sitting Room, Rachel sat to the side of the Room with a small number of other Patients who had the misfortune to be in Hospital over Christmas. The Hospital were very good upon this point and allowed families to visit all day and even held a small 'Party' Celebration for the Patients and their Visitors. Around the walls of the room were placed many chairs. Rachel was sitting watching television. Yet another re-run of films usual to Christmas then at Three O'clock, the Queen's Christmas speech, traditional, boring and put onto all Channels just so that no one could get away from it., so Rachel thought. Rachel had never really been much of a Royalist, she had more important things to worry about than who was flying off to which Country, meeting some World leader or other and waving at People. Rachel's chief concern was how long it was going to be before her body allowed her to walk again and enable her to be discharged turn home.

This was the first Christmas that they had been apart since Carl had married her and Rachel thought 'it sucks!' Along the wall opposite to where Rachel was sitting along with the others, were a line of tall windows running the length of the wall, which looked out over the gardens. Lined along in front of the windows were some more chairs, some of them occupied. At the opposite end of the room, away to the right, Rachel could see the tall Christmas Tree which stood opposite the doors in the centre of the end wall. The tree was decked out with baubles of a multitude of colours, tinsel hung from almost every branch, there was a fake snow sprayed here and there but mainly towards the top, where on top of the tree was a star.

The door opened and in walked Carl, Simon and Toby. Toby ran over to Rachel and hugged her hard, almost knocking her wheel chair over backwards. Toby had not seen his Mother since the day that she had delivered him to Toadford School and then had gone on to find herself in Hospital.

"Mom, Mom." Cried Toby, "Oh Mom, it's so amazing to see you."

"Wonderful to see you too Dear." Replied Rachel with a tear in her eyes. She had thought about this ever since Carl had told her that they would be coming to spend Christmas day with her, that if the accident had been a little more serious, that she would not be greeting her Son now and the family would be spending their first Christmas without her at all. She had thought about that scenario and that the last time Toby would have seen her alive would have been when he walked away from her in Toadford's Car Park and disappeared through the gate, but it was not now time for Rachel to dwell upon these thoughts, as she was still here and holding Toby in her arms.

"Hi Babe, hope you've had a good week, Love." Said Carl, a big beaming smile upon his face at seeing Toby's reaction to entering the room.

"Hi Darling, Physio has been OK, it's coming along well now. The Physio wants to try with me to walk without the bars. Said Rachel, smiling up at Carl.

"Hello Rachel, Merry Christmas." Said Simon, as he handed her a gift wrapped in silver paper.

"Merry Christmas!" Said Toby and Carl in unison, handing her two more gifts for Rachel to open and then smiled.

"Dad, just what I wanted, thank you. With the cold weather coming, a hat and scarf, it will help." Said Rachel. "Oh Darling thank you so much." She said to Carl as she opened his box to reveal a necklace of white stones.

"OH Sweetheart' I love it, your first!" Said Rachel to Toby as she unwrapped his clay cup, which he had thrown and turned in his art class at Toadford.

"Does it mean you will be home soon Mom?" Asked Toby.

"Yes, but will be a little while yet, we have to see how my walking goes without the bars. I have been doing some Gym work to strengthen my legs to help get me walking again. What are you doing with yourself while your Dad is out at work?" Said Rachel.

"Granddad is helping me with my Homework and next week I'll be going to Keiron's house." Said Toby

"Ah yes, I remember now, you're staying at your friend's house for the rest of the Holiday, so that its easier for your Dad to go to work and for Granddad to do what he needs to do." Said Rachel.

At the centre of the room had been placed a number of tables together for the Christmas Dinner and Tea. A space had been left so that Rachel was able to put her wheel chair into it and sit up to the table. The time came when a group of Nurses walked into the room and after they had finished a dozen Carols, a Christmas message was read to them by Dr Frost, looking rather comical in his white coat with Stethoscope around his neck and red Father Christmas hat upon his head with a white fury bauble upon it.

The Nurses too were wearing similar hats, all but one who was wearing a black hat with a white bauble and a word emblazoned across it in white;

"HUMBUG"

This was a rather aging Nurse named Doreen, who didn't much care for Christmas. She thought it too commercialised and didn't believe in the Christmas message. Doreen would rather that Christmas was forgotten. The giving of gifts she didn't hold with, she thought that it was a waste of money, as she also thought that all the merriment and celebration was too. It was Doreen's opinion that the 'Idiots,' who dressed as Father Christmas to hand out presents to deserving Children, should be better put to work with more important uses, rather than encouraging the next generation to continue the outdated, money grabbing tradition of Christmas.

"So what if two thousand years ago a baby was born in a desert town." Thought Doreen. It was Doreen's opinion; "So what if the neighbours had nothing to do but to 'black their noses' and come to see the Baby, so that they could then tell everyone (who wanted to listen), 'that they were there.' Doreen had opinions about most things, which were usually the opposite of everyone else's. She tended to keep herself to herself, just doing her duties and mumbling to herself as she went around her Ward. Doreen had only come into the room because Sister had told her to, if it was her choice, she would have carried on around her Ward bringing trays carrying plates full of Christmas Dinners to the Patients who were unable to leave their beds to join in with everyone in the room. Doreen didn't have to stay long, just until Dr Frost had given his Christmas Speech. Doreen then lifted her rather spacious behind off the chair where she was sitting, which seemed to groan with relief as she stood up upon her thick tree trunk legs.

She walked out of the room plodding along, her bulk in her Nurses uniform, bobbled along with the 'Humbug' hat which sat upon her collar length straight mousey brown hair. She scowled at the gathering in the room as she waddled through the door and they were now all taking their places at the tables. Doreen was going to shovel down her Christmas Dinner (Which was the only part of Christmas that she supported), while sitting at the Nurse's Station in her Ward.

In the room, as yet another 'usual' Christmas film began upon the TV screen, the Christmas Dinner was brought into the room and placed upon the table. Doreen had already been to collect her 'bit of everything', piled up upon her plate. Upon the tables appeared Roast Turkey, the hugest that Toby had ever seen, there was also a Roast Beef Join, Pork Joint and Gammon Joints, mountains of vegetables and Roast Potatoes, Cranberry Sauce, Redcurrant Sauce, Jelly, Bread Sauce with Turkey, beef and Pork gravy. There was vegetarian 'meatless' meat Loaf for the Veggies who were present, with Vegetable gravy for them.

A cheer rang out when Dr Frost stood and began to carve the Turkey. A collared Hospital Chaplain said 'Grace' and the feast began. Doreen sat at the Nurse's Station; most of the cheeks of her overhanging backside were too large

193

for the chair which she was sat upon. She sneered as she heard the cheer and stuffed yet another forkful of Turkey, Beef, Pork and Sprouts into the overly large gaping hole in her round face which she called her mouth. Her face was almost permanently a shade of red with two piggy little blue eyes looking out from the folds of skin around them. The stubby sausage like fingers gripped her knife and fork as she harpooned the menagerie of meats and vegetables which festooned her plate and rammed them into her Cake Hole. She wasn't bothered about not being able to watch the Christmas films, as most, apart from the Movie Premiers, she had seen umpteen times before. While Doreen was upon the Ward she didn't allow talking while she was eating, so the only sound which was audible from the Ward was the clinking of knives and forks upon the plates from the Patients in the beds and from Doreen.

Back in the 'Party Room', all merriment abounded. The Patients, Staff and Patients families seated around the tables chatted, eating and nattered muffled through mouthfuls of food. There were multitudes of BANGS and 'Oooh's', as Christmas crackers were pulled and snapped to reveal slips of paper with silly jokes upon them, which everyone had heard before, but still laughed anyway. People all around the tables put upon their heads many colours of Party hats which they had won from the Christmas crackers and some of the Family's Children had finished their main course of Christmas Dinner and were playing with small plastic toys which had fallen out of the crackers. All this time, Toby was enjoying this Christmas Party with Mom, Dad and Granddad. It was a better Christmas than he had envisaged when he had been told about Rachel's Accident. Her Physiotherapy was progressing and She was and getting better each day. It would not be long before Rachel was allowed to return home and continue her recovery there.

Toby picked up a Christmas cracker and held it up in front of Rachel with a smile. Rachel smiled back and took hold of the other end of the cracker and they both pulled. The crape paper stretched and so did the 'snapper' inside. Suddenly with a loud BANG, the two ends of the cracker tore away from each other in each of their hands. Toby looked at his half and found that he had the largest piece of the cracker, which contained a pale blue Party hat, which Toby unfolded and put upon his head; a small plastic whistle and a slip of paper carrying a joke. Toby unfolded it;

"What is Black, white, yellow-black, white, yellow-black, white, yellow?" Asked Toby, reading from the slip of paper.

"I have no idea?" Replied Rachel from opposite his seat at the table.

"A Canary crossing a Zebra Crossing." Laughed Toby and Rachel together. It didn't hurt so much now when Rachel laughed, the bruising to her abdomen and chest had gone in the months that she had been recovering. The breaks in her hip, leg and arm had healed bone wise, but it was just now a case of some physio exercises in the Gym and her walking exercises to strengthen her legs and hip to enable her to be able to walk again. As the doctors had told her, she may be left with a slight limp, it was this which was giving some difficulty in learning to walk again, as her balance had to reboot itself to compensate with walking with the limp. Rachel then pulled a cracker with Carl and won its contents. She then put upon her head, the yellow Party hat which she found in her half of the cracker and read out the joke from her slip of paper.

""How do you milk a Bull?" She asked.

"I don't know, I wouldn't think of trying?" Replied Carl, pulling another cracker with Simon. Carl won the contents of this cracker.

"Very carefully." Said Rachel. Carl read out the joke upon his slip of paper.

"How many Psychiatrist does it take to change a light bulb?" He asked.

"I don't know?" Replied Toby, giggling.

"Only one, but the light bulb has to really want to change." Laughed Carl, putting upon his head the purple Party Hat.

"My turn." Said Simon, pulling a cracker with Dr Frost and winning the contents; "What do you get if you cross a sheep with a Kangaroo?" Simon read from the slip of paper   and putting upon his head the green paper hat.

"We don't know?" Replied Carl, Rachel and Toby all together with a giggle.

"A Woolly Jumper." Laughed Simon and they all laughed with him.

Just then, a couple of Kitchen Staff entered the room carrying a large round Christmas Pudding upon a tray each and another couple carrying a large jug of Cream and a large jug of custard upon each of their trays. Then placed upon the tables and began handing out portions of Christmas Pudding with custard, Christmas Pudding with cream or Christmas Pudding with both cream and custard. Toby was a recipient of the latter choice, his bowl had a portion of Christmas Pudding with both cream and custard, his Christmas treat. They all tucked into their Christmas Pudding while in the background, the TV still went through yet another traditional showing of a film, meaning that it had been shown every Christmas for the past ten years. Once the Dinner was over and everyone had sat watching the TV for about an hour, chatting; Dr Frost announced it was time for his Patients to have some rest, after all he said, this is a Hospital. So everyone hugged and kissed their relative goodbye and began leaving the Ward.

Toby, Carl and Simon said goodbye to Rachel, who gave Carl a big hug and a kiss, then Toby. They then walked out of the room with Toby waving all the way to the door. At the door, Simon and Carl gave Rachel a last wave, as did Toby and Rachel waved back. Then they were gone out of the corridor into the Ward and the Way Out. Behind them through the doors to the Ward, sat Doreen at the Nurse's Station, finishing her seconds of Christmas Pudding with cream and custard, upon her desk beside her was a plate of Cocktail Sausages as snacks throughout the rest of her Night Shift. Rachel was wheeled back to her bed by

Dr Frost, who didn't wish to disturb Doreen from her Christmas Pudding, after all, it was Christmas.

"That was your Son, Toby with Mr Morby, his Father?" Askes Dr Frost.

"Oh yes, Toby is almost fourteen, in July. He attends Toadford School." Replied Rachel.

"Ah yes, I remember now, it was from the School that you were travelling when you had your accident, was it not?" Asked Dr Frost.

"Yes, that's right." Replied Rachel. Rachel pulled herself up onto her bed, with help from a Nurse; !I attended the School in my youth and also Carl did, and his Father too. I met Carl at Toadford School in fact." Said Rachel.

"Ah, childhood Sweethearts, that's how it should be." Replied Dr Frost. DR Frost his goodbyes to the Patients and thanked them for making the Christmas Party so enjoyable and the Patients thanked Dr Frost for the Party. He then left the Ward to continue with his rounds in other Wards. Carl drove back to Pegasus House with Toby and Simon in the Landrover from Cranleigh Hospital.

"Oh Wow Dad, that was a great Christmas Party and so good to see Mom again. I hope she is coming home soon, so that we don't have to keep on going to the Hospital." Said Toby, smiling.

"Sure was Toby, and I second your wish. What did you get from under the Christmas Tree when Dr Frost handed out the Presents?" Said Carl.

Toby put his hand into a carrier bag which had been provided for him to carry his present home. He pulled his hand out and displayed his treasure.

"I got a PS4 game Dad, great of them to give us such awesome presents!" Replied Toby, showing the game package to Simon.

"That would be your Mom telling Dr Frost what you would like. They do a good job there and have decent Staff." Said Carl, "That's what the Children's Charity Collection tins are for at each Reception Counter; so that all through the year, they can receive donations and at Christmas, put the takings towards the Presents for the Children who attend the Christmas Party if their Parent or Parents are in Hospital. There are usually at least some Children attending the Party if the Patients are in Hospital. The Patients in the Hospital arrange with Dr Frost if there is a particular present which their child would like and where possible, he tries to obtain it. They also provide a special Christmas Party in the Paediatric Ward, for the Children who are unable to be at home for Christmas and unfortunately need to be in Hospital upon Christmas day." Said Simon.

"They are doing a god job on Mom, aren't they Dad, she's getting better all the time, isn't she?" Asked Toby.

"Yes Son, Mom is coming along nicely and Dr Frost is doing a proper job with her, rebuilding her fitness and her recovery." Replied Carl. Simon looked at Carl and knew what his Father was conveying to him. Carl turned into the driveway of Pegasus House and drove up to the house, parking the car next to Simon's BMW.

"Home again." Said Simon.

"Yep, soon it will be with Rachel." Replied Carl.

"Well, we won't need any Dinner now will we, not after Seconds at the Hospital of everything." Said Simon.

"I feel tired Dad, a long day tomorrow, I go to Keiron's house for the week. I think I will get and early night, with the early start tomorrow." Said Toby.

"OK Son, yes it has been a long day. I'll wake you at eight so you have plenty of time to get your things together and be ready to leave at nine. I just hope that Keiron gave you the right address for his house, I'm not too familiar with Topley Village, I don't get over there much." Said Carl.

"We'll go over in the BMW, Carl, would be good for all of us to meet Keiron's family, so that we know who Toby is staying with and to be able to let us know who we are contacting if Toby is unwell or something, just in case of course." Said Simon.

"Well then, good night Dad, good night Granddad, see you in the morning." Said Toby, giving each a hug.

"Good night Son, sleep well." Replied Carl.

"Good night Toby." Replied Simon. Toby turned and walked out of the Living Room where they had all been sitting.

"What did you mean 'to know who Toby is with, just in case?'" Asked Carl.

"He's a Prince of Alexandria, Carl, we must be aware of his safety at all times and know who he is staying with for that reason. The Marquis has broken through to this world before and are if it were not for the 'Guildsmen' and help from the Kalhron, Alexandria and this World would have been laid waste by the Thracian Army and the 'Shambols'." Said Simon.

"I know all that Dad, but Toby is a child of this World and he needs to be with his friends," Said Carl.

"I am aware of that Carl, this is the reason why the Kalhron have agreed that we are not only to inform Rachel and Toby of their true Heritage, but also we are to attempt to recruit his friends to our cause. We can induct them into the 'Guildsmen' as Junior Members to bring them up to speed with the situation threatening both Worlds or we can induct them into the Kalhron and train them for combat." Said Simon.

"Dad, they are thirteen years old, barley teenagers and you want to turn them into Wizards or warriors to fight for a cause which is totally alien to them. Hopefully it won't come to that." Said Carl.

"But Carl, you do not fully understand. If all-out War breaks out and the Thracian Armies find some means to break through into this World, as trained Wizards, we would stand more chance having them upon this side to counter, as long as possible, any attempted incursion by Thracian troops or Wizards until the full forces of Alexandria can reach them to take over the fight. Toby MUST know of his position, if you and I are lost against the Marquis, he will be Prince Royal; he needs to be aware of this Carl, you must understand and so Toby and Rachel must, that Toby is an heir to the Kingdom's Throne and this must be fulfilled to safe guard the Kingdom. Toby's friends must be inducted, as they have formed a close bond and to separate them would most likely create a distraction for Toby and put his safety in danger. He turns fourteen in July, Carl, he must then be transferred from his main classes at Toadford and attend the Wizardry Classes in the Wizarding Hall. He must learn sword combat and Wandlore and defensive Wandsmanship. He must learn Archery and Jousting to fight upon horseback or the back of a Dwarf Dragon if needed as part of the Kalhron. Once he has passed through the 'Skin' and been inducted into Alexandrian lineage, to become officially heir to the throne, once he has felt the Power of the Oracle run through his veins and strengthen him once he has learned to wiled a sword and Wand, he will be ready for Kingship. His Apprenticeship now must take place, as with the threat from The Marquis looming ever closer, Toby must be prepared, we must be prepared. It is natural that Toby should wish to talk to his friends about his adventures, if they are part of that adventure, then there would be less opportunity for errors. Obviously, we will have to swear them to absolute secrecy and only inform their Parents if their duties will involve going into combat. We can simply tell their Parents that we are taking the Kids to camp, if that arises and once all the problem of Thracia has been contained, we can cast a memory charm over them so that they remember nothing of what took place." Said Simon.

"And if Thracia break through into this World?" Asked Carl, incredulously.

"We will need to call upon all Guildsmen to defend Toadford, The Village and Pegasus House. The Army would most likely be called in if it becomes a vast Battle, to be fought; we will need to deal with that as it occurs. Once Rachel is home, we can explain it all to her, don't worry Carl, I will be with you and I will take full responsibility for her reactions and will convince her it is all necessary. When Rachel travels through the 'Skin', she will be restored fully to health; the power of the Oracle will heal her completely, so she will then understand our position and our necessity for the secrecy over the years. Rachel is an intelligent Woman Carl, once she has initially reacted to your news, we can start work together and build a secure Royal Family to lead the Kingdom of Alexandria. Once the Company has returned from Lord Barnabus, I will be dispatching small companies of soldiers all headed by a Captain, to all parts of The Commonwealth to gather together an Army from all of the Shires, which will crush the Insurgency and ambition of The Marquis. If either of us or both of us fall to this Insurgency, then Toby must be ready to take up his position and duty as Prince Royal and lead the Armies to Victory. My Ancestors made this situation Carl, if they had not created the Portal, not built this house up and Toadford School to hide each Prince until he is Fourteen and eligible as an Apprentice, we would not be in this position, it is our duty, now that the Portal exists, to safeguard the Prince and to safeguard this World from delivering an Evil tide which could wash away all of the Humanity in this World. Carl, we have to defend the both Worlds." Said Simon in total seriousness.

"I know Father, I am from your World, but I just don't relish the thought of breaking the news and now we need to include Toby's friends!" Said Carl.

"I'm afraid so Carl, Toby's friends must be included as it may be support for Toby to encourage him to succeed if he is accompanied by his friends, but also it lessens the opportunity for a slip up if Toby should accidentally tell them something of this World if we make them part of it, then any revelation is less important. Throughout the year, Toby's friends have proved loyal to Toby and each other and this is a quality we need in our troops. Toby has, alas, proved to be fiercely loyal to them also, which could cause a problem if they were separated for long periods of time. Obviously if they accompany him in classes, he will have less to tell them to let slip and their loyalty will grow together and be priceless if they are called into combat." Said Simon.

"So Toby's friends would be taught to become Wizards?" Asked Carl.

"Of course Carl, they would learn alongside Toby. It is the only way to help this work. When you trained, it was easier, because you had a couple of close friends and you were able to keep our secret. I know Toby may also be strong enough in mind to keep the secret, but with the Marquis moving across the land, I would rather not risk defeat." Said Simon.

"I know how important this is Father." Replied Carl, looking at the carpet. Carl had never been involved in any real Alexandrian conflict as peace had reigned throughout the time that Simon had been Ruler, but it was different now. They knew with the heavy Orc defeats which have already occurred, that the weapons they carry into conflict must be made and prepared by their Armourers; and that takes time, just as creating an Army full of weapons, suits of armour and other necessities, need time to be manufactured.

"Both sides would not last too long upon their present stock of weapons as it stood right then. The Wizards of The Kalhron will inform the Rulers of each Shire of the call to Duty and then when our messengers arrive at the Shires, there hopefully, will be the weaponry and men ready and waiting to join the fray." Said Simon.

"I think I'll turn in early too Dad, it was a long day and I have much to think about." Said Carl.

"Yes Son, we have got a lot to think about and it has been a long day. I will see you both in the morning, bright and early." Replied Simon.

Chapter Twenty Four - Topley Village

Toby's alarm clock rang out and his sleepy hand swung out from the bed clothes and landed upon the cut off button. It was eight O'clock as he had planned. He got out of bed and showered in his En Suite shower room then dressed in his blue Frackston City Football shirt and jeans, then went down stairs to the kitchen for Breakfast.

Toby made sure that his Ruc-Sac was packet properly along with his Lap-top bag and a couple of PS4 consul games, including the new one which he had gotten at the Hospital Christmas Party. It was a cold, crisp December morning. The Sun was not completely up yet and the frost lay heavily upon the ground. Toby loaded his bags onto the back seat of Simon's white BMW Seven Series and climbed into the back seat next to his bags, with Simon driving and Carl seated beside him in the front seats.

"You have the Post Code for Keiron's house, Toby?" Asked Simon.

"EX28 0TA." Replied Toby.

Simon pressed some buttons upon the instrument panel of the dash board and typed the Post Code into his 'Sat-Nav', after loading their current location into it and started up the car engine. Simon pressed another button upon the dash board and within a minute, all of the frost had disappeared from each of the car windows. Toby sat back in his big black leather seat and put the car phones from his MP3 player into his ears, so that he could listen to the album which Carl had bought him for Christmas, of his favourite Band, Green Boys. Then Simon put the BMW into reverse gear and pulled back to turn up along the driveway. He put the car into drive and accelerated away and out through the gates onto the Moorland Road, turning left onto Bogart Street and out towards the Moor. The 'Sat-Nav' told Simon to drive up onto the Moor, past the lane which led down through the Avenue of poplar trees to Toadford School, past the junction where Rachel came to grief with their accident.

They travelled on until the 'Sat-Nav' gave out an order;

"*TURN RIGHT AT THE NEXT JUNCTION*." Said the smooth metallic female voice.

"There it is, the sign post, it says 'TOPLEY VILLAGE', that's the turning!" Cried Toby from the back seat. Just then, the hedges to the right broke and a clear spot was visible, pointing down the lane where the clear spot was a sign post with a tall black and white Iron pale and white sign with a point, painted in black upon raised letters;

'TOPLEY VILLAGE 3'

Simon indicated to the right as the white BMW approached the junction and turned into Topley Drive.

"Getting close now, Toby." Said Carl, enthusiastically. Toby grinned from the back seat.

They drove for two miles along the hedge lined lane until another junction became visible with its black and white iron signpost which showed,

'TOPLEY VILLAGE 1'

This sign pointed down the newly visible lane to the left. As they drove along the lane, the hedges ended and they began to pass some very old cottages either side of the road. They then arrived at the Village Centre, The Square, where stood the Village Hall and next to it, the Parish Church of St. Andrew.

A two part Chancel, which showed the end part as being more recent than the first part, which was attached to a tall square tower, opposite the Church and Village Hall, stood the Fire Station with its one Tender at one end of the Square and past a row of shops, which included a Butcher and Baker was the small Police Station. Behind here was a row of cottages and the recently built industrial estate opposite the Police Station, upon the other corner of The Square, the Sat-Nav told Simon to drive out of the square and turn to the next right. Toby noticed that the road which had taken them into the Village was Lower Main Street and that the road away from The Square was Upper Main Street and now they turned into Manor Drive as the 'Sat-Nav' had instructed them to. Once again the smooth female voice announced that Simon was to turn left, just as Topley House came into view, which resembled Pegasus House. Keiron couldn't live there thought Toby, as the 'Sat-Nav' had told them to turn off before they reached the 'Big House'. A short drive along Mews Lane saw them pass a barn conversion house across the end of the lane with a Number three upon the gate post to the driveway, where sat the silver BMW in which Toby had watched Keiron drive away from Toadford in a week before.

"At least his Parents have a good taste in cars." Said Simon, as the 'Sat-Nav' finally announced;

"YOU HAVE REACHED YOUR DESTINATION."

"Yes, that's Keiron's dad's car, They picked him up from Toadford in it last week." Replied Toby.

"We'll be seeing you next, after next Term then Toby?" Asked Simon.

"I will be at the Hospital upon New Year's Eve, Keiron's Dad has agreed to bring us over to see Mom and let her meet Keiron and Polly for the day. Then

201

we'll go back to Keiron's house and return to Toadford from there next week." Replied Toby. Just then a blue Mercedes arrived and parked next to them in front of the house.

"Who's this then in the Mercedes?" Asked Simon.

"Oh, that's Polly arriving, her Dad has brought her." Replied Toby. Simon, Carl and Toby opened their doors and got out of Simon's car, as the doors to the Mercedes opened and out stepped Polly in her Purple coat and Cargal scarf with jeans and her Dad, tall with a Beige Trench coat and short black hair and clean shaven. Polly kissed her Father upon the cheek and said;

"I'll call you when I get back to School, Happy New Year."

"Happy New Year Pumpkin, see you next year." Said Mr Muggard and he hugged her. Polly removed herself from the hug and came running over to Toby standing next to Simon's BMW.

"Toby, so good to see you, did you have a good Christmas?" Squealed Polly, as she arrived next to Toby, just in time to wave to her Father as his Mercedes pulled away back up the lane.

"Hi Pumpkin, good to see you too, had a nice Christmas. We went to the Hospital and had Christmas Dinner with Mom and a small Party." Said Toby.

"Don't call me Pumpkin, only my dad calls me that." Said Polly sternly.

"Sorry Polly." Replied Toby.

"That's OK, no harm done." Said Polly, smiling again. Toby smiled back.

"Eh hem!" Coughed Simon from behind them.

"Sorry, err - - Polly Muggard, this is my Grandfather, Simon and my Dad, Carl. Said Toby quickly.

"Hello, pleased to meet you, I'm Polly, from Cranleigh." Replied Polly brightly.

"Hello nice to meet you, Toby has told us so much about you; nice to finally put a face to the name." Said Simon.

"Yes, nice to meet you Polly, did you have a nice Christmas?" Asked Carl.

"Yes thank you Mr Morby, just a family Christmas, just the way we like it." Replied Polly.

"Well time we were making our way in." Said Toby, motioning to Polly. Toby Polly, Simon ad Carl walked through the gate and along the path, through neatly trimmed lawns either side which were frosted like a Christmas cake, to the front door of the house. The outside had the Oak door which they were now standing at, which stood in a white washed wall with exposed wooden beamed frame work and a thatched roof. In the walls were two sets of leaded windows either side of the door. Above here were another four leaded windows either side of a single one above the door, in the upper storey. These were the windows to the Master

202

Bedroom of Bill and Daisy Mudley. Then the window of Thomas Mudley, Keiron's older Brother; then there were the windows of the landing over the stairs, the single one. Next to this was the window to Keiron's Bedroom and finally the window to his younger Sister's Bedroom, Leonie Mudley. Carl pressed the doorbell which gave a two tone chime. Behind the door, running feet could be heard and the door unlatched and opened. Standing there in the doorway was a thin girl of about twelve years old with blonde shoulder length hair and freckles.

"Hi Peeps, I'm Leonie, Keiron's Sister. I take it you're Toby." Said Leonie, pointing at Toby, "And you're Polly, I'll be joining you at Toadford Next term, what's it like there?"

"Yes that's right, I'm Polly and no we can't tell you what it's like at Toadford, Traditions you see, sorry." Replied Polly..

"Yeah, err – that's right, we're not allowed to tell others about the Traditions at Toadford and oh yeah, I'm Toby." Replied Toby.

"Tradition Spadition!" Snorted Leonine, "I just wanted to know what to look forwards to that's all – or not." Just then a hand took hold of Leonie's arm and gently eased her back into the hallway as Keiron stepped around her into the doorway. He politely addressed Carl and Simon as he was joined by his Father Bill.

"Leonie, you know we're not allowed to tell you about School." Scolded Keiron, "Hello, I'm Keiron, welcome to our house." He added, then turned to Polly and Toby. "Hi Polly, hi Toby, great to see you, got loads to show you inside."

"Hello, I'm Bill, this rabble's Dad. You must be Simon?" Said Bill as he welcomed the four of them.

"Yes, that's right. Topley Parish Council isn't it?" Said Simon.

Bill Mudley was tall like Keiron and had blonde thinning hair with gold rimmed glasses. He was wearing a smart pair of pale taupe trousers with a white shirt, which was open at the collar. Bill was in his mid-forties and had lived in Topley Village since he and Daisy had married over sixteen years earlier. Daisy was local to Topley Village and had met Bill when he was a delivery driver, driving for a Courier Company in Frackston. This was why he and Keiron were avid Frackston City fans.

"That's right, Simon, as you are from the Little Farthingworth Parish Council. Ah you must be Carl, Toby's Father, so nice to meet you. Said Bill, holding out his hand to Simon and Carl for them to shake.

"Yes that's right, I work as a National Park Ranger up upon the Moor." Replied Carl.

"Ah yes, must be an interesting job that." Said Bill. "no Mrs Morby with you then?" Enquired Bill,

"No sorry, Rachel is still in Hospital for a while yet." Replied Carl.

"Oh, sorry to heart that Carl, I hope that she recovers soon!" Said Bill.

"Oh Dad! You're forgetting , we're going to Mrs Morby on New Year's Eve, don't you remember?" Said Keiron.

"Oh of course, yes, what a Numbskull I am, totally forgot about that for a moment." Replied Bill, looking a little embarrassed.

"Well we mustn't keep you all out in the cold out here must we?" Said Bill and he motioned them to enter. They entered the Hallway, which was long and narrow, leading to the Kitchen door at the end. The walls were decorated with greyish green flock wallpaper at the top above a wooden Dado Rail, which was painted white, along with the bottom part of the wall. Upon each side of the Hallway, the walls were punctuated by two doors; and next to the door, the stair case rose up to a landing above them.

Toby took off his jacket to reveal his Frackston City shirt and Polly took of her Purple coat, putting her Cargal House Scarf into her coat pocket, revealing that she was waring a white Blouse with a large collar and over this a lilac jumper to go with her jeans and finished the outfit with a pair of Riding boots, Keiron took Polly's coat, dropped it then picked it up again and also took Toby's jacket from him and hung them upon the pegs which were fixed into to a strip of wood, which was screwed onto the wall of the hallway.

"Shall I take your coats?" Asked Keiron to Simon and Carl, who had not yet removed them.

"No thank you, that's OK Keiron, but we must be getting back." Replied Simon. Then Daisy appeared to greet the Visitors, having just emerged from the Kitchen, wearing a flowered dress which was partly obscured by a flour covered apron.

"Hello I'm Daisy, Keiron's Mom, nice te meet you'm all; they will be perfectly 'appy Noo Yere fer the week, we'll luk af'er theym fer 'ee." Said Daisy.

"Thank you so much, it's Kind of you." Replied Carl.

"No trouble at all." Said Daisy.

"Well, sorry but nice to see you, we must be off." Said Simon.

"OK, see you again at the Hospital, when we bring the Kids up to visit on New Year's Eve." Said Bill.

"See you next year, dad, granddad...... Oh yeah, sorry, see you on New Year's Eve." Said Toby.

Simon and Carl shook hands with Bill and Daisy, who also had some flour in her collar length blonde hair. They then turned and walked out of the door and along the garden path, past Bill's silver BMW and then with a click of his thumb, the car beeped and the doors unlocked for both Simon and Carl to climb into the

204

White BMW, which then roared into life and with one last wave from Simon and Carl, they drove away along the lane and turned right out onto the road which sent them upon their way back to Pegasus House; Bill then closed the door.

"Well now Leonie, wull ye shows Polly te 'er room, I 'opes that ye don't mind sharin' with her for the week, Polly?" Asked Daisy.

"Oh Mrs Mudley, I don't mind……" Began Polly.

"Please call me Daisy, Dear." Said Daisy.

"Oh yes, er right, I don't mind as I share a Dorm room with a class mate at Toadford." Replied Polly.

"…. And if you don't mind Toby, I've put you sharing in Keiron's Room." Said Daisy.

"That's OK, thank you Daisy, we share a Dorm Room at Toadford, so it will just be like school!" Said Toby.

"Oh good, we've got that settled, Keiron will show you to his Bedroom then Toby." Said Daisy.

"Thank you, Daisy." Said Toby.

Leonie led the way up the stairs to the landing above. The hallway had the stairs just inside the door a short way along next to the coat rack, under the right hand side of the hallway. Upon the other side, two more doors led into other rooms.

Up upon the landing, the rooms were at the front which showed a corridor either side to lead to the Bedrooms doors. First Keiron and Toby arrived at Keiron's Bedroom, which was first upon the right from the Stairs. Leonie and Polly walked further along the corridor to Leonie's Bedroom. Along the corridor, which ran the length of the back wall of the house, were windows which over looked a large back garden. This was maturely planted and there was a space for a decking which went across the back of the house, beyond this an area of lawn which was bordered by flower beds and then was an area which was used as the children's games area.

Beyond this was a vegetable and fruit garden; this was Bill's domain. To the left of this area, running its length, was a walled area which housed the fruit. There was a stone boundary wall and attached to this were a number of espaliered fruit trees; such as Apple, Pears and Peaches etc. In the centre of this area were standard Plum trees and Ballerina Cherry trees. Around this area was to found a number of raised bed fruit cages, which contained soft fruits like Black Currants, Red Currants and Gooseberries etc. Some fruit cages contained frames which supported Blackberry canes and Raspberry canes. To the right of this was an area consisting of raised growing beds which Bill used for vegetables. All that were present here at the moment waiting for the harvest were some Brussels Sprouts, Leeks, Parsnips and Cabbages.

Leonie walked into her Bedroom and was followed by Polly. Around the walls could be seen hanging numerous posters depicting all manner of 'gorgeous' Boy Bands, famous actors and young footballers. They were not of any particular team as such, Leonie liked them for their legs and these particular footballers were 'Super-Hot'. Leonie frequently lay upon her bed fanaticising about being the 'WAG' of one of the 'cool fit' Footballers.

Polly upon the other hand was not too impressed. She was not like most other girls, she was 'prim and proper' and didn't waste her time mooning over footballers whom she knew she had no chance with, so the thought had never occurred to her. Next to the wall, Bill had moved Leonie's single bed, so that he could bring in a camp bed and set it up beside Leonie's bed, this was to be where Polly was to sleep. She put her bag down and started to take some items out of it. Out came her homework books and a pad for writing, her pencil case and her Tigger' a teddy bear which Polly had been given as a four year old and had always been her treasure and had never been let out of her sight. She slept cuddling Tigger in her bed in the Dorm Room she shared with 'Bella. 'Bella was absent from the little gathering, because Keiron had told Toby and Polly that Bill and Daisy were only happy with one friend sharing a Bedroom and they pointed out to accommodate a third person in Leonie's Bedroom would be slightly over crowding it, so Keiron compromised in only inviting Toby and Polly, as they were the first friends that he had made at Toadford. Next to Leonie's bed, stood her bedside cabinet with her lamp upon it and a book with part of a bookmark protruding from the top of it. Also within the room was a wide hessian covered slatted wood wardrobe. A chest of drawers was near to Polly's camp bed and Leonie pointed out that Polly could use this for her clothes while she was staying.

"If you like, Polly, you can put your things into that Chest of drawers." Said Leonie.

"Thank you Leonie that would be most helpful." Replied Polly.

"Where do you live then, I know Keiron has told us that Toby lives in Little Farthingworth and that's only because he shares a Dorm Room with him at Toadford, he has told us about you but didn't say where you live?" Asked Leonie.

"I live in Cranleigh, my Father is an Accountant there and I am hoping to follow in his footsteps." Replied Polly.

"Brainy then are you?" Asked Leonie, "Keiron said that you are."

"Keiron would think an Ant was brainy compared with him." Replied Polly and they both laughed.

Down along the landing, Toby was making himself at home in Keiron's Bedroom. The rooms were identical in all but the furniture colour. Leonie's was pink and Keiron's was blue. There was also set up at the side of Keiron's bed, a camping bed which was for Toby's use. He had often gone on camping trips with his Parents, so Toby was used to sleeping upon a camping bed. The other immediately different thing noticeable about Keiron's Bedroom from Leonie's was that there was a distinct lack of Boy Band posters upon the walls, which were replaced with Rock Band posters and the footballer posters were not of a jumble of different players with nice legs, but all were of Frackston City players and there was also a distinct lack of pink in the room.

"This is my kind of room." Said Toby, looking around at all of the Frackston City posters upon Keiron's Bedroom wall; he had a duvet cover which showed some footballers and a huge badge of Frackston City in blue and had white trimmings. He had a Frackston City lampshade upon his bedside lamp which stood upon his bedside cabinet. Hanging from the ceiling were a number of completed and painted Aircraft model kits, upon a shelf unit to one side of the room were more completed Aircraft model kits. Also in the room there was a wardrobe, computer desk, book shelf unit and chest of drawers, which Keiron offered to Toby to use for his clothes during his stay.

"Oh yeah, I see you have the photo which Polly took on our first day at Toadford rather prominently displayed." Said Toby, looking at the bedside cabinet, which was standing next to the lamp and Keiron's alarm clock. The alarm clock was a Frackston City alarm clock of course. The photo of Keiron, Toby and Polly was framed. It was the photo taken by Polly of them sitting upon Toby's bed in the Dorm Room upon their first day at Toadford.

"Polly put it upon my Memory stick for me to print off when I got home. If you like, I can put a copy upon your memory stick for you so that you can print off a copy or I could print you off a copy while you're here?." Said Keiron.

"Oh yeah, please, thanks; the first meeting of the 'Terrible Trio', of course I'd love a copy." Said Toby, smiling from ear to ear. Toby was so excited to get a copy of the photograph because it was one of those things which marked the change in his life and was a record in some way of the transition to the new era in his life and a record of his first day at Toadford School, among his new friends. The photograph also was to Toby, a tangible memory of the day he met his new friends and became part of something, which he belonged to, something outside of Pegasus House. Toby smiled as he stood looking at the photo.

"If you want, you can use my Laptop to help you with any homework you want to work on while you're here." Said Keiron, momentarily breaking Toby's thoughts of the photograph.

"Oh, er – yeah, thanks Keiron, I do still have some bits and pieces to finish off." Said Toby.

"Well now you're settled in, we should go down stairs, I think to see Mom and Dad; it probably isn't too long until Lunch time." Said Keiron, "then maybe some games upon my Play Station." He added pointing at the TV and PS4 stood upon a TV stand with a DVD player.

"Yeah, that's a good idea, I've got some games I bought with me, including a couple that I got for Christmas." Replied Toby.

"Oh great, we can play those if you want to." Said Keiron, excitedly.

Toby tidied his things and put the clothes he had brought with him for the week into the chest of drawers and hung up his Uniform for their return to Toadford School the following week. Then they left Keiron's bedroom and walked along the landing to Leonie's bedroom. From inside there came the sound of Music, the 'Pop' sound of a Boy Band CD, one of Leonie's which she was playing. The boys could also smell the perfume of a girls Bedroom. Keiron knocked upon the door and a high voice called out;

"Come in Muddles."

Keiron opened the door and the two of then entered. Toby had never been in a girl's bedroom before, other tthan the Dorm Room of Polly and 'Bella at Toadford, and the amount of pink and Boy Band posters were a shock to his eyes for a short moment. Keiron then suggested that they all go down stairs to see his and Leonie's Parents and to see whether Lunch was ready. The four of them walked down stairs and Keiron led Polly and Toby into the door at the end of the hallway. The kitchen was surrounded by pale wooden storage cupboards along the lower left hand wall and other's fixed upon the wall above them. The work surfaces were of dark grey granite. Along the right hand wall of the Kitchen was the sink unit, washing machine and electric cooker. In the centre was a table with seats around it in a country style, six seats, a seventh had been added from another room which did not match the rest.

Seated at the table was Thomas, already tucking into a plate of ham sandwiches and a mug of coffee. Bill was seated at the top of the table and was also working himself through a pile of sandwiches.

"Hello you four, nice te see ye." Said Daisy, cheerily, "about ready fer some lunch are we? Good then. I 'ave cheese or 'am fer sandwiches, or mebe 'ee'd like summut else?"

"Oh yes, Cheese for me please, thank you Mrs Mudley." Replied Toby.

"It's Daisy me Dear," Said Daisy to Toby, "and 'ow 'bout 'ee me dear?"

"Would it be OK for me to have ham please Daisy?" Asked Polly.

"I'll have ham too please Mom." Chirped in Leonie.

"Same with me please Mom." Added Keiron.

"What wud 'ee like te drink?" Asked Daisy, "I 'ave Coffee, tea or Cola."

"Tea for me please, thank you." Said Polly.

"Coffee for me please. Thank you" Said Toby.

"I'll have Coffee." Said Keiron.

"Please?" Asked Daisy.

"Er- please Mom." Added Keiron.

"Cola for me please Mom." Said Leonie.

Daisy handed out the plates of sandwiches around the table and then brought the drinks over and handed them to each of the Children. She then sat down upon the chair at the opposite end of the table from Bill, with a plate of sandwiches and a mug of Coffee. They all sat munching away at their sandwiches for a few moments, Keiron, as usual using his hands like a JCB to Shovel the sandwiches into his mouth, cheeks like a Hamster.

"So where're ye farm Polly?" Asked Daisy.

"I live in Cranleigh; my Father is an accountant and I would like to follow in is footsteps." Replied Polly.

"Good solid career that." Replied Bill.

"She's a whiz at maths, leaves us lot behind." Said Keiron.

"That's because you're thick." Added Leonie and stuck out her tongue at him.

"And Toby, you live in Little Farthingworth?" Asked Daisy.

"Yes that's right, I live in Pegasus House, the big white house upon the end as you go up Moorland Road. My Dad is a Park Ranger for the National Park up at Cragmoor." Replied Toby.

"Your Grandfather is on the Council like me?" Asked Bill.

"Yes that's right, he's just been elected Chairman of Little Farthingworth Parish Council. He's also Lord of the Manor of Little Farthingworth, the Title has been handed down in the family for years." Replied Toby.

"So one day, yu'll be too wull ye Toby?" Asked Daisy.

"Maybe, I don't know? My dad will take the Title before me and who knows what is going to happen over time?" Replied Toby.

"Hee hee, Little Lord Toby!" Giggled Leonie. Thomas was sat eating his sandwiches and drinking his Coffee.

"Thomas is at Toadford, you must have seen him?" Said Daisy.

"I've seen him passing in the corridors." Said Toby.

"He's a third year, so we don't see much of him as he does different classes to ours and his Dorm Room is upon the floors above ours." Replied Keiron.

"Our Common Room is different too." Added Toby.

"Don' 'ee stop te talk te yer brother an' Toby then Tamas?" Said Daisy.

"Us 'Toffs' don't mix with 'Grunts', we've got more important things to think about." Replied Thomas in a grunt and went back to his Sandwiches.

"The ways of Toadford?" Said Bill.

"Did you attend Toadford, Bill?" Asked Polly.

"No I'm not from around these parts, I moved here to be with Daisy; I'm really from Taunton, but was working out of Cranleigh for a Delivery Compny." Said Bill.

We met when 'ee was a delivery man te the shop that I worked in next te the Post Office. Blackmore's it was then, like a Mini Mart; it closed down a few years ago and was converted to flats." Said Daisy.

So you're from Topley then, Daisy?" Asked Polly.

"That's right M'Dear, born an' bred. I was born in Cranleigh Hospital, but the family lived one o' the cottages, ye should've passed them as ye drove down yon lane inte The Village Square down from Topley Drive. I was livin' in the middle one of the three as ye drive down, upon the left hand side of the lane." Said Daisy.

"So you got Married here?" asked Poly.

"Yes, in the Parish Church." Replied Bill.

"Oh er, it mus' be eighteen yers now, since we wed en that little Church." Said Daisy, smiling at the memory of the happiest day of her life. Thomas got up from his seat and walked to the door.

"I'm going out for a while Mom, be out with Rob, so will be all afternoon. Will see you later for Dinner." Said Thomas as he walked out of the Kitchen door.

"OK Thomas, we'll see you later and mind it's not too late." Replied Bill, just as they heard the front door close.

"Well, at least he could have spent some time here, seeing as we have guests?" Said Dasy. Gruffly.

"You know what he's like Dear, all he thinks of is being with Rob when he's home from School and as he said, 'Toffs' don't mix with 'Grunts'."

"Would it be OK to leave the table please?" Asked Keiron.

"O' course ye can, Dear." Said Daisy.

"Want to come up and play some games, Toby?" Asked Keiron.

OK, sounds great." Replied Toby.

"Can I watch please?" Asked Polly.

"Suppose so, OK Polly." Replied Keiron.

"I'll come too." Said Leonie, excitedly.

"S'pose so, if you have to." Replied Keiron.

210

"Thank you, and yes, I do have to." Replied Leonie and stuck her tongue out at Keiron again.

Toby, Polly, Keiron and Leonie all left the Kitchen table and went back upstairs to Keiron's Bedroom. Keiron switched on his TV and PS4 and they waited for it to start up. While waiting, Toby went to his bag and took out a PS4 game, 'Marauders', which he gave to Keiron, who took the disc out of the box and slipped it into the PS4. Keiron and Toby were sitting upon Keiron's bed, as it was more central to the PS4 and Leonie was sitting upon the camp bed with Polly.

"Not very comfortable this, for sitting on." Said Polly Squirming her bottom, trying to get comfortable.

"Use my desk chair, you'll be more comfortable there." Replied Keiron.

"What about me? 'm uncomfortable too." Whined Leonie.

"Go and get your desk chair from your room then." Said Keiron.

So Leonie got up and left the bedroom, returning a few moments later with a pink upholstered Office type desk chair and placed it down next to Polly. At last the game was uploaded and began. Keiron flipped through the load screen and onto the menu screen. He and Toby chose characters to pay as and the game commenced.

The game began slowly, with their characters needing to collect a series of gem stones and artefacts from certain locations around the area of the first screen. This they both achieved quite easily, being rather experienced at this type of game. Then they moved up a few levels as they completed game plays for each screen.

Now things began to get a little more difficult. First a single computer character, called 'A Marauder' kept running into their stashes of gem stones and artefacts and began stealing them. At this point they realised that they supposed to build Fortifications around their gem stones artefacts, in order that they try to prevent the theft of their gems and artefacts. So Toby and Keiron began 'buying' materials and tools from the Menu and began to build walls around their 'Treasures'. As they climbed the levels, more and more 'Marauders' appeared with ever increasingly more powerful weapons, so Toby and Keiron's castles got bigger.

Gradually, as the game progressed, Toby and Keiron moved up some more levels. Meanwhile, the girls become somewhat increasingly bored watching the boys play their game and decided to move to Leonie's Bedroom. They left the boy's Bedroom, who didn't seem to notice their departure, evidently too engrossed in their game. Leonie and Polly walked along the landing corridor to Leonie's Bedroom. The two girls entered and Leonie invited Polly to sit upon her desk chair, while she sat upon her bed.

"Did you know the boys before you started at Toadford, Polly?" Asked Leonie.

"Oh no, I live in Cranleigh, so I had never met them before I arrived at the school. It was quite by accident that we became friends, actually." Replied Polly.

"Do you make many 'accidental friends' then Polly?" Asked Leonie, rather mockingly.

"No of course not, but I only became friends with the boys while trying to find some refuge away from my Roommate, Arrabella. If talking were an Olympic sport, Arrabella would certainly win a Gold Medal every time. Well, I retreated from her babbling and knocked upon the door which was opposite to my Dorm Room across the corridor, where I found Toby and Keiron. They welcomed me in when I told them why I required a short term sanctuary and we began to be friends. It was when a Bully from Wombat House, broke my nose with a football, which he kicked straight into my face. Toby and Keiron were so gallant, trying to defend my Honour and Arrabella helped me to the Hospital wing to tend to my nose. This was what really bonded us to become friends." Replied Polly.

"Ooh, I bet that hurt!" Asked Leonie, knowing the answer and squinting a little at the thought of being hit in the face by a football and also to look a little more closely at Polly's nose, which due to the swift thinking of Arrabella, to whisk Polly off to the Sister as quickly as possible and Sister Ruth was able to set her nose properly and save Polly from much permanent disfigurement, in fact upon inspection, Leonie was merely able to discern a small bump upon the bridge of Polly's nose, which was hardly visible at all unless one was looking for it.

"Yes, it hurt very much, but because of Arrabella's quick thinking and Sister Ruth's skill at setting my nose, thankfully there is hardly a trace of the injury." Replied Polly.

Polly knew however, that she had checked the mirror as often as she could for the first few weeks after the break of her nose, just to be sure that it would heal properly and not leave her looking like a freak. Every so often, Polly still catches herself looking into a mirror, just to make sure.

"I think you're nice, Polly, would you be my friend too?" Asked Leonie, looking hopefully at Polly with her wide blue eyes, pleading.

"Yes, I think I could accommodate you with the others," replied Polly, smiling, "It would be nice to have a female friend who I can visit when not at Toadford."

"Oh goody! That's settled then, how wonderful! I'm so glad that you agreed. It will be fun to be friends. I start at Toadford next year too. It will be good to know that when I arrive there, I will already have a friend there." Said Leonie with a beaming smile from ear to ear.

"Oh that's nice to hear that you will be joining us next year as you may be able to help me civilise Keiron from his primeval life style." Replied Polly.

The two girls continued to chat and Leonie put on one of her CD's, inevitably it was of course a Boy Band CD. Meanwhile back in Keiron's bedroom, Toby and Keiron were becoming a little exhausted with the PS4 game and shut it down to take a break. Toby looked in his Homework notes and began to bring out the books and his memory stick in order that he would be able to make a start upon the list which his Lessons had given to him.

"Oh, you gonna do some Homework then Toby?" Asked Keiron.

"Yeah, thought that I'd make a start before being tempted to start playing upon the PS4 again." Replied Toby.

"I'll have another game if you don't mind, if you wish to use my Lap-top to do your Homework with feel free mate." Said Keiron.

"If I make a start on some of the stuff, then maybe you can make a start on yours tomorrow or sometime, you could use my notes to help you along a bit, as long as you don't make your answers exactly like mine, the Masters won't think you were copying me." Said Toby.

"Yeah, I'll put my own style to mine, just in case. Well, I wouldn't be copying as such would I, just using your notes to help me put my work together, after all, how do the Masters know whether I had looked up the same sources as you and made similar notes" Said Keiron.

"You wouldn't be copying, as you would be writing your own work down slightly different to mine, just using my notes to help you would save you some time to complete the work," Said Toby.

"Right OK, you get going on the notes and I'll see what you have when you've completed then and written out your work from them." Said Keiron, as he started up the game again and selected solo player and continued with his saved progress.

Toby got to work, he turned on the Lap-top and went into the web explorer to find the sites that he was looking for to get the information he needed for his notes. Toby worked at this for a couple of hours, while so he joined Toby at the Lap-top. Some of the notes which Toby had completed were upon pages which were stacked next to the Lap-top, so Keiron took out a pad and a pen, then began to copy down the notes, making some changes in the words which Toby had written to make his notes appear different to Toby's. As Toby wrote down new fresh notes, Keiron used his pages to help him which Toby had already written, to record his own notes. By the time Toby had finished taking notes for all the subjects of his Homework, Keiron was almost up to where Toby had stopped taking notes and shut down the Lap-top.

"Now we have the notes, we can both work upon our Homework separately. That should please them when we get back to Toadford in the new year." Said Toby, finishing the last page of notes.

"Yeah thanks to your idea, I might actually get the Homework finished and produce some better work and get better grades." Replied Keiron as he worked through Toby's remaining pile of notes.

Eventually, Keiron finished the last page of his notes and returned the original papers to Toby. Now they were able to work upon the task set out by each subject and accurately as possible, hand in top rate Homework at their leisure throughout the rest of the week of their Christmas and New Year Holiday.

In Leonie's Bedroom, she had decided to lay back upon her bed listening to her Boy Band CD's and reading some girls 'romantic' magazines and some comics, while Polly had been sat at Leonie's desk, borrowing her Lap-top and also, like the boys, working upon her Homework notes. She steadily ran through the list to take notes upon all the subjects before starting work upon the finished articles. Just as Toby had done, only, unlike Toby, Polly didn't have Leonie 'copying out' her notes, for as Leonie didn't start at Toadford for another nine Months, she had no Homework to work upon. After completing their Homework notes, Toby and Keiron left the Bedroom and Keiron knocked upon Leonie's Bedroom door and called through;

"Are you two ready for Dinner? We're just upon our way down to get ours." Said Keiron.

"OK Muddles, on our way!" Called Leonine back through the door.

Keiron and Toby then walked onto the landing and went down stairs. They then walked to the door to the right of the hallway, facing the Kitchen at the end of the hallway next to the Kitchen door. Keiron opened the door and walked into the room, followed by Toby. Inside it had a beamed ceiling with white washed in-between each beam. The walls were papered with flock wallpaper similar to that upon the upper parts of the walls in the hallway. There was a single light at the centre of the room, which was an electric chandelier. Around the room were a number of glass fronted display cabinets, some with collectables in Porcelain and other ornaments and some with crockery and accessories within them. At the centre of the room was a large table, which Bill had put up an extra leaf to. Around the table was seven seats, the six seats which were associated with the table and one from the Kitchen table set. The table was set for seven people, with knives and forks placed next to place mats which depicted colourful flowers upon them and also there were coasters next to the place mats for the diners to put their drinks upon during dinner.

Toby, Keiron Leonie and Polly stood looking at the table and looking out of the window at the centre of the rear wall, which opened to allow entry to the conservatory beyond. In the Conservatory was some cane-work furniture, a sofa and some chairs and a coffee table with some trees in pots, only small trees with oranges and Lemons upon them either side of the doors which led out onto decking and into the back garden. Daisy and Bill both entered the room having exited the Kitchen carrying plates of food, which they put down upon the table.

They went back to the Kitchen twice, to bring out bowls of vegetables and potatoes. For the plates there were mats to put them upon and coasters for every one's drinks.

There was a bottle of wine for Bill and Daisy, for each of them to take a glass from and bottles of cola and glasses for the children. The food was dished out and the wine and Cola poured. As at Lunch time, Bill sat at the head of the table with Daisy opposite and along the left side of the table sat Thomas, Keiron and Leonie; then along the right side of the table sat Toby, and Polly.

Before the meal began, Bill called ever one to Pray and said 'Grace', once this was done, the meal began. Bill carved the meat, Pork for himself and Daisy, Beef for Thomas, Leonie and Polly, for Keiron and Toby, a couple of slices of each. Meanwhile, Daisy dished out the vegetables and poured the drinks, then everyone began to eat.

"Lovely Meal Mother." Said Thomas.

"Yes Mom, fankths for the meal." Spluttered Keiron through his customary mouth full of food. Daisy scowled at him and said;

"You're welcome."

"Manners Muddles." Chirped Leonie.

"Thut up Nipper." Spluttered Keiron through his mouthful of food.

"I take it he shovels it in at School then does he?" Asked Bill to Toby.

"A little," Replied Toby.

"Ooh, a little!" Exclaimed Polly, "he's like a human JCB."

"Couldn't put it better myself," Laughed Bill, they all joined in the laugh, all that is except Keiron, who didn't find it remotely funny.

"If you're starting at Toadford next September, Leonie, where do you currently go to School?" Asked Polly, trying to ignore Keiron shovelling in another mouthful of food.

"I go to St. Margaret's Middle School in Cranleigh, it's an all girl's School, so we don't have any smelly boys around to ruin it." Replied Leonie and shot her tongue out at Keiron. Being born only a tear apart, Keiron and Leonie had very much grown up together, they had quickly become rivals in most everything. This was the banter between the two of them.

"I finish at St. Margaret's in July then after the Summer Holidays, I join you at Toadford in September." Beamed Leonie.

"You probably won't see much of us, as being the second years then, we'll have different classes and have a different Common Room." Said Toby.

"But there will be days off. Like Weekends, won't there? We could get together then couldn't we?" Asked Leonie pleadingly.

"If we don't have too much Homework or anything, I suppose there would be time that we could meet up to spend some time together." Said Polly.

"Not if I can help it!" Muttered Keiron behind his hand, to which he received one of Polly's disapproving looks and another bout of sticking out tongue from Leonie.

"Now now, young lady, its rude to stick your tongue out at people, we've told you before." Said Daisy, sternly.

"He deserves it." Replied Leonie in a low mumble, looking sheepishly at her Mother and then giving Keiron a look that Polly would be proud of.

After they had finished the meal and desert, they excused themselves from the table and went in through the door to the left of stairs. This was the Living Room, where they found the walls papered with pale blue with a lower half of white. Around the room were more display cabinets with more ornaments in them. There were also some book shelves with a number of books upon them. There was a window, which looked out upon the front garden and entrance gate to the house. The window was flanked upon either side by deep blue curtains. Upon the wall opposite to where the door was, there was a large forty inch TV held onto the wall by a bracket.

In front of this were a pair of three seater sofas and a couple of armchairs, which were all pale blue. The carpet, which the furniture was stood upon, was a natural beige colour and between the seats and the wall, there stood a coffee table which had a magazine rack next to it. Leonie walked forwards and jumped into an arm chair, while Keiron indicated to Toby and Polly to join him sitting upon the sofa upon the right next to Leonie's arm Chair. Keiron stretched out and picked up the TV Remote Control and then switched on the TV. He pressed the button for 'Menu' and they looked down the list for something to watch, which they all agreed upon!

"Oh look there, Channel 104, they've got show jumping from Wembley Arena, put that on." Said Leonie.

"Bor-ing." Replied Keiron, running down through the Channel play lists.

"Oh Look, 'James Bond' on Channel 114." Said Toby, "Is it the one where he falls in love with a girl, saves her from the baddie and wants to marry her, but she dies?" Asked Toby.

"I think that you just described every 'James Bond' film ever made, Toby." Said Polly, rolling her eyes.

There was a sudden noise emanating from the direction of the TV, ,which indicated that Keiron had chosen to press the appropriate button and put on the film. It had not long started and was still in the titles, "You'll probably like it Leonie, all that hot Spy action and Romance, just your cup of tea." Said Keiron.

"Preferred the Show Jumping." Replied Leonie, rather crest fallen and folded her arms and sunk further into the arm chair . The three friends sat upon the sofa and watched the film while Leonie sulked a little in her arm chair. Polly sat and relaxed, allowing her head to fall onto Toby's shoulder. Toby just sat there and left Polly to rest her head and watched the film.

"Ooo that was a bit nasty!" Exclaimed Polly a little way into the film at a scene which was particularly frantic and bangy, with guns and car chases.

"Great film." Replied Keiron, glancing at Leonie with a small grin, who in turn spat out her tongue at him and turned her face away. They continued to watch and Polly continued to rest her head upon Toby's shoulder. About twenty minutes into the film, Bill and Daisy walked into the Living Room and sat upon the sofa to the left of where Toby, Keiron and Polly were seated. They said hello and started to watch the film, Daisy noticed Leonie sitting in the arm chair sulking and almost forcing herself to watch the film upon the TV.

"I take it there was horses upon the other channels and Keiron got to the remote control first?" Asked Daisy.

"Stupid Muddles!" Snorted Leonie, glaring at Keiron.

"It was a majority decision to watch the film." Said Keiron.

Thomas then came in and joined them, sitting in the other arm chair next to his Parent's sofa.

"There, that's the majority." Said Keiron.

"What Majority? Asked Leonie, snapping the words out at Keiron.

"Well, I want to watch 'James Bond', Toby does, I know Dad would want this film and of course, Thomas would want it , so even if all the females showed an objection, it would still be four against three, a majority." Replied Keiron Smugly.

What did you and Rob get up to?" Asked Bill.

"Just watching DVD's at his house and working upon our Homework assignments." Replied Thomas, not looking up from the TV screen.

"Well, if you all get the Homework's finished by tomorrow, that will give you the rest of the week to yourselves until New Year's Eve." Said Daisy.

"Yeah, that's the plan we thought of Mon." Said Keiron.

"What will you do next then?" Asked Bill.

"I thought I'd show Toby and Polly around the village and I thought I'd show them roundabouts, let them see the place." Said Keiron.

"Good idea." Agreed Bill, "But be careful of the old Iron mine upon Cragmoor Common, if you're going that way." Said Bill.

217

"Yeah will do Dad." Replied Keiron.

"I'll come too!" Chirped Leonine.

"If you have to!" Replied Keiron.

"Yeah, that will give Polly a bit of female company, won't it." Said Toby.

"Yes, that would be nice." Agreed Polly.

"Well if you're planning to take your Sister with you Keiron, keep an eye upon her and make sure that she's safe at all times for me will you please." Said Daisy.

"OK Mom will do." Replied Keiron with a sigh, "as long as she doesn't keep winging all the time."

"I don't winge." Came a muffled answer from the direction of Leonie's chair. She had turned to watch the film, reluctantly, with her head back in the arm chair and her face against the chair back facing the TV. There was a tinkling of teenage music and Thomas' mobile went to his ear.

"Yup, uh yeah, uh yeah, OK, uh yeah, see you outside the Church then Bro'." He said into the Mobile and then pressed the call end button and replaced his mobile into his trouser pocket.

"Was that Rob?" Asked Daisy.

"Yup." Came the reply.

"Are you meeting him tomorrow?"

"Yup."

This was the usual conversation with Thomas. All the while he was responding to Daisy, his eyes never left the TV and the film. Thomas was the Muddley's first born. He was in the third year at Toadford, two years above Keiron, Toby and Polly. Here were the visible scenes of the 'Traditions' of Toadford School, as Thomas had demonstrated that 'Toffs' or Third Years have little or no time for grunts, so by the time that Leonine arrived in September with the new batch of 'Grunts', Thomas, being a 'Cardinal' or Fourth Year by then would by tradition, treat the 'Grunts' as their slaves or simply have nothing to do with them at all. At this time, however, Toby, Keiron and Polly would only have become 'Weeners' or Second Years, so they would still be able to help 'Grunts' get around the School etc. Once Thomas will have reached the 'Seniors' the following year, they simply don't take much notice of anyone, as their time is taken up with preparing for Exams and preparing to leave Toadford School. Thomas was practicing for the September term, where he would ignore his brother and Sister at School, unless he had been made a prefect, and then he would delight in giving them orders! Eventually the film finished and Keiron suggested that they go up to his bedroom and Leonine suggested the same to Polly.

"Well, thank you for the meal and for letting us stay" Said Polly to Daisy and Bill as they stood to leave the room, "good night."

"Yes, thank you from me also and goodnight." Added Toby.

"That's alright M'Dears, youm welcome any time. Jus' let us know when 'ee'll be commin'." Said Daisy.

"Goodnight Mom." Said Leonie, kissing Daisy upon her right cheek.

"Yeah, er g'nite' Mom." Said Keiron and Daisy pointed to her cheek, reluctantly Keiron kissed it too.

"G'night te you'm all, 'ave a pleasant sleep an' see all o' 'ee en the Mornin'." Said Daisy.

"Yeah, goodnight all, see you in the Morning." Added Bill.

When they got up to the Bedrooms, Keiron led Toby into his room and then went into his en-suite Bathroom. He washed and changed, then came out into the Bedroom dressed in his checked pyjamas and blue dressing gown, then placed his clothes into a blue basket by the door. Toby then went into the en-suite and changed into his pyjamas, Frackston City ones and a Frackston City dressing gown.

"Nice threads." Said Keiron, admiring Toby's night ware.

"Dad got them for me from the Stadium Shop." Replied Toby.

"Toby sat at the desk and borrowed Keiron's Lap-top and so began writing his assignments for his homework. Meanwhile Keiron lay back upon his bed and began watching TV with the volume turned down, so as not to disturb Toby too much.

In Leonie's bedroom, much the same rituals had taken place, with Leonie and Polly both now seated at the desk while Leonie watched Polly working upon the Lap-top and starting her homework assignments in their night dresses and dressing gowns. Before long, Polly had completed three of the five assignments they had, working from their notes, while Toby had completed only two. Then it was time for them to go to bed. Leonie took off her dressing gown to reveal a night dress which had a picture of a Boy Band upon it and Polly revealed a cartoon Rabbit upon hers. The two girls got into their respective beds;

"Goodnight Polly." Said Leonie.

"Goodnight Leonie, see you in the morning." Replied Polly, and Leonie turned off the bed side lamp, plunging her Bedroom into darkness. In the other bedroom;

"G'night Keiron." Said Toby.

"Night Mate," Replied Keiron and turned his bedside lamp off and then his bedroom too was in darkness also. So ended their first night at Keiron's house.

Chapter Twenty Five – Investigating the Village

Next Morning, Toby was awake early at seven thirty. He had showered and had dressed in a pale blue T Shirt and a pair of jeans. He had sat down at Keiron's desk, after taking out his Homework notes from his Ruc-Sac and continued to work upon his Homework assignments. Meanwhile, the lump of bundled bed clothes upon his Keiron's bed continued to snore.

At this time in Leonie's Bedroom, Polly was also awake and had showered in Leonie's en-suite Bathroom and dressed in lilac T Shirt depicting a Teddy bear and a pair of Jeans. Polly had been working upon her homework assignments. By ten o'clock, Polly and Toby had both almost completed their homework assignments, when the first stirrings began, then they had finished and their assignments were completed. Eventually, Keiron and Leonie had emerged and arisen, dressed in a lilac T Shirt and jeans. It was now time for the four of them to go down stairs and get their Breakfasts. They entered the Kitchen where Bill and Thomas were already seated at the table eating their own Breakfast, a mixed grill each.

"Good Mornin' M'Dears," said Daisy, "an' what can I get ye fer yer Breakfast?"

"Good morning, would it be alright for me to have a bowl of cereal please Daisy?" Asked Polly as Daisy was taking more eggs and Bacon from the refrigerator.

"Of course M'Dear." Replied Daisy and poured out some cereal into a bowl and placed it in front of Polly.

"Good morning, may I have a fried breakfast please Daisy?" Asked Toby.

"O' course M'Dear." Replied daisy as she cracked and egg into the frying pan upon the cooker.

"Fry up from too please Mom…….. oh yeah, er ….. good mornin'." Said Keiron grinning.

"On its way Dear." Replied Daisy, already having cracked another three eggs into the frying pan. Daisy the flipped them and left them for a few moments before lifting then out of the pan and placing then upon the plates at the side of the cooker. She then replaced the eggs with two rasher of Bacon.

"Crisp for you Dear?" Asked Daisy.

"Yes please, Daisy." Replied Toby.

Daisy didn't need to ask Keiron, as she was used to cooking him a fry up Breakfast and knew that he preferred crispy Bacon. When the bacon was ready,

Daisy transferred this onto the waiting plates and put two pieces of bread into the pan to make fried bread.

May I have toast with mine, please Daisy?" Asked Toby.

"Yes o'course M'Dear." Replied Daisy as she placed two slices of bread into the electric toaster next to the cooker. Soon Keiron and Toby had their Breakfasts in front of them and had been joined by Daisy with a bowl of cereal. Leonie had passed a jug of milk to Polly, after pouring some upon her cereal. Polly then poured some milk upon cereal and the passed the jug onto Daisy.

"Are you enjoying yourselves at Toadford?" Asked Daisy.

"Oh yes, apart from a few teething problems, I think we've generally settled in quite well so far." Replied Polly with a sweet smile.

"How's our Keiron getting along then" Asked Bill.

"I think we're getting along OK, being Roommates and we're on most of the sports teams together, I think we are getting along fairly well." Replied Toby.

"Yeah it's been good this season, playing Football and Cricket for our House. We're in the House Cup Finals against Wombat." Replied Keiron.

"Oh so glad you're getting along so well Son and amazing to think that you're in the House finals." Said Bill.

"Have ye lived en Cranleigh long, Polly?" Asked Daisy.

"I was born in Cranleigh, at the Local Hospital. "Replied Polly.

"And were you born at Pegasus House, I take it, like most of the Morby's before you?" Asked Bill.

"Yes, I was born at the House, as was My Father and Grandfather." Replied Toby.

"So do you like living at such an old house, Toby, must be difficult to remember your way around?" Asked Daisy.

"Oh not really," Said Toby, "Mom, Dad and me, we live in the right hand ride of the house, like our own apartment, sort of thing, and the left hand side of the house is where my Grandfather lives.

Because he has to go away on business frequently, he stays in his side of the house and leaves us to the other."

"Don't 'ee ever come te ye then?" Asked Daisy.

"Oh yes, frequently, when he isn't away on Business, he usually has his meals with us and sometimes sits with us in the Sitting Room." Replied Toby.

"So Simon has the whole East Wing to himself?" Asked Bill.

"Well yes, but it is much smaller than our side of the house, I think the side which my Grandfather lives is Medieval and centuries old; I think our side was added much later." Said Toby.

"Must be cold in the winter, what with all the wind and weather blowing in off the Moor? It is here but as our walls are Cobb, it is much warmer here than many of the houses in the village. This used to be stables and a Tithe Barn, to the big house along the road, you would have passed it on your way into our street, it's called Topley House. Back along Topley House was the house of the Birbright family, had lived there for a few hundred years, like your family at Pegasus House, Toby. The Birbrights sold up during the forties when the last John Birbright out lived his sons, William and Michael, who were killed serving in Belgium during World War Two. He felt that with his sons gone, he had no need for a big house for their families to grow up in, as they would not be producing and family or heirs. The house is now a Hotel and the stables and Tithe barn were converted to houses; and we got the Tithe barn." Said Bill.

"Pegasus House has central heating in our side, so we don't have to worry about that. I don't know about Grandfather's side as I've never been in his part of the house." Replied Toby.

"You've never been in his past of the house then?" Bill asked Toby.

"Oh no, the door to his part of the house is always locked. I don't know if Dad has ever been in there, but I haven't seen him go in to there or come out." Replied Toby.

"You never know Toby, maybe he'll show you some time." Said Bill.

"Never know, maybe some time." Replied Toby.

But, of course, Toby had never seen the side of the House where Simon lives, as Simon had kept it quiet for his whole life so far. Rachel also had never seen into Simon's side of the house, even when she offered to clean for him, Simon told her he preferred to clean for himself. Since their marriage, Simon had treated the house as two defined halves, because this then shut out this World from his and ensured that no one knew about the Portal which lay beyond his door way in the hallway, which Simon locks with Alexandrian Magic. Simon uses a sealing spell upon the door as it is the only way to make the door way secure from both his world and ours.

Toby was unaware, at this time, that beyond that door in the hallway was a Portal of energy which transports anyone passing through it to a place which lies beyond our time and space which is caught up in a time bubble, where the era of this World was behind ours, almost medieval compared to our World and was inhabited by all manner of Evil and magical creatures, Elfs, Wizards and the Evil Lord, The Marquis.

The little group of four – Polly, Toby, Keiron and Leonie, all got up from their breakfasts after excusing themselves and walked out of the Kitchen into the hallway. They took down their coats from the rack against the wall next to the front door, Toby in his black jacket; Keiron in his blue 'Frackston City Jacket; Polly in her purple coat, after having recovered her 'Cargal' House scarf from the pocket and Leonie in her pale blue anorak. Keiron opened the front door, as Daisy walked out of the Kitchen into the hallway;

"Hello M'Dears, are we off to somewhere nice" Asked Daisy.

"Just thought that we'd go out and I'd show them around the village." Said Keiron.

"And I'm showing Polly around and keeping her company." Said Leonie.

"Well just remember, keep an eye upon your little Sister, OK." Sid Daisy.

"Will do Mom ." Replied Keiron.

With that done, Keiron showed them out of the door and out along the garden path. Keiron led them out along Mews Lane, which was where the his house was and past the 'Big House', before turning right to lead up to the Main Street.

"That's the Topley House Hotel, just there," Keiron pointed out to the others as they passed it before turning up to go to the main road of the village; "That's the 'Big House' that Dad told you about during Breakfast."

When they reached the Main Street, they turned to the left and walked along.

"Over there is the Police Station," Said Keiron, pointing across the road, "and here is the Post Office." He added pointing to the Post Office as they walked past it upon their side of the road.

They were now able to see in front of them, the curve of the Village Square as it went around in an oval with a tall towered Church in stone standing at the centre of the oval of which went around the Church with it like a kind of Island in the centre of the bustling shopping street. The four of them walked along the pavement and rounded a shoulder of the Village Square, where there was a road off to the left full of houses. They crossed over the road and passed the covered Market.

"That's the covered Market, they have some good stuff in there upon the stalls some times." Said Keiron, pointing it out as they walked around the Square. There were more small side streets leading off with more cottages. After passing some more small shops, they rounded the end of the Village Square. Walking along the other side, they found some more houses. After they had passed two side turnings which were leading off from the Square to their left, Keiron pointed out the Village Hall. They walked on along the Square and past the Butcher's shop, Mr Clancy and then the baker's shop, Mr Brown. Toby walked on slightly and then realised that Keiron had stopped. They looked around and saw that he was standing outside the Baker's window.

"Lardy Cake and cream buns!" he muttered.

"Always thinking of your stomach aren't you Muddles?" Replied Toby, grinning.

"I thought that we were having a guided tour of your village, Keiron, not your dietary needs." Added Polly.

"Sorry guys, got distracted." Said Keiron, apologetically, as he trotted to catch them up.

"Best pasties around in there." Keiron added.

"We get our pasties from Mr Franks, our Baker in Little Farthingworth, he makes great cakes too." Said Toby.

"We have a Supermarket in Cranleigh, where Mom buys all our food. Well most of it anyway, she gets the odd few things from the other shops in town." Said Polly.

"Mom likes a fresh loaf every day, so she buys them from Mr Brown's, as she can't get to town every day." Replied Keiron.

"Since Mom has been in Hospital, Dad has been doing the shopping, easy for him, as with me at Toadford, he only has to buy food for himself and my Grandfather. Most of the time, Grandfather is away on Business, so Dad just needs to feed himself. Of course, that has been different since I've been home from Toadford for Christmas, but now I'm here and will be going onto School from here when we return, then Dad doesn't need to think of feeding me anymore till I get home at Half Term. Hopefully, Mom will be back home from Hospital by then, so Dad will have the proper shopping to get." Said Toby.

"Oh I hope that your Mom is able to go home soon Toby." Said Polly with a smile.

"Yeah Mate, hope she's OK soon." Added Keiron.

"Thanks Guys." Replied Toby, and smiled.

"They walked up to the shoulder of the Square upon the west side and passed the Police Station. There they saw a notice which was asking whether any persons had information about a series of animal deaths out upon the Moor at Cragmoor Common.

"Hey, my Dad works out that way, they're sorting the Deer at the moment, while Dad is away on Compassionate Leave. I wonder whether any of the Guys he works with know anything?" Said Toby.

"You could call him, ask, maybe they have seen something." Said Keiron.

"I should think if they had, they would have informed the Police already." Said Polly.

"Yeah, maybe, but worth the excuse to call him, anyway." Replied Toby as he took his Mobile phone out of his pocket and dialled his Father's Mobile number. It rang and Carl answered.

"Hi Toby, got bored already have you? Want to come home?" Asked Carl as he chuckled.

"No nothing like that Dad. We're looking at a Police notice here, asking for any information about animal killings up upon Cragmoor, where you work, wondered whether the guys up there have heard or seen anything?" Said Toby

"No, I haven't heard anything from them while I've been on leave. But I go back to work in the New Year, so I can find out then; unless there's anything in the local newspaper. I'll have a look later for you. While you're on the line, I'm going on a trip into Barnstaple up north, during the week; Topley is on the way, would you Guys like a trip up for the day? It will be on Tuesday, going up for the Market and a look around the Town." Said Carl.

"Hey Guys, fancy a trip up to Barnstaple for the day on Wednesday?" Asked Toby, holding his hand across the Mobile.

"Why not, might be fun to have a look around, I haven't been there before." Replied Keiron.

"I've been a few times with my Father, I could show you around when we get there." Replied Polly, enthusiastically.

"Oh goody, a day out, YAAAY!" Squealed Leonie.

"Yeah Dad, the verdict is unanimously YES! Thanks, we'd love to go for a day out, may be spot something out upon the Moor upon the way through?" Said Toby, now speaking into his Mobile again.

"OK Toby, see you all on Tuesday, I'll be there about nine o'clock to pick you up, that should get there by ten." Replied Carl.

"OK Dad, see you on Wednesday." Replied Toby and ended his call.

"Oh yeah, a day trip out for our little group, pity 'Bella's not here." Said Keiron.

"Why do you fancy her?" Asked Toby, grinning.

"No....... what I meant was, she would complete the group if she were here; 'The Magnificent Grunts'." Said Keiron.

"But I'm not a Grunt!" Said Leonie with a frown which brought the freckles upon her forehead together like a big bruise.

"Not until next year, so you can be an 'Honorary Grunt' then." Replied Toby.

"I'M NOT A GRUNT!" Snapped Leonie, making a furrow in her ginger bruise of freckles.

"Its Tradition Leonie, we can't say why just yet, but we don't mean it as an insult. We are the 'Magnificent Grunts', it's just the name of our group, so you're not a full member yet, see?" Said Polly, trying to explain to Leonine without telling her the true reason for them being 'Grunts' and breaking a Toadford tradition.

"No Leonie, we don't mean it personally, of course you're not a 'little Grunt' really, but just for the purposes of the group." Said Toby, hoping that would stop Leonine from frowning.

"When I get to Toadford next year, I'll be a proper 'Grunt', won't I, and not just an Honorary one then?" Said Leonie, relaxing her frown just a little.

"Yes, That's right." Replied Polly, giving the boys a glance in relief that they had not broken the Traditions, "you will truly be a 'Grunt' then."

This put a smile back upon Leonie's face and the 'bruise' unfolded once again into a wide gathering of freckles across her forehead.

It's getting on for Lunch time, ,how about we head back for Lunch?" Asked Keiron, as his stomach had started to rumble due to looking into the baker's window.

"OK." Replied the other three altogether, their stomachs began to rumble at the mention of Lunch.

They walked out of the Village Square and back along Lower Main Street. Then they turned right into Manor Drive. They walked towards what they were able to see was a large Mansion type building with many windows across the front of two floors above the ground floor, above a columned portico porch in the centre of the frontage with steps leading up from the car park In front of the building. They then reached the street corner and turned into Mews Lane. They walked along the Cul-de sac, which was lined with a couple of ornamental Cherry trees either side of the road and passed the cottages upon either side of the road which were converted stables, these were number one mews Cottages and number two Mews Cottages. They walked up to Tithe Barn Cottage, which was a converted barn, where Keiron and Leonie called home. They went inside after Keiron had opened the door and walked along the hallway into the Kitchen. Daisy was there, as always at meal times, preparing Lunches.

"Hi Mom, no Dad or Thomas around?" Asked Keiron, sitting down at the table, almost falling off his chair and was joined by Toby, Polly and Leonie.

"No, M'Dear, Dad's gone a work, an' tom, 'ee's out wi' Rob, I think. They went a Cranleigh with Rob's older brother, Justin, in his car." Replied Daisy. She went to the Bread Bin upon the work surface, near to the Toaster.

"Would 'ee like some Sandwiches fer yer Lunches then, M'Dears?" Asked Daisy.

"Oh yes please." Said the four at the same time.

"Now then, let me see, three ham and a cheese wasn't it, I think that's right?" Asked Daisy.

"Yes, ham for me please Daisy, thank you." Replied Polly.

"And for me Mom.. er...please, thanks." Added Keiron.

"And mine's the third ham, please Mom, thanks." Chirped Leonie.

"Yes, Daisy thanks, mine is the Cheese Sandwich." Replied Toby.

So Daisy busied herself for a few minutes making the sandwiches and them over to the table, along with a cup of tea for Polly, a mug of Coffee each for Keiron and Toby and a glass of Cola for Leonie. Then Daisy joined them with her own plate of Sandwiches and a mug of Coffee.

"Where does Mr Muggard work?" Asked Polly.

"He's a Lawyer, M'Dear, works at Howard and Pole in Cranleigh." Replied Daisy.

"Oh yes, they have a large Office Building in the High Street in Cranleigh, don't they? I think I've seen it when I've been walking down the High Street." Said Polly.

"Yes, he's had to go into work this morning to collect some paper's to work upon for a case he's running." Said Daisy.

"Must be hard work being a Lawyer, I mean all the paperwork, the Court cases and what if you are asked to represent someone who you know is Guilty and they want to plead Not Guilty?" Asked Toby.

"Dad is always bringing home paperwork and disappearing into his 'Home Office', for hours to work upon them." Said Leonie.

Well Dad 'as te do that, Leonie, as the paperwork is fer Cases which are confidential and we are not supposed to know 'bout them an' their details." Replied Daisy.

"Well I hope he has time for us over the New Year, he has a family as well as a job." Said Leonie.

"He tries te make time fer us M'Dear, when he can, but his work is important an' does take up a lot o' his time." Daisy.

"He will OK for New Year's Eve wont he Mom , this going to the Office for some paperwork isn't gonna change any of that, is it?" Asked Keiron.

"No, Dad will be OK fer New Year's Eve. He's jus' workin' frum 'ome fer the next week or so, so that he can be here fer New Year's Eve and also not 'ave te go inte work 'til the new Year. He 'as an important Case goin' on, so he wanted te do somethin' towards it during his Christmas Break." Said Daisy.

"My Grandfather is like that, he spends a lot of time in his study in his side of the house or away on business. He is the Twinning Officer for the Parish Council, so he is often away on Council Business with the Twinning Committee. We are Twinned with a Village in France called 'Marianne' in Normandy, so Granddad goes over there quite a lot with the Twinning Committee. Being Chairman of the Parish Council, he also spends time in his study with Parish Council business." Said Toby.

"Yes, Bill is the same; he's on the Parish Council, so some o' his time is spent on Council Business in his Office." Replied Daisy.

Just then, the door opened and Thomas walked in followed by a tall thin boy with long straight brown hair which did not seem to have a parting to reveal his face, all but his nose protruding from it, and brown eyes were they visible. He was wearing similar clothes to Thomas, a T Shirt which depicted some rock Band or other's logo and event dates of same gigs for their tour, with a pair of jeans and a rather worn Denim jacket. He gave a rather weak kind of wave towards the Kitchen and Thomas made a move for the stairs, with Rob close behind.

"Did 'ee wan' some Lunch M'Dears?" Called Daisy from the Kitchen table.

"Ham Sandwiches, two pleas, with Colas, we'll be up in my Bedroom." Grunted Thomas as he climbed the stairs and went into his bedroom followed by Rob. The door closed and then the steady thump, thump, thump of the bass from the Rock beat which came from upstairs.

"Oh well, that's them occupied for a few hours, 'til Dinner time. Mind you, that doesn't mean that they won't go out again before Dinner." Said Keiron.

Daisy had made two rounds of Ham Sandwiches which were upon plates and there were also two glasses of Cola upon a the tray which she was carrying and she walked out of the Kitchen.

"Better take these up for them." Said Daisy, as she walked up the stairs and disappeared. Up upon the landing outside Thomas' Bedroom, Daisy held the tray in one hand and knocked upon the Bedroom door. A pair of hands appeared when the door was opened and they took the tray from Daisy. They retreated back into the Bedroom and then the door closed.

"Thanks." Daisy heard from behind the door. Once her hearing had stopped ringing due to the sudden onslaught of the music from the Bedroom when the door had been opened, Daisy then walked back down stairs and returned to the Kitchen to sit back down upon her chair at the table so that she was able to resume eating her Lunch.

"Well, that's them two Catered for, fer a foo hours at least, I 'opes." Said Daisy as she munched away at a Ham Sandwich. The group finished their Lunches and thanked Daisy for her trouble, then they left the Kitchen.

"How about we do a bit of exploring then this afternoon?" Said Keiron, looking at the other's expectantly.

"Sounds like a good idea." Replied Toby.

"Depends what you mean by 'exploring', doesn't it?" Asked Polly.

"Well, I've shown you the village inside the centre, so how about I show you some more of the village outside the centre?" Said Keiron.

"Well, yes, I think it does sound like a good idea," Said Polly, shrugging her shoulders, "It would be nice to see some more of where you live, so different than my town."

"Ooo an Adventure, goody!!" Enthused Leonie.

"It may be best if you wore a different coat Polly, just in case you get this nice purple one dirty." Said Keiron.

"I've got a jacket which I can wear." Said Polly and she then ran upstairs to Leonie's bedroom, followed by Leonie.

"I've got a jacket too." Said Leonie and got a pale blue jacket out of her wardrobe. Polly went to her bag and pulled out a pale lilac jacket and put it on.

"Nice jacket, Polly." Said Leonie, who's blonde hair showed up more with her wearing the pale blue jacket.

"Yes it is." Replied Polly, "One of my favourites. Yours is nice too."

""Thanks, I got it for my Birthday." Replied Leonie, "Which is 25 June, by the way."

"Oh, right, OK, I'll remember that." Said Polly, Smiling, she had picked up upon Leonie's hint.

"Mine is 30 April." Said Polly, and Leonie took a small book out of a drawer and wrote under 'P', 'Polly Muggard, 30 April Birthday'.

"What's your address, Polly?" Asked Leonie, holding the pen ready to write it down in her little book.

"35 Toll Street, Cranleigh, EX28 4QP." Replied Polly, "Oh and my E Mail Addy is pmuggard@yahoo.co.uk."

"Oh thanks." Smiled Leonie as she wrote this information down in her book. "littlemiss21@yahoo.co.uk is my Addy, and you know my address, it's the same as Keiron's.

"Thanks. "Said Polly and produced her own little book and wrote down what Leonie had told her. The two girls then left the Bedroom and joined the boys back downstairs.

"We ready now then, OK? Off we go." Said Keiron and led the way out of the front door.

"Where to now then, Keiron?" Asked Toby as they all walked out of the garden gate onto Mews Lane.

"I'll show you the old Quarry up from the village centre." Replied Keiron.

"You know Mom doesn't like us to go up there, Keiron, it's dangerous." Said Leonie, in a whisper.

"Yeah Shrimp, that's when we were kids. I know my way around there now, been up there many a time." Replied Keiron, "and if you think of telling Mom, I'll just tell her you were with us and it was your idea."

"I……." Leonie began to say, but stopped thinking about the consequences of her Mom being told that it was her idea to visit the old Quarry. Keiron just grinned at her, as though he knew exactly what she was thinking. Leonie looped her arm in Polly's arm and smugly answered;

"Doesn't matter, I've got my friend with me, don't bother me." Leonie looked up at Polly and smiled, Polly smiled back.

"Where abouts is it then?" Asked Toby.

"Oh it's along the road out of the village past the square and then left at the cross, rather than right to the main road and it's just though a filed along the lane a short distance away." Replied Keiron.

The four started walking and turned into Manor Drive and walked up to Main Street, and then turned left towards the village centre. They walked into the Square passing the Post Office and the Parish Church and then past the Village Hall around the shoulder of the Square and out onto Upper Main Street. Leading out of the village towards Topley Drive.

"How far is it to this Quarry?" Asked Polly.

"Not far, it's a little way up here then we turn left and it's a short way across a filed." Replied Keiron.

"He means a ruddy long way." Said Leonie.

"Oi, less of the language Leonie." Called Keiron.

"Well you say 'Ruddy' when you're angry or excited." Pointed out Leonie, her frown was back.

"Yeah, but I'm older than you." Retorted Keiron.

"Only by months." Leonie threw back at him accompanied by one of her trademark sticking out of her tongue.

"Still older than you, why Mom has put me in charge of you." Said Keiron.

This time, the tongue was vibrated as Leonie let out a huge 'raspberry' at Keiron.

They reached Topley Cross, where Upper Main Street met Topley Drive and Keiron turned left into Topley Drive. Toby and Polly saw the sign post opposite the lane, with a sign pointing down where they had just came from, which had painted upon its white arrow like sign;

TOPLEY 1 ¾

There were also two other sign which were aligned with each other pointing left and right of the post, which had a sign painted upon an upright sign upon the post, which read;

+TOPLEY CROSS +

To the right of the sign Post, pointing out towards the main road the sign read;

BARNSTAPLE	26
CRANLEIGH	20
CREDITON	20
EXETER	28
GREATER FARTHINGWORTH	18
LITTLE FARTHINGWORTH	10

The sign to the left of the sign post read;

TIVERTON	12

"It's just a couple of hundred yards along and across a field upon this side of the lane." Said Keiron as he led them down the right hand side of the lane until they reached a five bar gate, where the hedge gave way to an entrance to the field behind the hedge. There was a style next to the gate which was attached to a small piece of fencing, also a post which had a green arrow like sign at the top which had been painted to read:

PUBLIC FOOTPATH

Toby noticed that upon the post of the style that there was a 'Yellow Way' badge nailed to it, which confirmed this was a public footpath. Being the son of a Park Ranger, Toby knew all about the 'Yellow Way' marks which pointed out the recognised public footpaths with in the countryside and if they pointed out across a field, that a land owner had no rights to obstruct the entrance to the

231

footpath either end a sit crossed their land, or place a dangerous animal, such as a Bull in the filed which was marked as a 'Yellow Way' footpath.

The four climbed over the Style, Keiron rather fell over the other side as he dismounted it, much to the delight of Leonie, who laughed as he picked himself up. Then Polly went over the style, followed by Leonie and then Toby.

"Gentleman eh, letting the 'Ladies' go first." Giggled Leonie to Toby.

"At least someone has some Manners." Said Polly giving Keiron one of her looks.

"We need to keep to the edge of the field, as that's where the footpath runs, due to the farmer planting up the filed across the middle. You can see the path between the wire fencing at the edge and the length of ribbon between the posts along the edge of the ploughed area. Now, and this means especially you Leonie, please stay to the footpath, if you wander off it, look out for the Quarry edge, the reason why there is wire fencing along this side of the footpath." Said Keiron. He then led them off along the footpath around the field. A small coppice of Ash trees brought them out onto an open piece of the footpath, where it was quite visible that about five feet from the wire fence, which was about waist height, the ground just wasn't there. They stopped a short distance along here and looked out over the wire fence. Before them stretched out was a huge hole in the ground like a giant crater, where a meteorite had landed, although this one was man made. The Quarry fell away below them to a depth of about sixty feet and then it was filled with water. Polly was able to make out some ducks swimming upon the water and some wading birds around the edges of the water.

"Wow!" Exclaimed Polly, "Got to get some of this."

Polly then opened her bag and out came her trusted camera. Polly started clicking away in many directions across the Quarry and down at the ducks.

"OK, how about a group photo?" Suggested Toby enthusiastically.

"Yeah, good idea." Agreed Keiron with equal enthusiasm.

"OK, I will set up my camera now." Said Polly. They looked around and noticed a rock sticking out of the ground which had a rather flattish top to it, which was about waist height. So Polly propped her camera up upon the top of the rock, facing the edge of the quarry, then the four of them stood in front of the fence so that the camera was able to see some of the quarry behind them and the timer began to whir. As the flashing red light went out, with a click the camera shutter sounded.

"Great, our group photo number two!" Said Keiron,

"Yes, but we're missing 'Bella." Said Polly.

At first, Polly had none too keen with 'Bella, she saw her as rather a pain. When the Wombat attack took place at Toadford, 'Bella had thought quickly and managed to whisk Polly away while the two boys created a diversion, so that

232

Polly was able to obtain swift treatment for her nose and avoid a bad setting, after the football had broken it. The swift thinking and action from 'Bella and the Gallantry from the boys had touched Polly, now she flet that they were truly her friends.

"We can get one with all of us, sometime, when 'Bella can be with us." Said Toby.

Polly walked forwards to the rock and picked up her camera. She clicked some buttons upon the back of the camera and the Monitor lit up with the photo of the four of them standing with a view of the Quarry behind them.

"YAAY! Look there I am, I'm part of the gang." Said Leonie pointing to her likeness upon the Monitor, "Who's 'Bella?"

"Oh, she's our other friend at Toadford, my Roommate, she wasn't able to be with us here for our Holiday." Replied Polly.

This saddened Polly, that there had not been enough room at Keiron's house for 'Bella. Leonie's Bedroom was just too small to put two inflatable mattresses and she could hardly sleep in the boys Bedroom. It was a pity thought Polly, as they would have been all together and 'Bella would have been with them in the photograph.

"What's 'Bella like?" Enquired Leonie.

"Well, she is a bit bigger than me, actually more than a bit bigger, she has dark brown hair and glasses, Oh and er never stops chattering; apart from that she's a good friend." Replied Polly.

Across the wide expanse of the Quarry, a figure moved upon the far side along the edge. Toby was not able to see it clearly, so far away. The figure was hunched and walked with a limp and used a staff as he walked. Toby thought he was probably some old farmer out for a walk. Suddenly there was a red flash of light from the direction of the figure and he disappeared from view. Keiron looked at Toby and noticed him standing staring across to the other side of the Quarry.

"What's up Mate? Seen something interesting?" Asked Keiron, looking now to where Toby was watching. Toby continued to look across the Quarry, just in case, he thought, he may have been mistaken with what he thought he had seen. He also wondered whether the figure would return.

"I thought that I saw an old man walking along the other side of the Quarry. I thought that I saw a red flash of light, then I couldn't see him anymore?" Replied Toby, still looking across the Quarry.

"Probably saw someone taking a dog for a walk." Chirped Leonie, holding her hand up to her eyebrows, to shield her eyes, trying to look to see across the Quarry to where Toby had been watching.

"Maybe, but I don't think many dog walkers disappear in a flash of red light?" Said Toby.

"Maybe you just thought that you saw the red light, maybe it was a trick of the light?" Said Polly, who had brushed her long light brown hair away from her face and was also now shading her eyes to try to look over to where they all were watching; while the wind gently whisper her hair around behind her head. The four stood for a few moments with the light breeze kissing their faces and tousling their hair. They continued to look out over the Quarry, just trying to see whether the old man came back into view.

"Shall we go and have a look to see if there is anyone still over there?" Suggested Keiron enthusiastically.

"We will have to be very careful, we don't know who it is over there and the Quarry is quite dangerous. We would have to stick to the path like glue, which we are presently upon and follow it right around the Quarry to the other side, carefully." Said Polly, authoritivley

"You will need to stay with us and no wandering off, Nipper." Said Keiron to Leonie, all 'Big Brother' like, Leonie just frowned at him.

The ground was a little soft under foot as they walked along the path around the Quarry edge.

"Is this what you meant when you spoke of the possibility of getting dirty and so suggested a change of jacket? Well, while I was changing my jacket, I took the liberty of changing my Riding boots into Wellingtons, just in case." Said Polly.

"Well around the corner, a bit further along is a small shrubbed area which can get a bit wet and muddy at this time of year, especially when there has been some rain." Said Keiron.

"Well I chose correctly then." Replied Polly triumphantly.

As they walked now, towards another hedge, they noticed a style at its end nearest the fence, which was obviously their way forwards to the next field, which the Footpath cross over, upon its way around the circumference of the Quarry.

"It's a long way, when do we get there?" Whined Leonie.

"Not far now to where Toby thought that he saw the old man." Replied Keiron.

"Here it is!" Came a sudden cry from Toby, who was standing a short distance from the other three. Toby stood looking at the ground, puzzled? Keiron, Polly and Leonie ran over to him. First of all they stood and looked around for anyone, then not noticing anyone as far as the filed stretched, Toby pointed down at the ground, where there was an area of soil which was almost circular in shape upon which there was no grass. The grass around the area of this spot appeared to be brown, like it had been singed by a ball of heat.

Toby looked up and gazed across to the other side of the Quarry to where they had been standing when he thought that he had seen the old man.

"Yes, ,there look; that's where we were standing when I saw the old man and look," Said Toby pointing at the spot, which they could see had the soil inside the singed circle of grass back and as though it had been baked in a hot oven. "There, that was where the flash of red light was. It looks like it has cooked the ground where the old man stood!" Said Toby.

"Maybe it was aliens and they fried him with a ray gun?" Said Keiron, giggling.

"I don't know mate, but really looks weird! We checked the path across the field when we got close to here and there was no sign that he had gotten away that quickly, he didn't even pass us upon the path that we walked around upon, so he didn't go that way. He was walking hunched over with a stick, so he couldn't have gotten away very quickly, so we should be able to still see him in the distance if he had walked away, but he just seems to have vanished and left this, what looks like a burn mark in the grass; I didn't see him jump or fall into the Quarry either?" Said Toby.

"As I said, probably zapped by Aliens!" Replied Keiron, smugly.

"Don't be stupid, there are no such things as aliens." Replied Polly.

"I don't like this, can we go home now please?" Said Leonie, frowning again and taking hold of Polly's hand.

"If we go home, we'll never know what Happened to the old man, will we?" Keiron pointed out.

Toby took a few steps away from the burned spot, then suddenly as though he were walking into a solid wall of some kind, almost rebounded and fell to the ground. Polly, Keiron and Leonie ran to where he lay. His eyes were in the top of his head, only the whites showing and his breathing was shallow.

"Ruddy Hell!" Exclaimed Keiron, "now what do we do, we're miles from nowhere!"

"It seemed like he bounced off the air, just over there?" Said Leonie, pointing at nowhere, where Toby had 'bounced off'.

While Polly stayed with Toby, accompanied by Leonie, Keiron stood up and walked carefully over to the spot. He stood and slowly reached out his hand, searching for the something which had thrown Toby to the ground.

"Be careful Keiron, you saw what happened to Toby, don't be stupid, come back here." Said Leonie, with fear in her voice.

"Leonie is right, Keiron, we don't want both of you out cold when we're in the middle of nowhere." Agreed Polly.

"I'm OK, I don't seem to have found it yet?" Said Keiron. Just then his hand lightly flet something gently and he suddenly received something like an electric shock. He pulled his hand away sharply, looking at where he had just been touching.

"Here, there's something here, seems the air at this point is electric. That would explain why Toby was thrown to the ground." Said Keiron.

"Oh don't be stupid Muddles, we're in the middle of a filed, how can anyone one spot be electric, there would need to be an electric fence to make Toby 'bounce off' like that." Said Leonie, as she left Polly's side and walked over to where Keiron was standing. Leonie attempted to reach out her hand, just as Keiron had done.

"No Sis, this is dangerous." Called Keiron quickly, shooting his hand out to stop her. Keiron then reached out his hand slightly harder than before and flet the electric shock again, only this time he took a step backwards as the shock flet stronger.

"OW! My God, it seems to get more of a punch to it the harder you hit it, that explains what happened to Toby. He walked straight into it and was repelled by a stronger shock." Said Keiron, ,now shaking his hand a little.

"Think it's time we weren't here. I told you I didn't like it before." Said Leonie, now looking quite frightened. Just then Toby groaned, so Polly shook him a little.

"Toby, Toby, wake up, we've got to go now." She said.

"Wa, wa, watsgoin' on?" Mumbled Toby, as his eyes slowly found how to open and focus again.

"You were shocked by something over there," Polly pointed to where Toby had been thrown down and to where Keiron had found the electrified air. "You were thrown unconscious away from it." Said Polly as informatively as possible.

"what 'something'." Toby whispered.

"It's some kind of electric air? Don't ask me? You just walked against it and next thing we know, you were laying down there; you almost 'bounced off' thin air, mate." Said Keiron.

"Bounced off thin air?" Asked Toby, now sitting up and trying to stand. Polly gave him some support and helped him to his feet.

"Yeah thin air, you simply walked forwards, then 'bounced off'." Said Keiron.

"It's true, we all saw you." Said Leonie.

Toby looked towards Polly, standing beside him hoping that of all people, she would have a more plausible explanation.

"That's how it happened, just as Keiron said; it sounds incredible, impossible even, but it was just as Keiron told it." Said Polly, shrugging her shoulders.

"It would seem like there is something going on here, something we can't know about, something that scares me. It would be best, I would say, that we go home and figure it out from there somehow?" Said Polly.

"I agree, I've already said, we should go home twice, so now let's do it, before something even more strange happens." Said Leonie.

The four of them turned and walked back to the pathway and walked through the field back along the way they had followed to get there. They reached the style in the hedge and climbed over it. They then followed the path back around the fence around the first field that they had followed.

"I wonder whether this is an electrified fence surrounding Quarry?" Said Toby and reached out his hand slowly. Suddenly there was a spark of blue light which came out from Toby's fingers and snaked its way over to touch the fence.

"WOW! The fence is electric, I never knew that?" said Keiron.

"Don't be stupid, weren't you watching? The blue spark came from Toby and went to the fence, that means its Toby that is electric, not the fence?" Said Polly.

"Ooooh that's weird!" Said Leonie.

They continued walking and reached the style next to the five bar gate. They all climbed over the style, back onto Topley Drive and began walking back along the lane towards Topley Cross.

"I expect it's just static electricity that you picked up when you touched the, 'whatever it was' back there and collapsed." Said Polly.

"The 'whatever it was'? What is 'whatever it was'?" Said Toby, puzzled.

"Maybe the fence is electric and some static from the fence had somehow got stuck upon that spot and you got zapped by it when you walked into it?" Suggested Keiron as they turned the corner at Topley Close into Lower Main Street.

"What about the blackened grass spot upon the ground?" Said Leonie.

"Maybe that was a rabbit or something smaller and it was zapped away, being smaller?" Tried Keiron.

"What about the old man, he would have been about Toby's size, so why didn't he get zapped and we find him unconscious when we got there?" Asked Polly.

"Maybe he walked away passing a different spot?" Said Toby.

"Maybe he was abducted by Aliens and the burned spot upon the ground was made by their transport beam which took him aboard their ship." Offered Keiron , gesturing throughout with his hands excitedly.

"What space ship? We didn't see any space ship?" Offered Keiron, looking at Leonie mentally challenging Keiron to 'get out of that one'.

"It may have been cloaked, made to appear invisible?" Offered Keiron, looking at Leonie as though to say 'there, I've covered myself'.

"Well we don't know do we and won't know now, as the old man is gone and we are upon our way home." Said Polly, "Anyhow, space ships don't exist, apart from our own and there is no such thing as Aliens." She added authoritivley.

The four walked along Lower Main Street and approached the Square.

"We can always check it out upon the Internet when we get back, after dinner, of course." Suggested Keiron.

"It would have to be after Dinner, wouldn't it, Keiron? After all, stomach comes first as always, doesn't it?" Said Leonie.

They walked through the village centre and out onto Upper Main Street, along to the corner of Manor Drive. Before long, they were walking along Mews Lane towards the now familiar sight of Tithe Barn Cottage. Keiron let them in with his key and they went into the Living Room after hanging up their jackets in the hallway. In the Living Room they found Daisy sitting upon one of the sofas. Leonie almost jumped straight into the armchair which she had occupied the previous evening and Keiron, Polly and Toby sat upon the other Sofa.

Hi Daisy, I hope that you had a good afternoon." Said Polly in polite greeting.

"Hi Daisy." Said Toby, smiling.

"Hi Mom." Said Leonie, from the bundle which filled the armchair.

"Er ... Yeah, Hi Mom." Added Keiron.

"Yes M'Dears, I 'ave 'ad a lovely af'ernoon cleanin' an; makin' dinner like, only sat down a few moments ago, jus' afore ye came through the front door." Said Daisy.

"Oh that's good to hear." Said Leonie.

"An' what 'ave you'm lot been upta then? 'Ad an adventure or summat 'ave yer?" Asked Daisy.

"Oh we did a little exploring of the Village and round abouts." Said Keiron, looking towards the others.

"Well, as lang as yer didn' get inte any bother like, I don' wan' you'm fathers acallin' yere an' a tellin' me off fer not looking af'er you'm prapper like." Said Daisy.

"Oh we are OK, Daisy." Said Polly.

".....Only, you'm orta be a bit careful like, what with a gwain aroun' that ol' quarry, dangerous place that." Said Daisy.

How did you know we'd been around the Quarry?" Asked Keiron incredulously.

238

"Oh, Ol farmer Fry tol' me, 'ee was takin' 'is dug fer a walk along Lower Main Street, 'ee says, an' saw yer a gwain over the style inter that there Quarry field." Replied Daisy.

"Oh....... er ..... yeah, er ..... I was just showing Toby and Polly the Quarry, we stayed upon the path and just looked at it. Then we came home again." Said Keiron.

"You'm 'ome OK now M'dears, so don' yer go aworryin' no more, jus' be careful with yeh lil' Sister ifn yeh gwain places like that; yeh know there's some wild ol' places in these parts." Said Daisy, knowingly.

"We know that Mom and yes, we will be careful." Said Keiron, looking around at the others, thinking how it was a good thing that farmer Fry had not seen what had happened to Toby.

"Jus, you'm mind yerslefs, that's all I'm sayin', yeh should be ol' enough te know what you'm a dwain be now." Said Daisy. Daisy then got up from her sofa and walked to the door of the Living Room.

"Time you'm intrepid explorers got yer Dinners, ain't it? I mean, yer'll be a needin' all the energy fer yeh Expeditions won' yeh?" Laughed Daisy as she walked from the Living room, through the hallway and into the Kitchen.

After their Dinners, the four went up to Keiron's Bedroom. Toby and Keiron sat at the desk and Leonie with Polly sat upon chairs which they had brought out of Leonie's Bedroom to join them. Quickly Toby found his way through the start-up and onto the Search Engine, then typed 'Burned Grass Circles' and hit the Enter key. Then a list of websites appeared upon the screen page, including several sites which talked about crop circles, but Keiron waved Toby on as they were far too big to be the burn mark upon the field. Toby found a site for the local Newspaper website. This read that there had been found remains of small animals which had appeared to have been butchered, up upon Cragmoor Common. The article also went on to say that they had been found along with small circles of stones which appeared to have been heated and cracked, nearby larger circles of burned grass, which were of a size in which a man would be able to stand in. They also looked at a site which talked about the phenomenon of ball Lightning. Most interesting though, however, was that they seemed to always be drawn back to the Local News Paper website and the strange story of the happenings up upon Cragmoor Common.

"These stories seem to be saying that it is similar to what we found up at the Quarry?" Said Polly.

"Except that there's no mention of anyone walking into 'Nothing' and being electrocuted or flashes of red light?" Said Keiron, shrugging his shoulders.

"The thing is, yes, they seem to be similar and yes, there is no mention of the electric shock or red light, but remains were found, so the reports from these people have come across after the event, so they weren't present to see any coloured flashed of light. We were there to see red light flashes,, so we saw it. Maybe the others saw these remains and walked away from whatever would have shocked them without touching it. Obviously, I walked towards the thing which shocked me, so I got shocked, plus we were looking directly over at where the old man was and that's why we saw the red light cast and the man disappear? Suggested Toby, thoughtfully.

"What do you mean 'Cast'?" Asked Leonie.

"Well, I mean, when we saw it flash." Replied Toby.

"When you said cast', I thought of spells?" Replied Leonie.

"Well there is no such thing as Magic, so spells cannot be the answer." Replied Polly.

"Maybe the stuff up upon the Moor is not related to the Quarry and is just some camper or something staying the night, sleeping up there and killing some wild thing like a rabbit for their Dinner." Suggested Keiron.

"But the article said that there were several marks of burning?" Said Leonie.

"maybe it was a company of Covert Marines who were upon some type of manoeuvres and the fact that they were covertly means that they can't be identified. " Said Keiron.

"In a moment, we'll be back to your Aliens idea." Said Polly to Keiron.

"Well... er .... It's still a possibility, maybe it was Aliens?" Said Keiron.

"And there it is!" Sighed Polly, rolling her eyes.

"Well what do you think, 'Clever Clogs', don't see you coming up with any good ideas." Said Keiron sharply. Polly just gave him one of her unimpressed looks.

"Seems the only way to find out is if we visit the place where the finds were upon Cragmoor Common and see whether they are the same as the Quarry." Suggested Toby.

"That's miles away!" Replied Leonie.

"It would be possible if we go along Cragmoor Drive, they don't say how far along it is to where they found the signs, but we could have a look to try to find them and compare them?" Suggested Keiron, trying to get back into Polly's good books.

"Well, if we wrap up warm and spend all day at it, we could possibly give it a try." Said Polly.

"We'd need to take a packed Lunch, stop off at the old Ropdon Farm to eat it and make that a resting point." Said Keiron.

"If it's not aliens he's thinking about, it's his stomach as usual." Said Leonie.

"Well Nipper, we do have to think of a good place to stop for our Lunch break, as that would be what we were needing if we are to out all day upon the open Moor." Said Keiron. Leonie just stuck her tongue out at him.

"OK right, we need to leave fairly early then don't we, so best if we get to bed early and set our alarm clocks, for - -say, what?" Said Toby.

"How about seven O'clock, then we can be ready for Breakfast by eight and then, maybe leave about Nine O'clock?" Suggested Polly.

Yea Sounds like a good plan Polly, that would give us plenty of time to prepare our packed Lunches ready to leave." Replied Toby.

They all agreed and so Leonie and Polly retired to Leonie's Bedroom and then went to bed. Toby then shut down the computer and closed its lid. Then Toby and Keiron both changed into their Pyjamas, and got into bed.

"Hope you know what you're in for tomorrow Mate, its ruddy miles up to Cragmoor Common." Said Keiron.

Well, we're getting a break at that farm aren't we?" Replied Toby.

"Yeah, it's derelict, a ruin, we have to be careful there though, old machinery and tools around, like, and some people say that it's Haunted." Said Keiron.

"Well we will be there during the day, so don't think that should be much trouble." Replied Toby.

"You never know. Good night Mate." Said Keiron.

"Good night, Keiron." Said Toby. Keiron turned out his bedside lamp and they both settled down to sleep.

"Do you know what Keiron is talking about, Leonie?" Asked Polly, lying in her camp bed next to Leonie's bed.

"Not really, I've only ever been up that way in Dad's car, so I'm not too familiar with it. I do know that the farm that Muddles mentioned is a ruin, so we shouldn't be disturbed there while we have our Lunch." Said Leonie.

"So, we shall have to rely upon the boys again? Oh well, let's pray that we are still here tomorrow night. Goodnight Leonie." Said Polly.

"Goodnight Polly, hopefully will see you tomorrow?" Said Leonie and she turned out the bedside lamp. Them settled down to sleep.

Chapter Twenty Six – The Cragmoor Adventure

The morning arrived with the crash of the alarm clock upon Keiron's bedside table. Toby got up out of bed with early morning energy which he rather didn't recognise. He simply put this down to the excitement of going out for the day with his friends upon the Moor and the anticipation of what they would find.

As Toby returned to the Bedroom from the en-suite Bathroom, Keion was stirring from his bed. Toby changed into his day clothes, a T Shirt showing the logo of a Rock Band and Jeans; over which he put a Cardigan, so that he was able to take it off if he became too hot. Keiron blearily stumbled into the en-suite. Toby sat at the desk and went over his notes from the Local News Paper reports. He noted that Keiron had been crudely doodling some flying saucers onto the paper 'beaming up' figures of old men; Toby smiled. He looked towards the door of the en-suite and heard the swish of the shower curtain and the shower turn on and the water cascade over Keiron.

"UUG .. er …. OOH … Oh crap … er what time is it?" Mumbled Keiron through the water pouring down his face.

"It's twenty past seven, better get going if we're going to keep to Polly's schedule." Replied Toby.

"Spa … twenty past ruddy seven, who's stupid idea was this?" spluttered Keiron through the shower of water.

"Yours." Replied Toby, enthusiastically.

"Oh …. er …. yeah, I remember now. Next time I have a ruddy stupid idea, kick me won't you!" Said Keiron.

"Will do Mate." Replied Toby, smirking.

The door to the en-suite opened and Keiron walked back into the Bedroom, a little less bleary eyed than when he went into the en-suite. He put on a blue T Shirt with the Frackston City logo upon his chest and Jeans. He too put on a Cardigan, also just in case he needed it. Keiron stood with a towel drying off his hair as best that he could when there was a knock at the door.

"Come in Polly." Called the boys in unison.

The door opened and there stood Polly in a white blouse, lilac jumper and jeans. Leonie stood behind her dressed in similar clothes, they walked into the room and joined the boys. Leonie didn't wait for either of them to move and plonked herself down to sit upon Keiron's bed. Toby stood up and moved to his bed, allowing Polly to sit in his seat at the desk.

"Ever the Gentleman, thank you Toby." Said Polly smiling.

"We ready to go then?" Enquired Leonie, looking from one to the other.

"Have you got the information, Toby?" Asked Polly, smiling.

"Oh yes, I have Maps which show the common and where the remains were found." Replied Toby.

"Good, we shouldn't get lost then!" Replied Polly.

"Brekkie then folks!" Exclaimed Keiron and got up to walk to his Bedroom door.

"Oh you and your stomach." Moaned Leonie.

"OK, Breakfast and make our packed Lunches, then we should be ready to set off for nine O'clock." Said Polly.

The four of them left Keiron's Bedroom and walked down stairs and into the kitchen. Upon the table were two fried breakfasts, two bowls of cereal and drinks. Daisy stood at a work surface with four polythene boxes laid out, enough slices of bread for a stack of four sandwiches each, and was just finishing off putting on the top slices upon the bottom ones and cutting them placing them into their respective boxes, along with an apple in each and a packet of crisps."

"Thank you very much, Daisy, this has saved us a lot of time this morning." Said Polly.

"Yes, thank you Daisy." Agreed Toby.

"Yeah, er …. Thanks." Echoed Keiron.

"Well, I 'eared you'm lot a talkin' 'bout an adventure las' nite; out fer the day yeh says. So I thought like, I'd save yeh sometime an' see you'm all off, OK. Where's You'm a gawain then?" Said Daisy.

"I'm taking them up to see the old farm up at Ropdon, Mom." Said Keiron.

"You'm mind youmsleves up there my boy, 'tis dangerous what with all that ol' machinery layin' aroun', like." Said Daisy.

"yes Mom, I know, don't worry, we'll be careful." Said Keiron.

"Put the maps into your Ruc-Sac, Toby, don't let Mom see, she'll start asking more questions again." Whispered Keiron, so that Toby slipped the maps into his Ruc-Sac while Daisy was just finishing the last of the sandwiches.

After breakfast, the group left the house and Keiron indicated to them to turn right out of Mews Lane into Manor Drive and out into Upper Main Street. All the way along Mews Lane, Daisy watched them go from the door step, until they turned out of the lane. At Upper Main Street, they turned the corner walking away from the village centre.

"Now we go this way." Said Keiron, pointing along the road away from the village. They walked along the lane, some birds were singing in some of the

243

gardens. The low winter Sun seemed watery and was having trouble rising in the sky. The sky had a few clouds but was mostly clear, which was making the day feel slightly crisp.

"I wonder what we will see up at Cragmoor?" Said Leonie dreamily.

"Most probably nothing." Said Polly.

"Maybe a blast crater where the thruster from the Alien ship took off?" Speculated Keiron.

"Keiron, there will be no crater, no ship, NO ALIENS! Aliens don't exist." Said Polly with authority!

"OOH! Keep your knickers on! Wh-who says that Aliens don't exist?" Replied Keiron.

"There hasn't been any evidence to prove that they exist, it's all nonsense!" Snapped Polly.

"There hasn't been any proof that they don't either!" Replied Keiron.

"It's the 'God Question' again, isn't it?" Said Toby.

"What do you mean?" Asked Polly.

"Well, most people don't believe in God, as there has never been any tangible proof to say that He exists, whereas people who do believe, state that there has never been any proof that He doesn't. It all down to faith really." Said Toby.

"What? We should have faith in Aliens?" Asked Leonie.

"No, what I mean is, that either one believes in them or one doesn't." Said Toby.

"Ever the Diplomat, eh Toby." Grinned Keiron.

"Well, I like to be one, who doesn't!" Stated Polly, shooting one of her looks at Keiron.

They continued to walk along Upper Main Street until they reached the corner of Cragmoor Drive, which was opposite the foot of Crosscombe Hill, past the houses. Atop the hill was placed the lighted cross, which was always placed at the top of the hill at this time of year. The cross was not lit at this time of day as they walked past it, but it did command attention.

"There is a cross at the top of that hill, is it always there?" Asked Toby.

"Yes, during Easter and at this time of year. That's Crosscombe Hill, and when it gets dark, the cross lights up. It can be seen right across the Village." Said Keiron

"Who puts it up there?" Asked Toby.

"A group from the Church in the village put it up there, when it is done there is a Choir from the local Primary School who sing Hymns at Easter and Carols at Christmas around it and what they call the 'Cross Ceremony'. Then the Church congregation with the School Choir, walk down to the Church carrying torches for a service. They did it just before Christmas, before you arrived." Replied Leonie.

"Did you take part?" Asked Polly.

"I used to, when I was going to the Village Primary School, but I don't know, I don't have tine so much, with Homework from Middle School and from next year, I'll be at Toadford, so I will have even less time for it." Replied Leonie.

"Did you take part?" Polly asked Keiron.

"Not Ruddy likely! I wasn't in the School Choir and I wasn't going to freeze to death just to sing around a Cross at the top of a hill." Replied Keiron.

"No Muddles, you're so uncultured aren't you, even from Primary age." Scoffed Leonie.

"Yeah, well, I wasn't a little Angel, was I Sis?" Said Keiron.

"How long has the Cross been put up there?" Asked Toby.

"Oh, hundreds of years as far as I know, I'm not sure if anyone knows actually how long it's been put there?" Said Keiron.

"It's just one of those village traditions which everyone takes part in but doesn't really know how long it's been going on." Replied Leonie.

They then turned their back upon the cross and began to walk along Cragmoor Drive. For just less than a mile was a row of old looking cottages, like houses they had passed before, showing signs of Christmas decorations in their windows and Holly Wreaths upon their doors. Then, past the cottages, they began to reach open countryside as hedges appeared either side of the lane and pavement ran out.

"It's just up here aways, Ropdon Farm, we can stop for a rest here and have some food." Said Keiron.

"Is it very dangerous?" Asked Polly, worriedly.

"Not really, if you're careful. That was just Mom being Mom. It's derelict and hasn't been lived in for years, that's why Mom was worried and of course, because we've got Nipper along with us." Replied Keiron.

"Mom's worried you'll get into a muddle, Muddles and lose me or something." Said Leonie.

"Well if you keep close and stay with us, that's not gonna happen, is it Sis?" Said Keiron.

245

They walked on some way further and before long came to an opening in the hedgerow. Here was the entrance to the farmyard. Hanging from a wall which took the place of the hedgerow and ran the full length of the front of the farmyard, was an old wooden sign, upon which was barely visible an old painted wording:

"ROPDON FARM"

The stone wall was rather overgrown with long grass and the remnants of weeds which had long since gone to seed, There was a large wide gap to one side of the wall, where stood a pair of large old weather beaten five bar gates which were secured by a large rusted padlock. A long track led into the farm from this gateway and to the right of the gates, behind the wall, was an overgrown garden area, which had been the front garden of the farm house, while it was occupied and worked. Then standing there was a large stone house. There were faded and peeled remnants of green paint upon rotten windows of broken glass across the front wall. This had at one time been the living room of the farm house. Around the side of the house was a porch and door. This was the main door into the farm house. Away along the yard lane into the farmyard stood a number of outbuildings, partially standing, including a rusting old cattle barn. They walked up to the door and Keiron turned the door knob and opened the door with a loud creak, leading the others into the farmhouse.

As they entered, they were hit by the smell of age, abandonment and neglect. Inside the door was a short hallway, with a mouldy old over coat still hanging, covered in cobwebs, upon an old wooden coat stand. Next to this was a grimy cobweb covered old mirror upon the wall, which was at the base of the stairs, to the right of the hallway. The walls were covered, mostly, with grimy old damp wallpaper, which had peeked off to reveal large black mould patches upon the plaster of the walls, which in some places had some fair sized cracks.

The floor was covered in a dirty, grime covered carpet, or the remains of; along the walls at the skirting boards in some places, they could see the mushroom heads of fungi sticking up out of the carpet. Bridging the gap between the ceiling and the walls were a canopy of cobwebs. At the end of the hallway was a door, which was open, and through which was noticeable some old Kitchen cupboard units, so that must be the Kitchen. To the left of where they stood was to be seen two doorways, one open, which was to the front of the building and most likely the Lounge, and the door to the back upon the left was most likely the Dining Room. They made their way, carefully, along the hallway, into the Dining Room. Inside was nothing other than an open fireplace in a wall which once again was covered in grimy unrecognisable wallpaper, most peeled off and dirty cobwebs were everywhere. They then looked into the Kitchen, were was empty of furniture but there were work surfaces, which were covered in grime and cobwebs, but were a place to sit down once they had been brushed off. Polly found an old stiff hand brush in a corner and used it to brush off a couple of the work surfaces of cobwebs and grime. Then they jumped up and sat upon the areas which were now slightly cleaner than the rest of the Kitchen. They put down their Ruc-sacks and took out their lunch boxes. This was, they thought the best place to sit and have their Lunch, ,as it was a little chilly outside with some gusty winds. They thought it best that they wait here for a short time to see if the wind calmed down.

"This place is filthy." Complained Polly with a screwed up face of disgust.

"It would be, it's been empty for years." Replied Keiron.

"Why was it suddenly abandoned like this?" Asked Toby.

"Something about the Son of the family shooting his entire family and being hung for Murder, so as there was no one left to inherit the farm, it was just abandoned." Explained Keiron.

"That's terrible!" Said Polly.

Yeah, over the years, anything of any value was taken by locals who thought that it was abandoned for a length of time and no one was alive to claim the stuff, at night, no one was around, people would just walk in here and take whatever they wanted. As it is said around the village that because of the killings which were carried out here, that the ghosts of the family members haunt the farm and it's also said that because the killings were so horrific, that the Son went to Hell and stalks the farm in demonic form looking for more souls to take." Said Keiron.

Leonie looked a little chilled at this story, Polly was her usual self.

Don't be silly Keiron, ghosts and Demons don't exist," She said with her usual tone of authority, "And you're scaring your Sister".

Leonie gave a nervous smile to Polly.

"Do you believe in anything, Polly?" Asked Keiron, grumpily.

"Science has never proven this and mostly the stories have been put down to drunks, people high on drugs and to just plain liars who make up the stories." Replied Polly.

"Science doesn't have to explain everything, what about 'Quantum Physics'? That describes things which the established laws of Physics say are impossible, yet they are real and happen!" Said Keiron.

"That's different, they explain 'Quantum Mechanics, which are things previously thought as impossible, which experimentation has since proved." Replied Polly.

"Well ghosts and Demons come under this rule, it's just no one has managed to produce proof to explain them scientifically or their existence other than the world of alleged eye witnesses." Said Keiron.

"There have been plenty of 'Ghost Hunters' who have tried to produce proof with scientific experiment and equipment but have come up with nothing." Replied Polly.

"What do you think Toby?" Asked Keiron.

"I don't think anything, I haven't seen one, but not seeing it doesn't mean it doesn't exist; although the fakes and failed experiments using specially constructed equipment made to get results has come up with nothing; I guess I just don't know?" Said Toby.

"Always on the fence aren't we Toby?" Snapped Keiron frowning.

"Well at least Toby has an open mind to look at things from both sides." Said Leonie.

"Do you fancy him, or something, Nipper?" Asked Keiron.

"Don't be stupid Muddles, I hardly know him." Snapped Leonie, frowning at Keiron, then going red blushing.

"Leave Leonie alone Keiron, she's just giving her opinion, like the rest of us. She's too young to think of things like that; why, are you jealous?" Said Polly.

Keiron didn't answer, he just scowled at Polly, who gave him one of her looks in return.

"It's not only you who can give those looks then, Polly?" Said Toby to Polly and she laughed, which ended up with them all laughing.

Soon they decided that it was time to leave the farm and continue on up onto Cragmoor Common, to see whether they could find anything up there to explain the reports. They packed up their Lunch boxes and Polly took out her camera, which was forever with her and she set it up so that she was able to switch on the timer and line them all up for a photo. She clicked the shutter and the camera whirred. Polly then ran into line and smiled. The shutter clicked and there was the first photo containing Leonie as part of the group.

"Don't mind Polly, she carries the camera everywhere." Keiron told Leonie.

"Yes, I got some shots while you weren't looking, of all of you while we were having lunch." Replied Polly. Polly then stopped as they were leaving the farmyard and took a photo of the house and then of the out buildings and Cattle barn further down the farmyard.

"OK then, finished, let's get going." Said Polly.

She put the camera back in her pocket and they walked out of the farmyard and turned to their left and began walking along the lane again away from the Village. The lane began to rise slightly as they walked up hill approaching the Moor above them.

After a while, they reached the main Barnstaple Road and crossed over to the far side of the road. There in front was a five bar gate in the hedge. Over the gate they could see the Moor stretched out in front of them. They climbed over the gate and then were able to see without the hedge blocking their view, the expanse of the Moor stretching out in front of them all around for miles. As to be expected, the ground was hard compacted soil with tough short grass growing upon it. This was kept low by the grazing sheep and Ponies which were dotted about across the Moor. To the right, in the distance, they could see the large stone edifice which rose up out of the Common like a huge rockery.

"That's the Crag, it's called 'The Old Crag' by locals, why this is called 'Cragmoor Common', I've never been there, only seen it from here." Said Keiron.

"Wow! I've never seen it before." Relied Polly.

"I usually go past here in the car, so I usually just see hedges." Said Toby.

To the left, in the distance, they could see a line of tall Poplar trees running along the edge of the Common.

"See those Poplar trees along the horizon over there?" Said Keiron, pointing across the Common to the far side.

"Oh yeah, I can see them." Replied Toby.

"What are they then?" Asked Leonie, putting her hand over the brows of her eyes to attempt seeing more clearly.

"That's Poplar Drive, which leads up to Toadford School, over there." Replied Keiron and pointed where the line of threes would end in the distance.

"I can't see it?" Said Leonie.

"Of course you can't see it from here, its miles away over there and it's the other side of a huge Gorge which goes along over there." Replied Keiron, pointing along the horizon towards the Old Crag.

"Well, we can't see any problems here, ,so we could go over to the Crag to look, we may be able to see more from there too, as it will be up high." Said Toby.

Then they began to walk across the common, towards the Crag. As they walked, the closer that they got to it, the Crag seemed to get larger. As they walked across the Common, Polly took her camera. She asked them all to stop for a moment and pose, so that she was able to take a photo of each of them individually with the Old Crag in the background.

After some while, they saw that they were approaching the base of the Old Crag. Then, to their total surprise and Horror, they found two sheep Carcasses with the legs and breast missing; all that remained was the back bones, fleeces and heads. Polly and Leonie took a sharp breath and looked away covering their eyes. The boys made a suggestion to move on away from the gruesome sight around the base of the Old Crag. They found a rocky pathway wide enough for two to walk, which seemed to be leading up the face of the Crag. They thought that this was just what they needed and began to walk along the pathway, gently rising up the face of the rock stack as they went.

"Seems like we have found what we were looking for." Said Keiron, puffing a little as he walked along the path.

"Yeah, sheep carcasses. It's not Big Cat kills, as they eat the breast meat but don't generally take the whole of the ribcage and legs, leaving just the backbone and head." Said Toby.

"Yeah, looks really strange that, don't it?" Replied Keiron stumbling upon a piece of rock in the pathway.

"Well we don't wish to look thank you! Said Polly, walking arm in arm with Leonie." We don't exactly wish to smell them either, they stink and are covered in flies."

"The smell of Death!" Grinned Keiron, looking back over his shoulder. Polly shot him one of her unimpressed looks.

Those poor sheep." Said Leonie, with a tear rolling down her cheek.

"Well, unless it was Foxes, but again, they may take the meat but don't usually go off with the ribcage and legs, leaving the head and backbone behind. Foxes would normally attack the lambs though; a full grown sheep would ordinarily be too big, unless it was sick or lame. To leave that kind of remains usually means a pack of animals or something really big!" Said Keiron.

"So what do you think did this then?" Asked Toby.

"Dunno? But if it wasn't a pack of animals, then it must have been something ruddy big." Replied Keiron.

They climbed a little longer along the pathway and came to an area where there was a wider piece of ground and to one side against the cliff of the rock, a ledge running along a short length which was long enough for them all to sit upon.

"Wow! I hadn't realised how high we were while we were climbing, just look at that view!" Said Toby as the surveyed the view from where they were. They had climbed about one third of the height of the Crag, about a hundred feet and were rewarded with a view across towards Toadford, which was still too far away to be seen ; Poplar Drive was visible as a line of bare branches and trunks along in front of them. They looked to their left, and was able to see the hedgerow, the road and beyond this was visible Crosscombe Hill with its cross at its top which overlooked the rows of the houses of Topley Village.

"See there, at the end of the field at the foot of Crosscombe Hill, that large house on the end of the short lane, that's our house!" Said Keiron pointing down towards the Village.

"Oh yeah, I can see it now!" Agreed Leonie, smiling.

"Glad we got to sit down, I was getting tired." Said Polly as she took a bottle of orange juice out of her Ruc-Sack and took a swig of it.

"I can see the Church too, the tower in the Village centre. I can't see the Quarry from here though," Said Toby.

"you won't see that from here Mate, Tugmoor Wood is in the way covering it up; that's the Woods which you can see just behind the Village, they're in the way even though the trees are bare, they are so thick that they are covering up the view of the Quarry. Maybe higher up they may give way to a view of the Quarry." Said Keiron.

"Higher up! We're going higher up?" Asked Leonie with surprise.

"Can't See the Carcasses from here." Said Toby.

"No, they'll be covered by foliage from this height." Replied Keiron.

"Good, I don't want to see them anyway," Said Leonie.

"Or smell them." Added Polly, Making a face. Wrinkling up her nose and pinching it with her thumb and finger. Leonie laughed.

"Over there, also behind the trees of Tugmoor Wood are the remains of an ancient Iron Mine. In Medieval times, it's said, they mined Iron ore from there and the Mine was still being worked until the late 1800's, no none knows for sure how old it is, maybe even dates to Roman times?" Said Keiron.

They sat there upon their ledge drinking for a while and eating their Sandwiches and crisps, which they hadn't eaten at the farm and then decided it was time to go up a little farther to see whether they were able to see anything else. As they walked along the pathway and climbed gradually higher, they spotted what looked like a cave or something in the rock face ahead of them. They walked up to it and took a step back. The stench was powerful, a stench of some type of animal or something and of stale blood. Then to their horror, they noticed around the entrance to the cave was strewn a huge pile of animal bones.

"'OH MY GOD! What is that stench and what is all that?!" Chocked Polly, throwing her hands up to her face with shock. Leonie covered her mouth with her hands and turned to retch.

"Oh Ruddy Hell! I think we should get out of here before anything comes along and puts us upon the pile with the other bones." Said Keiron.

"Yeah, good idea Mate, let's get the girls away from here and then get back and let the Authorities know about this place." Said Toby.

"Yes please, let's go and get out of here." Agreed Polly, still with her hands over her mouth and nose, trying not to be sick again.

"Come on then, I'm scared now." Said Leonie, she turned around and was sick again.

They started back down the path, a little more quickly than they had climbed it.

"Careful, don't go too quickly and trip!" Said Toby.

"Don't worry, we won't." Replied Polly, who was trotting down the pathway, holding Leonie's hand.

Before long, they reached the foot of the path back upon the Common and began to walk back away from the 'Old Crag' towards the five bar gate and the Village. They got about halfway across to the gate, when suddenly in front of them they saw a figure with greenish grey skin, filthy looking with ragged clothes, a metal hat of some kind, crudely made and then a gust of wind blew in their faces and the caught its scent in their nostrils and recognised the stench from the cave. The figure had black blood around its mouth wore filthy looking ragged clothes. This is what was killing the animals. The figure looked up and shouted ;

"Manous!" Then he began to charge at the four terrified friends.

"What does he mean 'Manners'?" Stuttered Keiron.

"Who cares about MANNERS? Run!!!" Shouted Toby.

With a terrifying scream, Toby, Keiron and the two girls began running from the figure charging at them, who now seemed to be holding up a large piece of metal above his head. They ran away but Toby had an idea which he hoped would get them to freedom. He suggested that they try to run at an area, so that possibly, they may be able to effectively turn their chaser around and make for the five bar gate with the figure chasing from behind, so that he chases them towards the gate.

The figure before long realised what they had in mind and decided to chase across and cut off their dash for the gate. Just then, the figure stopped the chase and put the metal thing back into its scabbard upon its belt, the boys realised this was a sword. He then pulled out a bow over his shoulder and notched an arrow.

"Jesus Christ! He's got a bow and arrow! What's this Nutter doing?" Shouted Keiron. There was another almighty scream and the boys looked in horror as Polly hit the ground behind a rock. Keiron looked at Toby and both had a horrific thought run through their minds. They ran over to the rock, expecting to see a lifeless body of Polly pierced by an arrow, but were relieved somewhat to find her crouching behind the rock with Leonie trying to stay hidden. Sticking out of the turf a few yards away was the shaft and fletching's of an arrow. Just then another arrow thudded into the ground narrowly missing Toby's head, bringing another scream from both Polly and Leonie.

"We have to get out of here somehow?" Said Toby.

"Yeah, but how? With some Nutter taking pot shots at us with a bow and arrow, we're really going to get far aren't we ?" Said Keiron.

"He had to stand still while firing, all we have to do is get to the gate and get out of range while we try to run there." Suggested Toby.

They all suddenly stood up quickly and started running, zig zagging towards the gate the boys made sure that the girls were in front of them so that they were able to shield them to a small degree. Suddenly a scream ran out!

"TOBY NO!!"

Toby heard Polly's cry and looked around just in time to see the arrow flying straight towards him. He found himself concentrating hard, crossed his arms in front of him, possibly to shield his face from the arrow.

"Better to get it in the arm rather than the face!" Toby cried

"GO AWAY!"

There was a blinding blue flash of light surrounding Toby and a beam shot out and the arrow disappeared!

This momentarily confused the attacker, fatally, as though from nowhere, just like the attacker had been; the Old Man appeared dressed in a long robe of deep blue. He held out in front of him a stick in his right hand and shouted something in a language unfamiliar to the four friends:

"MORTE TOTALIS."

There was a bright red light which streaked out of the old man's stick with a scream from Polly, Leonie and a roar from the attacker, he appeared to glow red and then exploded! Cowering down, the four caught sight of a glimpse that the old man picked up the bow and arrows, which the attacker had been holding when he was thwarted and then with a blinding Golden flash of light, he disappeared,

"Whoa! W … w .. What just h happened?" Stammered Keiron pointing wide eyed first at Toby, then at where the old man had disappeared.

They were rooted to the spot for a while, then Toby slowly walked over to where the old man had been standing. There was type of ash upon the ground in places.

"W … w .. where are y .. y .. you going?" Asked Keiron, "And what the Ruddy hell did you .. er .. him .. er .. everyone do?" Stammered Keiron.

"I'm frightened, can't we just go?" Said Leonie, crying, tears streaming down her face.

"Yes please, can we just go, in case anything else happens." Said Polly, hugging Leonie, who was crying into Polly's chest.

"I just want to see, … I just want to s.. see." Said Toby, walking shakily towards the spot where the old man disappeared and the attacker 'exploded'. When he arrived there , at the spot, he saw what he had expected.

"Come and see … quickly, c .. c .. come and see!" Called Toby.

Keiron gingerly got up and slowly walked to meet Toby. There upon the ground where Toby pointed without saying more, was a burned grass circle, still smouldering.

"T .. t .. that's it, t .. the burned grass, the red flash of light, that's what we saw at the Quarry." Stammered Toby.

"Y .. y .. Yeah Mate, I see what you mean." Said Keiron, who went to put his hand upon Toby's shoulder, but then remembered the arrow and withdrew it, "T .. time we were going, Mate." Said Keiron.

They walked back in silence and joined up with the girls, Polly was white faced and had tears down her cheeks, Leonie was still crying. Keiron helped them up and they put his jacket around Leonie. They walked away in silence towards the gate, just Leonie's sobs and the wind was all they were able to hear.

Before long, they reached the gate, Leonie was holding Polly's hand as Keiron was walking with his arm around Polly, her arm which was not holding Leonie's hand was also around Keiron's waist. Beside them walked Toby alone, silently, just starting ahead of him.

Thoughts ran through his head, red flashes of light, the old man, the attacker exploding, the Quarry. They reached the gate, Keiron lifted Leonie and helped her over the gate, by now, her crying had stopped. Then Keiron helped Polly to climb over and then climbed over himself. Toby then climbed over the gate, although the other's weren't entirely sure that Toby was aware that he had climbed over the gate. They walked back along the main road, Polly's hand in Leonie's and her other arm back around Keiron's waist. They walked back along the main road to the junction of Cragmoor Drive, then down the lane past the farm. They momentarily stopped to look at the farm but none of them wished to enter after what had happened up upon the Moor and the stories which Keiron had told them while they had been eating their Lunch.

They walked on until they came once more into the houses. They turned into Upper Main Street and as the light was beginning to turn to twilight, they were able to see the cross upon the top of the hill lit up with lights as they passed. Silently, Leonie made a wish, as too did Toby. They eventually turned into Manor Drive, then Mews Lane and arrived back at the house. Keiron let them in with his key. They walked in and went straight upstairs to Leonie's and Keiron's Bedrooms. They all had showers to ease their shock and clean up their day and then changed their clothes. It was now six O'clock in the evening, they had been out for most of the day. Keiron sat and looked at Toby, while he pulled on his jumper.

"What happened back there?" Asked Keiron, still a little shaky with some fear in his voice.

"You saw what happened." Replied Toby with equal shakiness in his voice.

"I mean with you Mate, I mean the arrow?" Said Keiron.

254

"I don't know; Polly screamed, I looked up, put my arms up to shield my face and thought 'go away', and it went?" Replied Toby; he sat upon the camp bed while Keiron was sitting in his desk chair.

"It went away alright! A huge flash of blue light came from you like, like a force field or something and the arrow disappeared. Then that old man appeared out of nowhere, shouted something and a red flash like sparks came out of the stick he was holding then that Nutter with the bow and arrows exploded." Said Keiron.

"We saw the burned grass again." Said Toby, now dressed in jeans and a green and blue jumper, different from the way he was dressed out upon the Moor.

"Yeah, that was weird." Answered Keiron, shaking his head.

"It's all weird." Replied Toby.

There came a knock at the door, the two boys almost jumped out of their skins. Keiron let out a little fart,

"Are you decent?" Came a voice through the door, which sounded like a muffled Polly speaking.

"Yeah, we're OK, come on in." Replied Keiron.

"Ahem!" Coughed Polly as the door opened and she entered with Leonie, standing in front of Keiron.

"Oh right, yeah." Said Keiron and he got up from the desk and sat upon his bed to allow Polly to sit down upon the desk chair which he had vacated. Leonie sat upon Toby's bed next to him.

"You could always sit here next to me, like Leonie is next to Toby?" Said Keiron, rather hopefully to Polly.

"What for? I have a seat." Replied Polly.

"Oh right, OK then." Said Keiron, looking at the floor; Polly acknowledged this reaction and sighed audibly. She got up from the desk and walked over then sat down next to Keiron upon his bed. He lifted his arm and Polly gave him one of her looks, he lowered the arm again.

"What happened out there today?" Asked Leonie.

"I don't know, it must have been a dream?" Said Toby.

"That Guy who attacked us, he looked like a tramp, but had armour and weapons? He looked like he had been living rough up there a long time." Said Polly.

"Are you OK now?" Asked Keiron.

"Yes I think so, not every day one has an arrow shot at one and lives to tell the tale." Said Polly.

"Know how you feel!" Replied Toby.

"That light from you, Toby, that must be what that shock did to you, it must have super charged you or something?" Said Polly

"And the Guy exploding? The old Guy firing at him with a stick, then he exploded in a ball of light, what's that all about? Magic?" Said Keiron.

"There's no such thing as Magic … or Ghosts or Aliens or things …." Said Toby, looking at Polly; she looked at the floor.

"I don't know anymore, there must be some explanation for it all?" Said Polly.

"I'm starving, must be Dinner time, hope Mom saved us some." Said Keiron.

"We'd better get down, but not a word about what we saw, Mom would go crazy and ground us for life." Replied Leonie.

"Come on let's go." Said Keiron.

Leonie and Toby stood up and walked to the door and went out onto the landing. Leonie led the way to the stairs. Polly caught Keiron's sleeve briefly, indicating to hold back. Leonie and Toby disappeared down the stairs and Polly was left with Keiron upon the landing.

"I just wanted to say something before we went down stairs to join the others." Said Polly.

"What is it?" Replied Keiron.

"It's about the 'arm thing', I mean your arm. I know we walked back from the Common with our arms around one another, but I was upset, really upset and welcomed the comfort. I wanted to say, we are friends, just friends, close friends if you will, but that's all. Please, Please, don't read anymore into it OK. I didn't wish to say anything in front of the others to save embarrassment, you OK, but we're just friends, OK." Said Polly.

"OK Polly, I understand, just close friends. But please know that I'm here for you, when you need a friend, like today. Thanks for not wanting to embarrass me." Said Keiron.

"I hope you're not too disappointed, but quite frankly if you don't mind, I'm too young to be thinking of 'Boys' just now, I'm only fourteen in six weeks' time. I just didn't want you to think anything more of me putting my arm around you. Thank you for understanding Keiron, I appreciate it." Replied Polly. Then she stepped forwards and gave him a hug. For the first time, Keiron felt her hug, smelt her hair and perfume, the first time he actually thought of her as a 'Girl'. Polly then stepped back and broke the hug.

"Can't we get Dinner now?" Said Keiron, once they had stopped hugging.

"OK Muddles, you've got a stomach to fill up." Laughed Polly; Keiron laughed too and they walked down stairs holding hands, Keiron smiled at Polly and she smiled back.

The next day, the four thought it best if they didn't go on any adventures, just in case. Toby was still at a loose end wondering what had happened and where the 'Force field' had come from, how did he make it. Since he had fell by the top of the Quarry and blacked out, he had felt like he had more energy, he had felt fitter and looked in the mirror and noticed that his body seemed to have toned up. When he thought about it, the reflexes he had, he had spun around and rebuffed the arrow quite quickly. What did this all mean, what was he supposed to do with this new found ability.

They spent most of the day helping Keiron to complete his homework, ensuring that he wrote it all in his own words and made sure that he didn't simply try to copy theirs. By the time he was finished, they had helped him to produce a reasonably good piece of work which should get him a good grade, they hoped. The rest of the time they spent either taking their meals or playing Play Station. In Keiron's Bedroom, he and Toby were playing their usual fantasy games and in Leonie's Bedroom, they were playing more 'girly' games. Then it came to New Year's Eve, they had their Dinner and all got ready for their visit to the Hospital.

Chapter Twenty Seven – The Hospital Visit

They arose that morning, showered, changed and went down stairs for their Breakfasts, the usual routine. They made sure that they had packed everything that they wished to take with them, into their bags, which they were carrying. They put them into the car boot and then they got into the car and sat upon the back seats. It was Bill's Silver BMW. The three, Toby, Keiron and Polly, waved eagerly from the car and Leonie, who was staying behind, waved back from the porch.

Overnight, the weather had closed in a little and it was decidedly chillier now. Bill was driving with Daisy sitting in the front passenger seat.

"Pity Leonie couldn't come, if it were Toby's Dad's Landrover, Leonie would have fitted in and could have come too." Said Keiron.

"Well, we don't have a Landrover, Keiron," Said Bill, "Maybe I should have put her onto the Roof-Rack?" He laughed, they all laughed with him.

"I could just picture that." Laughed Toby.

Bill drove off along Mews Lane and out onto Manor Drive. He drove out of the village past Tugmoor Wood and Poplar Drive, which led to Toadford School.

"There's Tugmoor Wood." Said Keiron as they drove out of Topley Drive and down towards Little Farthingworth.

"That's my House, Pegasus House, there along the driveway, behind the trees." Said Toby.

Soon they reached the Village Centre and turned into Cranleigh Street. They passed Tugmoor Farm and headed down the lane to Cranleigh. As they neared to the edge of the town, Polly let out a squeal!

"Oh goody, we'll soon be in my neck of the woods!" Chirped Polly.

They drove down the lane and eventually entered the town of Cranleigh.

"The Hospital is over to the right of the Town Centre, over near to the Library." Said Polly, with authority.

"You should know where that is, shouldn't you Polly?" Laughed Keiron.

"Which one, Library or Hospital?" Asked Toby.

"Library of course, with all that swatting up you do with your books. I bet you've got a season ticket for the Library, haven't you Polly?." Giggled Keiron. Polly simply shot him one of her looks along the back seat of the car with Toby strategically between Keiron and her.

They arrived at the Hospital and Toby lead them to the lifts and up to level two and onto the Ward. Sitting with Rachel in the TV Room were Carl and Simon.

"Hi Dad." Said Toby, waving, then trotting up to them at the couches facing the TV.

"Hi Toby, all OK with you?" Said Carl.

"Hi Toby, enjoyed your visit with Keiron?" Said Simon.

"Hi Granddad, we've had a good week, shame it all ends after the weekend." Said Toby.

"Good morning Mr Morby, and of course Mr Morby." Said Polly first to Simon and then to Carl.

"Hi Polly." Replied Carl.

"Hello Polly." Replied Simon.

"Good morning Mrs Morby, I hope that you are feeling better." Said Polly to Rachel.

"Thank you my Dear, I'm feeling a little better, yes." Replied Rachel to Polly.

"Hi Mom." Said Toby, with a big smile.

"Hi Toby, the Physio says my progress is coming along and I will be able to come home in a few weeks. Then I'll just need to come in for Physio and a few check-ups after that.

"That's great news, Mom." Said Toby, smiling.

"It's not quite ready, but soon I'll be better." Replied Rachel.

"Hi Mrs Morby, I'm Keiron, it's me they've been staying with." Said Keiron, "Good to know you're getting better,"

"Hello, I'm Daisy, glad te meet 'ee." Said Daisy, "Glad te see 'ee lookin' better."

"Well, we won't rush, but nice to meet you Keiron." Replied Rachel.

"Thank you for having our little rascal." Said Carl to Bill, who was standing with them.

That's no problem, they've been a pleasure to have around, that's when they're not off gallivanting upon one of their little 'adventures 'around the village." Said Bill, Daisy giggled.

"Had many adventures have you?" Asked Rachel.

"Oh ... er ... A few, around the village, just getting to know the place." Said Toby, nervously looking from Keiron to Polly.

"I'd like a drink, would anyone mind anyone mind if I went to get one?" Asked Toby, glancing at Keiron.

"I'll help to carry them if anyone would like one?" Replied Keiron.

"Yes that's a good idea, I'll have a white Coffee with sugar please." Said Bill, "Same for Daisy."

"Same again." Said Simon.

"May I have a white Tea without sugar please." Asked Rachel.

"Me too please." Said Carl.

"I'll come with you to help and I would like to see what they have before I decide." Said Polly.

The Three got up and walked out into the reception area to the drinks machine. Toby put in the money and pressed the buttons for each drink, then he came to Polly's turn and she chose a Coffee, white with no sugar.

"You could have asked for that up in the ward?" Said Keiron.

"I wanted to be part of the parlay." Said Polly.

"Thing is, what do we do with this? How can we deal with it? If we go to the Authorities and tell them everything, they wouldn't believe us?" Said Keiron.

"Yeah, I was thinking about that?" Said Toby.

"How would we explain it? OK, there was a tramp or deranged person who had been living rough and killing the animals for food, living in that cave upon the Old Crag, so far so good. Then he attacked us, first with what looked like a crude looking sword and then a bow and arrow, that's OK so far. Then how do we continue? Oh Mr Policeman, suddenly an old man appeared as though from nowhere, pointed a stick at the Lunatic, a spark shot out of the stick and he exploded. The old man then picked up his remaining weapons, and then vanished in a bright golden light? Oh yes, and by the way Mr Policeman, before we forget, Toby here was able to disarm the Lunatic of one shot, when he fired an arrow at him and Toby shot out a bright blue light and made the arrow disappear before it hit him! How on Earth do you expect anyone would believe us?" Said Polly, not her usual self.

"How would anyone believe that?" Came Simon's voice from behind them. The three turned around and almost dropped the drinks in their hands.

"I thought that I would come and give you a hand as you were taking a while, but this is much more interesting," Simon added.

"We'd better go back in with the drinks before they get cold." Said Toby.

The three walked past Simon gingerly and went back into the ward to take the drinks to the others. Simon gave them a look which Toby had never seen upon his Grandfather's face before. It was a look that said 'I know your secret, but I have a bigger secret.'" Simon joined the rest at Rachel's bedside and gave Carl a look to say 'we need to talk', motioning to Toby, Keiron and Polly.

"So theses 'adventures', been anywhere fun?" Asked Rachel.

"Oh, around the Village, looking at places we haven't seen before, like the old farm at Ropdon. It's supposed to be haunted, be we stayed there for a while and had our lunch and didn't see any ghosts." Said Toby.

"Did you explore the farm much?" Asked Carl.

"Oh no, there's a lot of dangerous machinery rotting away there so we kept away from the barns and such." Replied Keiron.

"How about the Moors?" Said Simon giving them a knowing look.

"Briefly," Replied Toby. Simon's look bore into him, he could almost hear Simon's thoughts, 'what did you see there?' Toby seemed as though he were in a trance as he sat there thinking of their narrow escape up upon Cragmoor Common.

"..... and we could see right across the Village from up there, even Tugmoor Woods." Said Keiron, Toby caught the end of his speech from Keiron as his trance was broken.

"There is a star above the Village; on top of......... what is it called?" Said Polly, turning to Keiron.

"Crosscombe Hill," Replied Keiron quickly.

"Oh, Oh yes, erm Crosscombe Hill. The Cross is made from a framework in the shape of a cross, which has many lights attached to it, so that in the dark it glows, making a cross shape above the Village, shining out." Said Polly.

"So, did you all enjoy yourslef?" Asked Rachel with a smile.

"Oh er, yes we had fun," Said Toby, looking at Keiron, who glanced at Polly.

"Time please I'm afraid, Visiting time is over, sorry." Said Nurse Jenkings as she walked through the Ward and approached Rachel's bed.

"Yes, I do feel a little tired after so many visitors. Well I will see you when I get home," Said Rachel, looking at Toby.

"Dad's agreed for us to go to Polly's house for half term, so I won't see you until Easter." Said Toby, "I'll call you though, frequently."

"That will be nice." Replied Rachel.

"Then I'll be back at home for a few weeks before Keiron and Polly came to stay for a while during the Summer Holiday." Said Toby.

"Yes, I should be up and around by then, so I'll look forward to you all being around, we could have some fun." Replied Rachel.

"Well, bye Dear, Happy New Year, I'll see you on Wednesday." Said Carl and kissed Rachel goodbye, hugged her and made room for the others.

"OK love, Happy New Year," Said Rachel, See you soon."

261

"Goodbye Rachel, Happy New Year, see you when you get to come home." Said Simon.

"Thanks Dad, Happy New Year to you too." Replied Rachel.

"Happy New Year." Said Toby, Keiron and Polly together.

"Happy New Year to you lot!" Replied Rachel and giggled.

"Happy New Year Mrs Morby, so good to meet you." Said Bill, Daisy smiled.

"And to you too Mr and Mrs Mudley, so nice to meet you and thank you for putting up with our Toby for the week." Said Rachel.

"Oh Don'ee mention it M'Dear, been a pleasure te 'ave their company." Replied Daisy, "An' its Bill an' Daisy M'Dear."

"And I'm Rachel." Said Rachel, smiling.

They all then waved to Rachel, who waved back, then they walked out of the Ward. Toby turned and waved as they went out through the Ward door and out into the Reception area.

Rachel lay there thinking about their visit and of when she would be back home again and the wrongs with her body had fully healed. By this time, her Physiotherapy was coming along nicely. She was able now to walk across the Ward with the help of Crotches. Hopefully, she thought, I'll be able to walk better without the Crotches soon and possibly get back to the job of Teaching at the School. With these thoughts, Rachel lay with her head upon her pillow and drifted off into a deep sleep.

Rachel found herself sitting upon a small caved stone stool. Beside her stood many disgusting creatures; Orcs, Goblins and other ugly things. Then a voice boomed out and Rachel tried to cover her ears with her hands, but found them manacled, it was impossible to raise her hands higher than her mouth.

"You will bring me the Enchanted One." Boomed the voice. Rachel looked up sheepishly and saw the great face of the Marquis, his red bloodshot eyes bore into her, to her very Soul.

I will never give him to you." Replied Rachel, gritting her teeth and trying to sound fierce.

"You will not need to give him to me; your ransom will be that he will need to save you, so that just you being here will bring him to me." Said the Voice.

Rachel felt the heat of his breath and smelt the fetid breath as he spoke.

"You'll never get him, he'll never fall for your traps......" Screamed Rachel.

Rachel sat up suddenly in bed, sweating. She looked around her and saw the Hospital Ward of other empty beds. Then Rachel told herself that she was really dreaming. Where did that all come from? She thought; Rachel then settled down and went back to sleep.

The little Party walked out through the Reception area into the car park. Simon and Carl stood beside the Landrover and the rest by the BMW.

"Well goodbye then, Happy New Year to you all. Said Simon, "I'll see you when you return home, when you're with your friends Toby, then you can tell me much about your trip onto the Moor."

"Happy New Year." Said Carl.

"Yes, and to you too, "Replied Bill, he and Daisy shook Carl's hand.

"Happy New Year Dad." Said Toby, giving Carl a hug.

"Happy New Years, Son." Replied Carl.

"Happy New Year." Said Keiron and Polly together.

"And to you too." Said Simon and Carl.

The New Year greetings over with, Simon and Carl got into the Landrover; then Toby, Polly, Keiron, Bill and Daisy got into the BMW. The Landrover drove away with a toot of its horn.

"Are you three settled then?" Said Daisy from her front passenger seat, buckling up her seat belt, after waving off the Landrover.

"Yeah, we're OK back here, all strapped in." Said Keiron, again, Toby was sitting between him and Polly.

"Off we go then." Said Bill.

The BMW pulled out of the Hospital Car Park and Bill drove them back to Tithe Barn Cottage. When they got back, they went to the Bedrooms to put away their bags after hanging up their coats in the hallway.

Toby sat and thought for a few moments. As they had passed Pegasus House while leaving Little Farthingworth upon their journey back to Topley, he had noticed the lights of the house flicker through the skeletal branches of the trees of the hedge and he thought about his Father and Grandfather being there and celebrating the turning of the old year to the new. He thought about himself being with his friends and celebration with Keiron's Brother and Sister and Parents.

Toby also thought about his Mom, Rachel sitting in the TV Room of the Hospital watching the New Year Show and having some Nurses around her who were roistered on for that shift, giving a little cheer along with the Nurses, who would rather be at a party with other Patients who would rather be with another Party. Toby thought of Rachel wishing she was at home with the rest of her family celebration the New Year. A small tear gently slid down Toby's cheek.

"....... Then Mom and Dad will let us stay up to see in the New Year, aint that great?" Toby suddenly heard Keiron saying. Then remaining where he was, took no notice of Keiron.

"Sorry, I was lost in thought." Said Toby.

263

"You've been doing that a lot just lately, anything I can help with?" Said Keiron.

"No it's alright Mate, thanks for asking." Replied Toby.

"Time to go down for Dinner, then Mom and Dad will allow us to stay up to see in the new year. What are we doing tomorrow?" Said Keiron.

Soon it was approaching the time, upon the TV was the 'New Year Show', with the scene in Westminster of St. Steven's Tower. The camera zoomed in onto its clock face as the second hand approached Midnight. The crowd could be heard loudly chanting the countdown of seconds. The second hand met the other two and momentarily all three hands of the clock face pointed directly upwards to the twelve position and appeared to look like one clock hand. The chimes burst into song and then;

… BONG! BONG! BONG! BONG! BONG! BONG! BONG! BONG! BONG! BONG! BONG! BONG!

Went the clock as 'Big Ben' struck to herald Midnight. The crowd let out a huge cheer and fireworks began shooting into the air from everywhere. The Camera switched to a view of London Bridge with a shower of Fireworks shooting up from the Bridge in every colour of the Rainbow. A view from Fleet Street showed St. Pauls Cathedral lit up with Fireworks, making it resemble how the Cathedral had once looked during World War Two 'Blitz' of London. Another view from the cameras showed Tower Bridge lit up Fireworks and beside the Bridge, the Tower of London covered with bright coloured lights flashing.

"HAPPY NEW YEAR!" Everyone cried together and Toby, Keiron, Polly, Bill, Daisy, Leonie and Thomas held up their drinks and made a toast to the New Year to herald it in.

"Here's to the New Year with new adventures." Said Polly smiling to Toby, Keiron and Leonie.

"Here, here!" Replied the three of them together. Once all of the excitement had died down and the celebrations were mostly over, it was time for everyone to retire to their respective Bedrooms. Within Keiron's Bedroom, the boys ended their day together.

"Happy New Year Mate!" Said Toby to Keiron as he lay in his bed.

"Yeah, Happy New Year Mate!" Came the reply from Keiron's bed.

"Yeah, it will be when we beat the Wombats in the Finals and win the School cup." Said Toby.

"Yeah, too true Mate. Goodnight Toby, see you next year." Said Keiron.

"Goodnight Mate." Replied Toby, then they both settled down in their beds and went to sleep. Meanwhile a similar scene was taking place within Leonie's Bedroom.

"Happy New Year, Polly." Said Leonie from her bed.

"Happy New Year, Leonie." Replied Polly from her bed.

"What are we doing tomorrow?" Asked Leonie.

"You mean later today? Well, I don't know, we will have to ask and see what the boys are doing and decide from there." Replied Polly.

"See you later then, Polly." Said Leonie.

"Yes, see you later." Replied Polly.

"Goodnight, Polly." Said Leonie.

"Goodnight, Leonie." Said Polly. Then the two girls settled down into their beds and fell asleep.

The next couple of days went by much the same as the last, with the group of friends visiting the village or walking around. Then it was the day of the trip to Barnstaple. The group were up early and Breakfasted ready for the trip out. They heard the Landrover as Carlo pulled up outside the house and then the doorbell rang. Keiron went to the door with Toby following close behind, Keiron opened the door.

"Hi Mr Morby." Said Keiron to Carl, standing at the door.

"Hi Dad, have a good time at New Year?" Said Toby, stepping out from behind Keiron.

"Morning Boys, yes Toby, me and Granddad had a good time at New Year, did you? Said Carl, thinking how he had enjoyed Simon's company but also in part of him, had thought about Rachel alone away from the family for the first time. Simon had supported him in his thoughts and reassured him with the truth Toby was now approaching his Fourteenth Birthday in the Summer, that he was of age in the Warding term and now he was at Toadford, they would all need to become accustomed to his absence from the house. Carl had accepted this advice, even if he still felt uneasy about it, and felt a little better. Simon had also reminded Carl of the importance of Toby being told his true identity and that this was especially important this year for one thing, because of the growing trouble and threat from Thracia and The Marquis. The other thing was that it was important that Toby know the truth, due to his need to begin his Apprenticeship and training as a Wizard following his Fourteenth Birthday.

"Morning Boys, yes, are you all ready yet?" Asked Carl.

"Come in please, we're almost there." Said Keiron.

"Thank you," Said Carl as he stepped through the door. Keiron and Toby lead Carl into the lounge, where seated upon one of the couches was Daisy and upon the other couch was Polly. Leonie occupied her usual arm chair.

"Do'ee set down now, we don' wan' 'ee a clutterin' up the place, do we now." Said Daisy, not taking her eyes from the TV; Carl sat upon the couch, next to Daisy.

"Morn' Carl, 'ope you'm 'ad a gud Noo Yere." Said Daisy.

"Yes thanks Daisy, hope you did too." Replied Carl.

"Oh yes, we 'ad a gud time yere we did, din' we you'm lot?" Said Daisy.

"Yeah we did." Smile Toby.

"We're ready now Dad, just got to get our coats." Said Toby as Leonie entered the room after going to get her Ruc-Sack. They all stood up from their seats, those already had their Ruc-Sacks. They all stood up from their seats, those already had their Ruc-Sacks packed them up and carried them out to the coats, along with Leonie. They all took their coats down from the rack and put them on. Keiron then opened the front door and they walked out onto the garden path.

"You'm lot 'ave a gud time now an' enjoy youmsleves now." Called Daisy as they walked along the garden path to the gate.

"we will." Smiled Keiron.

"See you later Daisy." Said Toby.

"See you'm later, Mom." Said Leonie, who stopped at the door to give Daisy a peck of a Kiss upon her cheek, then she caught up with the rest of the group as they arrived at the Landrover.

"See you later Girls." Called Daisy.

They reached the Landrover and Carl checked they were all there. Then Polly, Leonie and Keiron climbed into the rear seats of the Landrover and Toby got into the front passenger seat. Carl climbed into the driver's seat and they all buckled up their seat blets.

"We already then?" Said Carl.

"Yeah' all belted up and ready." Said Keiron.

The Landrover roared into life and with a last wave to Daisy upon the door step, Carl pulled away from his parking space and the Landrover drove off along Mews Lane and out into Manor Drive. He drove out into the Village Centre and out along Lower Main Street to turn out into Topley Drive and then out turning right onto the Moorland Road.

Chapter Twenty Eight – The Day Out

The Landrover drove along the Moorland Road and soon they were able to see over the hedges, the Old Crag, towering above the landscape around it. They recognised the piece of Moorland in front of it where they had been attacked and Toby had let out a force of light which had prevented him from being hit by an arrow. They also remembered the attack from 'the Nutter' with the bow and looking at the Old Crag, they remembered their climb up it and the cave upon its far side full of bones.

"There, that's Cragmoor Common, where those strange stories had come from, of mutilated bodies of animals being found." Said Carl.

"Yeah, don't remind us." Thought Toby.

"That huge stone crop you see there a short way from us is The Old Crag. Back along, some years ago, it was alleged that some Satanic Rites or some such rubbish were performed upon the Crag, but the Local Authorities of the time put a stop to it all". Said Carl.

The Landrover chugged along and finally left the Old Crag behind, disappearing into the rear view mirrors. A short way along the road and they saw some wire enclosures with a team of men trying to keep a small Stag calm to tranquilise it.

"That's the Veterinary Enclosure we rebuilt and secured. We capture the wild Deer, treat them if they need it and then let them go back out onto the Moor. Said Carl.

Toby, Keiron, Polly and Leonie were more interested in this, as it took their minds off the Crag, so that they were able to leave that memory behind. Carl drove on and shortly, they saw that they had entered a town. It was Tiverton; they had stopped in a Car Park and were able to see a Café in front of them.

"Time for a short break, half an hour, OK!" Said Carl.

"Yeah, OK Dad." Replied Toby.

They all got out of the Landrover and walked over to the Café. They entered and found a table to sit at.

"Right OK then, what does everyone want to eat?" Asked Carl, as he handed out Menus to the three teenagers and Leonie. They studied the Menus for a few moments, then they made up their minds.

"Sausage and chips for me please, if that's alright, Dad," Asked Toby.

"That's OK, Toby." Said Carl.

"Same for me too please." Asked Keiron.

"Right, so OK, It's two sausages with chips so far?" Said Carl, turning to the girls.

"Would it be alright for me to have a small chicken salad please, Carl?" Asked Polly, brushing her hair from her face.

"Yes, that's fine, Polly." Replied Carl, smiling.

"And the same for me please." Smiled Leonie, her blue eyes sparkled among her freckles.

A waitress appeared, somewhat pretty with a slim figure, shoulder length brown hair and blue eyes. She wore a white blouse, black bow tie and black skirt. She walked up to their table and stood, waiting. She took out her order pad and pen. She then prepared to take their order.

"Are you ready to order, Sir?" Asked the Waitress. She thought of what it would be like to live up in London, where all the cool people live and the wages were much more than just the legal minimum wage. An aroma of delicious grilled Beef Burgers, Onions, Bacon and Chicken wafted throughout the café, especially when one of the waitresses walked in or out of the Kitchen door.

"Yes please, we'll have two sausage with chips, two small chicken Salads, please, oh … and er … yes, a Gammon with chips too. What drinks, Guy?" Said Carl. Toby looked at each of his friends and asked them.

"Colas all around?"

"Yes please." Came back an unanimous reply.

"Right OK, may we also have four Colas and a mug of Coffee; white, no sugar, to add to the food please?" Said Carl. The waitress wrote it all down upon her order pad and walked away to the Kitchen and disappeared through the door, again the aroma of the food intensified as she pushed the door open and walked through.

The Kitchen doors were next to the counter which had a glass box full with cakes and pastries within it, for take away or eat in, The Tables were situated opposite the counter beside a long length of large picture windows which looked out across the Car Park. Around the walls of the Café were hung many pictures of racing cars, motor bikes, comic strips and more. There were also a multitude of ornaments which were located around the café upon shelves. One ornament in particular caught the eye of Toby, who sat watching it. Keiron was absent mindedly looking out of the window at Carl's Landrover. Still looking at the ornament, Toby asked;

"Can you see that ornament over there next to the end of the counter, up there above that table upon the shelf?"

Keiron stopped at the Landrover, Leonie and Polly stopped comparing rugs and other pieces of jewellery, Carl stopped watching the Kitchen door, they all looked where Toby was indicating.

"What're we looking at?" Enquired Keiron.

"Up there above the empty table, upon the shelf, is that an ornamental Puma?" Asked Toby.

"Yes, that's right." Replied Carl.

The ornament was about six inches tall and about twelve inches in length. It was matt black apart from staring yellow eyes and sharp white teeth.

"Oh yes, this is where there have been reports of Wild Cats being sighted or animals being found killed by then." Said Carl.

"Wow! So do you think that the people have reported sightings." Said Carl.

"Have there only been sightings though, hasn't anyone had proof?" Asked Polly.

"No one has brought forward definite photographic proof, if t that's what you're asking. Some people have shown sketchy photos taken at distance, but there are none which clearly show the cats in detail." Said Carl.

"do you believe the Stories?" Leonie asked Carl.

"I Can't say for sure, working up upon the Moor all of the time, I haven't seen anything myself, but some of the Guys have said that they found the remains of a number of animals which they say the cats have been feeding upon, like sheep." Replied Carl.

Before long, the Waitress returned with a tray carrying two small Chicken Salads and two glasses of Cola. A Second blonde, slim Waitress appeared with another tray carrying two Sausages with Chips, a Gammon with Chips, two more glasses of Cola and a steaming mug of Coffee. These were all deposited in front of their respective dinners and then the two Waitresses walked back to the Kitchen doors with the empty trays and disappeared through them. Upon the table was a group of assorted sauce bottles, sugar bowls, salt and pepper pots and a vinegar bottle. One by one, these sauces and other seasonings were put upon the meals. Keiron, as usual, seemed to put a bottle of hot Chile sauce upon his.

"So did you have a good time together for this holiday?" Asked Carl.

"Oh yes, it's been great fun." Replied Toby, looking from Polly to Keiron,

"Best fun was up upon the Moor …-" Began Leonie, Keiron almost choked upon his mouthful of Sausage, which he had been chewing. Carl looked at Leonie and Toby, Polly and Keiron gave her a very stern look. Recovering herself, she spoke on;

" ….. I mean the Old Farm, just before the Moor, you know, Ropdon Farm. We went exploring and had our Lunch there." Finished off Leonie, a little sheepishly.

"Did you find much up there, while you were 'exploring'?" Asked Carl.

"Oh just some old machinery and abandoned old broken tools and such, the things were so old, they would have only been any use to a Museum." Added Toby.

"You should be careful around that old place, can be dangerous with all that old machinery around." Instructed Carl.

"So you didn't go up upon the Moor then?" Asked Carl, raising an eyebrow.

"We did have a quick look but didn't have much time, so we came back to Keiron's house." Replied Toby.

"Did you see anything up upon the Moor, anything interesting?" Asked Carl.

"No, not really; loads of sheep, the Old Crag, bit of scenery, you know ….-" Said Toby.

"Nothing unusual?" Asked Carl.

"Not that we saw?" Replied Keiron, looking from Toby to Polly.

"It's just that there have been some strange reports just lately of animals being killed by some form of Predator?" Said Carl.

"Er …. Well, we didn't see anything?" Lied Toby, going slightly pink faced.

"Well, if you do go up there 'inspecting' and do see anything, let me know immediately, yeah?" Said Carl, looking from Keiron to Polly and then Toby.

"Will do Dad." Replied Toby.

After they had finished their meals, Carl paid at the counter and they returned to the Landrover. They drove out across the Canal Bridge and out onto the A361 road. They continued upon their journey, leaving Tiverton behind. By now, the weak January Sun was in the sky, with not much warmth issuing from it. Either side of the road was Heathland of Heathers and Furze bushes, beyond which they were able to see the high ground of the Great Common leading to Hawkridge and Withypool.

The Landrover rumbled on as they reached the large round – a – bout which to the left led South to South Molton, to the right, Brayford and the Moor, straight ahead, to their destination, Barnstaple.

"I bought us all Lunch back there, ,I known it was a little early, but I have to take the car around to have it checked over. So I'll drop you lot off at the Bus Station and pick up there about three O'clock." Said Carl.

"OK Dad," Replied Toby.

The Landrover turned off from the busy duel carriageway and followed the A361 past the Industrial Estate, with its DIY Warehouses and Super Markets, along past the Old Brunel Railway Station, now being used as a Church. They went across another round – a – Bout, which took them past some more houses, the Army Centre and across another mini round – a – Bout, through some traffic lights at a Pelican Crossing. They then turned right past the impressive façade of the Bus Station and some flats, a Night Club and some empty Offices. They then turned left along the road at the front of the Bus Station stands and around by the Disabled Centre so that Carl parked outside the CAB Office. They unbuckled their seat belts and Toby, Keiron. Polly and Leonie got out of the Landrover.

"See you then. What are you four going to do here then?" Asked Carl.

"Oh just have a look around, see what's about." Replied Keiron.

"I've never been here before, will be nice to explore." Said Leonie, enthusiastically.

"I've been here a few times with my Father, when he's had to visit upon Business, he lets me look around while he's in a meeting." Said Polly.

"That's good then, you will be able to show us around and remember the way back to the Bus Station, when we need to go back to meet up with my Dad at three O'clock." Said Toby.

Polly thought that this made her feel a little important to their day's enjoyment. She thought that it gave her a little power over the others, as they did not know their way around, SHE did! This would mean that Polly was in charge of where they went and what they did, which suited her very much.

Carl drove away to the waves from the four friends. Then Polly showed the others that they needed to walk along the alley type street to their left, which was Silver Street. Along Silver Street, they saw a closed down printers works, a jewellery shop, a Removals Company with their office and garage, which held their two huge Removals vans emblazoned along their sides with their company name. Further along, they passed some old houses, which were converted to offices and a Computer Repair shop. There was an old pub, which looked 'rather dodgy', followed along Wells Street by a Hotel Car Park and opposite, the main Hotel in the Town Centre. At the end of Wells Street, they walked out into Boutport Street; well technically, this was actually Lower Boutport Street. They walked out of Wells Street and had a Department store to their right and the frontage of the Hotel, with Dickensian style Bay windows and a name panel above the door inscribed with 'The Royal and Fortescue Hotel' in Gold Leaf.

Toby noticed a shop in the row opposite from where they were standing. Making sure that they crossed the road safely, they walked up to a shop window. It was not difficult to cross this road at this point, apart from the Taxis getting in everyone's way. It was a one way street and so only traffic from one direction would affect them, other than some idiot riding a bicycle the wrong way up the one way street.

The street here was curved around following the old path of the Town wall from Medieval times. The street headed off to the left, past the junction with the High Street and down past the Hotel and a row of shops upon each side of the road and a small café, to Barnstaple Square. The group noticed that the shop Toby had seen was a Toy shop called Youings. It connected to and formed a long 'sectioned' shop front around the corner into the High Street junction. The shop appeared to be split into separate sections but all of the same shop. The sections had windows which from their Dickensian design, showed that the shop had stood there for over a hundred years, as was told by a guided legend over the shop fronts which stated this fact. Toby was looking at the toy shop window.

Looks like their toys are rather childish, I think, let's move on shall we?" Said Toby, Polly agreed, as did Keiron and Leonie, which was rather unusual as being, maybe the only time the two siblings had agreed upon something for quite a while! They walked away to their left from the toy shop 'section', in the direction of the square. In the other direction, to the North, ran a street lined upon both sides with shops, cafés and Cinema, leading eventually past the junction with Boutport Street 'proper', towards the Post Office and Market. The direction in which they were walking, to the South, lead them towards the High Street, where Leonie and Polly were 'itching' to get to for the main shops and shopping Mall.

The next shop 'section' they came to, to Toby's delight, was a model shop. Toby looked through the window and saw piles of model kits. In the window were a number of model kits which were marked down with sale prices. Also in the window was a miniature railway track, made circular and had a scale sized railway engine running around in circles. Toby looked at Polly and then back to the back to the shop window.

"May I have a look in here, to see what they have got please?" Toby asked Polly, giving her a big eyed 'Puppy' look and smile.

"Yes, OK then, but don't take too long, remember there are loads of more shops to see and we only have time enough until we need to head back to the Bus Station to meet your Dad." Replied Polly, but who was really thinking, don't take too long, the girls need time in the High Street for THEIR Shopping!

The Bell went 'ting' as Toby pushed the door open into this 'Aladdin's cave' of treasure. It was nice, actually to be inside in a warm shop, out of the cold breeze blowing along the street. They stopped a little way into the shop. Toby's and Keiron's heads turning to take in the view, the only place where model kits and train sets were not piled from floor to ceiling was either the door and window or the counter. Behind the counter stood the shop keeper, manager of this section of the shop. He had fair hair which he whore in a 'Boston DA' style, wore a 'cheese cloth' shirt and jeans, with large turn ups at the ankle.

Toby stared open mouthed at the stacks of model kits from floor to ceiling.

272

"Wow! Exclaimed Toby, Keiron gasped, speechless and Polly looked at Leonie; both girls rolled their eyes and giggled.

"May I help you?" Asked the shop keeper.

"They are just looking, for now." Replied Polly, still giggling.

Toby and Keiron scanned the stacks of model kits like bar code readers, finally. Toby found three model kits which he liked. He picked a 1:72 scale Sopwith Camel Fighter plane, and 1:72 scale British Aerospace Hawk, Red Arrows and an 1:72 scale Eurofighter. Toby looked at the points listed upon the boxes, decided that he had already got all but three of the colours; Matt Black, Air Force Grey and Olive Drab. Toby went to the counter and took the colours he needed out of the rack next to the counter. Keiron picked out a nice Boeing B17G Flying Fortress and its relevant paints.

"You can help me paint the parts, if you like, while you're here for the next couple of days, Toby." Said Keiron with a smile.

"I'm putting mine into my luggage and storing them there until I go home at Easter or may just give them to Dad, when he picks us up at three O'clock, so that he can take them home and put them in my Bedroom ready for me when I get back at Easter." Said Toby.

"It would be better to give them to your Dad to take home, Toby, that way they will be safe and waiting for you, when you go home." Suggested Polly.

"Yeah, that's the best idea, I think, thanks Polly." Replied Toby with a smile. Toby and Keiron took their model kits and paints to the counter.

"Hello, have you any cement to stick them together, please, two tubes." Asked Toby to the shop keeper.

"Here we go." Replied the shop keeper, turning to a shelf behind him and placed two tubes upon the counter with Toby's model kits and paints.

'"Is that all for today then Sir?" Asked the shop keeper.

"For me? Yes, ,thank you." Replied Toby. The shop keeper totalled up Toby's bill and put the kits, ,paints and cement into a carrier bag.

"That will be £25.97 please," Said the shop keeper.

Toby put his debit card into the slot and tapped in his PIN Number. There was a whirling sound and then a receipt appeared.

"Thank you, please call again," Said the shop keeper, handing Toby his bag.

"Have you another two tubes of cement, please?" Asked Keiron, smiling. The shop keeper placed the tubes of cement, along with Keiron's model kit and paints, into a carrier bag, handing the bag to Keiron.

Then they turned to the door. Toby and Keiron, both with big smiles upon their faces and clutching their precious bags of goodies in their hands. Then they walked out of the model shop. They turned to their right as they left the shop and passed the next window, which was a Tobacconist, 'section' of the shop.

"I don't think we will be needing anything in THERE!" Exclaimed Toby, scowling at the window which was filled with advertisements of numerous brand of tobacco and smoking memorabilia.

"No thank you!" Exclaimed Leonie, scrunching up her nose too.

"Filthy things!" Exclaimed Polly, scrunching up her nose too.

"They walked into the next street around the corner, following the line of the shop fronts. This was the High Street. The next 'section' was a confectionery shop, this pleased of all them.

"Do you mind if we go in here, please?" Asked Leonie, enthusiastically, looking at Keiron.

"Just you try to stop us." Replied Keiron, laughing.

They walked into the sweet shop and were excited by what they saw. Inside to the left of the door, were racks filled with boxes of chocolates and fudge. There was a chilled drinks fridge and shelves full of chocolate bars. To their right was the shop counter and behind it were shelves filled with large jars of loose sweets of all kinds. In the middle, between the drinks fridge and the counter, stood a table with sale packets of chocolate bars and boiled sweets.

Toby chose some Sherbet Lemons, loose, some packets of chocolate bars from the sale table and a packet of mints. Keiron chose some Sherbet Flying Saucers and packets of chocolate bars from the sale table. Polly chose some Sherbet Lemons and just a couple of packets of chocolate bars; Leonie chose the same. They all paid for their sweets and left the shop back into the chill breeze. They turned to their right and their journey to the High Street began!

They walked along the High Street, moving towards the North, the icy wind gently breathed towards them, which made them glad that they had chosen to wear their coats and scarves. Each had a different hat. Keiron's scarf had 'FRACKSTON CITY FC' embroidered in blue, edged with white along its centre in large letters. His hat was embroidered with the Frackston City Emblem at the front. Polly was wearing a type of 'Russian' style fur hat (Synthetic fur of course!) and Leonie was wearing a pink woolly hat and scarf. Polly was also wearing her Toadford School scarf, as was Toby.

"Let's find somewhere to go into, to get out of this wind." Suggested Keiron, as his cheeks became ever more pink from the sting of the chill air.

"I'll show you something, it's quite interesting." Replied Polly, "following me Chaps and Chapess." She added bossily.

Leonie smiled, thinking that she liked being called a 'Chapess' by Polly, as this indicated to her that she belonged within their group. Leonie and Keiron had not really seen eye to eye all that often while growing up, being so close together in age; they were natural rivals. Now it would seem, that they had the newly formed group of friends to have in common with one answer at last.

Polly lead them along the High Street, passing a number of different shops upon each side of the road along the way; a jewellers, HSBC Bank, many charity shops, a few expensive looking clothes shops, a 'Bookie', a Picture Framing shop and a Kitchen shop, There was also a large Italian style Pizzeria, which Polly pointed out would mean all of them would require a 'Gold card' if they considered buying anything in there. They eventually passed a Wimpy Burger Bar, which Keiron was upset by.

"Can we go in there, its sacrilege to leave nice juicy Burgers behind! " Said Keiron.

"I want to show you something interesting, we can come back after and get a snack and drink." Said Polly, rather Bossily.

"We could get some shopping and look around at the rest of the High Street and come back to finish off in the Wimpy Bar before heading back to the Bus Station, if everyone is agreeable?" Suggested Leonie.

"Good idea." Agreed Polly with a smile.

"Sounds OK to me." Said Toby.

"S'pose so, I might be able to last that long before being carried off upon a stretcher racked with hunger." Said Keiron miserably.

"Drama Queen!" Exclaimed Polly and gave Keiron one of her looks!

"OK then, we'll finish off in the Burger Bar," Stated Leonie.

They then followed Polly away from the Burger Bar and into a footpath with Iron gates, Keiron with a little less enthusiasm than the others, along the footpath they arrived at the Parish Church.

"This is the Parish Church, built in 1100AD but rebuilt in 1369, this is a pretty nice Church," Said Polly.

"Can we see inside?" Asked Toby.

"Of course we can." Replied Polly.

Polly led them into the Church, which had two isles beside the Knave leading up to the Rood Screen and then the Altar behind. Around the walls were many plaques which spoke of wealthy local people commemorated long after their deaths. Polly then led them back outside and they walked along the path again.

"That spire was added during the rebuild in 1679 and it is twisted due to being built from 'Green wood' which twisted over the years while it seasoned." Said Polly.

"Swallowed a guide book, have you Polly?" Keiron said to Polly.

275

"No, but I did some reading up upon the Town before we came." Replied Polly irritably.

"It's good to learn something about the places you see, adds to the memory of the visit." Said Leonie, supportively.

"It's the other building which is interesting." Said Polly, pointing in front of them at a small stone building.

They walked to a stone gateway and up some stone steps to a large oak door. This led inside a small passage with stone stairs heading down. Next to these was the main chamber of the building. They walked into a chamber and were greeted by a fairly short, roundish man with very short black hair and wisps of grey, with glasses. He wore a vintage looking costume, Britches with a frilled shirt and red waistcoat, which had a badge pinned to it, inscribed, "MICHAEL VOLUNTEER."

"Good afternoon, I'm Michael and would be happy to answer any questions you have." Said The Guide, Michael.

"Hello, we're just looking." Said Polly.

"The building was built as a Chancery Chapel, but was rebuilt and converted after it closed as a chapel in 1453 and became the Grammar School for the Town." Began Michael.

"Wow! It's really old then?" Asked Toby.

"Oh, it's older than that. There originally would have been a small chapel built here upon this site, possibly of wood to begin with and later in stone. It was discovered that there was a crypt underneath the building, still left from the original chapel, which was reported to have dated from the sixth century A.D.

This would have been the original chapel to the Town before the Norman Conquest. The Church next to here was added later by the Normans after they captured the Town in 1068AD, this room was the main room used by the school as a classroom." Said Michael.

"Cool, so old." Said Keiron.

"Lots of History in the Town, we have a Heritage Centre over by the River, you can find out more of the History there if you wish. You would need about half an hour or so to go around the exhibition." Said Michael.

"Sorry, we're a bit short of time today, but will remember that for another visit." Said Polly.

"Thanks for the information." Said Toby.

You're welcome." Said Michael.

They left the chapel and walked around the side path which led them out onto a street of small shop units, called Butchers Row. Opposite was the famous

'Barnstaple Pannier Market. The street was throbbing with people going in and out of the shop units. They were filled with a café, Deli, fish monger, cheese shop, two Butchers, a Green Grocer and Baker.

The market was within a covered building with a glass and Ironwork roof, not unlike the Crystal Palace had been in London. Inside, stalls made up three rows along the length of the market with many different sellers plying their trade. There was many Green Grocers selling fruit and vegetables, some Butchers, Trinket stalls, tool merchants and a stall for Batteries, cigarettes accessories and that type of thing. There were a number of smaller farmers selling from stalls. Also in one corner was a café and the other end showed a fudge shop and another café. There was also a stall selling German food, like huge sausages, Pork Burgers and things like Schnitzel. There was also a stall ran by a Nepaelse chef who sold curries and other food, such as Bhajis and Samosas. Within the Market were people everywhere. The stalls were full of customers. Above the Market at the High Street end was the Town's Guild Hall.

The group moved on from the Market and now found themselves with Department stores and others, the real Hub of the High Street. Here a short way along from the Market was the Shopping Mall of the Town, Polly led them into the first entrance they arrived at.

"Oh look Leonie, there's our Shop!" Exclaimed Polly, pointing out a girls clothes shop a short way into the Mall. They walked into the racks of clothes and trying on some. They walked around about the clothes they were trying on. Polly walked out of the changing room with pair of cream jeans." Cool" Muttered Keiron, who for the first time noticed Polly's figure and how good she looked in jeans.

"Well thank you kindly, Keiron." Replied Polly.

"Yes, very nice." Said Toby.

The girls changed into some more clothes and paraded for the boys.

"Nice stuff." Said Toby as Leonie walked out modelling a frilly blouse under a brown jumper and brown jeans, topped off with a brown corduroy hat.

"S'Okay s'pose." Said Keiron.

After many of these changes, the girls decided upon their clothes and took them to the counter, paid for them and gratefully received the buldging carrier bags which held their purchases.

"Where now?!" Asked Toby.

"THERE!" Said Leonie pointing to a jewellery shop and trinket store. They crossed the Mall to the shop where Leonie and Polly immersed themselves into hand bags, braclets, earrings and much more. They eventually emerged back into the Mall and showed the boys their purchases.

"Nice." Said Toby, (which seemed to be becoming a 'catch phrase.'),

"Not bad, if you like that kinda thing." Shrugged Keiron.

"Let's check out the rest of the Mall." Suggested Polly.

They walked past numerous Mobile phone shops, a restaurant, which Polly pointed out to be too expensive for them, some Department stores and a Book shop. They looked in the book shop for anything interesting, found a spice and herb shop further along the Mall, they found sweets were sold there, but were expensive. They then walked out onto the High Street again, where Toby noticed a rather largish book shop down on their left.

"Yes Ok, but don't be long, then we'll make our way down to the Burger Bar." Said Polly.

They walked into the book shop where they found shelves up to the ceiling full of books, all in sections. Toby headed straight to the 'Fantasy' section where he stared at the all of the books upon the shelves. Toby picked out a book from the latest fantasy series and then took it to the counter. They then walked out of the shop after Toby had paid for the book and back out along the High Street.

"A good days' shopping?" Said Polly.

"Oh yes indeed." Replied Leonie, smiling.

"Same here? Said Toby, holding up his bags.

"And me." Said Keiron. They spent a great deal of their Christmas money, but held some back for the Burger Bar a few shops along. When they arrived, a waitress showed them to a table for four and put menus upon the table. The four scanned the Menus. The waitress returned holding her electronic order pad, then asked for their order.

"Hello, I'm Trina,, what would you like?" She asked. She was about five feet seven had light brown hair tied in a Ponytail and was wearing a black uniform.

"I'll have a Cola and a Quarter Pounder with cheese, please." Said Toby.

"And the same for me please." Said Keiron, grinning.

"I'll have …. er .. right, a Ham Berger and a Cola, please." Asked Polly scribbled the orders down upon her pad, tapped it with the stylus and pressed a button to enter the order.

"It will be along in a few minutes." Said Trina and walked away.

Toby was sitting next to Keiron, opposite Leonie and Keiron was sitting opposite Polly. There were salt and Pepper shakers, a vinegar bottle and sugar bowl in the centre of the table between them.

Before long, Tina arrived with another waitress, named Elaine. Tallish, slim and with a blonde Bobb hair style. They each carried a tray which held two plates with Burgers and two glasses of Cola upon each of them.

278

"There we are, Cola and Ham Berger." Said Trina, placing a plate and a glass in front of Leonie.

"Thank you." Said Leonie, brightly.

"And for you Dear." Said Trina, placing the same in front of Polly.

"Thank you." Said Polly.

"A Cola and a Quarter Pounder with cheese you said, Sir." Said Elaine, placing a plate and glass of Cola in front of Toby.

"Thank you." Said Toby.

"And also for you sir." Said Elaine, placing another plate and glass in front of Keiron.

"Thank you." Said Keiron, smiling. At last, he thought, I can fill my belly!

The waitresses then walked away with the trays. Leonie and Polly picked up their cutlery and cut the Burger bun into pieces, then with their knife and fork, picked up the prices and began to eat their Burgers. Toby and Keiron held their Burgers in their napkins and then proceeded to bite huge chunks out of them, holding them in their hands.

"The JCB is off again." Laughed Leonie, looking at Keiron. Polly laughed too.

"It's how to eat Quarter Pounders." Replied Keiron, between mouthfuls.

"Yes, well we're Civilised." Retorted Polly, holding up her cutlery for Keiron to see.

"It's not been a bad day so far, has it?" Said Toby, finishing the last of his Burger.

"Yes, it has been a good day, I've really enjoyed myself." Replied Leonie.

"Yes, it was well worth coming. " Said Polly.

"Yeah, we won't get a day out like this for a while." Said Keiron.

They finished off their Burgers and drank their Colas, then paid at the counter. They left the Burger Bar, laden with carrier bags and walked down the High Street.

"It's a quarter to three, we should get to the Bus Station well in time for your Dad, Toby." Said Polly.

"Yeah, thanks for showing us around Polly, if I come here again with Dad, I'll know where everything is." Said Toby.

"There's that Hotel across there, and the side street at the side of it." Said Keiron pointing across from the end of the High Street. They crossed over and walked back along Wells Street and Silver Street to the Bus Station. They turned the corner just as Carl drone round to the front of the Mobility shop. He parked up and they hurried over to the Landrover.

"Hi Guys, Yeah, they serviced her, she's OK." Said Carl.

"Hello Mr Morby." Said Polly as they began to climb into the back seat.

"Hi Polly, enjoyed youmsleves I see, have the shops got anything left in them after you lot have finished raiding them?" Replied Carl.

"Would you take a bag home with you Dad, please, and put it in my room for when I get back at Easter?" Asked Toby.

"Will do, leave it in the back and I'll know which one." Said Carl.

"Everybody ready." Asked Carl, the four put their seat blets on, Toby in the front passenger seat and the other three in the rear seats. Toby passed his bag with the models, cement and plaints backwards and Polly put it into the back of the Landrover. Toby held onto the book, he would take that back to Toadford with him when they returned on Monday.

Carl turned the recognition, revved the engine a little and then pulled away from the parking space. They drove out from the Bus Station, out along past the Army centre and Carl pulled into a Petrol Station, a short way along. He got out and stood filling up the Landrover. Then he replaced the nozzle and walked over to the office and paid. He returned to the Landrover and got back in.

"All full up now, so off we go." Said Carl.

He pulled back out of the Petrol Station and turned left at the roundabout. Keeping to the main road, they passed the old Brunel Railway Station, then some shops and offices, then a Burger bar. They then passed the industrial Estate, then there was a sign pointing towards Tiverton, they were back upon the A361.

"Get much while you were there?" Asked Carl.

"Oh, got the new Fantasy Book, some models and the paints." Replied Toby.

"I got a model too." Said Keiron.

"We got some clothes and accessories." Said Polly.

"Then we finished off in a Burger Bar." Said Leonie.

"So you had a good day then?" Asked Carl.

"Oh yes, we had fun." Replied Polly.

"What're you all doing tomorrow? Said Carl.

"After we make sure we're packed properly, we might just have an easy day, as it's our last before we return to Toadford." Replied Polly.

"Yeah, Keiron wants me to help him paint his model, so we'll probably have a relaxed day of it." Said Toby.

"I go back to school too, for my last two terms. Then after the Summer, I go to Toadford as well, we'll all be together." Said Leonie, smiling.

"Hope you all have fun. You are going to Polly's for half Term, is that right?" Asked Carl.

"Yes, me and Keiron are." Replied Toby.

"Oh, I'm sure I could fit Leonie in my room, the boys will be sharing the spare room." Replied Polly.

"You'll have to get Dad to bring you with him when we are collected from Toadford then Leonie, he may have to take us to Polly's as there won't be room in her Dad's car for all of us." Said Keiron.

"So I can come?" Squealed Leonie, her eyes bright.

"If Mom says it's OK and Dad can bring you." Replied Keiron. "My Parents won't mind if Leonie is Polly's Bedroom."

"Whoop Whoop!" Cried Leonie, now she really felt she belonged.

"They continued their journey until they reached Tiverton, then Carl turned off to go through the town. They go onto the Exeter Road and soon turned onto the Road down across the Moors. As he drove across the Moors, the sky became black and the car became dark. Carl glanced around and saw that Leonie, Polly and Keiron had fallen asleep in the back seats; Polly had fallen asleep with her head upon Keiron's shoulder. Carl turned to Toby and saw that he too had fallen asleep. It had been a long day and was now heading into the evening.

Eventually, Carl drove through Cragmoor Common and turned off into Cragmoor Drive when he saw the sign for Topley Village. He passed the star upon the houses and then turned off into Manor Drive. A short way along, before reaching Topley shining House, Carl turned into Mews Lane, turned around and parked outside Tithe Barn Cottage. He shook Toby gently in his seat.

"OK, we're back." Said Carl.

Toby opened his eyes sleepily and sat up in his seat. He turned to the others and shook Keiron.

"We're back, Mate." Toby said, Keiron just grunted.

"Keiron, we're back." Toby said again, this time he sat up and in doing so woke up Polly from leaning upon his shoulder. With the movement of Keiron and Polly, Leonie also woke.

"Are we home?" Asked Leonie, rubbing her eyes.

"Yes, we're here." Replied Keiron, climbing out of the Landrover.

"Had a good trip?" Asked Carl.

"Yes thank you, Mr Morby, thank you for taking us today." Said Polly.

"Don't mention it, I had to go anyway. Glad that you had fun." Said Carl.

"Thank you, Mr Morby." Said Leonie.

"It's Carl, Dear." Replied Carl.

"Thanks Carl, we appreciate it." Said Keiron.

"That's OK Guys." Said Carl.

The others began to walk towards the house and Carl started up the car again.

"Well, see you at Easter then, Son. Look after yourslef and don't get into any trouble. Hope you win your Football Cup." Said Carl.

"Thanks Dad, we'll have a good go at that. Thanks for today, see you and Mom at Easter." Replied Toby.

Carl put the Landrover into gear and pulled away waving; Toby waved him all the way up the lane until he turned back out onto Manor Drive. The other three waved from the garden gate. Toby walked to the gate and they all walked up to the door, where Keiron opened the door with his key and let them in, classing the door behind them. Daisy walked out into the hallway where the four had put down their bags of goodies and were taking off their coats and hats.

"Did 'ee 'ave a gud time?" Asked Daisy.

"Oh yes Mom!" Squealed Leonie, jumping up and down.

"We had a great time." Said Keiron, holding up his bag.

"Did 'ee enjoy youmzleves Toby, Polly?" Asked Daisy.

"Oh yes thanks, Daisy." Said Polly, holding up her bags.

"Yes thanks." Replied Toby.

"Thank yer Dad fer me, Toby, fer puttin' up with these two rascals fer yon day." Said Daisy.

"I will, thanks." Said Toby.

By the time they had taken their bags up stairs and unpacked them, it was time to have Dinner. After Dinner, they spent the evening watching television and showing Daisy the things which they had bought during their day out. It was then gratefully time for bed, with all the day's events. They were quite happy to go upstairs and crash out in bed. Almost as soon as they had pulled up their duvets and their head had hit their pillows, they were asleep.

The next day, Toby and Keiron were awake early to get their cases and bags packed ready for the next day before breakfast. In doing this, It would give them more time to spend upon one last days outing and painting some of the parts of Keiron's model kit.

They went for a walk out to the village after lunch and decided to look a little further, as it was their last day. They walked out of the village centre again along Lower Main Street and this time turned right rather than left, as they had to reach the Quarry. Keiron showed them a gate which led into a Bridleway through some trees, the further that they walked into the trees the thicker they became until they were completely enclosed by them.

"Where are we?" Asked Polly, who wasn't familiar with the area at all.

"We're in Tugmoor Woods." Replied Keiron. He fumbled in his jacket pocket and brought out a piece of red coloured wool. Keiron then tied it to a branch of a bush beside the path. "Just so that we know which way it is to get back out again, as the wood can get quite dense so we may get lost if we stray off the path."

"Would it be that difficult to find our way back?" Asked Polly.

"Not if we're careful, but as we get to the centre of the woods, it does get confusing if one doesn't mark the pathway and direction to retrace our steps." Replied Keiron.

"If you put the markers upon the left of the path, we'll know that if we keep them you our right when returning. We'll know which way we're going." Suggested Toby.

"Good idea Mate, we need to find our way out quickly as we've not got all day to be in here and need to be out of the woods by the time it gets dark." Replied Keiron.

"Best we don't go too far in then. I think." Said Polly.

"Good idea." Replied Toby.

As they walked on, the light became more dappled and all they were able to see was dancing shadows and glimmers of light around them. They were able to hear the rustling of the wind through the trees and bushes. Sound was different, as different as the light was in here. The tall trees around them; Oaks and ancient Beeches scattered with Ivy covered around Ash trees, Holly and Hazel; this was ancient woodland. Sound echoed around the trees and it was difficult to know from which direction the sound came from.

"It's a bit scary in here." Said Polly, looking all around like she was scanning the area.

"A bit dark too." Added Leonie, squinting, trying to look into the depths of the forest more easily.

"We'll be OK as long as we stick to the path, we will only need to turn around and walk back the way that we came in." Said Keiron.

"They walked a little further on through the trees and Keiron pointed out a large Oak tree to their right. He tied a piece of wool to a bush upon the left side of the path just before the tree. The ground that they walked upon was rich soil mixed and covered with the rotted and now rotting leaves of Centuries. The smell wafted to them as they walked along and kicked up the leaves upon the surface of the path, a rather sweet musty smell, like mushrooms. Around and about, where the Sun's rays reached the floor of the woodland, there were many plants here. None were in flower yet, save for the Aconites and Hellebores along with the Snow Drops.

"I found this a while ago when I was exploring here; that's when I discovered it was best to keep a Marker for my way out of the woods." Said Keiron.

"It looks like an old Oak tree." Said Toby.

"Very old." Added Polly.

The trunk was tall and gnarled like stone. It seemed solid, also like stone. It was as round in diameter as the four of them standing side by side and in front of them there appeared to be crack in the bark.

"There seems to be a crack there, look, it looks like it goes in line straight across for a couple of feet and then comes down to the ground on both sides; it …. it looks like a door!" Said Toby.

"Don't be silly; trees don't have doors in them." Retorted Polly.

"How do you know if all trees don't, examined many trees in great detail in Cranleigh, have you?" Said Keiron, with a grin.

"It may be a town and not a Village, Keiron, but we do have trees in Cranleigh, they don't only grow in the countryside. I'm pretty sure all the ones I've ever seen don't have doors in them." Replied Polly, giving Keiron one of her disapproving looks, This was something of a common practise by Polly, just by giving a person one of her looks, she was able to transmit a feeling of distain, anger, disgust and fascination or emotion without even speaking to them.

Just then, they heard a rustling behind them. Slowly, Toby turned around to look. With thinking, Keiron stepped over in front of Polly and saw a smallish young Deer Stag standing a little way away from them upon the other side of the pathway. Toby and Polly looked in awe at the creature. He stood some four feet tall at shoulder with a defined looking face and a pair of large antlers upon his head. Leonie was rooted to this spot, unable to speak. Keiron was being careful not to spook the Dear. Without thinking, almost subconsciously, Toby slowly moved towards the Stag. The Stag continued to chew away happily at the undergrowth and ignored the four friends standing in its presence.

Before long the Stag shifted its feeding location and Toby stopped dead still, hardly daring to breathe. He was now only a matter of ten feet from the Stag. It was only then that the Stag noticed there was company. He looked at the group and then at Toby. Polly began to fear that the Stag would charge Toby and gore him with its antlers; she momentarily turned her face into Keiron's shoulder.

284

When there was no cry of alarm from Toby, she looked back. To everyone's disbelief, the Stag walked a couple of steps nearer, still looking directly at Toby and then bowed its head low stretching out its front legs. Without thinking, Toby slowly bowed to the Stag, then straightened up. The Stag then moved away before leaving at a trot into the trees and away out of sight.

"Oh my God! What just happened?" Asked Leonie, excited at what she had just witnessed.

"Toby, that Stag just bowed to you and then ran away, what the ruddy Hell was all that about?" Asked Keiron.

"I d .. d .. don't k .. know? I've seen Stags and other Deer when I've been with dad up upon the Moor, but they've never bowed to me before?" Replied Toby, completely confused.

"Do you think it's something to do with that door?" Asked Keiron.

"I've told you already didn't I, trees don't have doors?" Said Polly, sternly.

"Who are Ye? Why are ye trespassing' at ma hoose?" Said a voice from behind them.

They all turned slowly around to see who it was that had spoken to them. Again, they were confused, in awe and were completely at a loss as to what was before their very eyes.

Standing there before them was a short man of about four feet in height, or maybe a little shorter. He had big hands in which he held an old Oak staff which was delicately and skilfully carved. He was wearing a white frilly shirt with pale brown Britches which were held up by a thick black leather belt with a large golden buckle, shaped like a small Dragon. He was wearing a red felt hat which was slightly tall and had around it a thin black strap similar to the one around his waist with its own square golden buckle. He was wearing over his shirt a waistcoat of dullish red leather which matched in colour, his ruddy cheeks. He had long bushy white beard, underneath a reddish purple bulbous nose. His eyes were like two coals beneath his thick white eyebrows. When he spoke, it was vaguely sounding a little like a Scottish accent.

"Are ye deef? I'll ask ye agin shall I? What are ye doin' trespassin' at Ma Hoose?" The little man said.

"We're not trespassing and did you say Your House?!" Asked Polly with a little surprise in her voice.

"Aye Lassie, that's what I said, at Ma Hoose." He replied, sternly.

"We were just walking in the woods and saw a Deer Stag." Replied Toby.

"Are you a Midget?" Asked Leonie, rather forthrightly.

"Leonie! Don't be so rude!" Ordered Keiron, not knowing what the man may do or how he would reply in return. The man plumped out his chest and stood as though to attention.

"Nay Lassie, I aint no Midget, I'm a Dwarf, if ye please? One o' the line o' Gartharic The Golden Hand." Replied the Dwarf.

"So is Snow White around then, can we meet her?" Asked Leonie.

"Who?" Replied the Dwarf quizzically.

"Oh .. er .. it's a children's story about a Princess and Seven Dwarfs, sorry, don't you know it. Haven't you heard of it or read it?" Asked Polly.

"Nay Lassie, I dinna read much, no with living in yon woods in a tree." Said the Dwarf.

"I don't see any tree house, sorry I'm Polly, Polly Mugford." Said Polly, looking up into the branches of the tree.

"Angharad, Son of Gilgarad at ye service, Lassie." Replied the Dwarf.

"I'm Toby, Toby Morby." Offered Toby, holding out his hand for Angharad to shake, which he did with a thoughtful look upon his face.

"Ah, so ye woold be ye Laird's Clan then ma boy, bein' a 'Morteby,' that would explain why Skybolt there bowed down to yer then." Replied Angharad.

"Why did he bow down to Toby?" Asked Leonie, quizzically.

"A'cause yon Stag recognised Master Toby there, as bein' o' ye Laird's Clan. It's an animal thing, see, they are able te see things that we no can see or feel." Explained Angharad, vaguely, as he actually didn't think it correct to mention The Royal Blood out in the open air too much.

"My name is Keiron Muddley, I've never noticed you before in the woods?" Said Keiron, holding out his hand for Angharad to shake.

"I've no let ye notice me Laddie, but I've seen ye a few times lookin' aroond." Replied Angharad. Keiron went red in the face at the thought of his being watched whenever he went for a walk in the woods.

"And I'm Leonie, I'm Keiron's Sister." Said Leonie.

"Pleased te make yer acquaintance ma Dear." Said Angharad, with a slight bow. "Wood y'all like te come an' 'ave a cup of' tea wi me."

Toby looked at his watch, which prompted Keiron and Polly to do the same, he noticed that time was against them.

"Terribly sorry, please excuse us, but don't think us rude or anything; we can't stay, I'm afraid. We have to get back home. We go back to school tomorrow and we need to get home before its dark." Said Toby, apologetically.

"Oche aye ma Laird, I understand. I take it that ye are o' Toadford School, yes?" Asked Angharad.

"Yes, we all go to Toadford School, except Leonie." Replied Polly.

"And I will be starting to go there in September." Added Leonie.

"Well, ye are all welcome when ye come, now that I know ye and that ye are wi' yon Young Master.

"Yes, well we'd had better be getting back, thank you for your kind invitation. Sorry we can't accept today." Smiled Keiron.

"I'll see ye soon then, 'ave a nice time o' it at Toadford." Said Angharad.

"Goodbye then, have a nice evening." Said Polly.

The four of them then began to walk away, with a wave back, which was returned by Angharad. They walked a short distance and Poly felt obliged to turn to look back, as did Keiron, just in time to see a door closing, yes – a door close in the trunk of an old Oak tree, where the split had been, it closed with a chink of light and then disappeared.

"I thought that you said that trees didn't have doors?" Said Keiron, grinning. Polly walked in silence for a few moments, contemplating having to admit that she was wrong, letting Keiron win, showing that 'Muddles' was more intleligent than she was. This thought gave her pimples. Toby and Leonie were listening hard, to try and see whether Keiron couldn't claim victory because her silence would indicate that he had outsmarted her.

"Well it must have been a trick of the light, you did notice the change in the light in there I suppose?" Replied Polly, trying to put some logic into her answer, she walked on with her nose in the air feleing victorious.

"How do you explain Angharad then? Where did he go to and did you see the way he was dressed?" Called Keiron after her, quickening his pace slightly to catch up with her. They emerged from the dull dappling light of the wood into the open world with proper daylight, It was beginning to get dull as the time was getting on and a chill breeze had blown up since they entered the woodland.

They continued along the forestry pathway towards the road.

"He must have a cottage or hut or something nearby and he was obviously an eccentric." Explained Polly, confidently.

"So you didn't see the door in the tree close when we were walking away from there then?" Continued Keiron.

"As I said, it must have been a trick of the light." Insisted Polly.

"There's been some really strange things going on this Holiday!" Said Toby.

"Spooky." Giggled Leonie.

They climbed the gate back over onto the road and then headed off back along Lower Main Street, back into the village centre. It was beginning to get dark as the street lights were beginning to glow orange as their timer switches turned to the 'On' position. They walked through the Village Square with the Church upon one side and some shops upon the other, then they left the Square where some shops upon the other, then they left the square where some shop keepers were taking displays back into the shops and locking up the doors to go home.

"Yeah, back to school tomorrow." Said Keiron thoughtfully.

"Won't be long before we have the Cup Final against Hatchel House, that should be a breeze," Said Keiron.

"Yeah, let's hope we don't pick up any injuries before then, we have five months until we need to play." Said Toby.

"Actually, we're in January now, so you have four months, the Cup Final is an May not June." corrected Polly, happy to be right about something again.

"Hatchel are still going to get a ruddy good thrashing which ever month it is that we will be playing them." Said Keiron.

"Try to avoid Taylor if you can as much as possible; he'll be really gunning for you to get you suspended or injured as much as he can before the match, just to see you miss the Final, because he has to". Advised Polly.

They walked out of the village centre and onto the lane up along Upper Main Street, out towards the cross which was shining up on top of its hill. They reached Manor Drive and walked along until they turned into Mews and walked up to Tithe Barn Cottage. Keiron let them in with his key. They stopped to take off their coats, hats and scarves and then went upstairs to freshen up.

Not long after, they entered the kitchen where Daisy had a big pan of stew steaming away upon the cooker. Upon the table were bowls laid out with spoons by their sides and a large bowl of bread rolls in the centre of the table. They sat down at the table and waited patiently.

"'Ad a gud aft'noon 'ave thee M'Dears?" Asked Daisy, ladling out the stew into their bowls.

"Yes thanks Mom." Replied Keiron.

"We went for a walk in the woods." Said Leonie.

"Was that they'm woods on te way out o' the village?" Asked Daisy.

"Yes, that's right." Replied Toby.

"Oh, Oi've 'eard stories 'bout theym woods, you'm shuld be careful ifn you'm be wantin' te gwain into theym woods now," Said Daisy.

"What type of stories?" Asked Polly.

"Oh, Oh youm wouldn't want to know all that gossip see." Said Daisy.

288

"Yes we would !" Replied Keiron.

"Please tell us." Begged Leonie.

"Well, some stories of strange things, lights, folk, disappearing and such like, see." Said Daisy.

"It's very dense in there so Keiron used pieces of coloured wool to retrace our journey back out." Said Polly, who was quite impressed that Keiron had taken the time to think about something and come up with a simple but effective answer to keep them safe from getting lost.

"'Ave you'm all got yer stuff ready fer the new term then at School?" Asked Daisy.

"Yes, thanks Daisy, we're all sorted out, we packed our things this morning before we went for our walk in the woods." Replied Keiron.

"'Ave you'm packed ready fer tomorrow, Leonie Dear?" Asked Daisy.

"Yes Mom, I don't have any more homework to take back so I've just got my new books for the term and stuff." Replied Leonie.

"what do you do about changing over from St. Margaret's, Leonie?" Asked Polly.

"Oh, I don't have placement exams this term, because I won't be there next year to place into option classes. I will just do lessons the same as everyone else. The course work marks though, will be sent onto Toadford for the subjects covered there so that my course work grade can be credited to any work that I do there." Replied Leonie.

"So you'll just leave in July and then start at Toadford in September?" Asked Polly.

"Yes, that's right." Said Leonie, grinning.

"We will be 'Weeners' when you arrive, so we will be on higher tables in the Dining Hall and will have different lesson to you, so we will most likely only see you at break times." Said Polly.

"That's OK Polly; I'll have my head full with finding my way around the School for lessons and homework, probably, to think of much for the first few weeks. Meeting up in the Break times sounds good though, then I'll become a full member of your gang, so you'll need to take a new group photo, won't you Polly?" Said Leonie.

"Yes, that's right, I always carry my camera around, so that'll be able to get the photo of our complete team, including you and 'Bella when you arrive at Toadford," Said Polly.

"Yeah, that'll make five of us, that'll be cool!" Said Keiron.

"YAAAAY!" Squealed Leonie.

289

After Dinner, they went up to the confines of Keiron's Bedroom, a little squashed with four People ad a camping bed. Leonie was borrowing Keiron's Lap-top with Polly to try looking up any references for 'Strange things at Tugmoor Woods;' meanwhile, Toby and Keiron were painting Keiron's model kit, painting the parts. At present, Keiron was painting the fuselage pieces while Toby was concentrating upon painting the smaller pieces.

The girls were carefully going through all of the links which the Lap-top was putting upon the screen.

"We've found a few stories of disappearances from years ago on some of the sites which we've looked at. We've printed some of them off for us all to read." Said Polly.

"There were a lot of stories where people had sighted strange creatures, so they said." Added Leonie,

Polly and Leonie handed out copies of the printouts from the Laptop to Toby and Keiron. They went through them, studying them, taking notes.

"A number of them mentioned the meeting or seeing 'a strange old man', smallish, who seemed to disappear when they looked away; Hmmm I wonder?" Asked Toby.

"Wonder that?" Asked Leonie,

"The thing I Wonder about is Angharad." Said Polly.

"Yes, just what I was thinking." Agreed Toby, nodding his head.

"Angharad?", Asked Leonie quizzically.

"Yeah, the little Guy in the Woods, you know, who walked away and went into the door in the tree." Said Toby.

"Or appeared to." Interjected Polly.

"That would explained the reports of the strange small old man who appeared to vanish when they looked away; he vanished because he went into the door in the Oak tree." Said Toby.

"Or appeared to." Repeated Polly.

"Yes, appeared to, alright, but it would still explain the reports." Said Toby making his port.

"How about the reports of strange Creatures?" Asked Keiron.

"I don't like the sound of that." Said Leonie rather worriedly.

"We didn't see any, only a Deer." Said Toby.

"And Angharad." Added Keiron.

"Yes, but he was just a small old man, not exactly a strange creature," Argued Polly.

"Next time we're all there, we could have a better look." Said Keiron.

"Careful how we go, remember what happed up on Cragmoor, that tramp who attacked us, if there's strange creatures around it, may not be wise to go too far into the woods." Suggested Leonie.

"We won't know unless we look." Replied Keiron.

"Yeah, but all the same, we could look, but be watchful at all times." Suggested Polly.

"Good idea." Replied Toby.

"'S'pose, it would be interesting to see properly what we can find in there to answer some of our questions and the stories." Agreed Leonie.

They thought it time to adjourn their meeting and go to bed, as they had an early start in the Morning. Bill would leave early for work and drop Leonie off on his way, while Daisy would take the other's to Toadford, he would disappear with all the other Toffs.

Chapter Twenty Nine – The Wizard Lord

The morning came with early light spreading across the ground. Huddled under their blankets in their beds, the soldiers were stirring. Some had already taken to the duty of lighting a fire and had put a large pot upon it. They tended to their injured while Sentries surveyed the perimeter to their camp looking for signs of movement and forewarning of another attack.

No one was at all badly hurt, just bruises and the odd cut, graze or gash from a sword which was sown up and patched with lint and healing herbs. The Master sat, surveying the area and the damage to his company. He was slowly, carefully inspecting his mighty sword 'Petrach' for any damage and to look for bluntness of its keen edge. The blue glow of its power had subsided indicating that there were no Goblins or Orcs nearby and it now sat in his hands, dull as any other sword.

Men now were gathering at a small brook in front of their camp which bled into the main Meerlandse River, having taken off their armour carefully, slowly, keeping an eye upon his sword, watching for any signs of its blue glow showing and being on alert for the need to fix his armour back on and take up his sword. He took the sword the few yards to the brook and placed his hands into the water. The cold of the water soothed his face as he brought two cupped handfuls up to it and buried his face in them. He washed his aching arms and broad chest and then stood in the water to feel it caress his legs.

Once he felt more revived, he walked from the water and heard the sound of thundering hooves. He glanced at his sword, standing beside the water's edge and took note that its blade still did not glow blue. He walked up the small slope of the bank, to see the return of the Regiment. General Thomas, Captain Manos and General Listus.

The four came to a halt in a cloud of dust and dismounted their horses and Pony, allowing a Soldier to lead each one away to be tied up and fed, watered and brushed down. Looking around him, it was obvious to the Captain that there had been a skirmish here the night before. The four dismounted and General Thomas, Lucius and general Listus walked to their tents. Captain Manus dismounted his horse and secured it, and then he walked over to the Master's tent. The Master stood and saluted.

"How goes it Youter, what tiding do you have for me this crisp frosty morning?" Said Captain Manos as he arrived in front of The Master's tent. The Master stood and saluted.

"Mighty grievous my Lord, we were attacked by a raiding party of Goblins last night. We fought with might, Sir; we drove them off back out of the Village and back into hiding. No doubt to plan another attack tonight." Replied The Master. The Sun was trying to make its way through the cloud and momentarily caught the Captain's breastplate and sparkled. A Soldier had brought a seat out of the Master's Tent. They were folding wooden seats, easy to carry in the saddle packs. Captain Manos sat down as did The Master upon a folding seat of his of his own.

"I see, the men have had a hard fight by their Manner. But for the telling of this fortune, we should be away from here and make for Mount Vernon by way of the Marsh of Gorr." Said Captain Manos.

The Master wiped his wet hair out of his eyes; as the wind had begun to blow the jet black, slicked hair dry and around his face. He then called a Soldier boy to come over to him, who duly saluted and then proceeded to help the Master replace and strap his armour back on. The Captain then rose from his seat and closed it up and the Master turned and picked up his seat. Then he and The Captain both walked over to the General's tent, to speak with General Thomas. Once there they greeted him and then the three of them walked over to where the Regent was seated outside a tent which had hurriedly been prepared for him. He sat at a small fold up table and greeted the three saluting figures as they put down their folding seats and sat down with the Regent. Soon after they were joined by General Listus.

"By the tidings of the night, it would seem that we should elect to travel by way of the Marsh of Gorr to eventuate ourselves to reach Mount Vernon." Said The Master.

"We encountered speculation and interest at the Inn Yester night, interest which necessitated in that we take into our conference the Tavern Landlord, to see us through 'til Morn'. If we take the road, we will be too obvious to another raiding party. If we are careful and do not rush, we may transverse the Marshes without harm and so avoid open ambush from Goblins or any other foul creatures the Marquis sends our way." Replied Captain Manos.

"We will need Scouts to look out a path through the Mires and to keep watch upon our flanks for Goblins and such." Suggested General Thomas; they all agreed.

"We must make happen our arrival at Mount Vernon and then our part of this Royal Mission will be fulfilled. This must be our main interest now." Said Lucius.

"At the end of all this, my men shouldst be greatly Honoured." Said The Master.

"Oh that you can be assured of yes Master Youtir, they will be just that. Yourslef also, Master Youtir, will be greatly Honoured upon our return, once our part in this mission and the risk that they placed upon themselves to fulfil it." Said Lucius.

"we must be away at the first opportunity." Said General Thomas. The meeting broke up and they walked back to their respective places. The Regent to his horse, and Captain Manos, General Thomas to his horse. General Listus to his Pony and the Master to his tent. The Soldiers returned to his tents and began to pack away their things, after they had walked away carrying their folding seats with them.

They broke camp, after they had all packed up, bagging up their things and tents and strapped them upon their saddles. The Master too packed up his bags and strapped to his saddle. The company again formed and began their ride towards the village centre.

It was still early morning in Millslade Village; the company slowly rode through the streets of the village, past silent cottages and beyond the Church. They hoped that travelling through the village so early, that they may miss the people and be gone before anyone stirred to see them. This way, they would be able to charge track and take the Moorland was way out across the stretched landscape and man eating Mires of the Marsh of Gorr.

As they rode past the Mighty Cracken Inn, Captain Manos remember that there was an air of distain throughout the bar as they had sat at their table. It was noticed the talk between the man at the bar and the Landlord. If the Regent had not cleared their way by paying with Gold. In one corner of the Tavern, seated alone with his tankard of ale, a solitary figure, clothed with a rough grey cloak and hood; he simply sat sipping from his tankard.

The sign creaked in the early morning wind which also blew upon their scarves, which were wrapped around their necks. Dust was blowing around a shutter slammed back and forth upon a Bedroom window of the Inn. With each crack against the cracked wall, flaked with age and worn white wash, the worn timber of the shutter split a little more. They rounded the Church, its stone square Tower loomed before them casting a shadow across their path. They travelled along the dusty lane out of the Village Centre through the outer laying farms. They past the last small gathering of cottages, then they rode as quietly as possible through the fields along the lane past the stone walls which lined the lane. They reached a junction in the lane which led them through a farmyard. There were old and leaning gate posts at the entrance and to their left was an old rickety farmhouse. A sign which swung precariously from an old knarled post was only just legible as stating that this was Clitohney Farm. It looked and smelled old. The farmhouse had no glass to its windows, which were few; rather it merely had shutters of cracked Oak to shut out all that the weather and Seasons would throw at them. The roof of the house was of old thatch, which was laying a little thin now and most likely housed very much most of the rodent and bird population for miles around.

The Riders were taking this route at this early hour to hopefully avoid the many spies which it was evident upon their journey had been sent into these shires to gather information and prevent the building of forces by the Alexandrians. This had become more noticeable and lately more dangerous as they had worked their way across the shires towards their journey's end. Opposite the farm house stood three barns of Cobb and wooden frame construction. Once

294

again they merely had shutters for window covers and many of these were hanging from one hinge. The whole farm gave the air of neglect and the need of repair. The barns were thatched like the house, and housed a number of farm implements such as ploughs, of which there were three. It was strange to understand how a farm which was wealthy enough to house three ploughs should be left to this state of neglect? They suddenly became aware of a young maid, average height, slim and dressed with a rather old looking slightly ragged dress and blouse. The neckline showed her slightly bronzed skin underneath which was achieved by many hours outside for work in the Sun. She was standing next to a well with a wooden pail in her hand and looked surprised at seeing a company of fully packed and armed Soldiers approaching her through the farmyard.

"What be your business here My Lords? We are but a poor hard working farm of no consequence to no one, Sir." Asked the Girl.

"What be your name Maid?" Asked Lucius, as the Company came to a halt a short way in front of her.

"I be Lucy, M' Lord, daughter o' Yeoman Mc Traivick, owner o' yere farm. What be your business 'ere wi' us? Ye came fully armed, a small army, wi Dwarfs? We 'ave nay trouble 'ere Sir." Said Lucy.

"We are on a Royal Mission my Dear Miss Mc Traivick, we are simply passing through and would gladly ask you, please, do not mention our presence to any soul." Replied Lucius.

"We look for the path leading us out to the Marsh." Said General Thomas.

"M'Lord, 'tis dangerous out across yon marsh o' Mires, ye would surely die if ye tried te cross wi'out knowledge o' them Mires." Said Lucy.

We wull know oor path, Missy." Said General Listus.

"M' Lord Dwarf, if ye would know yer path across the Mires, then ye would no' 'ave asked which path te take." Replied Lucy.

"He means My Dear, that as we are rigorously trained Soldiers of the Highest arms, that we would find a path." Said Lucius.

"Aye, er … yes Missy, that es what I wuz sayin'." Agreed General Listus.

"You seem to know your wits, My Dear." Said General Thomas.

"Aye M' Lord, I may be a poor farm girl but I assure you, Sir; I am no' bereft of thought." Replied Lucy.

They rode forward, closer to the well and a soldier climbed down from his horse and walked over to where Lucy stood. He took the pail from her hand gently and then stood it upon the rim of the well. He dropped the pail of the well down into its depths and they heard a loud echoing splash as it hit the water far below. The Soldier then began to wind the handle of the well and the rope dangling into it went taught.

"You do not need to assist me Sir, I have been drowning pails of water from this well all my life as far as I can remember back along." Said Lucy.

"My name is Norius, My Dear." Said the Soldier, still turning the handle.

"What?" Reacted Lucy.

"My name is Norius, Norius de Campandre." Said the Soldier.

"Yes well, Norius, as I said er …. I can draw water for myself." Said Lucy catching the pail as it reached the top and open air after its journey up from the depths of the well. She poured it into a pail which stood beside the well. Norius then dropped it back into the well.

"One more I should think." Said Norius, as with a splash he began to turn the handle again and as before the rope went taught.

"My name be Lucy, Sir Norius, please be a usin' it, no' 'My Dear', I was gi'en ye name te be used, so please be addressin' me this way." Said Lucy.

"Yes, thank you Miss Lucy." Replied Norius, as the second pail of water arrived at the top of the well.

"Ye'll find yon Marsh if ye continues te ye path at ye far side o' yonder yard an' gwain through yon red gate. This will see ye out onto yon Marsh, be sure te praperly secure ye gate once ye 'ave all passed, te no' let out our sheep or other animals onto ye Marsh, or my Father would no' be as courteous as I 'ave been, I can assure ye." Said Lucy.

"We will not be here long enough to meet your Father, I'm afraid Miss Lucy, but give him the Prince Royals Blessing for me and thank you for your help." Said Lucius.

"Might I ask who is givin' such a High Blessing te my Father?" Asked Lucy. The Regent drew back his tunic and revealed the hilt of his sword 'Telos', with its glittering green Emeralds in the morning light.

"I am Lucius Thamley, Regent of the Kingdom of Alexandria, First Minister to Prince Royal Simon de Morteby of Alexandria." Said Lucius and replaced his tunic over the sword hilt, just in case any spies were watching.

"Sire, she may be a spy, thou revealed us.?" Said General Listus with a suppressed expression upon his face.

"Aye,, there is that General, but I would wager that if she were a spy and did wish to ambush us, we would already be dead by now." Said Lucius.

"I will bid ye goodbye, my Lord Regent, fer I 'ave many Chores o' my day ahead o' me." Said Lucy, with a small courtesy then picked up the pail of the water and walked towards the farm house.

"I bid thee goodbye and Bless you Miss Lucy." Said Norius, giving a small bow.

"Safe journey Sir, er …. Norius." Said Lucy, lifting her skirt slightly and giving a small courtesy to Norius. He walked back over and remounted his steed, then the Company began their way across the farmyard and out into the pathway upon the other side of the yard. Once again, they began to pass a number of stone walls which enclosed some fields. At the end of this pathway, they found the closed gate, painted red gate. They lifted the latch and passed from farm track to barren Moorland. Once all were through, remembering their warning, the last Soldier through made sure that the gate was closed. Once through, they found themselves upon an open barren Moor, populated only by a covering of thin tough grass and tufts of Heather.

"So where now?" Lucius thought aloud.

"You may follow me across the Mires, My Lord, or take up valuable time and be in much more peril to attempt youmsleves." Said a voice from their right hand side.

The Soldiers all drew their swords, some Dwarfs drew Battle Axes and some swords, some also drew bows.

"Halt with your anger, My Lords, for you need me to lead you across,, the Marsh." Said the figure. He was seated upon a white horse, which appeared to have golden hooves, then the men noticed that the horse in fact had a single twisted Silver horn protruding from its forehead. The figure sat upon an ornately carved saddle, he was dressed in britches of grey wool, his tunic and other clothes were covered by slightly ragged grey cloak and hood. He dropped his hood, to reveal the face of a young man with a strong jaw, fair hair and blue eyes.

"Who are you Sir, why should we follow you?" Said Lucius, rather pompously.

"I am Callinius, Apprentice to his Lordship Wizard Barnabus The Enlightened. I shall show you across the Mash of Gorr to our Master's dwelling place. You may otherwise ignore my offer and pick your own way across more slowly and more dangerously and most likely die in the progress." Said Callinius.

"Aye ye riding yon Unicorn, Laddie?" Asked General Listus, with astonishment.

"I am Sir, 'tis the steed given to the Chief Apprentice of My Lord Wizard." Replied Callinius.

"How do you capture and tame the creature? 'Tis a legend, a fable? " Asked Captain Manos.

"Tis beautiful." Added Norius, quietly to himself.

"A Unicorn is the most useful way to cross the Mires safely. She sees their depths and is able to sense a safe path. To answer your question,, My Lord Captain, to capture her takes strong magic, as she has strong magic herself. One never owns a Unicorn, one never fully tames a Unicorn, one simply borrows her for a while. If you Gentlemen would follow us in single file and do not wander,

297

we shall safely cross the Mires and Cliothedes will have done her job," Said Callinius.

"Do you not have another name, like Barnabus has the Enlightened?" Asked Captain Manos.

"Not as yet, My Lord, I will only receive my Colour of Magic and Song of Eternity once my Apprenticeship is completed." Replied Callinius.

"We thought of you as a spy for the Dark One." Said General Thomas.

"I assure you Gentlemen, I am no spy of Thracia, Cliothedes would never allow me upon her back if this were so. She would kill me, ran through with the horn." Said Calinius.

With that said, the Company sheaved their swords and Axes, and proceeded to follow the grey figure of Calinius across the misty ground. As they travelled out across the Marshes, the mists made the air chilled. The mist seemed to hang in the air and reluctantly part like a net curtain as they rode through it. The sure feet of Cliothedes led them through Mires either side of them as easy as riding along a road.

Suddenly from their right side a rush of figures sprang out from cover behind some rocks. Swords drawn, they advanced upon the Company. There was a large number so the Soldiers dismounted to take on the leading group at the front, while Dwarf archers fired waves of arrows into the rear of the attacking pack, to pick them off as they tried to back up their fellows at the front. The rear was falling fast under the constant shower of arrows. The Soldiers drew their swords and stood their ground, as Calinius had told them, do not leave the pathway shown to them by Cliothedes.

They parted and their foes were recognised, more Goblins and Orcs. Orcs did not usually tolerate fighting alongside Goblin's but when ordered to by the Marquis, they had little choice.

The Goblins were, as some would regard, ugly creatures. They had rather elongated skulls, pointed in some way at the back, their noses were thin and long, piggy like grey and filled w ith sharp pointed teeth. They were around five feet six inches tall, like a Dwarf, but had spindly arms and legs. They were capable of a sort of Magic, but having Alexandrian swords to fight, their type of Magic was too low to use in a skirmish.

The front line rushed the Soldiers and swing their swords. Goblin steel is much prized for sword blades but wielded by a Goblin, was a formidable weapon to face. They were though, facing Alexandrian swords and Dwarf battle Axes, the finest made.

The first soldiers held up their weapons and deflected the blows from the Goblins who were attacking them. Eyes now burning with a green glow, the anger within the Goblin was rising with every blow that was blocked and parried.

One Soldier, well trained well given strength to be patent, simply parried each blow and refused to allow the Goblin through his guard.

He swung, it was blocked; he swung again, another block; he trusted, a parry. Now the green anger of the Goblin was losing control. He swung and swung and swung. The Soldier blocked all of his attempts. Until now a swish of an Alexandrian blade came into contact. A Sizable gash now showed upon the face of the Goblin, his left cheek oozing green blood. His eyes narrowed; swish, block; swish block; thrust parry; swish block; swish duck.

"ARGHHH." Cried the Goblin, wide eyed as he felt the searing pain as the Soldiers sword sliced into the Goblin's shoulder and neck. Green blood spurted out and poured down his chest. His green glowing eyes faded to nothing more than two grey unseeing pools of dead flesh, he then slumped to the ground. More and More Goblins fell before the Soldiers, cut down by Alexandrian swords. The rear ranks of Orcs became eventually piles of bodies as flight after flight of arrows showered upon them cutting them down where they stood. The Master, General Thomas and Captain Manos cut their way through the ranks of Goblins, the swords 'Mandrake', wielded by General Thomas; 'Angil' by Captain 'Manos' and 'Telcos' by, wielded by Lucius, with its green Emeralds flashing in the Sun with each blow, tasted much Goblin Blood.

A Goblin came upon Manos, wielding its Goblin steel sword, swinging it around its head with its right hand and brandishing a round wooden shield to protect his right side. Manos with his Alexandrian armour, shield and sword 'Angil', blocked and trusted, parried, trusted then lunged and the Goblin stopped as though frozen and slumped to the ground, Manos placed his right foot upon the Goblin's chest and drew his sword 'Angil' from the body of the Goblin like from a stone. Mandrake crushed down and a Goblin's skull cleaved in two,, drenching General Thomas' Alexandrian Armour with thick green Goblin Blood.

Before long, the enemy army had been so badly depleted that they withdrew and ran. Some succumbed to the Marsh and found the Bogs and Mires which claimed them, whereas the remaining Goblins and Orcs fled leaving the Alexandrian Company to tend to their wounds. General Thomas had the Soldiers stack what Goblin and Orc bodies they were able to find and they burned them. They set camp and bedded down for the night. Next morning the Company packed away their camp and continued upon their journey to the edge of the Marsh of Gorr. Beyond this, they reached two outcrops of rock, as high as small mountains. To the left was Mount Kalem and to the right, Mount Vernon. Between the outcrops was a long narrow passage, which appeared to be swathed in mist.

"My Lords, we must transverse the passage. Beware, all is not as it seems as we pass through. My steed has the power to shield us for only a short time, but we must be wary of the spirits which dwell within the Mists." Said Calinius.

Calinius began to lead the Company through the passage between the rocks upon his Unicorn. As he rode forwards, the mist around them parted to allow them through and then drifted closed behind them. They moved slowly through the mist the rear ranks keeping watch behind for any sign of Goblins or Orcs. The pathway upon which they were travelling was full of small rocks which the riders found it difficult to stop their horses from stumbling upon. The Unicorn with its almost translucent white skin and golden mane, tail and golden hooves walked the pathway as though it were a flat lawn. Waves of Aura could be seen emanated from the Unicorn pushing the mists back away from the Company. Behind them, shadowy shapes moved around in the mist and they could hear faint wailing and moaning swirling around them.

"Do not venture beyond the influence of my steed, the spirits be hungry, my Lords." Said Calinius.

"Not only the spirits be hungry, there are some weary Soldiers who be hungry Master Calinius." Replied General Lists.

The company upon their horses and ponies continued to follow Calinius upon his Unicorn. All around them swirled the mist and the moaning and crying spirits swishing around, being kept at bay by the Aura emitting from the Unicorn. They looked around them and looking up either side of the Passage were tall rock cliffs. Around them were piles of rocks and brushwood scrub. Part way up the cliffs grew grey grass like growths waving in the mist.

They eventually reached a rather more rocky area along the Passage where a great outcrop towered up upon their left side. It appeared like a huge chimney stack of rock and at its foot they were just able to make out a dark entrance to what looked like a cave.

The Company rode up to a small flat plateaux at the cave's entrance where stunted short trees were growing and tied up their horses and ponies. The Soldiers camped with the horses guarding the entrance and Calinius led Lucius, General Thomas and general Listus into the mouth of the cave.

Once inside the cave above them guarding the entrance, stood four great stone Gargoyles. Before them was a great vaulted chamber which was circled by tall candlesticks with large tall candles upon them. The candlesticks were silver and richly carved with Runic symbols. Around the walls stood great panels of Quartz which glowed from impossible light sources. All around the walls were carvings of Magical Creatures.

They crossed a stone bridge which spanned a seemingly bottomless crevasse. They then walked through a large stone archway which was covered in carvings of many Runic symbols. Lucius and the Generals looked up at the vaulted roof and archway with a look of awe upon their faces. They entered a huge chamber, also with a vaulted roof and panels of Quartz. Around the Chamber were a pile of books, some with spines which were cracked, giving away their age, also this was betrayed by the layers of dust upon them and the cradle of Spider's webs

300

hanging all around them. In one corner stood a stand with a perch on top, where sat a large bird with red and gold feathers and a parrot-like beak.

All around the walls were massive book shelves filled with leather bound volumes and niches holding statuettes and bust of different ancient Wizards. Strange instruments accompanied them of all shapes and sizes. The bird turned its head and looked at the trio, he squawked.

"Ah, I have been expecting you, my Lords. Please enter my humble abode." Said the ancient voice of a figure with his back turned to them. They crossed the chamber, across a marble floor marked with the compass points and a ring depicting Zodiac signs. The figure was seated at an untidy mess of papers upon a large carved desk. Beside the desk was a number of easels which held boards with papers, illustrated with formulae and equations, each a different piece of work.

The figure was tall, old and lined with age, long white hair and a long white beard, dressed in an ancient grown of deep blue with embroidered golden motifs and Runic symbols upon it.

"My Lords, I have been awaiting your visit." Called Barnabus, still facing away from them.

"My foresight tells me that we are experiencing a serious vexation, there have been raids upon Calistria and also upon Parlemann and Petros Shires." Said Barnabus in his ancient voice, "These are but scouting visits, designed to draw us into conflict, designed to weaken the outer shires of the Kingdom and bite away at the Skin."

"We are not properly prepared for battle, my Lord Wizard; we have already suffered two attacks ourselves from small bands of Goblin, Orc and Troll. We have lost one of our own during these skirmishes." Replied Lucius.

"For this reason I sent out my apprentice upon Cliothedes, my Unicorn, to aid you through the Mires and the Enchanted alley to bring you safely to here." Said Barnabus.

"We lost Calistria te a very strange force o' Orcs an' Goblins M'Laird Wizard, a surprise attack whuch left ma kin as aught but Refugees en a foreign land. We 'ave, by Yon Grace o' ye Laird o' yon Shire, established a new settlement in the Shire of Karlsburg." Said General Listus.

"Yes General, they were trying our defences, hitting our mines to deprive us of our economy." Said Barnabus.

"Aye my Lord Wizard, without means te pay fer armoury and weaponry; where would ye Marquis think an army would be bought with no wages?" Said General Listus.

"There is no need to be thinking of problems there General, the Coffers of the Alexandrian Treasury would pay an' Army for some considerable time. We need to strengthen the Skin and the borders of each Shire." Said General Thomas, "'Tis true my Lord General, with my foresight, I have been able to council His Majesty had ordered that Messengers be sent out throughout the Kingdom and Shires to build an Army to defend the entire Commonwealth of Shires, to build a force to defend against the entire forces of Thracia." Said Lucius.

"I shall call for the Wizard Council to convene and take the message to their Shires and ally with Alexandrian Army upon the ground." Replied Barnabus.

Barnabus leaned upon his staff, made from what appeared to be Petrified wood. It was twisted and knarled with elaborate carvings from the centre to the hand figurine at the top, which appeared to be gripping a large Diamond.

"It is time Gentlemen that we make our plans to recapture Calistria and restore her to her rightful people. There is much work to be done and much to be prepared." Said Barnabus, "I will send my apprentice with you upon Cliothedes to guide you back through the Enchanted Valley and across The Marsh of Gorr. They will then make their way to Alexandria to await my arrival."

Lucius and the two Generals bade farewell to Barnabus, Calinius disappeared from the chamber. Listus and the Generals walked back under the archway and across the bridge then with one look behind, out of the cave into the daylight beyond. Captain Manos and the Soldiers outside stood to attention and all saluted. Calinius then walked out of the Cave, accompanied by Cliothedes the Unicorn. He mounted her and waited for the Soldiers to pack away camp and for Lucius and General Thomas to mount their horses and for Lucius and General Thomas to mount their horses and for General Listus to mount his Pony. With all packed away and mounted, Calinius began to retrace their steps through the Enchanted Valley. Once again, all around them outside the influence of the Unicorn's Aura, the mist and spirits swirled around them, being kept at bay by the Aura of Cliothedes. A spirit reached out to a Soldier half way along the column, who resembled Alkan; the Soldier recognised the face of the spirit and reached out. Suddenly the face of the spirit changed to that of a skull in a hood, a hand took hold of the Soldier who was lifted screaming from his horse into the air. Calinius, with cat like reflexes drew his wand 'Tallius' and fired off a repellent curse at the spirit. A streak of green light flew from his wand and hit the spirit who dropped the Soldier with a shriek and he fell rather heavily to the ground. The Column stopped while Soldiers around him helped him back into the saddle of his horse.

"There you see Gentlemen why it is so important to keep within the Aura of Cliothedes. The spirits can be deadly if you give them the opportunity. Your soldier was lucky this time, if the spirit had been able to rise further into the sky, it would have dropped him from a much greater height,, most certainly unto his death, to join with the spirits here within the mist." Said Calinius, placing 'Tallius' back into its sheath within his Robes.

The Company, led by Calinius, continued upon their journey through the mist until they emerged from the Valley out onto the Mash of Gorr. All around was high grass, strong, bright green from the moisture which was readily available due to the Bogs and Mires which they found surrounding them.

"Please keep in the footsteps of Cliothedes; she will lead you across the Marsh. Cliothedes is able to sense where the Bogs and Mires lay, before she reaches them; so Gentlemen, if you keep within her footsteps once more, you will safely cross the Marsh." Said Calinius.

The Company slowly, in single file, followed Cliothedes across the Marsh. All around them, they were able to see the damp surface, which covered in weed, looked just a solid as the path which Cliothedes was treading. Underneath the surface weeds though, lay bottomless Bogs, waiting to suck man and horse deep underneath them.

Eventually, they reached the far side of the Marsh and found solid ground upon the Moor once again. They trotted on now, finding the familiar gate which led them back into the farm track and into the village of Millslade. Before the Company left the Moor, Calinius pulled up upon Cliothedes' reins.

"I must bid thee fine fellows farewell from here. I must not allow the villagers to see Cliothedes this close to the Agents of the Marquis. I will see you Gentlemen upon your return to Alexandria. To you Gentlemen Dwarfs, we will meet again once more as we battle to regain your Homeland of Calistria. Said Calinius.

"Fare well Calinius, and thank you for leading us safely to here. We will see you once again upon our return to Alexandria." Replied Lucius.

"Thank you Calinius, for making it possible for me to return home and defending me from the Spirits." Said the Soldier whom they had almost lost in the mist.

"No need to thank me Sir, I was but reforming my duty." Replied Calinius.

"We thank ye Sir Calinius, fer yere brave offer te fight alongside us te regain oor Homeland." Said General Listus.

With no further delay, a wave of his hand, to the amazement of all who saw it, Cliothedes reared into her hind legs and from either side of her saddle, at the shoulders, two pure white wide wings sprung out. With but four beats of her mighty wings, Cliothedes along with Calinius upon her back rose into the air and flew away. The Company watched as they disappeared far into the distance.

"Wull ma Dear Sirs, me thunks its aboot time fer a Dram ere too en yon Inn now that oor business wi'Ye Wizard Laird is completed." Said General Listus. Seemingly, once business of any kind is satisfactorily concluded, Dwarfs generally liked to cement the deal over 'a dram ere too' in the nearest tavern.

They rode away from the farm track and joined the road up past a row of cottages upon either side with fields in between. They rode into the village Square and off to their left were the familiar sight of 'Ye Mighty Cracken' tavern. They tie up their horses and ponies outside the Tavern and after watering their steeds, the Soldiers and Dwarfs walked into the Tavern. They sat at a number of tables around the bar; the Barmaids came over in their dull grey dresses and puffed sleeved blouses wearing white bonnets, table by table and brought them some Mutton Stew and Ale. The Generals, Captain Manos and Lucius Thamley, sat at a table of their own. A Barmaid came over to their table and gave a little courtesy.

"Gud day te 'ee M'Lords, 'tis gud te see yees again so soon; will yerbe aneedin' a bead fer yon night, Sirs? Asked the Barmaid cheerfully.

"No thank you Mary, all that we require is a good helping of your Mutton Stew and some of your finest Ale." Replied Lucius.

"Thank 'ee M'Lords, I shall deal with that d'rectly." Replied Mary enthusiastically. She walked away and disappeared behind the Bar. Next across the Tavern walked the Landlord, towel over his shoulder.

"Gud day te 'ee Gentlemen, so fine te see 'ee again so soon, I 'opes you'm 'as an enjoyable stay 'ere in our 'umble little Tavern." Said the Landlord.

"Good day to you Jan, we are but passing through at this time, but we hope that you have a good day." Said Lucius, as he handed a couple of Gold coins to the Landlord.

Thank 'ee Sir, that'll cover everything for 'ee an' Yere Company which travles with 'ee." Replied Jan. He then disappeared from them also back to the Bar where he sat upon a stool supping some Ale from a tankard and speaking with a couple of men.

The men looked like most other men who frequently visited village Taverns on the outer fringes of the Shires. They were most likely labourers of farm lands, dressed plainly with stout boots. Lucius looked to make sure that no one was over hearing them and then turned to the other companions at his table.

"General Listus, will you be leaving us as you journey close to your new settlement or will you be journeying with us back to Alexandria?" Asked Lucius.

"Nay Sire, me an' ma men wull be ridin' fer home once we be close enough. Ye tidings we bring fer oor King be far too important te tally lang an' forsake oor mission." Replied General Listus.

"We will be separated somewhere west of the Connarch Bridge, south of Karlsburg City." Said Lucius.

"So we go by means of Karlsburg Shire then; doesn't that take us close to the Connarch Mountains, where the troll descended from to kill our Brother Alkan; is this a wise path to take?" Asked General Thomas.

"We ere less likely te be attacked by Ye Dark Laird's minions if we ere a force, so it wud be prudent te journey thus way together, then split up af'er passin' beyond yon mountains, where it be somewhat safer." Said General Listus.

"I agree Gentlemen; this would be the route to afford the entire company the most protection en force. We don't want to stay around here too long, following our reception upon our Journey inward; so we need to clear the mountains and reach the home of General Listus before night falls upon our outwards journey." Said Captain Manos.

"So it is agreed then Gentlemen, we are away over te oor new settlement across yon river, then ye journey back te yer Prince Royal wuth all oor tidings, brought frum ye Laird Wizard." Said General Listus.

"We agree, Aye." Said Lucius. General Thomas and Captain Manos together.

"So wuth that oot o' ye way, let's get doon te a wee Dram ere Too." Added General Listus.

After they had eaten their fill of Mutton Stew and drank their Ale, they left their table. Captain Manos walked over to the tables where the Company were seated, they were now singing folk songs and some were finishing their Mutton Stew.

"Now Lads, 'tis time that we were moving on, so finish up your Ale and your orders are to form the Company outside once you have your steeds." Said Captain Manos.

The Soldiers and Dwarfs stopped their merrymaking and stood to attention saluting their Captain; the Dwarfs finished their Ale, and then saluted. The Company then made their way out of the Tavern and walked around to the stables. Here they received their horses and ponies from the stable hands and mounted them. The Company then rode them around to the front of the Tavern and formed files lined up outside. Lucius, the Generals Listus and Thomas along with Captain Manos, met the Company outside of the Tavern. The Stable hands brought around their horses and pony; they then mounted them and stood in front of the Company.

"Men, we ride for Millslade Bridge and over to Karlsburg Shire to the Dwarf Settlement. Have you all abound?" Asked Captain Manos. The Company Saluted in agreement.

"Company Aboot, quick step – away wi ye." Called General Listus. The four Officers turned their steeds to face the road to the North, followed by the ranks of the Company.

The column of the Company travelled the road out of Millslade Village led by Lucius and the Generals. Captain Manos brought up the rear. All along the road, they were extra vigilant as the road bordered the river Meerlandse and approached Millslade Bridge. They stopped and grouped into ranks as the

Generals and Lucius held up their left hands to signal that the Company were to halt.

"Men of the Alexandrian Guard, I speak also to our Brother Dwarfs, we may tally here for a silent prayer for our courageous lost Brother, who lays across the river and is commemorated by his monument.

We The Royal Guard and fellow Dwarfs do pray for the Soul of our departed Brother, Alkan; who was taken from us by Dark deeds, Alkan – AMEN." Said Lucius.

"Alkan – AMEN." Said the Company, men and Dwarf together as one.

The Men and Dwarfs stayed there for a few minutes in Silent Prayer, each soldier and officer saying his own silent prayer. When they were all ready, Lucius once again led the men and Dwarfs away from the Gorge of Alkan, until they reached Millslade Bridge. Some of the Soldiers peered over the Bridge as they crossed to see the remains of the Mountain Troll still lying in the river like a large stone weir. They slowly rode across the bridge, keeping vigilant in case there was another Troll replacing he who lay at the bottom of the Gorge.

Once safely across the bridge, they turned North once again and rode swiftly beside the Gorge and the river, now travelling through the Shire of Oxshott and onwards into the Shire of Karlsburg. They showed their pace slightly as they reached the junction of the road to Karlsburg City, close to the Connarch Bridge. Once again, they were extra vigilant as they turn onto the road, riding North Westward now, away from the Bridge.

"We should be extra vigilant aboot 'ere M'Lairds, as across yon Bridge lays ye road te ye Mountains o' Connarch. Those yonder mountains are best known te house Mountain Trolls an' 'tis likely te 'ave been ye origin o' oor deed friend who now resides at ye bottom o' ye river beed." Said General Listus.

The junction showed a clear road back to the Bridge, the Mountains standing tall against the sky in the near distance. No Trolls were evident, as they were not crossing the Bridge; they had no intentions to check under the Bridge. They turned and continued to ride the road swiftly until a short distance along the road, leading southwards.

"Fallow me Gentlemen." Said General Listus, indicating with his left hand down the road which joined at this junction. They rode along this road for a few miles until they began to see either side of the road, collections of small cottages, timber framed with cob walls, stretching out in front of them as they entered the edge of the village.

The Cottages had small low stockade fences around them and a courtyard with paddocks. Around the village could be seen fields which had been cleared and cultivated, filled Cottages had orchards within their stockade and fruit gardens. They travelled further into the village and as General Listus and his Company of Dwarfs rode deeper into the village; so many Dwarfs came running from the fields, the cottages and their other means of work. There were Taylors, Bakers, Blacksmiths and women and children Dwarfs came running to greet them.

At the centre of the village, the Company were greeted by a large stockade fence, with a Ha-Ha around it. Across the Ha-Ha was a wooden drawbridge.

"Gentlemen, welcome te yon Palace o' King Boranius of Calistria, Ruler of Dwarfs." Said General Listus, proudly.

"Tantak onui Listusa." Called General Listus, the drawbridge creaked and began to lower across the Ha-Ha.

It was only now as they crossed the drawbridge, being led by General Listus, that over the side of the drawbridge, they were able to see hundreds of razor sharp points of carved wooden poles driven into the Earth of the Ha-Ha with their deadly points sticking upwards, just ready with prospective impaling should any of The Company make any false move and fell from the drawbridge. The Company rode off the drawbridge and crossed through the main gate of the stockade. Above them, they could see great Iron doors upon either side of the Gatehouse, suspended above them with sharpened base edges to them, huge guillotines poised to be dropped upon an enemy who would so much as attempt to cross the threshold of the Gatehouse and hope to get through in one piece.

"We Dwarfs 'ave tightened ye defences an' security o' ye Palace 'ere. Since ye Palace en oor hame wuz destroyed. I'd like te see any o' thee ugly Orcs oor Goblins try te breech oor Gates ye noo" Said General Listus., a little boastful.

The Company passed through the Gatehouses and out into a large open Bailey stretching in front of them. The surface of the Bailey was made up of cobblestones and hay spread around. Along the Inner edges of the stockade fence were a number of Cobb and wooden framed buildings; some looked like houses while others were barrack type buildings, some stables. At the centre was another stockade and gatehouse. This was surrounded by a Moat, which lay between two rings of Stockade fencing. At the centre of the second Inner gatehouse was another drawbridge, which led out through to an Inner Bailey. Again its surface was of cobblestones and hay spread around. Here were to found more Cobb and wooden framed buildings. Along the Stockade just beneath the top, around the Inner Stockade and Outer Stockade fences stretched platforms of wood and scaffolding made as walkways for Archers to stand and fire over the Palace in needed. At the centre of the Palace was the King's Keep. A circular wooden building with three towers, at the corner, so to speak, of the Keep, stood upon four points, four tall look out towers, which could be used by Archers to defend the Keep in the event that it came under attack, if the outer defences had failed.

The Company rode into the centre of the Inner Bailey, where grooms met them and they dismounted from their horses and ponies. The Grooms took away the horses to a certain stable block and the ponies to another. The Dwarf Soldiers who had ridden in with General then were dismissed and walked away towards the Gatehouse.

"Men,'tis now we are safest as we can be, be off with you for the night and join yoursleves with your Dwarf Comrades." Said General Thomas.

He dismissed the men and they saluted, then turned and were led by the Dwarf Soldiers out into the Outer Bailey to the Barrack Area.

"We shed oor armour an' weapons 'ere Laddies, an' then it is te ye Ale Hoose fer us,, 'ame it is an' ye're welcome te sup a Dram ere too wi' us this nicht." Said the Dwarf Captain, Figdly.

The Royal Guard Soldiers gave a cheer and followed the Dwarfs to the allotted Barrack block which they were to use for the night.

"Now Men, we thank thee Captain Figdly, we must unburden ourselves of our weapons at the Barrack Room and then we will gladly join you." Replied Captain Manos.

The Armour of the Dwarfs and weapons were sent to the Black Smiths whose furnaces around the Outer Baily sent smoke up into the air at intervals around the Stockade. There, the Armour and weapons would be checked, cleaned and sharpened, then stowed in the Armoury until needed once more. The Armour and weapons of the Alexandrian Company were serviced by the Blacksmith and then brought back to their Barrack to be stowed until next day when they would be required to wear it upon their journey back to Alexandria.

Chapter Thirty – The Royal Meeting

After the Soldiers and Dwarf Guards had walked away out of the outer Bailey and the Drawbridge had been raise once more. General Listus led Lucius and General Thomas to the main doors of the Palace Keep. All around them, the smell of Turf fires coming from both the cottages which made up the Village beyond the Stockade, the numerous Black Smiths, Bakers, and other workers around the Stockade and Village, the Keep along with the Kitchens beside it. Also mingled in with the smell of Turf was were the smells from the cooking of many different meats.

The Guards opened the great doors of the Palace and bowed as the Trio walked through, saluting them. They walked into an Anti-Chamber of wooden panelling draped with tapestries. There was a set of wooden Panelled double doors with a shield and Coat of Arms depicting three stars in Rouge upon an Argent Ground. They were shown through the doors by yet more Guards and walked into a large semi-circular room, a Great Hall, bedecked in flags of all colours and tapestries depicting hunting scenes and victorious battles. There were a number of tables covered in golden lined white table cloths and with wooden benches either side. At the centre of the rear of the Hall was a large table set with all kinds of meat and other foods imaginable.

At the table sat two male Dwarfs and two female Dwarfs, the central two, finely dressed in furs and leather with crowns of gold and jewels upon their heads; the male with red hair and beard and the Female with long red hair. To either side of them, to the right of the first Male sat a younger male Dwarf who had not much of a beard and red hair, to the left of the first female Dwarf sat a younger female with long red hair. The Trio bowed low as a trumpet sounded to herald their arrival, blown by Dwarfs who were dressed in coats which bore the arms of the Dwarfish Kingdom of Calistria.

"Welcome Gentlemen, ma Laird General Listus, We ere most pleased te see yer return an' We greet ye ma Lairds also." Said the Older male dwarf wearing the most ornate crown.

"Hail Sire, I bring ye Yon Regiment o' Alexandria; M'Laird Lucius Thamley an' General Thomas o' ye Royal Guard o' Alexandria," Replied General Listus, straightening himself up again.

"Ma Lairds, I am Boranius, King o' Calistria, Laird o' Dwarfs; beside me, ma Beautiful Wife an' Queen Marion; to ma right, ma Son and Heir, Prunce Milos o' Calistria an' te ma left, that is Queen Marion's left ye see, ma Daughter, Pruncees Surignan o' Calistria." Said King Boranius.

Upon their heads, Prince Milos wore a small crown with Garnets around the rim and Princess Surignan wore a golden Diamond and Platinum Tiara. Queen Marion wore a golden crown studied with diamonds and Turquoise. She wore a long gown of white with golden threads embroidered around it. King Boranius sat resplendent in a golden and white enamelled Armour with red fur lined cape. Prince Milos wore Silver Armour with a purple fur cape. Princess Surignan wore a long white gown with emeralds embroidered around it. The Trio were waved to join the table by King Boranius and indicated to begin to feed themselves from the menagerie of meats and other dishes available upon the table.

"Sire, we bring you word from the Wizard Lord Barnabus. He has foreseen more attacks, he will be convening a meeting of The Kalhron to discuss their options and how they are going to fight to free Calistria and restore you unto your rightful Shire Kingdom. My Lord, the Prince Royal Simon de Morteby, has sent me as his representative to discuss the matter with you and to bring his pledge of support to retake Calistria." Said Lucius. He held out his sword, 'Telos', to King Boranius, to reveal the glittering emeralds along its pommel and the large emerald at the top.

"I am Lord Lucius Thamley, First Minister of Alexandria and Royal Regent. Alexandria is at your service your Majesty." Said Lucius. King Boranius took the sword from Lucius and examined it closely. The Silver blade showed etched scenes of battle and the legend written in Runes ;

"I AM TELOS of ALEXANDRIA"

ELFIN HANDS MADE ME"

"Hmmm, fine workmanship, Elfin made, speaks te me saying "Alexandria Had Me Made' an' names yon sword as 'Telos', truly ye sword of the Regent of Alexandria. Rise Sir Lucius of Calistria, serve us well M'Laird Knight'." Said King Boranius as he dubbed each shoulder with Lucius' sword, 'Telos'.

"I shall serve you well your Majesty, as will Alexandria. Replied Lucius.

"General Listus, We dub thee Sir Listus of Calistria, Rise Sir Knight." Said King Boranius, dubbing General Listus upon each shoulder with 'Telos'.

"My Laird Sir Knight, I had te use yere sword fer thus service , as Dwarfs dinna carry swords, but Battle Axes. I thank yer fer its use." Said King Boranius, handing 'Telos' back to Lucius, who then sheathed it back into its Scabbard.

"How fares Toridius The Gold; Sire; I have not seen him this long time that I have been away?" Asked General Listus.

"He fares well, Sir Knight, he keeps hemsel' locked away en hus Lair these days, concoctin' something oor other te fight ye fulthy Orcs an'Goblins. frum yer tidings o' Sir Knight Lucius, he wull most likely, be travellin' te ye Laird Barnabus fere ye meeitn' o' yon Wizards." Replied King Boranius.

"If ye now sit at oor table M'Laird, an' tell us that ye'll be ready te defend us an' retake Calistria, where were ye Shire Armies o' Alexandria an' ye Kalhron te defend us when Calistria fell, an' wus taken frum us?" Asked Prince Milos, somewhat bitterly.

310

"The attacks were so swift and ferocious, before we had word, Calistria, Parlemann and Petros Shires had fallen to the Dark Lord. The Passageway through Calistria Shire is most like the means which Thracia used to send the Mountain Trolls into the Mountains of Connarch and how we were surprised and lost a man at Millslade Bridge. Said Lucius.

"We were further attacked by Goblins and Orcs in the night near to Millslade Village, which means that this Passageway is very much the very probable means of their travelling this deep into the Shires, by using the Mountains as their cover." Added General Thomas.

I see my Lairds, I did not know this, I apologise ef ma werds were heatful te yer, followin' yere loss, but see oor loss Gentlemen, is but greater." Said Prince Milos.

"We have journeyed far, facing much Peril, to reach you and to bring unto you the tidings from the Wizard Lord, Barnabus and from our own Majesty, Simon de Morteby, Prince Royal of Alexandria." Said Lucius.

"Aye M'Laird Regent, fer that we ere grateful. It wood be ye dream o' all Dwarfs en freedom, te return te their own beloved Calistria. Oor Royal Family barely escaped wuth Oor lives an' many good Dwarfs wuz lost en ye struggle te survive. Ye Laird o' yon Shire, in which we stand, shouldst be thanked an' herein, all Dwarfs shouldst be mire grateful, was full te the heart wuth kindness, to give us thus land te settle upon, te create us a new hame. Fer oor return te oor own rightful land an' Shire, all Dwarfs wood be so much eternally grateful te Alexandria," Said King Boranius.

"The Prince Royal Himself, His Majesty, has bade us to bring unto you, his invitation into his plans to defend the Kingdom return to you and your Kinsmen to your rightful Shire." Replied Lucius.

"We are preparing a full force Army to win your Heritage back for you and return you to your rightful Throne, seated there within your own Throne Room, within your own Shire. This though may take some time to arrange and magnify our ranks to carry out many expeditions, covertly, into the Shires nearest to the Thracian border, to scout their movements and especially, where it is possible, scout into Calistria itself, to see how far their infiltration has reached and to find signs of their plans to attack other Shires. There will also be stockpiles of weapons at strategic locations throughout the Shires, to help arm them if the Thracian Army has called Battle into action." Added General Thomas.

Wull M'Laird Regent, ef ye Dark Laird shallst send huis Army o' Evil Warriors again' us, then We shall - wuth ye help o' all ye Shires, defeat them oor die trying. I pledge te yer, M'Laird Regent, if any Shire shouldst need support, the Dwarfs of Calistria shall be their support." Said King Boranius.

"There's no' much time te prepare, if agents o'ye Dark One ere already abroad en yon Shires an' we 'ave already lost ye two Shires te Ye Marquis' control, then Preparations really must begin immediately." Replied General Listus.

"Ye must stay thus nicht at oor hospitality M'Lairds, then ye shall be refreshed mayhap te travel upon yer return te Alexandria." Replied King Boranius.

"Oor Staff 'ave prepared Rooms fer yer te sleep en fer t'nicht, te lay doon yer heeds; please be rested Gentlemen." Said Queen Marion. "

"We thank Thee, your Majesties and hope that we are well rested for our journey back to Alexandria." Replied Lucius.

Next day, early, the King and Queen of Calistria made sure that Lucius and General Thomas had Well breakfasted and had their horses brought around for them. They bade their farewells to the King and Queen and then rode through the inner Gatehouse into the Outer Bailey and then rode through where they found their Company of Men, the Royal Guards, already mounted upon their horses and waiting to begin their journey. Lucius and General Thomas said their last farewells to General Listus. Then General Thomas gave the signal, Captain Manos shouted the order and the Company rode forwards out of the main Gate and on their way back to Alexandria, with the Master saluting at the rear.

Back in the depths of the cave back at Mount Kalem, among the huge piles of books and scrolls, smothered with their layers of dust, stooped an ancient figure. He stopped over a crystal ball, looking deeply into it. The crystal ball stood propped up upon a circular plinth which was circled with Runic Symbols all around it. This stood upon a table, made from Marble with a flat top, again single leg of Marble like a column, which was carved as Ivy growing twisting up around it.

"Much stirs in the lands, much which shouldst not be here, not in the Shires." Muttered Barnabus to himself.

The aged Wizard shuffled over to a large looking bird bath, again carved with Runic symbols and Ivy leaves of Marble. He placed his hand into the water of the bowl and began swirling the water in a clockwise direction. As he swirled his hand, a light appeared in the water, a pure white light which began to become brighter as Barnabus swirled his hand. This was his Foretelling Font. Here he was able to see into the future, if it wished to reveal itself, or to see into a prophesy or prediction. Wizards of the Shires, when it was necessary to call together the Kalhron, the Wizard Council or Army. A shaft of pure white light shone from the centre of the Font and hit the ceiling of the cave, many feet above,

"Kalhronus Altran Whamarnus Patria." Called Barnabus. He held his hands up over his head, arms out stretched and the blinding pure white light pulsed out and for a few moments filled the cave. The light cleared, Barnabus stood by his Font in his cave. A rumbling sound became apparent, then one by one, twelve streaks of coloured light appeared as though from nowhere. There were two streaks of blue light, three of gold light, three of red, two of green, then one each of White, yellow and silver. The lights cleared and standing before Barnabus were twelve Wizards, The Kalhron, Wizards of The Shires.

Lingle The Blue, Wizard of Beershire, wearing Robes of pale blue; Toridius The Gold, Wizard of Calistria, wearing Robes of gold. He was without a Shire as such but lived in exile in Alexandria. Then there was Karlov The White, Wizard of Holcombeshire, wearing Robes of white; Cerentine The Red, Wizard of Volmsbadshire, wearing Robes of deep red; Ludwig The Bald, Wizard of Karlsburgshire, wearing Robes of Yellow; Peter The Green, Wizard of Oxshottshire, wearing deep green Robes. Michael The silver, Wizard of Morehamptonshire, wearing Robes of Silver; Marchleot The Brown, Wizard of Deerforestshire, wearing Robes of brown; Zenos The Grey, Wizard of Parlemannshire, wearing Robes of grey and in exile at Alexandria; Manios The swift, Wizard of Woodcarmshire, wearing Robes of pale purple; Takalos The Honourable, Wizard of Petroshire, wearing Robes of claret, living in exile at Alexandria. He had been living within the Infirmary due to serious injuries sustained during the attack upon Petros by Thracian Armies. Next Nikos The Charmed, Wizard of Queensboroughshire, wearing Robes of pale green; these twelve along with Barnabus The Enlightened, made up the Kalhron.

"Minsarek Kalhronus Calronaii." Said Barnabus.

"Minsarek Kalhronus Calronaii." Replied all twelve Wizards together in unison.

"Gentlemen Wizards, I have summoned you all today with grave news. As you are aware, we have suffered many incursions into the Shires by agents and Armies of Thracia. Due to its age, 'The Skin' has become noticeably fragile in places and is now vulnerable to attack. It has become apparent that some areas of our Shires have been sadly lost to Thracia, I speak of course, about Calistria and Petros along with the Shire of Parlemann. These first Shires would appear to have been targeted and taken for specific strategies; The Shire of Calistria was an obvious target to cut off and hurt our economy by depriving us of the Galem Gold for our currency, also hoard up the coffers of Thracia. The shire of Parlemann was a strategic target as it now gives Thracia covert access to the Mountains of Connarch, which is why a delegation from Alexandria was recently attacked twice by Thracian Warriors during their visit to this very cave. The Thracian Forces who attacked the Company were able to enter this area by means of travelling over the Mountains from Parlemann. These Mountains, it would appear, may be very much the home of many Thracian Warriors from Orcs, Goblins and Trolls, which have already been noticed. The Shire of Petros was most possibly targeted as a means to covertly enter other Shires by sea and to complete a whole swathe of land taken from the Commonwealth of Shires.

We will be called upon to fight in this war, because believe me Gentlemen, this is a war in which the Marquis will use all of the means to hand to attempt to defeat the Commonwealth, and he will use Dark Magik to defeat us, so we must

313

be ready and active with our own magic to defeat him and his Forces. For this war, we will need to recruit more Apprentices, it will be a rushed Apprenticeship with much to be completed in a short time, and also the training will need to quickly establish the Apprentices as Duellers, defensive spells and offensive spells like Binding, Immobilising and total Paralysis are needed to combat the Thracian Troops. For some creatures, a simple stunning spell will not be enough. This means for the first time since our last battles against The Marquis, it will be necessary, Very regrettably, to teach the Killing Curse.

It is not a curse I myself am very fond of, but the Marquis will not hesitate to use it, neither will his Minions or The Shambols. So as a very last resort, no matter how it pains us, we must be prepared to teach the Apprentices to use thought and hand Magic, so as to avoid speaking a curse if possible and casting by thought alone. Obviously, there are some creatures upon the Dark One's Forces who can manipulate minds and read them, so it would be necessary to bring the apprentices up to the standard needed to cast thought curses very quickly, to try to help avoid their intentions being detected when Duelling." Said Barnabus.

"Master, we have no Shire to protect, many of our people were lost to the Dark One; Our Magic School was destroyed and I now live in Exile. I have no Apprentices to teach, the Thracian Army, when ransacking our Shire, took away all of my Apprentices into captivity." Replied Talakos The Honourable.

"It wuz ye same en Calistria, oor poor Apprentices, dragged away by yon dirty filth Orcs an' Goblin's." Said Toridius The Gold.

"In Parlemann it was also the same." Said Zenos The Grey.

"I am aware of this; therefore, you Wizards will help train others. It may be useful for you Toridius, to if you were able to help Lingle with his Apprentices, as your People are at present holding a piece of land in that Shire to build a new Community." Said Barnabus, "For you Takalos and for Zenos, it may be a good thing for you to join with me and to train the Apprentices in Alexandria."

"Yes My Lord, this would be a goodly plan of action for us to undertake." Replied Zenos The Grey.

"It may be a good course of action to take, to join two or more Classes together, where the smaller number of Apprentices are to be found. This would give these Apprentices equal amount of opportunity to learn. If Manios The Swift were to join The Apprentice School at Deene Forest with Marchleot The Brown, this would take the Apprentices away from near the border with Thracia, hopefully making them safer. If Nikos The Charmed were to do the same and take his Apprentices away from Queensboroughshire, this may help. If Nikos joined up with Peter The Green at Oxshottshire. If Michael The Silver were to leave Morehamptonshire and travel with his Apprentices to be allowed to teach in Cragmoorshire, this relocation would help.

314

If Toridius The Gold were to join with Lingle The Blue of Beershire, this would help move the Calistrian Apprentices away from the possible risk of attack from the Mountains of Connarch, also if Ludwig The Bald joined up with Cerentine The Red in Volmsbadshire, this would be the same, to minimise the risk of attack from the Mountains. Alas you Takalos will return for a little while longer to the Infirmary to heal yourslef, your Apprentices will be added to Karlov The White's, so when you are fit again you will join him with them. Zenos, your Apprentices will come to Alexandria along with you to join with mine and will complete their Apprenticeship." Said Barnabus.

"Agreed my Lord, 'tis a most ingenious plan to bring those most at risk away from the Borders." Said TakalosThe Honourable.

"You must all now be away and prepare your Schools to join the Kalhron." Said Barnabus. With that said, a flash of blue light saw Lingle The Blue disappear from the Chamber. Flashes of red light saw Cerentine The Red, Marchleot The Brown and Takalos The Honourable leave the Chamber, Takalos to the Infirmary. Then flashes of Gold light saw Toridius The Gold, Manios The Swift and Zenos The Grey disappeared, There was a flash of White Light and Karlov The White disappeared. Michael The Silver disappeared in a flash of silver light while a flash of Green light saw Peter The Green leave the cavern. Finally, a flash of Blue light saw Nikos The Charmed leave the Cave.

Barnabus was now alone in his Chamber; he held his staff above his head and the Crystal began to glow.

"Removoratum," Barnabus called out in a strong voice. The Chamber was filled with a bright white light, books, scrolls and instruments flew themselves into various compartments of a strange oak chest which lay to one side of the Wizard's bench. Scroll after book after instrument flew into various of the multiple compartments, as one filled, it appeared to just drop into the one below, without damaging its contents. Once the Chamber was cleared of all books and scrolls etc, all that was left was the perch with the red and gold bird sat upon it. Barnabus lifted up his arm and held it out at just above hip height with a slightly bent elbow.

The bird squawked and flew down from his perch and landed upon the arm of Barnabus. Once he had landed, it was time for Barnabus to wave his left arm, the one without the bird upon it. The perch leapt into the air and miraculously disappeared, lowering itself into the top most compartment of the trunk. Then the trunk lid swung up and over clamping shut with a thud and a click as it locked firmly closed. Barnabus turned to the bird;

"Well old friend, time we were leaving." Said Barnabus. The bird turned its head slightly to one side and looked at his Master. Barnabus banged his staff three times upon the ground;

"IlTravailus Duchi." Cried Barnabus and with a bright golden flash of light, Barnabus, the bird and the trunk had disappeared. All that was left there in the cave was silence, a few moments later and the candles went out, plunging the Chamber into darkness.

In a largish Chamber of the Castle at Alexandria, there was a bright flash of golden light and an audible 'Plop' from the air. Barnabus appeared with the bird upon his right arm, the trunk appeared beside him.

"Exgorio." Cried Barnabus. The compartments of the trunk all appeared one after the other and disgorged their contents. Books, Book cases and scrolls leapt out, put themselves against the walls of the Chamber and formed piles once more, as though they had never moved. The perch came out and stood next to the desk and then the instruments and Foretelling Font followed by the crystal ball upon its stand.

"Ah, you see, isn't magic wonderful Felius, when used properly?" Said Barnabus to the bird, who squawked his reply.

"Home from home my dear boy, necessary of course, however irritating to have to move everything. I was fond of that old cave; mayhap we will return there one day soon, eh Felius?" Said Barnabus. Felius just sat upon his perch and let out another squawk.

Chapter Thirty One– Spring Term

Next morning was a hive of activity throughout the house as Bill and Leonie got ready to leave after their breakfast. Leonie was already in her Uniform of blue jumper, white blouse and black skirt; all ready to go to her new term at her own School. This and the Summer term would be Leonie's last at her present School, before she too would be joining the others at Toadford School.

"See you Leonie, will probably visit during the Holidays; have a good time 'til then." Said Polly cheerfully.

"Thank you Polly, I'm looking forward to seeing you again." Replied Leonie.

"See you soon Leonie." Said Toby.

them.

Toby, Keiron and Polly waved her good bye as she got into Bill's BMW and drove out of the lane. They had their breakfast and made sure that all they needed was packed in their bags. Toby had given his Laptop bag and model kits to Carl during their return from their day out to Barnstaple to take home for him, so he only had his Ruc-Sack and suit case with his clothes and books for the next term in

After they were quite sure that all was in order and they were fully breakfasted, Toby, Keiron and Polly followed Daisy and Thomas out to her car, parked out upon the Lane. They opened the passenger doors after Daisy had opened the boot and they had placed their bags into the hatch-back and Daisy had closed it up again. Toby, Polly and Keiron climbed into the back seat and strapped themselves into the Ford Focus and Thomas climbed into the front passenger seat beside his Mother and pulled his seatbelt across him and clicked it into place.

"Ready for your next term Grunt's?" Asked Thomas, grinning sarcastically.

"Ready as you are." Replied Keiron.

Polly gave Thomas one of her looks. Daisy settled into the driving seat, a click then roar and the car pulled away from Tithe Barn Cottage. They drove down through the village where they saw the people bustling around their daily business; there was a School bus at its stop with a multitude of children boarding it. Out of the village they went along Upper Main Street and turned into Topley Drive and passed the gate leading to Tugmoor Woods. They sat in the back seats and watched it go by; wondering about what there could possibly be in there wondering whether it was just stories told by people who wanted a bit of media attention and their fifteen minutes of fame.

"OK young Lads an' Lasses, time we was leavin' fer school." Said Daisy. Bill would be taking Leonie to her School. Bill started the engine of the BMW and made sure that Leonie had her seatbelt secured properly. Then it was with a cheer, time for them to leave. The BMW pulled smoothly away from Tithe Barn Cottage and drove away down Mews Lane and then turned into Manor Drive a few moments later. Keiron took out his time table for their first week back and opened it out, to check their Rota.

"Thank you so much, Daisy, for putting up with me, with us. I've enjoyed my stay here and have been made to feel most wlecome. Said Polly, with a smile. She had changed into her School Uniform after breakfast, grey jumper with Cargal emblem over a white blouse with black skirt and wearing a Cargal house tie.

"Yes, thank you daisy, I have enjoyed my stay very much." Added Toby, in his School Uniform; grey jumper with Cargal emblem, white shirt, Cargal House tie and black trousers. They would put on their gowns when they reached Toadford School.

"So yer time as Grunts ees headin' fer its finale then, yer first yere almost over?" Said Daisy.

"Not quite Daisy, we still have spring and Summer terms to finish off yet. Spring term finishes with the Finals of the School Cups in Football and Rugby, whereas we finish Summer term with the Cricket Final." Said Toby.

"So fram Easter onwards, you'm plays yer Cricket season, endin' with the House Cup Final afore yer finish fer the Summer Holidays?" Asked Daisy.

"That's right Mom." Said Keiron.

"An' are parents allowed to these games, to support their Sons?" Asked Daisy, hopefully.

"Only the Finals, not the qualifying matches." Said Toby.

"And we're in all of them, or will be when we win through the qualifying for the Cricket matches and reach the Final, we will be in all of them." Said Keiron.

"So yer think you'm will reach the Cricket Final then?" Asked Daisy.

"We've got a good chance as the top player for the Wombats is suspended until the end of the year from playing in any of the qualifying games of any of the sports and from taking part in School sports day, because he deliberately kicked a football into Polly's face." Said Keiron.

"He did what? I bet that 'urt, Polly." Said Daisy.

"Yes it did, broke my nose, but with Nurse Pauline's help and quick thinking from my Room-mate 'Bella, the Nurse was able to reset my nose quickly and so stop it from setting wrongly." Said Polly.

"Who was this thug?" Asked Daisy.

"Just one of the School Bullies who thinks he's hard." Said Keiron.

"Yes, these gallant boys stood up against them for me, to give us time to get away to the Hospital." Said Polly.

"Oh, gallant were you boys? You must be good friends then." Said Daisy.

The 'Hatch-back' then turned out of Manor Drive into Upper Main Street and headed towards the village centre. They passed through the village Square and past the Post Office and Church. Parked outside the Church was the School Bus for the Comprehensive at Cranleigh, where the Students attended whom didn't attend Toadford School. Stretching back from the bus was a line of Children in their School Uniforms, with their Cranleigh College badges upon their Blazers and some of the girls wearing their skirt hems a little higher up than was regulation length. Before long, the 'Hatch-back' was heading away from the village centre passing Tugmoor Woods as they went. They drove the short distance along Topley Drive and turned out onto the Moorland Road, heading towards Little Farthingworth.

They eventually changed their train of thought and realised that they were heading along the Poplar tree lined Poplar Drive, approaching the Car Park of Toadford School. Then there they were, the Gargoyles which stood upon the tops of the gate posts and along the wall at intervals. The Ford Focus drove through the tall gates and into the Car Park. "Here we go!" Cried Keiron. The Trio then broke into song, Well ...... Polly and Toby did, with Keiron trying to keep up.

♫♪   ♫

We lead the pack and strive to win,

To One and all our members are Kin;

♪   If threatened by an enemy Cur,

♪

♪   The Soldiers of our House will stir;

We'll make a stand 'gainst man or mouse,

To always win for Cargal House.

♫   ♫

"That sounds good an' Patriotic." Said Daisy.

"Yes, it's our House Song, for Cargal House." Replied Polly.

"Well, Lady an' Gents, 'ere we are." Called Daisy as they entered the gates, with their Gargoyles atop the gate posts.

The 'Hatch-back' then entered the now familiar span of gravel with its central fountain and brick wall across the end of the Car Park where stood the solitary

Oak door at its centre. Daisy parked the car and with a flourish of doors and legs, they all poured out of the car and collected their bags from the boot. Quickly, the Students were decanted from their cars, Daisy making sure that they all had their things from the 'Hatch-back's boot, their suit cases and Ruc-Sacks.

"Well then Keiron, we'll see 'ee at Easter then. Have a good time 'til then, Son." Said Daisy, giving Keiron a big hug.

"I will Mom and tell Dad I'll be studying hard through Half Term and send him my love and to Leonie." Replied Keiron.

"Thank you for a lovely stay and the lift, Daisy." Said Polly with a big smile.

"Yes, thank you, Daisy." Added Toby.

"Don't 'ee worry, pleased to 'ave 'ee an' I was bringing Keiron back anyway, so good to 'ave met 'ee both an' 'ave gotten to know 'ee, now we know better who Keiron was talking about in 'is letters." Said Daisy.

'Bella had already arrived; her Mother had already dropped her off and left. She stood by the fountain at the centre of the Car Park waiting to see the others arrive. She came running over to the Ford Focus when she saw them get out and take their bags out of the boot.

"Oh wow, you're here. Oh ,,, my … God, did you have a great Christmas? How was it over at Keiron's house? What did you get up to?" Asked Arrabella. Her eyes twinkling with excitement as she spoke.

"'Bella, you're rambling again." Said Polly, primly.

"Oh Gosh! Sorry, I have to stop doing that." Replied 'Bella.

"We had a good time at Keiron's house; sorry there wasn't enough room for you to come, we missed you though – " Said Toby.

"Did you really miss me? " Asked 'Bella, with a smile.

"Yes, we did; hopefully, there will be enough room for you at Pegasus House during Easter, if you're allowed to come over and stay for a visit?" Said Toby.

"Maybe not Easter, but maybe Summer?" Replied 'Bella.

"OK, maybe Summer." Replied Toby

"Maybe 'Bella could share with Leonie, if she was allowed to come and stay?" Said Keiron.

"Er, Mom… this is our friend Arrabella, Polly's Room Mate." Said Keiron.

"Noice te meet 'Ee M'Dear." Replied Daisy, holding our her hand for 'Bella, who shook it.

"Nice to meet you too." Replied 'Bella.

"See you all again soon M'Dears, 'ave a gud time at School an' gud luck wi' yer Finals en Sports Toby, 'ope yer wins." Said Daisy.

With that, they gave her a last smiling wave before she got into the 'Hatch-back' and pulled away with a toot of the horn. Soon they had waved off Daisy and walked through the gate and across the bridge through the courtyards and into the main building. They went to their Dorm Rooms to settle in and unpack before Assembly and the first lessons and the task of handing in all their homework begun.

The Trio turned to walk over to the Oak door. Through this, they entered the walled Courtyard with the porch way. They entered this and began to cross the covered bridge over the Gorge to the first Gatehouse.

"I wonder how long this bridge has been here?" Asked Keiron.

"Oh most probably as long as the School, or if thinking of it as once being a medieval Fortified Manor House, probably longer than it has been a School." Replied Polly.

"It's more of a Castle; our house, Pegasus House, is an old Medieval Manor House, but it doesn't have all these Turrets, Towers and Gatehouses and it doesn't have a big covered bridge across a deep Gorge either." Said Toby.

"Well Fortified Castle, Manor House, Castle, same thing really; unless built by a King or Baron. Most Lords houses were fortified during medieval times, so...... Castle and Manor House would have often been much the same thing really." Said Polly, with her usual 'Know it all' tone of voice.

"We could ask some Teachers, after all, if we are going to call tis place home for the next four years, we may as Well learn something about its History." Said Toby.

"Yeah and about that strange outer Bailey which is forbidden to us and those locked gates behind the sports fields." Added Keiron.

"Yes and those locked doors within the Gatehouse." Said Toby.

"Yeah, maybe with a bit of luck, all the Magnificent Grunts will be together in the same place at the same time, including Leonie." Said Toby.

"You two do realise that next year, Leonie does indeed transcend from being an 'Honorary Grunt', to becoming a fully-fledged Grunt; that being the case, we will become Weeners, Ergo, - it ceases to be the Magnificent Grunts, but becomes the Magnificent Grunt and - Weeners. We would need to draw up a new name for our Group." Said Polly.

"How about 'The Cygnet Investigators'?" Said Keiron.

"Why 'Cygnet'?" Asked Toby.

"Yes Well done Keiron, playing upon the idea of the young swan, the emblem of Cargal House." Agreed Polly.

"Not just a pretty face." Beamed Keiron.

"Not even a pretty face." Returned Polly.

"I think that the 'Cygnet Investigators ' fits just right; Well-done Keiron." Said 'Bella.

"How about 'The Cygnet Committee?" Suggested Keiron.

"Why 'Committee'?" Asked 'Bella.

"Because there are five of us now and I think that constitutes a 'Committee'." Replied Keiron, pausing to wait for the acceptance of his good idea again, which didn't come.

"Cygnet Committee it is then." Said Polly.

"At least someone appreciates me around here." Mumbled Keiron.

They opened the gate and walked through into the Courtyard. There waiting for them were their House Masters, who then asked them to line up in their respective Houses in their years.

The four Houses all lined up, they began to enter the porch way and then across the bridge led by Wombat House. They walked into the porch and onto the bridge across the Gorge. Either side of them were rows of columns at intervals which held up the roof of the bridge. The columns were circular and the roof was braced with Oak beams.

"I'm always amazed walking over this bridge, that it's here. It's a long way down that Gorge." Said Keiron, looking through the columns as they walked.

"There was, according to the records, a drawbridge at the centre, to help prevent the 'wrong people' from crossing and entering the Castle." Said Polly.

"Where is it now?" Asked 'Bella.

"It was replaced when the buildings became a school, that's when the full span of the bridge was completed." Replied Polly.

They continued walking across the bridge with Keiron peering out of the arches between the columns frequently. They reached the far side and arrived at the main Gatehouse. Tall and imposing, built in solid stone, the large tall Oak doors were opened and Wombat House led the School into its depths.

Inside was a flag stoned pathway which led through the doorway and through a passage way out through an arch into another courtyard. Either side of the Gatehouse walkway set into the stone walls were the two Oak doors, as usual, being locked.

They walked through the open Iron Gates out of the arch into the next courtyard, and then saw the outer Oak door open and the Wombat Students walked through out of the Gatehouse. They found themselves in a small Bailey, enclosed by high stone walls. To their right they were able to see a large range of stone buildings and to their left they were, across some lawns, some Staff Cottages, which housed some of the Teachers and Grounds Staff.

Ahead of them, along the stone path lay the Main Gatehouse to the Inner Bailey. This they reached and were led through.

"I wonder what It is that is so secret about those doors and why there is a Tradition at the School not to tell ones children about the place if they attended here?" Said Keiron.

"Traditions are mainly about control of the Truth, Keiron. It would seem that when looked upon, many of them, are put in place at Toadford to protect the outside world from the Truth. Possibly only a small number of Students each year are made aware of the truth by means of competition or otherwise, so the truth is metered out upon a 'need to know' basis." Lectured Polly.

"The doors may be part of the 'need to know' policy then?" Asked Keiron.

"Yes." Said Polly.

"Like the big gates at the back of the Main Bailey and sports fields."

"Yes."

"Like the gates over beyond those stone buildings."

"Yes."

" – and the restricted section of the Library."

"Oh for God's sake – YES!"

Polly almost shouted the last 'Yes', much to her embarrassment and the amusement of the other Students directly behind them. Keiron jumped backwards a little at that 'Yes! and didn't answer, simply looking at the ground. They walked through the Outer Gates to the Inner Bailey and crossed to the stone steps of the Main Entrance to the School Building. Once through the Main doors and into the Great Hallway of the Main building, the Students Houses were split into two lines. To the left, the lines consisted of Wombat House and Farley House; to the right, the lines consisted of Cargal House and Hatchell House.

The line containing the four friends walked up the stairs to the right and along the landing until they reached the outer door to the Cargal section of the Dormitories. The Prefect at the head of the line unlocked the door and led Cederick Thybold, Chief House Master of Cargal House and the rest of the Cargal House Students into the passageway. There lining the walls were the paintings and photographs hanging framed of past and present Cargal House members, who had achieved greatness for the House.

They reached their dorm Rooms and unlocked their doors;

"Well, we'll just get settled in and will see you two in a short time for Assembly." Said Polly to the boys.

"OK then, see you soon." Replied Toby. With that he and Keiron disappeared into their Dorm Room. They dumped their Ruc-Sacks and suitcases upon their beds and began to empty them into their respective cupboards, draws and receptacles.

Toby placed his Tablet out onto his desk and Keiron did also. They put their time tables for the new term out with their Tablets. Keiron tucked his shirt in and there was a knock at the door. Toby opened the door to find Polly and 'Bella smiling at him.

"Come in, we're just about ready to get going down to Assembly." Said Toby, as he and Keiron finished putting what they needed for their morning's lessons into their Ruc-Sacks. It was time to start their new Term.

"Are you two ready?" Asked Polly.

"Yes." They replied together.

"OK, let's get down to Assembly then." Said Poly and led the way out of the Dorm Room and out onto the landing.

"Good to be back." Said Polly, smiling as they walked down the stairs.

Not long left now, 'til we finish for the Summer Hols." Said Keiron.

"We've only just got back and you're already looking forwards to going away again.!" Exclaimed Polly with surprise.

"Just thinking of when we can all meet up, including Leonie, as the 'Cygnet Committee, that's all." Replied Keiron indignantly.

"They reached the bottom of the stairs and crossed into the corridor which led down past the Hospital Wing, The Headmaster's Office and the Boys Shower Room and Toilets.

"Phew! Boys jock straps!" Giggled 'Bella holding her nose as though she had a peg upon it, as they passed the boys Shower Room. They then entered the Great Hall, where as usual, the Hall was decked with many tables to contain the four Houses and an additional table at the top of the Hall and sat at the appropriate table for their House and year. Toby sat with Polly opposite Keiron and 'Bella.

"Ooh, back at our usual table." Gushed 'Bella. She was happy to be at Toadford and to belong to the Cygnet Committee; it was the first time she had flet at home, that she belonged. 'Bella had grown up very much feeling that she was a loner, that she didn't belong. Now this group of friends had accepted her and made her part of their group. Also being part of the great Toadford traditions thrilled her so much.

Inside the Great Hall, the rest of the School had now congregated upon the tables. At the head of the Hall, the Staff were seated at the table and were waiting for the Headmaster to arrive.

"Good Morning school," Announced Parfinkle as the hubbub died down within the Great Hall." Welcome to the new Term here at Toadford. This Term we will be heading towards the Exams at the end of the next Term so you will all need to be revising. Also during this Term, we will have the Finals of the House Football Cup and House Rugby Cup. We have time before these Historic challenges both Athletic and Scholarly, so best we work hard and triumph. Have a great Term." Said Parfinkle.

A Closing Prayer was said and then the Assembly dispersed. The Cygnets went to their respective classes; 'Bella and Polly to Home Education and Toby with Keiron to Metal Work. Down at the workshop, Toby and Keiron worked upon their pieces for end of Term Exams. Tom Taylor, as usual, tried to cause trouble for Toby again.

"Wonder if Morby will be fit for the Football Cup Final?" Sneered Taylor.

"Not if we flatten him first?" Laughed Delbert Eldridge, who was joined laughing by his brother's Gaynell and Dexter and Tom Taylor. Aaron Pooke stood grinning and pulling his extended index finger across his throat in a cut throat motion.

"You won't be playing, Taylor, so who are you to talk? Or you Gay-boy" Said Keiron.

"Shut your mouth Muddles, or do you want us to shut it for you? Grunted Gaynell Eldridge.

"You just signed your death warrant Muddley." Said Gaynell through his gritted teeth.

"Are you mad Keiron, picking a fight with the Eldridges?" Whispered Toby.

"So after you smashed that arrow, you're frightened of the Eldridges?" Asked Keiron in a whisper.

"I don't know what happened there and don't know how it happened; how I could control it or even whether it will happen again?" Replied Toby, still whispering.

"Oh My God! I thought that you could handle them like you did that arrow?" Whispered Keiron dispiritedly.

"I don't know how I did that or if I can do it again, I tell you; Oh Muddles, now we're in trouble." Whispered Toby.

They silently worked upon their projects, trying to keep out of eye line of the Eldridges and Tom Taylor. Who were frequently looking in their direction and grinning. As the lesson progressed, Keiron became more and more apprehensive, as within the Workshop were housed many tools which could possibly be used as weapons in a fight.

The Eldridge Triplets were well known for utilising objects to use as weapons in a fight. Around the Workshop, apart from the Workbenches, with their vices attached, were panels where a number of sets of tools were hanging. To one side of the workshop, was a door leading to a walk-in store room, which held stores of metal and the larger tools.

Eventually the lesson ended and it was time to head to their next lesson. Toby and Keiron, luckily, were able to leave the Metalwork Room before any of the Wombats were ready. The next lesson was Biology in the Science Lab, the other end of the building towards the front. They had a free period before then so Toby and Keiron left the corridor from the Workshop and walked, hurriedly, the few yards to the stair case which led to their Dormitory Wing. They were half way up the staircase when the Eldridges and the other Wombats were at the bottom. Just at that moment, Tom Harnatt walked out of the corridor into the hallway and the Wombat Students moved across to their staircase. By the time they reached the landing, Toby and Keiron had disappeared into the door to the Cargal House Wing. They walked into their Dorm Room and collapsed onto their own beds, respectively.

"Oh Hell! What do we do now, how can we avoid them indefinitely, we only just got away with it that time." Said Keiron, staring at the ceiling.

"We, Wh-at do you mean We? You got us into this, but Oh yes, it will be We won't it, I mean they won't miss their chance to bring me into it, will they? After all, Tom Taylor would love to see the Eldridges take me out, wouldn't they? I would miss the Sports Finals and more likely spend a long time in Hospital." Replied Toby, also staring at the ceiling.

"Maybe if I apologised, that may end it?" Suggested Keiron, hopefully.

"Are you serious!? You called Gaynell Eldridge 'Gay boy'; do you really think that saying 'sorry' will really make it all better?" Replied Toby, disbelievingly.

"Just a thought." Said Keiron.

They sat up upon their beds and then stood up and put away their leather gloves and leather aprons, then they sat back down upon their beds, putting their Biology books in their bags.

"How about if we see whether Polly and 'Bella are in the Common Room yet? Maybe they can take our minds off the problem." Said Toby.

"Yeah, maybe, just for now." Replied Keiron with an audible gulp. They stood up from their beds and put on their Ruc-Sacks over their shoulders. Then they walked out of the Dorm Room and walked along the corridor, lined with the 'Famous' past Cargal House paintings and photos.

Part way along, Keiron pointed out that he had noticed that the Girls door to their Dorm Room was closed, so they didn't know whether the girls were back or in the Common Room or were still at their lesson. Keiron tried to knock upon the door, he got no answer; so he caught up with Toby, who was standing in the corridor, looking at a photo of a young boy whom was standing with the House Football Cup in his hand, dressed in the Cargal House Football kit. The name plate pinned underneath the Photograph read, as Toby was already aware;

"Carl Morby Cargal House

House Football Cup

Winners"

Toby looked at the framed photograph hanging there upon the wall for a good few moments, thinking about his own photograph, which may possibly be added to the line up along the wall. Then he thought now being taken out of the Finals of the Cricket, Rugby and Football, would mean that he would not play in these matches; so win or lose, his portrait would not be added to the existing archive. He thought of how Keiron's ill thought outburst may have ended his possibility of hanging his photo, joining that of his Father's, hanging upon the Cargal House Dorm Wing wall for all those existing and future Cargal House Students to see, Father and Son together.

He couldn't be mad at Keiron though, he just thought that what he had seen at the hill upon Crag Moor would just be enough, as Muddles wouldn't think properly before opening his mouth, Wombat's might catch them alone without others around or without being within the vicinity of a Master. If they could avoid the Wombats, especially the Eldridges, until the summer, at least they would have the Summer break to look forward to a Wombat Free Holiday. The sports would be a difficult task avoiding the Eldridges though.

"Sorry Mate, I just didn't think before I opened my mouth, just being Muddles, I'm afraid, as always." Said Kieron apologetically.

"That's OK Mate; it's done now, so all we have to do is deal with the situation as it arises as best we can. Better look out for Polly and 'Bella, the Wombats will most probably target them with bullying, being our friends." Said Toby.

"Yeah, I didn't think of that, did I? Oh my God, what have I done?" Whispered Keiron, with a look of terror upon his face.

"I think we'll come to that when we face it Mate." Replied Toby, trying to be a little supportive, but not succeeding too well.

They then turned the corner into the Common Room. Here they found that Polly and 'Bella had not returned from their lesson. They walked into the Common Room and both crashed down upon a couch in front of the Fireplace. The fire was happily burning away in the hearth. Toby was laying upon his back looking at the stone vaulting of the roof of the room, the ceiling made up from lathe boards between the vaulting ribs which were white washed.

It was running through Toby's mind about the strange powerful energy burst. Was it just that occasion which he was able to shoot down that arrow, or was it a permanent ability he now had? Keiron was laying on the opposite couch, thinking of different ways to avoid the Eldridges and other Wombats. They both looked up at the Common Room door which opened and in walked Polly and 'Bella, who crossed the room to the fire place where they joined Toby and Keiron at the couches.

"Budge up." Said Polly, tapping Toby's legs, which he duly lifted off the couch and moved to a sitting position to allow Polly to sit down next to him. Upon the other couch, Keiron had done the same to allow 'Bella to sit down also.

"You two look like you've lost something?" Said Polly.

Not yet, but it won't be long before we do." Replied Toby.

What does that mean?" Said 'Bella, who of course was not aware of the incident at Cragmoor.

"He's only gone and got our death warrants signed with the Eldridges." Said Toby, indicating with his head nodding towards Keiron.

"I told you Mate, I didn't think before blurting it out, sorry." Replied Keiron in a pleading tone.

"Didn't think about what?" Asked 'Bella, surprised.

"I thought that when the Eldridges threatened and bullied us, that Toby could use his new power that he destroyed the arrow with to defend us?" Pleaded Keiron. Toby and Polly looked at Keiron very sternly with deep frowns upon their faces.

"Oh – er – oops – er – sorry Guys, ah – er yes, 'Bella, you see – er, um, it sort of happened while we were at my house over Christmas and New Year. There was this accident see, then this homeless guy had been living rough upon the Moor, it looked like and we obviously disturbed him – er – um, and yeah – he got sort of angry, like, and fired an arrow at Toby. Toby was great, he sort of jumped up and fired some kind of bolt out of his hand and the arrow blew up!" Stuttered Keiron. Toby and Polly's frowns lessened a little as Keiron had not mentioned the Old Man blowing up the guy with a flash of red light from his stick which he was holding.

"A Bolt? A Bolt? A bolt of what?" Asked 'Bella.

The look which Toby and Polly were giving Keiron was in a way as to say 'you started this, now get out of it and don't mention the Old Man or the Gnome in the tree.'

"Well, it was sort of like a bolt of light, blue light and the arrow just blew up before it hit Toby." Continued Keiron.

"Yes, but as I said before Keiron, we don't know if that was a one off shot or not, I don't want to be facing an angry Trio of Eldridges if it was a one off and I can't do it again and send out a bolt to stop them." Said Toby.

"Where did this bolt of light come from?" Asked 'Bella. Toby and Polly rolled their eyes at Keiron and knew that with the way the conversation was going, that they would have to tell 'Bella everything.

"It's like this 'Bella, when we went for a walk up to an old Quarry, near to where Keiron's house is, we saw across the Quarry, an old man. He seemed to be making bolts of light appear from nowhere, which we thought, of course was impossible." Said Polly.

"You mean you thought it was impossible, but we were soon proved wrong." Chimed in Keiron to one of Polly's darkest looks.

"Yes, thank you Keiron. We went around the Quarry to see what he was doing and he caused a huge red flash of light and disappeared." Continued Polly.

"Disappeared, Really?" Squealed 'Bella.

"Yeah Really." Added Keiron.

"Well when we got there, he was gone and all we found was a scorch ,mark upon the grass….." Continued Polly."

"Scorch marks? Maybe he was playing with fire works?" Suggested 'Bella.

"That was what I was thinking until Toby sort of stumbled and there was a bright blue flash of light and Toby was laying upon the ground. He seemed to be knocked unconscious for a short while and when he awoke, we decided that it was best to go back to Keiron's house." Said Polly.

"Yeah, when we went for a walk the next day, we found some homeless guy and he tried to attack us. When he fired an arrow at us, I don't know why, I just thought 'no you don't mate' and suddenly, a bright blue light seemed to come out of my hand as I raised it towards the arrow, then it just exploded; the arrow that is, not my hand, see." Said Toby, showing them his hand.

"Oi Mate, keep that away from me, that's a lethal weapon that is." Said Keiron squirming back away from Toby's hand.

'Bella sat in shock, she was speechless, which for 'Bella was some feat, in fact it could be said that it was bordering upon being a miracle.

"How did that happen?" 'Bella eventually said.

"We don't know, it just happened?" Replied Toby.

Has it happened again, it might be too dangerous to try anyway if that bolt of light destroyed the arrow the way it did, if I try to defend myself against the Eldridges, then the same may happen to them.

An arrow is one thing, obliterating Human Beings is another. That could be looked upon as Murder and I am no Murderer." Said Toby, rather seriously.

"Of course you're not a Murderer Toby, I just thought you may try it out somewhere safe, just to know whether it is still there and whether you can control it. It wouldn't be nice if you accidentally used it and something horrible happened." Said 'Bella.

"Trouble is, there isn't many places around this part of the School that may be safe enough to try it, especially to try to do it where we won't get caught." Said Toby.

"You can think of explaining that if you were caught. 'Oh sorry Sir, I was testing to see whether I was able to still produce a blue light to fire at something and blow it up'. Any Teacher hearing that would want us locked up." Replied Keiron.

"We'll just have to try to stay out of the Eldridge's way or have to deal with the situation if we can't." Said Toby. He was now watching the dying embers in the fire grate.

"It is right though, I mean check to see if this is real and not just the one off shot; just supposing something did go wrong, it just doesn't bare thinking about." Said Toby, still looking at the fire grate.

"But what is this 'Power'?" Asked 'Bella. Toby shifted uneasily in his seat and moved his gaze from the fire grate to the rug upon the floor in front of it.

"We don't know, as we said we don't even know whether the incident up upon the Moor was a one off or whether the 'Power' is permanent or just temporary for a short time." Said Polly.

"What we should do, if Toby and Keiron can stay clear of the Eldridges, in the meantime, is maybe look out for some place around the grounds, where we are allowed to go, which we are able to be unobserved and Toby can try to see if he still has the 'Power'." Said 'Bella.

"Yes, that would be a good idea." Agreed, Toby, Polly and Keiron.

"So as soon as we can, we should find a place where we can't be disturbed." Said 'Bella.

"Well, time for Biology Class, so we had better be getting along there; have you got the books you need, you two?" Asked Polly rather Motherly.

"Yes, we've got our books." Replied Toby and Keiron in unison, holding up their Ruc-Sacks. Then the four friends stood up from their seats, left the Common Room and walked down to the class rooms for their Biology Lesson.

After the Biology class, Toby, Keiron Polly and 'Bella made their way out of the class room as quickly as possible and made their way to the Great Hall for their Lunch. They had a free period after lunch, so that if they were able to avoid the Eldridges, they may be able to get outside secretly while the Eldridges had their next lesson and find a secluded spot for Toby to try out and see whether he had still got the 'Power', in a place where, hopefully, either the Eldridge Triplets or anyone else would see what they were doing.

Inside the Great Hall, the Students sat in their House lines at their year tables. As usual, no matter what the threat seemed to be to him, it didn't seem to be putting him off shovelling his Lunch down his neck. 'Bella and Polly sat disbelievingly watching him between mouthfuls.

"I thought that he was traumatised and terrified? Doesn't seem like that now, does he, shovelling half of the World food production into his mouth." Said Polly rather distastefully.

Keiron stopped stoking his boiler for a brief moment and turned his head towards Polly and 'Bella. He was looking through his blonde fringe, eyeing them through his glasses. Keiron then slowly placed his knife and fork upon the plate in front of him, almost laying them in the Baked Beans and slowly took off his glasses. He turned them around in his palm and picked up a serviette from the table beside him. He then proceeded to wipe clean his glasses, removing some Bacon Fat and Tomato Sauce. Keiron looked down at his plate as though to take stock of his remaining Lunch and noted that he still had some roast Beef, Cabbage, Sausages and Baked Beans to finish off. This he had collected from the serving trays and filled his plate before coming over to sit at the Cargal Grunt's seats.

"It's alright for you lot, I've got to bulk myself up quickly, before the Eldridges get a hold of me. So far I've managed to give them the slip, but that can't surely last for long. I'm doing more exercising too, to try to bulk up a bit, so I can run away from them faster. Don't forget, we've got a Rugby Final to play against them coming up soon and I think a bit of cushioning may well help when they squash me flat." Said Keiron. Then he picked up his knife and fork and continued working his way through his plate.

"Well, all I can see is that you will simply bring about a Heart attack with all that fat and cholesterol going into your veins my lad." Replied Polly, 'Bella giggled.

"My Lad? What's that all about? I just told you, I'm doing extra exercises to cope." Said Keiron, after swallowing yet another mouthful of his Lunch.

"To burn that lot off, you would need to be racing trains my Dear boy." Scolded Polly; this time it was Toby's turn to giggle and almost choke upon his Roast Beef.

"He is exercising more at least, I hope he's fit for the Rugby Final and the Football Final in May." Said 'Bella.

"After what he said to Gaynell Eldridge, he'll be lucky to survive to be fit enough for the Rugby and Football Finals." Replied Toby.

"Well, let's hope this weird plan works and you're both fit enough to win both Finals and win us the School Year Cup as well as the Football, Cricket and Rugby trophies." Said Polly.

"Hey don't include me in no 'weird plan', it's him who is gorging himself." Said Toby, rather indignantly. He looked into the Hall, checking upon the Eldridges.

"So we don't think that sneaking outside during our free period to try to find out whether your 'New Power' is still present, rather than reading up upon our work for our next lesson, isn't just in the slightest way a bit 'weird' then, Toby?" Asked Polly, raising an eyebrow, trying to make her point.

"Ouch!" Said 'Bella, screwing up her face and shrugging her shoulders, indicating her acknowledgement of Polly's stinging remark. Toby rolled his eyes and looked at Polly.

"Yeah well, it wasn't me who put us into this situation Polly, is it? So that is why I said that; I meant when I said about not including me in his 'weird plan'." Replied Toby, holding back his anger as best that he could.

"OK, well – if we're going to have to get this done, we had better make a move, the Eldridges will be making a move to their next lesson soon and if we want to get outside away from them before they can leave their seats at the table, let's get doing then, we only have just over half an hour." Said Polly. With that said, all cutlery was placed upon the appropriate plate and bowl, then they all arose from their seats. As they walked towards the man doors of the Great Hall, the Eldridges upon their Wombat table watched the four Cargal Grunts go.

"Wha' d'ye thanks 'ees 'appenen' ower there then Bro's?" asked Gaynell Eldridge to Delbert. Delbert always seemed to be the Triplet's 'Ring Leader', whenever there was any trouble, Delbert Eldridge would almost certainly be found at the middle of it all, Dexter and Gaynell seemed always be there to back up Delbert.

The Triplets were also back up Muscle for Tom Taylor, when he swaggered around the School building up any type of following, but also in fear of him.

"Seems t'me like, that its 'bout time our Gaynell got 'Pay Back' fer acallin our Bro' names like that four-eyed runt did," Said Delbert as the four Cargil students exited through the door of the Great Hall.

"Yeah, can't wait fer t'grind that Muddle's bones inta flour." Gaynell replied

The four friends; Toby, Keiron, Polly and 'Bella, walked out through the porch and down the steps to the pathway in the Inner Bailey. They stood upon the pathway working out which way to go and where the best location would be for Toby to try out his test!

"Well if we try it out over by the great Hall, the Teachers and most of the students will be still in there and might see something." Said Toby.

"Where would be the best place then?" Replied 'Bella looking all around.

"What about 'round the opposite side of the Castle?" Suggested Keiron.

"What about the Caretaker, wouldn't he see anything from his Office there?" Replied Polly.

"That's it you see, he's in the Great Hall with everyone else and the Staff room would be empty as the Teachers are all in the Great Hall finishing their Lunch too." Said Keiron.

"We had better start quickly, so that Old Gabby doesn't come back to his office too early." Said 'Bella.

They then quickly walked away to the right of the entrance and followed the wall around the corner along the side of the wall. Here they were rather sheltered by the Towers of the Offices. They stood while Keiron placed a stone upon the ground about ten feet from Toby and stood back.

"Watch out, be careful Keiron." Said 'Bella, with concern in her voice.

!S'OK, Toby's not ready yet." Replied Keiron. Toby stared at the stone and held out his hand. He Concentrated, nothing happened.

"Keiron pick up the stone, stand to the side and throw it gently towards me." Said Toby.

"Be careful you two." Said Polly a little worry in her voice.

"We know what we're doing." Replied Keiron, picking up the stone.

"That's just the thing, isn't it? You DON'T actually know what you're doing." Replied Polly, again, sounding rather 'Motherly'. Keiron gently threw the stone under arm towards Toby. Toby again concentrated, nothing; he jumped sideways as the stone landed just beyond where he had been standing.

"Try throwing the stone directly at me, see if that helps?" Said Toby, nervously.

"Are you sure Mate?" Asked Keiron with a tremble in his voice.

"Oh do be careful you two." Implored Polly, really getting nervous now.

Toby stood and concentrated upon a spot some five feet or so in front of his face, but held his hand down this time. Trying to clear his mind and just think of the spot. Keiron stood to one side and took a deep breath; 'Bella closed her eyes not daring to look. Keiron drew back his right arm and released the stone. It flew through the air directly towards Toby's face like a missile. The stone reached the spot some five feet from Toby's face; Toby instinctively raised his hand in a reflex action and a blue bolt of light shot out forwards from his fingertips. And the stone disintegrated before their eyes. They all stood slightly in shock for a short while; it was a few moments before anyone spoke.

"Well, that er – sorts that question out then. It would appear that you do still have the Power Toby, only one thing is, it looks like you can only use it when

333

your safety is threatened. So it would seem that you can't use the Power unless you are actually being attacked?" Said Polly.

"Thing is, if I am under direct attack, how could I use the Power against the Eldridges? I couldn't blast them apart, a Human Being?" Replied Toby.

"Why not? They deserve it. They're just scum." Added Keiron.

"But I couldn't just blast into another Human Being,,,,," Began Toby.

"That's a matter of opinion." Poked in Keiron.

"Yes Mate, but I couldn't just blast them, that would be Murder." Said Toby. They all sat down upon a couple of benches at the side of the Bailey.

"Have you thought about not worrying about firing bolts of energy but rather harnessing the energy and using it like a shield, for protection, rather than aggression?" Asked Polly.

"I would need a lot of practise, but hopefully, that would be possible." Said Toby.

"What did you think about when you fired the bolt of energy when the stone blew up? Asked Keiron.

"I, I just cleared my mind and concentrated upon the spot where the stone blew up." Replied Toby.

"What about concentrating into your mind and thinking about there being a wall in front of you, maybe the stone would bounce off? If you concentrate upon a spot for the wall across in front of you, and it didn't work, you chose a spot slightly closer to fire a bolt , maybe it would work." Suggested Polly, all excited.

"Yes, it just might work if I can train this thing like it. Said Toby.

"How exciting." Gushed 'Bella.

Toby and Keiron stood up from the bench which they were sitting upon and walked to the centre of the Bailey. Keiron found another stone and stood to one side.

"Ready Mate." Asked Keiron.

"Yeah Ok." Replied Toby. Keiron drew back his right arm as before and threw the stone directly towards Toby. Toby again brought up his right hand, this time he pictured in his mind a brick wall standing between himself and the stone. The stone travelled through the air until it arrived at about five feet from Toby's face. The stone suddenly bounced backwards and fell to the ground. Polly and 'Bella cheered.

"YAAAY! You did it Toby, you did it!" Shouted Keiron, jumping up and down with delight.

"Yeah, but I need to practise quite a lot to make sure it's constant. Maybe I can develop it into different shields?" Said Toby.

"At least now we know that if the Eldridges throw a punch at you or anything else, that as long as you keep your cool, you can block it like with the stone and make them stop." Said Bella.

"Yeah, that's if Toby doesn't panic and blow their arm off." Added Polly.

Toby and the other three burst with laughter, their tension lifting as they knew that the Eldridge threat had been lessened. Toby and Keiron sat back down upon their bench,, Polly and 'Bella were sitting together.

"Looks like you will need to practise a lot and get the Power under your control; otherwise the Care Taker will be scraping bits of the Eldridges off all the walls." Said Keiron, and laughed.

"Eew, Eldridge jam." Said 'Bella, laghing.

"Yes Toby, you can't risk using the Power untrained. You must learn to control it for safety sake. If you react to a situation the wrong way, it could be terrible." Said Polly, a little element of fear in her voice.

"Yes Terrible." Echoed 'Bella, quietly.

It was then time to get their revision for their next lesson. They sat revising for the rest of the free period before making their way back inside and to their next class. Over the next few weeks they somewhat successfully managed to avoid direct confrontation with the Eldridges, until that is the day came for the Rugby Trophy Final.

Early that Saturday, Toby and Keiron awoke and met Polly and 'Bella in the Common Room. As from Monday, their 'Half Term' began and they would be collected after the match by their Parents. They were sitting in the Common Room in front of the fireplace upon the couches. The Rest of the team were sitting or standing spread out around the Common Room.

"Well, it's almost upon us, almost time to face the Music." Said Keiron.

"Hopefully, I can use the 'Barrier' part of the Power to block them from getting too close enough to make contact and make an attack." Said Toby.

"After all your practice, hopefully you'll keep cool enough to remember to just use the block." Said Polly.

"I'll try to put a block in front of Keiron if they try to attack him if I can." Said Toby.

Thanks Mate." Replied Keiron, trying to smile.

"I can't promise it will work in the heat of the moment, but I'll give it a go." Added Toby.

"Oh I hope we thrash them." Said 'Bella.

"Yeah well, if we survive until then, we should have a good chance to win the Football Trophy, as the Wombats won't be playing us, so no Tom Taylor or Eldridges to contend with." Said Keiron.

The four friends left the seats and began to walk around the Bailey towards the back of the building. Keiron and Toby had their hands in their trouser pockets. Their minds were stuck upon the thought of the danger which the Eldridge Triplets now posed to them, especially Toby and Keiron on or off the Rugby Filed and trying to avoid them until the Rugby Cup Final, ,which was now only a week away, would not be easy.

"It won't be easy to get through the week avoiding Tom Taylor and the Eldridges. I hope we can survive it and the Rugby field." Said Keiron as they rounded the corner and walked between the Kitchens and the back of the School. It was around here where Tom Taylor had kicked a football into Polly's face and had broken her nose, so this area of the school grounds didn't hold many happy memories for Polly. It was this incident which earned Tom Taylor his suspension from taking part in any sports event for any sport at the School the whole of that year. That was why the Wombat team were knocked out of all of the sporting finals except that of the Rugby Cup Final and why the Wombats wouldn't be facing Cargal House in the Final of the Football Cup.

Also, due to the attack upon Polly, Wombat House had been docked 100 House Points from their total for the year, which brought them close to Cargal, being only fifteen points ahead.

"Yes, and we hope that the trouble you two have caused with the Wombats doesn't spill over and start them coming after us, don't we 'Bella?" Said Polly, giving the boys a look of daggers. They walked into the back doors to the main School building and rounded the stairs leading to their Dorm Section. When inside, they once again headed for the Common Room until their next lesson.

Chapter Thirty Two – The Rugby Cup Final and Year Ending

The day had finally arrived for the Rugby Cup Final. Toby and Keiron awoke at their usual time and were soon down in the Great Hall tucking in to their Breakfasts.

As usual, Keiron's plate had piles of sausages, eggs, Mushrooms, beans and fried bread upon it with a liberal dollop of brown sauce. Toby's plate was similar but not filled so high.

"You two boys are never going to digest that lot by this afternoon." Said Polly in astonishment. She and 'Bella had only placed two sausages, egg, beans and two rashers of Bacon upon their plates.

"Of course we will, its Rugby, so we need all the protein we can get." Replied Keiron, piling six rashers of Bacon upon his plate and adding another handsome dollop of brown sauce. He passed the platter along to Toby and he added some rashers of bacon to his plate.

"You boys will end up with stitches eating all that food before the match." Said 'Bella, chewing upon a piece of sausage.

"Still plenty of time before we play yet. We'll have a light Lunch before the match, so we're making up for it now." Replied Toby.

"Yeah, and it may not be just your stomachs in stitches after the Eldridges have gotten hold of you upon the Rugby filed." Added Polly.

"Please, don't remind us!" Pleaded Toby, wincing just thinking about it.

"Don't worry, we'll ask Sister Ruth and Nurse Pauline to keep a special eye out for you two, after the Wombats have finished with you." Giggled 'Bella. Toby and Keiron looked at the floor and Polly frowned.

"Well. Let us just hope that the school medical team will not be needed in that respect." Said Polly, smiling at the two boys opposite her across the table.

Soon it was time for the group of friends to go to the Cargal stand of the Rugby Field. Here they should be safe for a while with the other Cargal House Students and some of their Parents, who were gathered to watch the day's matches. Today, Saturday, it would be the matches of the Cup Finals for the Seniors and Weeners in the morning and Grunts in the afternoon. On Sunday, the next day, it would be the turn of the Cardinals in the morning and the Toffs in the afternoon. So for the time being, Toby and Keiron were able to join the rest of Cargal House in supporting their Seniors in their Cup Final. Then they would be joining Mr Marden for last minute training and team talks before Lunch. Then it would be their turn after, the Grunts Cup Final. Toby and the others found their Parents as they entered the pathway up to the Rugby Field. Bill and Daisy had already found Thomas, Leonie spotted them and ran over to them.

"Hi Guys, so good to see you." Said Leonie, gleefully.

"Hi Leonie." Said Toby.

"Hello Leonie, how are you?" Replied Polly.

"Oh, OK now I've seen you, Polly. I won't have to put up with the horrid Rugger on my own now you're here." Said Leonie.

"Hi Sis." Said Keiron.

Hi Bro, wow, you're playing in the Cup Final, cool." Said Leonie.

"Leonie, this is 'Bella, our other friend whom couldn't be with us at Christmas." Said Polly, introducing 'Bella.

"Hi 'Bella, nice to meet you." Replied Leonie, smiling.

"Hi." Said 'Bella, returning the smile.

"Hey you lot, how about us? Called Bill. The group walked over to Bill, Daisy and Thomas.

"Hi Dad, Mom, glad you could come and watch." Said Keiron.

"Hi Bill, Daisy, glad to see you." Said Toby

"Hello Bill, Daisy, happy to see you again." Said Polly.

"Mom, Dad, this is 'Bella, our other friend whom couldn't make it at Christmas." Said Keiron, indicating to 'Bella.

"Nice to meet you." Said Bill.

"Yes M'Dear, nice to meet you at last." Said Daisy.

"Hi Thomas." Said Leonie.

"Yer." Replied Thomas, monosybilically.

"Hello Polly." Said Daisy.

"Hello Polly, hope you're well." Said Bill.

"Hello Toby, gud luck this af'ernoon." Said Daisy.

"Yeah, good luck, give 'em Hell." Added Bill.

"How come you two are in your team strips but Thomas isn't?" Asked Leonie, quizzically.

"Oh, he doesn't play Rugby and his team didn't get into the Final for the Toffs. The Toffs is tomorrow between Farley House and Wombat House." Said Keiron.

Oh that's a pity, we could've had both our boys playing . Said Bill.

"Don't think so." Mumbled Thomas, looking at the ground.

"What are the other matches then?" Asked Bill.

Well, in about twenty minutes, once we're all in our seats, it's the Senior Cup Final first, Cargal Versus Hatchell Houses; that's followed by the Weeners Cup Final, Hatchell Versus Wombat, before Lunch, then after Lunch, it's us, The Grunts Cup Final, Cargal Versus Wombat Houses." Said Toby.

"What're your chances d'you think?" Asked Bill. They looked at each other.

"Well, if we can avoid too many tackles from the Eldridge Triplets, without their front man, Tom Taylor, we may have a chance, but just a slim one. Said Keiron.

"Well, you'm boys jus' do yer best an' let's see that Cup en yer 'ands." Said Daisy.

"Think we should be looking for a seat, as you said, match starts in twenty minutes." Said Bill.

Then Toby spied Carl walk out from the pathway from the back porch of the School. He ran over to Carl and greeted him. At the same time, 'Bella noticed her father also and ran to greet him.

"Hi Dad, glad you could come." Said Toby.

Hi Toby, how are you?" Replied Carl.

"Nervous, never been in anything like this before." Replied Toby.

"You'll be OK." Said Carl.

"Better catch up with the others, the Muddley's have gone to save our seats." Said Toby, hurrying Carl up.

Hi Dad, great that you could come ." Said 'Bella.

"Hello Arrabella, you look happy." Replied Peter, her Father.

"Let's follow Toby, Keiron's family are saving seats for us, first match starts in about twenty Minutes." Said 'Bella, tugging at her Father's arm.

They caught up with Carl and Toby and 'Bella introduced them to her Father. Peter Snoop was an Accountant for a Finance Company in Frackston, where 'Bella lived. She lived in Frackston with her Mother and Father and was an Only Child. When they reached the Rugby Field, Keiron was watching for them. He showed them up to the seats in the stand where they found the others seated.

"Hey everyone, this is my Dad, Peter." Said 'Bella, smiling.

"Hello everyone." Replied Peter.

"Hi Peter." Replied everyone in unison. 'Bella sat next to Polly, who was in turn next to Toby.

"My Dad's an Accountant, like yours Polly." Said 'Bella.

"Well that gives us something in common doesn't it." Replied Polly.

Before they knew it, the Tannoy sounded around the stands.

"Ladies and Gentlemen, Students, we are gathered here today for the Toadford School Rugby Cup Final for the Senior Year. Our opponents today are Cargal House Versus Hatchell House. You will see that our teams are identifiable by their shirts as such; Cargal House are wearing the green and silver shirts and Hatchell House are wearing the gold and silver shirts. The sides have been gathered upon the pitch, the toss of a coin reveals that it will be the Cargal House team who kicks us off." Came the narration from the Tannoy.

The teams lines up as the School band and choir sang the School song. Following this, the teams took up their positions upon the pitch. The whistle blew and the match began with the Cargal Scrum Half kicking the ball out from his twenty two yard line.

"Here we go! Come on Cargal House!" Shouted Bill. The crowd cheered as the ball was punted forwards and the Hatchell Fullback made a clean catch shouting "Mark!"

He then kicked the ball up the field and watched it cross the touchline some five metres beyond the centre line. The game went on like this back and forth until five minutes before Half Time when Cargal House made a break through with a Try. This was then converted to make the score Seven to Nil.

Half Time arrived after another try from Cargal House and two Penalty conversions from Hatchell House, making the Half Time score Cargal - Fourteen Points to Hatchell House - Six Points, During the Half Time break, the parents and Students were served with sandwiches and refreshments.

"Well, looks like the Cargal team have it in the bag." Said Toby

"YAAY! Cargal," Cheered 'Bella.

"Yeah, that's if Hatchell don't come back from this." Added Keiron.

"Let's hope that you can win like this too this afternoon." Said Polly.

"Well, our match will be different to this, we have the Eldridges to cope with." Said Toby.

The second half of the Match was much the same as the first; Hatchell House dug in to defend their line and Cargal House began to press harder with scrums and Line-outs. Eventually, Hatchell back line cracked again and Cargal House ran in another try; to the delighted cheer from the Parents and Students seated in the Cargal stand. The Hatchell Kicker managed another Penalty Conversion, but it was too little too late. The final whistle sounded to a roar from the Cargal stand

and it was Twenty One to Nine; Cargal House had won the Senior Rugby Cup Final. The Captain raised the Trophy to a huge cheer from the Cargal stand. Wombat House won the Weener's Rugby Cup Final, which equalled the House Points earned by the Cargal Win.

Before they knew it, the time had come. Mr Marden gave them their final briefing before he let his Rugby team of Cargal House Grunts walk out of the changing rooms, which were separated from the ones at the rear of the School Building and were under the stands. The Cargal team lining up with the Wombat team outside their changing rooms ready to walk out of the tunnel onto the pitch. Just before they were given the signal to walk out of the tunnel, the Eldridges gave a knowing look over to Toby and Keiron with broad grins. The two lines of players, one line in green and silver halved shirts and white shorts, were Cargal House, a swans head emblem upon their left breast; and another line of Deep Blue and silver hooped shirts and deep blue shorts with a Boar's head emblem upon their left breast, the Wombat House Team.

They began to firstly walk, then trot out of the of the dimly lit tunnel into the sunshine outside. Led by their Captains, Peter Cougher for Cargal House and Aaron Pooke for Wombat House and the Referee and his Linesmen, who were contracted in for the day to afford total fair play and the non-existent opportunity for either House to call Biased upon each other. They took up positions upon the pitch, the crowd around the stands were getting excited and cheering.

"Oooh, I do hope they do well." Said 'Bella, jumping up and down.

"I really think they will try their utmost hardest." Replied Polly, rather more sedately. It was after all, now that they would find out whether with all the excitement and nerves of the actual event, whether Toby would be able to concentrate enough to use his 'Power' to safeguard himself and/or Keiron from the crunching tackles which they expected from the Eldridges. The toss of the coin resulted in a kick off for Cargal House and the hopeful tactics, allowing for the weight and strength of the three combined Eldridge Triplets within the scrum, that their kick off would either find a mark from one of the backs or fullbacks or that Steve Logan would be able to kick directly into touch.

The whistle blew and Steve Logan decided to try for a kick direct into touch, with the hope that this would result in a Line-out deep into the Wombat's half of the pitch. The last thing that Cargal House would be wishing for would be if the kick resulted in a scrum.

The ball was well connected with Steve Logan's boot in his drop kick and it sailed spinning away high into the air and looped out into touch, just short of the Wombat's twenty two yard line. The resulting Line-out was thrown in by Dexter Eldridge. Toby was lifted into the air by Michael Pullman, one of the Cargal Props and pawed the ball down to his left to be cleanly caught by Peter Cougher who then promptly fed the ball out and back along the line to the Cargal backs, which then began to run with the ball. As they entered the Twenty Two yard area, Andrew Martyn was brought down with a crashing tackle from Gaynell Eldridge. It took a few moments for Andrew Martyn to regain his wind and composure before the game continued with an immediate Ruck being formed around him. Peter cougher made the step over as Wombat's tried to push them over. Then Caine Malling came in sideways and grabbed the ball just before Peter Cougher was able to get hold of it. The shrill whistle blew and the Referee ran over and indicated that it would be a Penalty kick to Cargal House. Amid strong protests from Wombat players, Steve Logan was handed the ball, who then placed it upon a divot which he had punched up with his boot and aimed the point of the ball in a standing position towards the Wombat's goal. Steve Logan stood up and took a step backwards and then walked sideways in an arc around the ball, Steve then looked up at the goal posts to gage how far away they were and how hard and high he would need to kick the ball to complete his task. Steve took a deep breath and then stepped forwards, swinging his right leg and his boot connected perfectly with the ball which hurtled through the air in a long arc and sailed over the central crossbar of the goal post. A huge cheer rang out from the Cargal stand as the Parents and Students celebrated the first point upon the score board for Cargal House. Thanks to Steve Logan's Penalty conversion, Cargal now led by a score of three points to nil.

The teams regrouped and the Wombat's Kick off restarted the match. The ball was well placed by Nigel Cooke so that the ball bounced inside the touchline and bounced across it. The Referee blew his whistle and indicated for a Scrum. This was not what Cargal House had wished to see. The Referee called the two sets of props to form the Scrum with the Forwards behind them to complete the pack.

"Alright Guys, let's keep it clean, this is just a School match after all." Said the Referee.

The props locked arms and bent forwards waiting for the signal. The forwards locked in behind them in the pack; the two sides braced themselves, the Referee signalled bringing his hands together and called;

"Brace."

The two packs crashed into each other, the props shoulders from either team buffeting to create the Scrum.

"No collapsing now Lads, let's get this done." Called the Referee.

The Scrum took the strain and as expected, the Wombat pack was the weightiest and must powerful thanks to the Trio of Eldridges being part of the front row. Toby fed the ball in as straight as he could, a leg darted forwards beating the three Eldridges by millimetres and swinging backwards with the ball under the foot as Alvin Munce, Cargal House Hooker dragged the ball backwards with the ball under the foot as Alvin Munce, Cargal House Hooker, dragged the ball under the feet of the Forwards behind him in the second row of the Scrum. The Eldridges gave another push with their combined weight and size to attempt to push their side of the Scrum over the ball, but the Cargal pack held on just long enough for the ball to be pushed backwards out of the pack into the grateful hands of Toby Morby.

Toby, the Cargal Scrum Half, had turned around behind the scrum to collect the ball from his pack and to feed it out to the line of Cargal players to his right, spread across the field away from the Scrum. Toby took hold of the ball and instinctively dived out and 'Bullet' passed it out along the line away from the Scrum.

"Pulverise him!" Shouted Dexter Eldridge as the ball flew out along the Cargal line and the Wombat pack made a last surge forwards with the intention of trampling Toby before he was able to roll out of the Scrum's path. Alas Toby had indeed already rolled out of the Scrum's path; also as it broke up, the momentum of the Scrum came to a sudden halt and the Eldridge Trio almost tripped to fall flat upon their faces, also they very nearly almost brought the forwards in their second row crashing down upon them.

Rather than the Wombats making a surge, it was actually the Cargal team who made a surge up the pitch, entering the Wombat's half of the pitch, still passing the ball along the line towards the opposite wing they came face to face with the Wombat defenders. Each time a tackle was attempted, the Cargal player running with the ball had released it, passing it along to the next in line. After the Scrum broke up, the Cargal Forwards then made another line for the ball to be passed along once it had completed its journey along the first line.

The Cargal line had reached the twenty-two yard box before the Wombat's had any luck with slowing the progress of their opponents. The ball found its way into the hands of Steve Logan, who before being felled like a pole-axe by Gaynell Eldridge, was able to chip the ball forwards over the heads of the Wombat defensive line, Toby, who was a few steps behind Steve in the line, ran forwards, keeping the ball in flight in his sight at all times and allowed the ball to drop over his shoulder into his hands. Toby then sprinted forwards and dived forwards with his out stretched hands bringing the ball down across the base Line into the Try Area. The Cargal part of the crowd went crazy! Polly, 'Bella and Leonie were squealing with excitement and delight, jumping up and down; the parents, especially Carl Morby, cheering loudly.

"Try!" Shouted Bill with a cheer, Daisy was now more interested as she caught sight of Keiron congratulation Toby for scoring the first Cargal try. This meant that just before half Time, Cargal House had a lead of Ten Points to Nil as Steve Logan had once again converted the try.

Shortly after Nigel Cooke for Wombat House took the drop kick to restart the match, the Referee raised his arm straight up above his head, pointing his fingers upwards and indicated that the next time that the ball entered touch that it would the end of the first half and they would be at Half Time. During the early second half of the match, the play went much the same way as the first, with Cargal having most of the possession. As the half went on, Toby received the ball from a Line Out and was immediately pounced upon by Dexter Eldridge. Without thinking or hesitating, Toby held out his right hand and swiftly moved it backwards behind him. To his surprise, Dexter found himself suddenly seem to move backwards as he swung his arms, resulting in him grasping at empty air. Up in the Cargal Stand, the majority of Parents and Students thought that Toby had sold Dexter a daft side-step; but a giggling Polly and 'Bella knew differently; Toby had used his 'Power' to sweep Dexter aside and prevent him from tackling him, Toby ran forwards with the ball, chased this time by Gaynell Eldridge.

"C'mere Morby, I'm gowaina squat yer, likes a fly." Shouted Gaynell.

Toby once again ran on and swept his right hand behind himself as Gaynell closed in. Gaynell dived for Toby's legs only to find himself falling spread Eagled face down in the mud. He looked up from his mud bath with a round face black as a Miner and cursed Toby as he ran on. Now Toby was free of the Eldridges, he sped on until confronted by Delbert Eldridge, who allowed Toby to pass his shoulder and wrapping his arms around his legs. Toby flet that all his momentum had suddenly came to a halt, as though he had hit a brick wall. Instinctively, Toby twisted as he began to feel himself falling and passed the ball out to his left and backwards as Peter Cougher overlapped him, catching the ball and speeding off down the wing the last ten yards and then diving over the Try line to place the ball across for another Cargal House try. Steve Logan then stepped up to once again convert the try and with a roar of cheers from the Cargal Strand, it was announced and displayed upon the Score Board that Cargal House now had a handsome lead over Wombat House of Seventeen points to Nil!

Now all Cargal had to do was to defend their line and prevent the Wombat's from scoring in the remaining ten minutes and they would be Champions. The match was important as it carried a prize of fifty House points for the winner and if Cargal were able to hold off the Wombats for the remaining ten Minutes, this would result in the Cargal House moving ahead of the Wombats in the House point totals, in line to win the Toadford School Cup.

The game was restarted with a drop kick from Nigel Cooke for Wombat House. Despite the attempt to mark the ball, it bounced near the touch line into touch. Another Scrum to Wombat House, another time for the Cargal Pack to attempt holding off the power of the Wombat Pack consisting of the three front row props being the Eldridge Triplets. The years of being brought up upon a farm and the farm work which they did there, despite being only fourteen years of age, had made the Brothers larger and stronger than most other fourteen years olds, just their daily life upon the farm had been like a daily work-out since they were ten years old.

When their Parents were away from the farm, the brothers rather cruelly used a Calf; which they would lift up around their shoulders and use the poor animals for weight training, dripping their knees and squatting then standing again, reportedly. If Hargus and Hettie were home, then the Brothers would use

344

conventional weights in a converted barn which Hargus had fixed up for them. His idea being that providing his Sons with a 'Gym' to work-out in would pay him back through all the work which the Brothers would be able to do around the farm as they grew and became fitter and stronger.

The weighty Scrum, with Cargal legs getting tired, began to push forwards very firmly.

"C'mon Boys, push 'em 'ard….. Hmmmmm!" Shouted Gaynell Eldridge from within the Scrum. The Wombats began to dig their boots into the Pitch, front and back row roaring and pushing harder.

"Eave boys, 'Eave." Shouted Dexter Eldridge as the Cargal props and second row simply flet like there was a juggernaut pushing then backwards deep into their Twenty-Two yard area, dangerously approaching their Try line.

The backs fanned out behind the Scrum waiting for their for their need to defend their Try Line if necessary. Keiron among them, standing centrally between the goal and the line of Cargal Backs. The scrum made one more heave for the Cargal try line and then the ball emerged out from the back of the Wombat Pack. Immediately, Craig Pharram, stand in Scrum Half for Wombat House, snatched up the ball and drop kicked it over the heads of the Cargal back line. The Wombat forwards broke from the scrum and rushed forwards, blocked by the line of Cargal backs. The ball flew over the head of Keiron and cleared the Cross bar of the goal. A loud cheer rang out from the Wombat House Students. The Score was bellowed out by the PA System and upon the Score Board as Cargal House Seventeen to Wombat's three; with just five minutes to play, that meant that the Wombat House team had to go all out to Score as they needed two tries within five minutes simply to draw level and to force extra time.

"C'mon Cargal." Shouted 'Bella, jumping up and down. This prompted a chorus of the same being repeatedly chanted by the Parents and Students in the Cargal Stand. This, in turn, prompted a loud bout of booing being emitted from the Wombat House Stand.

"Get youmsleves a moovin' an' get that there ball over the line." Shouted a figure in the Wombat Stand. Stout stocky with an old yellowish green suit on with yellow check and thinning wiry red turning grey hair with a bald forehead on top of his head, a bulbous red rose and blue piercing eyes; Hargus Eldridge had come along to egg on his three Sons.

The game re-started with Steve Logan kicking for touch from his drop kick. The resulting Line-Up was won by Cargal and the ball sent out along their attacking line. The players passed the ball along each tried to block the progress of the Cargal team with every move they made towards the Try Line. Each time a Cargal player received the ball, he momentarily checked for a way forwards, if he could not see one, then passed the ball onto another player, making sure to keep possession of the ball. The Wombat's were getting frustrated and beginning to lose their cool. The ball passed again and again between the Cargal players, keeping Possession, stopping the Wombats getting hold of the ball and running any tries in. Then it happened, what the Wombats were dreading. The Referee checked his watch and held his right arm straight up above his head with his fingers held tightly together; the signal that eighty minutes had been reached and that the next time the ball crossed a touchline or a Penalty was awarded, then the Match would be ended. Parents and Students in the Cargal Stand became very excited as they recognised the signal from the Referee. Polly was not very up on the rules of Rugby, she knew that the ball was allowed to be carried in the hands and that the ball must be passed backwards by hand and could only be passed forwards if it were kicked. That was about all that Polly knew of the rules of Rugby and what a Try was. She asked her Father what the signal meant and why everyone was getting over excited.

"Why is the Referee running around with his arm up in the air?" Asked Polly.

"Because he's indicating that next time there is a dead ball of any kind; like going into touch or a Penalty, that the match will end." Replied John Muggard, Polly's Father. At hearing this information, Polly joined in with the cheering and jumped up and down with 'Bella.

Finally the ball was passed to Steve Logan who turned a quarter turn and kicked the ball high and over the touchline to his right. The Referee lowered his arm and then blew his whistle with two short peeps followed by a long peep. This is the signal that the match had ended with the score Seventeen Points to Three Points. Toby, Keiron and the Cargal team had won the Grunts Rugby Cup Final. It was the first that Toby had been involved in anything like either. He dropped to his knees where he stood with the Cargal Stand cheering out his name and Cargal – Cargal. Eventually, the Players walked to the tunnel of the Stands, where Parfinkle was waiting beside a pedestal which housed on top of it the Grunts Rugby Cup, a shiny Silver Trophy. Toby had never won anything like this either. The two teams stood in their lines either side of the pedestal. The Cargal team members, including Toby and Keiron, eyed the Trophy grinning while the forlorn looking Wombat House team were rather sulking and also eyeing the Trophy, but theirs was not a look towards it of joy but of jealousy and envy. Parfinkle walked along the line of Wombat's, each bowing his head as Parfinkle reached him and then looped a medal upon a ribbon over his head. Then once all of the Wombats had received their medals as runners up. Parfinkle moved over to the Cargal team and walked along their line, they bowed heads again and as before, Parfinkle placing a medal upon a ribbon over each of their heads. Then once this was complete, Parfinkle turned to the Pedestal and lifted the Silver Trophy and turned to face Peter Cougher, Captain of the Cargal Grunts Team.

"It is with great pleasure that I, Cragus T Parfinkle congratulate you and your team for becoming the Grunts Rugby Cup Champions and award you the Grunt's Rugby Trophy. Well done everyone and well done to the runners up." Said Parfinkle as he handed the Trophy to Peter Cougher, who received the Trophy and thanked Parfinkle; then Peter turned to face the Cargal Stand and to a roar of cheering from the Stand lifted the Trophy up over his head.

After this, the two teams walked into the tunnel leading to the Changing Rooms, the wombats rather disconsolate with their runners up medals around their necks and the Cargal, team all smiling, walking back with each of the team players taking turns to carry the Trophy. They reached the changing room for their team as Toby took hold of the Trophy. This felt good, Toby was enjoying the winning feeling and enjoying carrying a Silver Trophy; he wanted to do this more often.

The Cargal team members showered and changed back into their clothes. As there were Parents present at the School, they had been told to wear their School Uniforms just for this weekend. The Cargal team emerged from the Changing Rooms and left the stands, walked to the School building. Inside the made their way along the Hallway and then turned to look at the Trophy Cabinet to their right, looking at the space where their Trophy would soon be proudly standing with the 'Cargal House' name inscribed into the plate around the pedestal; showing that all who looked at it in the future, that this year Cargal House won the Grunt's Rugby Cup.

They could hear chattering in the hallway and some general hubbub coming from the corridor to their left just before the main entrance. They walked along the corridor with the Hospital wing to their right and the Offices of the Sister, Secretary and Head Master to their left. As they walked along the corridor the sound of the hubbub was getting louder. They passed the girl's toilets and shower rooms; Steve Logan ran over to a closed door to his right and tried it to see if it were locked, "Don't bother Steve, there won't be any girls in the Shower Room today, it'll be empty, they will all be in the Great Hall." Said Peter Cougher, who knew exactly what Steve Logan was up to.

"Tell you what mate, that was a fantastic side step you gave Dexter Eldridge, and again with Gaynell, so funny to see him face down in the mud." Laughed Andrew Martyn, who had played as opposite Winger to Peter Cougher. As they walked into the Great Hall, they were hit by the rise in volume of the hubbub, the whole of the tables for Cargal House Students erupted into a huge cheer and the Rugby team walked over and took their places at the Grunt's table, proudly displaying their winners medals around their necks. The Wombats across the Hall at their tables were scowling across at the Rugby team and their medals.

"What happened to you lot, you should've pulverised them, what's the point of you being your size if you let wimps like Morby dance around you like Ballet dancers?" Chastised Tom Taylor.

"You can talk, you weren't even playing!" Replied Nigel Cooke.

"You know I'm banned from playing." Protested Tom Taylor.

"Yer, an' 'oos fault es that then, eh?" Asked Dexter Eldridge.

347

"Shaddup!" Snapped Tom Taylor.

"You Guys were brilliant." Said 'Bella back on the Cargal table, as they sat down.

"Good on you Grunts." Called the Captain of the Seniors team from his table.

"Thanks Martyn, well done to you too." Replied Peter Cougher, Captain of the Grunts team.

Then there was a tapping of a stick upon wood; everyone looked up to see Parfinkle standing at his Lectern preparing to speak.

"Good evening everyone, Ladies, Gentlemen and Students. It gives me Great pleasure to present unto you our three gallant Cup Winners from today's matches; Cargal House, your Seniors Rugby Champions." Said Parfinkle. The Cargal Seniors Rugby Team arose from their seats and walked to the front of the Great Hall amid loud applause and cheers from the Cargal tables.

"May we now have the Wombat House Weeners team, who are the Weener Rugby Cup Champions this year? Finally, may we have the Cargal House Grunts?" The Wombat Weeners team walked out and stood with the Cargal Seniors team, all standing with their Winners medals hanging from the ribbons around their necks.

To more applause, very loudly from Polly and 'Bella, Toby , Keiron and the rest of the Grunt's Rugby team walked to the front to join the other teams, proudly displaying their medals around their necks. Once all three teams of Champions reached the front and stood together, Parfinkle once again introduced them.

"I give you our Champions!" Shouted Parfinkle.

There was an enormous burst of applause from all around the whole of the Great Hall, Toby and Keiron stood smiling. It was at that moment, out of nowhere, that Polly felt happy to be part of their group and to be friends with two of the boys receiving respect from the entire School for their achievement that day. Parfinkle motioned for the teams to return to their seats, once he had decided that they had milked enough applause for their work.

"Let us enjoy!" Announced Parfinkle, to the sound of applause from the Master's table, along with all of the Students House tables. The doors opened and the Kitchen Staff appeared, bringing Silver salvers full of sausages, pies, chips, boiled and roasted potatoes, roasted chickens, beef, and lamb, vegetables and all manner of delicious food. The teams had regained their seats and immediately Keiron tucked in, filling his plate with some of almost everything.

"Here goes the Human Shovel again," Said Polly, rolling her slate blue eyes. I've just expelled a lot of energy, I need to regain it ready for the Football Cup Final." Said Keiron through a mouthful of Roast Lamb.

"We've got Cricket qualifying matches first." Toby reminded Keiron, also through a mouthful of Lamb.

Oh Yeah, sorry Mate, I was forgetting that." Replied Keiron.

"Don't look now, over there .... ! Began Polly, tilting her head a couple of times, discreetly towards the Wombat Grunt's table. Of course, when one tells a teenage boy not to look, the result generally, is that evidently, they look!

"I said DON'T look, are you deaf?" Scolded Polly. What they had looked at was what Polly had noticed; which was that the Wombat's Grunt table were all staring eerily towards the Cargal House Grunt's table, especially towards a small group of friends. Tom Taylor sat prominently at the centre of the Wombat Grunt's table, watching with a thin grin upon his face.

"Ugh, he gives me the creeps!" Stated Polly.

He thinks he's handsome and irresistible." Said 'Bella, with a slight sneer in her voice and the corner of her top lip curled up.

"Well, he's in a minority of one with that opinion; he's the ugliest boy in the School." Added Polly.

You're forgetting the Eldridges," Said Keiron matter of fatly.

"Oh, er yes, well, I was forgetting those Gorillas." Said Polly, correcting herself.

It was not often that Keion was able to correct Polly, and less often for Polly in herself stable, prim and proper manner to accept being corrected, especially by Keiron. Polly held no grudge against Keiron for correcting her the way he'd done so in the Great Hall. After all, anyone may have heard and that would have knocked Polly down from her pedestal.

The weeks which followed had fewer lessons in them as the Cup teams from the Houses needed some practice and training time. During this time was also played the Girls Grunt's Netball Cup Final, which was won by Cargal House, as predicted, Polly Muggard (Goal Shooter), was the highest scorer ending at Twenty One Points to Twelve Points. Cargal House were cheered off the court, especially Polly, who had received a great many 'High-fives'; from other girls and even older members of Cargal House from higher years.

The Cricket Score was as predicted a comfortable win for Farley House, where Toby was not out for a hundred and sixty five runs, leaving the rest of the team to put together the rest of the Cargal Score line of Three Hundred and Eighty Six runs all out and Farley House then managing Four Hundred and Five runs, very easily beating the Cargal Score. Once again after each House Cup Match, a feast was held within the Great Hall.

Then there was the Hockey final, where Polly was seriously injured when the Wombat striker, Virginia Cornett, swing her stick and with a crunching sound and nausea to Polly, who collapsed vomiting onto the green grass of the pitch screaming between mouthfuls of vomit. A stretcher was bought onto the pitch and they carried Polly off and straight to the Hospital Wing. After looking at Polly's now ballooning swollen ankle, Sister Ruth declared Polly's injury to be too much over the capabilities of the School Hospital Wing. So Made Polly as Comfortable as possible with some Pain Killers and waited for an Ambulance to arrive and take her away to Hospital in her home Town of Cranleigh, to give her an X Ray.

The Referee meanwhile, had shown Virginia Cornett a straight red car, which was a rare event during House Hockey matches. It was felt very strongly by the Cargal Grunts and some of the older Cargal Students that Virginia had deliberately followed through with her hockey stick after knocking the ball away from Polly as she closed in upon the Wombat's goal. Alas, without their leading striker, the Cargal Girls lost their way and the match. Of course, cheating is the way that Wombats celebrated everything, just to rub it into their 'Loser' opponents. The air in the Cargal House Grunts Common Room was thick enough to cut through.

Everyone was waiting for the next to speak first. The shock of Virginia Cornett's attack upon Polly, who they thought was deliberately attacked despite Virginia's refusal to accept the Referee's decision at first and protests of innocence and the inevitable threats of what her father could do to them 'if' she told him who the Referee was, talked to friends of his at the Police and made him be brought before him in his Magistrates Court. All of this of course, made no impression upon the Referee, he'd had worse threats than that from Professional Hockey teams who he regularly officiated for.

Virginia could still be heard shouting her mouth off as she walked away from the pitch towards the back of the School building and the Changing Rooms. As the Hockey pitch was not in the 'Stadium' of small stands which was used for School Football or Rugby House Matches, the Hockey players had to use the School Changing Rooms for changing and showering, rather than the rooms beneath the stand of the School Official Playing pitch. It would be Virginia's fate to be interviewed by Parfinkle and then have suitable punishment given to her. Virginia trudged through the School carrying her sports bag with her along the Hallway and turned left before the entrance doors to walk along the Corridor until she reached the Girls Shower Room, upon her right. She entered and disrobed of her sports kit. Virginia stood under the shower and washed away the Hockey match. She then put her Wombat badged uniform back on and proceeded out of the Shower Room and walked along the corridor to eventually stop outside the Head Master's office to await sentence from Parfinkle. She knew that she most likely faced a lengthy ban from all sports activities for many months, as Tom Taylor had been given and also it was suddenly dawning upon her; possible Suspension or even expulsion from Toadford School for the manner in which she shouted at and Threatened the Referee for sending her off when she had committed a serious injury to Polly.

350

Craigus T Parfinkle turned into the corridor from the Hallway and strided up to his Office door, unlocking it with a latch key. This was not the first time since she had been brought to his Office while being at Toadford School. Parfinkle silently walked into his Office and closed the door behind him. He walked into his Office and closed the door behind him. He walked around behind his desk, opened a draw and took out an A4 brown file with the name CORNETT V written at the top. Parfinkle had decided to keep all of the files of the trouble makers and Bullies close at hand in his own desk draws.

"COME!" Called Parfinkle loudly, as Virginia heard through the door while she stood outside the Office waiting her fate. Virginia stonily faced and silent opened the Office door and entered. Silently Parfinkle motioned for her to sit down upon the chair which he had placed in front of his desk. To begin with Parfinkle opened the file before him silently looking through the reports from the Masters about Virginia's behaviour, but none of these previous complaints match up to this one; this was the Daddy of them all.

Virginia Cornett squirmed in her seat, fiddled with her fingers and showed, as Parfinkle hoped, a frustrated Teenager seated before him.

"Miss Cornett, I am extremely concerned about your behaviour since joining us here at Toadford School. I like to run an efficient School Miss Cornett, that is not easy when I have to deal with Students like yourslef. I was alarmed at the way in which you attacked Miss Muggard......" Began Parfinkle.

"Didn' attack 'er, jus' mistimed me tackle is all, not attacked 'er." Interrupted Virginia, trying to look all innocent.

"Did you interrupt me Miss Cornett? I know your Father is a Magistrate in the City, but I really do not see this as a lifelong protective blanket for you to make threats with whenever you do not get your own way or find yourslef in trouble." Said Parfinkle.

"I didn' attack 'er I tell yer, she fell awkward like." Replied Virginia with the same careless meaning as whenever she talks to members of Staff.

"I beg to disagree Miss Cornett... Began Parfinkle again, this time beginning to show annoyance upon his face,

"Didn' attack 'er OK, I tell yer t'was an accident is what it was." Said Virginia, bland Teenage drawl as usual, monosybilically.

"Again you interrupted me when I was speaking, Miss Cornett. Again this attitude. I am sorry My Dear, but you leave me no alternative other than to Suspend you from school for a period of Three Months, not including the Summer Holidays, while an investigation is conducted into what our next step would be . It is possible that Mr Crabbin, the Referee, may wish to report your threats of causing the dishonour of being falsely arrested by Police Officers, who are no doubtable friends of your Father, and bringing him to Court upon false Charges and be sentenced by you Father simply for carrying out his duties for which he had been employed today, as being very serious indeed. If you are charged for attempting to Pervert the Course of Justice and suggesting that the Police are happy to commit Purgery in a Court of Law and that Your Father would be Compliant to this Purgery, then I would have no hesitation to Expel you from Toadford School." Said Parfinkle, sternly.

"S'OK, don' bother me none." Said Virginia without a care upon her face or in her voice.

"So I will be calling your Parents to come to the School to collect you, meanwhile, you will now go up to your Dorm Room and collect your belongings. Please leave nothing behind in case the latter scenario becomes necessary." Replied Parfinkle.

Virginia got up from her seat and walked straight out of the Office, leaving the door open for Parfinkle to have to get up from his seat and walked over to close, Virginia climbed the stairs to the landing where she stopped at the Wombat Wing's outer door. She then opened the door with the keypad and entered, going to her Dorm Room. Dad would get her out of this like always. She thought to herself as she closed her suitcase around her clothes. She placed the books and other smaller belongings into her Hold-all and then walked out of the Dorm wing and out of the front entrance and so out of the School to the Car Park beyond the bridge and Oak door. Maybe this was going to be the last of Virginia Cornett which Toadford School would see; possibly.

"Back in the Cargal Common Room, after the match, 'Bella sat crying upon a couch with Keiron while Toby sat alone upon the other in front of the fireplace. Just then, Parfinkle was seen to leave Thybold's Office, next door and walk briskly from the Dorm Wing. Just then Thybold came into the Grunt's Common Room and addressed all of the Students.

"I have some sad news for you all, I'm afraid. Polly Muggard, as you know, was taken to Cranleigh Hospital this afternoon following an injury during our ill-fated Cup Final against the Wombat's in the Hockey Cup Final. I must inform you that Miss Muggard suffered a fractured Ankle, caused by Virginia Cornett of Wombat House's overzealous use of the Hockey stick. Sadly Miss Muggard will be away from Toadford School until after Easter, while she recovers from her terrible ordeal. Some good news, if it can be seen that way, Virginia Cornett has been Suspended from School until a meeting can be convened and may possibly be facing expulsion from Toadford School; so please take note that Violent Conduct will not be tolerated at this School or rewarded." Said Thybold, sternly, frowning with the last line of his speech. Once he had noted the acknowledgement of the Grunts before him. Thybold then returned to his Office.

"Ruddy Hell!" Exclaimed Keiron, "Another Wombat bites the dust for attacking Polly and I thought that she was popular?!"

"Yes, well she is popular, with all of the Cargal Girls and indeed some of the Farley and Hatchell Girls, but not with the Wombats, they hate her for being your friend, Toby, and because of what happened to Tom Taylor." Said 'Bella.

"What! Why would they hate her for that?" Asked Toby Aghast.

"Because you're popular, more brainy than Tom Taylor, more better at most sports than Tom Taylor and because Cargal humiliated Wombat House, who expected to win the Cup with three huge Eldridge Gorillas playing Rugby for them." Said 'Bella.

"I can't help it if he's not quite as good as me, I just try to do my best, as my Dad has always told me to. I can't help it if Tom Taylor isn't quite as good as me?" Said Toby, pleadingly.

"We know that Mate, it's just them Wombats think they're everything. Anyone who stops them being 'top' of everything and best of everything are their enemies." Added 'Bella.

"It won't be the same without Polly until Easter." Said Keiron, gloomily.

"We'll definitely miss her." Said 'Bella.

"Won't be anyone to answer all of the questions in class." Said Keiron, nudging Toby.

"Don't be so nasty Keiron." Scolded 'Bella, Keiron Grinned.

The time was now upon them, the final days of the School year. The Grunts Cricket Cup had easily been won by Cargal House, with Toby scoring just short of a Century in runs. The Easter Holidays had been long, well seemingly long to Toby, Keiron and 'Bella, as they had missed Polly. She had written to them to keep them up to date with her progress and they wrote back to keep her in touch with the events occurring at Toadford.

After the Easter break, Mr Marden had put up the Cargal Football players through extra training. The Football Cup Final was more important in Mr Marden's eyes, as Cargal were now fifteen points behind Wombat House in the House Points chart. If Cargal House beat Wombat in the Football Cup Final, then they would rise to the top of the House Points chart and would win the School Cup.

One morning, the week before Half Term, Toby and Keiron sat at the Breakfast table in the Great Hall shovelling the contents of their plates into their mouths as usual.

"Ehem." Interrupted a voice. Toby and Keiron looked up from their plates to see 'Bella standing before them.

"Why don't you sit down 'Bella, what's keeping you?" Asked Keiron, through a mouthful of Egg and Bacon. As he reached the end of his question, 'Bella stood aside.

"POLLY!" called out Toby and Keiron in unison, jumping from their seats dropping their knives and forks upon their plates; they ran to meet Polly, taking turns to embrace her.

"OK Guys, careful with my ankle please, hello." Said Poly giggling. 'Bella stood giggling as the boys and Polly took their seats at the table. 'Bella sat down as Keiron resumed shovelling in his Sausage Eggs and the rest of his Breakfast.

"Some things never change, do they." Said Poly, tutting.

"Welcome back Polly, we've missed you so much." Said Toby, excitedly.

"Yeah, welcome b'ck Powly." Mumbled Keiron through a mouthful of Bacon.

"Thank you for your usual greeting, Keiron, Bacon and all." Replied Polly.

"Well, we now have the Cygnet Committee complete again." Said 'Bella, looking from Toby to Keiron and then to Polly, smiling.

"All except Leonie." Replied Keiron.

"Yes, she arrives next term, then we will be truly complete." Added Polly.

The week went quickly for the group of friends, with Polly back beside them; the Wombats were wary of trying any tricks towards them, avoiding the attentions of the Masters before the all-important Football Cup Final against Cargal, the decider as to who won the School Cup. Following the meeting, Virginia Cornett had been saved from Expulsion, most likely by her Magistrate Father, she was Suspended for the remainder of the term and excluded from the Exams, receiving a 'Fail' mark for them all.

The Exams went by, Keiron being helped with his revision by Toby and Polly; his expectations of higher Grades than he would have otherwise received ordinarily showing, evidently. Toby also was expecting slightly higher Grades, thanks to some help from Polly to complete his revision comprehensively too. Before everyone knew it, the day arrived.

As usual, the Cup Final was held upon the Saturday following end of Term Classes. Some Students, who had no interest in football or Sports had already left to begin their Summer holidays being collected by their Parents. The remainder of the Students were breakfasting in the Great Hall.

"Well it's finally here Mate. Time to do or die." Said Keiron.

"Yeah, well with the Eldridges playing, it may well be something of the latter part of that quote that we should be guarding against." Replied Toby, nervously.

"Don't be too hard upon youmsleves boys, think positive. If you do get in too much of a tangle with the Eldridges, then simply use a bit of your power to brush them aside, to avoid injury that is, not to aid in scoring goals of course, that would be cheating." Said Polly.

"And we couldn't be seen cheating now, could we Polly." Added Keiron, mockingly.

"There's no pride in cheating, one doesn't achieve anything by cheating, there's no skill in that is there?" Replied Polly.

"No we must keep things all above board and legitimate, play fair and no cheating." Said Toby, winking to Keiron.

"You don't want to scoff down too much food now, not with the game later, you'll give yoursleves stitches and cramps." Said 'Bella.

"We've got plenty of time before the match to digest our food, it's only nine O'clock in the Morning, the match doesn't kick off until three O'clock this afternoon." Said Keiron.

"Yes, that may be, but you have last minute training this morning with Mr Marden and you don't want to appear too lethargic because you've eaten too much beforehand, you may end up being dropped from the team at the last minute." Replied Polly.

"Don't worry about that Polly, we don't have training until twelve O'clock and then its only light training just to finalise and tighten up tactics before we kick off for the match." Replied Toby.

After they had finished their Breakfast, the group of Cygnets left the Great Hall and walked up the stairs back to the Cargal House Common Room. There they, as usual, sat at the couches in front of the fireplace. Polly had taken her turn to fetch the refreshments from the drinks cabinet and was now sitting upon the couch beside Toby with her legs up, with bent knees, resting a book upon her thighs ready. Polly had put on her Cargal sports shirt and tracksuit bottoms, ready for when they would go out to the stand to watch the Football Cup Final that afternoon. Toby and Keiron were dressed in their Cargal House Football shirts of Green and Silver halves with the Swans head emblem upon their left breast and their tracksuit bottoms, like Polly had done. They were ready for their Training Session at Twelve O'clock. 'Bella was dressed in casual clothes, not sporty at all, a lilac T Shirt with the Cargal Swan's head badge and a grey skirt. She sat next to Keiron upon the couch opposite Polly and Toby. They all sat drinking their glasses of Cola and thinking of the match that afternoon, all that is, apart from Polly, who was stuck into her book.

"'Higher Levels of Thought Made Easy'." Said Keiron, peering at the book which Polly was reading, "Enjoying your bit of light reading are you Polly?"

"Leave her alone, Keiron, it's a pity that you don't educate yourslef a bit more often. Reading would help you get better grades." Scolded 'Bella.

"Hi you Chaps, all ready to face the Wombats this afternoon then?" Asked Steve Logan, arriving at their couches, clutching a glass of Cola, "Budge up, room for a little 'un there." Steve added, bumping 'Bella with his hips.

Steve Logan was the Goal Keeper for the Cargal Grunts Football Team. For a boy of fourteen, he was tall for his age, being five feet eleven. His height gave him the perfect credentials for being a Goal Keeper. He was starting to 'beef up' with weight training to help him block shots and a be stronger barrier between the Posts. Short light brown hair, rather spikey and with sticking out ears, rather like a trophy handles, piercing blue eyes and some freckles upon his cheeks. Steve too was also in his track suit, ready for training.

"Polly, this is Steve Logan, our Goal Keeper." Said Toby, introducing Steve.

"I Know, we have the same classes together if you remember." Replied Polly, dismissively, not lifting her eyes away from her book.

"You haven't talked much with us before." Said 'Bella to Steve.

"Just thought as our star striker was here, I'd make the effort to mingle upon this special day." Replied Steve with a smile.

"What do you think our tactics will be today, as Tom Taylor won't be playing?" Asked Keiron.

"Oh Marden will probably have us avoiding the Eldridges with Pass and Move tactics, so as not to give them the opportunity to catch one of us in possession and get to be tackled too easily. I think that's what this last minute training session is supposed to be about." Said Steve.

"Yeah, I think that would be our best tactic; Pass and Move. To minimise the chances of Wombats connecting tackles." Replied Toby.

"Possibly a chance in the Box or around it to draw the tackles in and win free kicks or even Penalties, if we play Pass and Move. They may make a lumbering attempt at tackling, because we would have already passed the ball on and end up with a late tackle." Said Keiron.

"Yeah, there's that too; good thinking Keiron." Said Steve.

They continued to chat like this until the Common Room door opened and Mr Marden walked in, also dressed in a Cargal House Track Suit, ready for their training session.

"OK lads, ready are we? Let's get out upon that training pitch and sort out a few things then shall we?" Called out Mr Marden. The boys, including Toby and Keiron, got up from their seats and all filed out of the Common Room, following Mr Marden.

The boys wouldn't be seeing the girls until after the match, so Toby and Keiron said their good byes to Polly and 'Bella, who in turn wished them good luck in their match. Then Polly and 'Bella walked out of the Common Room, down the stairs and out of the Entrance to meet their Parents in the Bailey ready to all go out to the School Stadium to watch the House Football Cup Final between Cargal House and Wombat House. It was nearing three O'clock and the

Parents with their Students were filtering into the Stadium, and taking their seats in their respective House Stands. In the Wombat House Stand, House scarves were permanently on display along with many House Pennants; shouts and abuse towards Cargal House could be easily heard emanating from the Wombat Stand. Within the Cargal Dressing Room, Mr Marden was giving his Cargal House team last second tactics and a team talk to motivate his players, like a manager at the FA Cup Final.

"OK, right boys, let's have a good clean game; tackle true and decisively but try not to make the tackles count to them, don't give away free kicks if you can help it. Toby, I want you to latch onto any forward balls, especially in the Penalty area. Watch out for those Eldridge boys, avoid them as best you can. We'll be doing as we practised during our training Sessions, our 'Pass and Move' tactics, so as to confuse the Wombats and draw them into late tackles so that we may get awarded some free kicks or possibly even Penalties. Now Lads, let's be having you, get out there and put that Cup in Cargal House Colours. Said Mr Marden. The Boys cheered and walked out of the Changing Room into the 'Tunnel' underneath the Stands. Meanwhile in the Wombat's Changing Room, Mr Sheldon was giving his 'Pep' talk to the Wombat House Team.

"Right, I want to see some hard tackling lads,,,,, that means you Messer's Eldridge, make sure the Cargal team, especially that Morby Kid don't get a shot at Goal. Make sure you get the ball to Nigel, seeing as we don't have Tom with us today. Nigel, you latch onto any ball or scoring chance that comes your way; just put that ball into that Cargal House net. Right Lads, let's get out there and bring the Cup home to stay in our colours." Said Mr Sheldon, decisively.

The Wombat team cheered and then joined the Cargal team in the 'Tunnel', lined up beside them in their Deep Blue and Silver striped shirts with Deep Blue shorts and socks. The Referee and his assistants stood in front of the two teams, the Referee holding the Match ball under his arm, then gave the signal and began to lead the teams out onto the pitch to be greeted by loud cheers from the stands, especially the Wombat and Cargal Stands.

Happily the Sun was shining and the sky was bright blue with only a few wispy clouds here and there. The two teams stood in a line either side of the Referee and his Assistants facing the tunnel, where they had just emerged from and waited for music the begin playing the School Song.

The Cargal House players sang along to the music, blaring from the speakers around the stadium. The Wombats just simply grimaced at the crowd. The School song could be heard being sung by the Students in the stands, all save the Wombat stand where booing could be heard. When the School song finally ended, a loud cheer rang out from all around the stands. Polly and 'Bella screaming out from the Cargal Stand.

"Come on Cargal House." Which was followed by the Students chanting rhythmically.

357

"Cargal, Cargal, Cargal." They shouted together. This was equalled by chants from the opposite side.

"Wombat, Wombat, Wombat." Repetitively from the Wombat stand. The Farley and Hatchell Stands were somewhat neutral, even though they did in some way support Cargal House as they mutually hated Wombat House. The teams then stood as the Referee tossed a coin into the air and the team Captains called for their preferred prediction of whether 'Heads' or 'Tails' would land face up when the coin landed upon the ground.

Cargal House Captain, Steve Logan, had called 'Heads', but to his disappointed look, the coin landed 'tails' up. The Referee asked Aaron Pooke, the Wombat Goal Keeper and Captain which end of the pitch he would prefer and whether he wished to kick off the match. Aaron chose to face down wind, so that Cargal would be playing into the wind and chose to kick off.

The teams dispersed to take up their respective formations upon their halves of the pitch and the Referee called to each team Captain who came forwards into the Centre and exchanged House Pennants. The Captains then returned to their positions upon the pitch and the Referee checked this was so, checked his watches and then blew his whistle. Nigel Cooke tapped the ball to Peter Grainger and he passed to the ball back to Dexter Eldridge who passed it to his Brother Delbert, who began to build up a move up field, passing to the ball back into Midfield to Marc Knapp, who slowly walked the ball forwards, dribbling while the Cargal Midfielders held off at this point, to get the players settled into the game and to find their barings and get used to the pitch and the feel of the turf beneath their feet.

Nigel Cooke tried to slip Keiron's marking and darted forwards as Central Midfielder Michael Pullman headed the ball firmly back up field into the Midfield, where it was controlled by Fred Manly in the centre who laid the ball back out to the wings passing to Andrew Martin upon the left wing who began to run the ball forwards towards Marc Knapp, who attempted to tackle Andrew but he had already returned to the ball to Fred Manly. Fred pushed forwards with the ball, who then passed it out to Peter Cougher upon the right wing, who side stepped a rather early lethargic attempt of a tackle by Dexter Eldridge who just managed to catch a glimpse of green and Silver shoot past him as Peter began a run down the wing, making for the goal line, showing Dexter a clean pair of heels, Peter reached two yards from the goal line and crossed a looping ball across the face of the goal, where Gaynell tried to jump for it but was a little too heavy to rise quickly or very high and watched the ball sail over his head and be met sweetly upon the forehead of Toby Morby, who directed it straight into the top right hand corner of the Wombat goal. A huge cheer erupted from the Cargal House Stand, the Parents clapping and cheering with their Student children cheering. Polly and 'Bella were jumping up and down excitedly cheering holding their scarves above their heads;

"Toby, Toby, Toby." Repeatedly.

Aaron Pooke picked himself up after thumping the ground following his failed dive towards the ball and picked it out of his goal net, he kicked the ball forwards so that the Referee was able to place it upon the Centre Sport for Wombat House to kick off once again for the second time in the Match.

"Where the Hell were you?" Shouted Aaron Pooke to Dexter Eldridge who simply turned his back and took up his position at left back once more.

"And where were you?" Aaron shouted at Cain Malling, who should have been covering the area where Toby had ran into to make the header.

Again, Aaron Poke received not much more reaction from his scolding of Cain Malling than he had from Dexter Eldridge. There was no time for any deeper conservation from his failing defence as Nigel Cooke one again got the Match under way by kicking off again. The second half began much as the first had, with each team taking things carefully; Cargal House covering their defensive line to avoid losing their lead over their opponents and Wombat's attempting to prevent Cargal House from adding to their lead and scoring again. A move began with Steve Logan, Goal keeper for Cargal House, throwing the ball along the left midfield, passed it out to Peter Cougher.

Peter Cougher ran down the wing and managed to swing his right leg to send the ball floating across the penalty area as Dexter Eldridge once again came charging in to a mistimed tackle. Peter Cougher felt and heard the crunching sound as a flood of seething pain flew through his lower leg. He felt his leg crumple beneath him as he sprawled to the ground, not consciously hearing himself issuing an ear splitting horrified scream. He rolled over and over a number of times before lying face down,, head propped up by his fore head, visibly crying into the turf of the pitch. The tackle from Dexter Eldridge had been two-footed, he had lifted his large muscular frame from the ground and slid into Peter with an almighty impact. His right boot making firm contact with Peter's left shin, completely taking his standing leg away with it, leaving Peter in a heap upon the ground. It was apparent very quickly that Peter's left leg was not laying very well upon the ground; in fact, it was quite noticeable that his leg, below the knee was actually lying at an unusual angle to the rest of his leg:

His left leg was badly broken. While this was taking place, Peter had not noticed that the cross which he had delivered had been met by Toby's head and had been sent sailing into the top left corner of the goal, well out of reach of the flailing arm of Aaron Pooke. A Sudden scream from Polly in the Cargal House Stand and pointing of her finger towards the stricken Peter Cougher, lying still upon the ground brought the attention of the nearside Referee's Assistant to his plight, while the rest of the Cargal House Stand terminated their celebration of Toby's second goal to notice and acknowledge Peter's Condition.

The Referee swiftly ran over to where Peter was still lying motionless upon the pitch, the Assistant ran across to the Referee and explained that he had seen Dexter Eldridge slide towards Peter as he had crossed the ball for Toby to head into the goal. When the two Officials looked down and acknowledged the injury to Peter's leg, the Referee swung his left hand to the pocket of his shorts and immediately held aloft a Red Card and brandished it at Dexter Eldridge. To the Boos and abuse from the Cargal House Stand, reluctantly after some subtle persuasion by the two Officials, Dexter Eldridge walked slowly from the pitch into the tunnel under the stands, his Cup Final was over.

Now the Referee arranged for the Medic team to bring onto the pitch a stretcher onto which Peter was lifted carefully and then he was quickly carried from the pitch to follow Dexter Eldridge from the pitch into the tunnel. From there, he would be taken directly to the School Hospital Wing, where Nurse Pauline would stabilise his leg with a more secure splint than the inflatable one which had been used by the Medical team, ready for his transferral to Cranleigh Hospital, where he would receive more comprehensive treatment for his broken leg and Physiotherapy to recover.

Dexter Eldridge upon the other hand, had been sent directly to the Changing room, where he would change and sit out the remainder of the Match alone, ready to receive the judgement of his House Master and team Manager, Mr Sheldon.

Peter Cougher was replaced by his Substitute bringing the Cargal House team back up to eleven players once more, but due to Dexter's early departure, Wombat House would have to finish the match with ten players. The tactics would change now, as a Midfield player was sacrificed to substitute with another defender to fill the gap at Left Back, which had been vacated by Dexter Eldridge,

Dexter, sitting alone in the Changing Room under the Stands, was able to hear the dull sound of muffled cheering from the Stands as the match continued without him. No winner's medal for him now probably, he thought and kicked the bench he was sitting upon.

Upon the Cargal House Stand, now that Peter Cougher had been whisked away from the pitch, Polly had stopped crying and was being consoled by Bill and Daisy Mudley and 'Bella. It had been rather a shock when beginning to celebrate Toby's goal, she had suddenly noticed the grotesque angle at which Peter's leg was lying as he had been motionless upon the ground.

With the Match marching on until the late minutes of the game, Cargal once again pushed forwards with their 'Pass and Move' tactics. After their loss of Dexter, the wombat's seemed to be more careful with their tackling, especially near to the Penalty Box. The ball moved fairly swiftly up the pitch as their 'Pass and Move' movement took them to a position just outside of the Wombat's Penalty Box, Fred Manly suddenly saw a gap and punched a direct through ball into the box with a side footed pass.

Toby sprinted forwards to meet the through ball, only to feel his legs suddenly in open air and come down with a splat in the mud close to the Penalty spot. Immediately, the Referee's hand shot out and he pointed to the penalty spot a few feet from Toby's head with a shrill blow of his whistle and a cheer from the

Cargal House stand. The Referee turned to Gaynell Eldridge and held up a yellow Card in front of his face. Gaynell had to be pulled away from Toby by Aaron Pooke, the Wombat's Goal Keeper before he was able to lash out at Toby as he picked himself up from the ground, to prevent Gaynell attacking Toby and leaving the Wombat team with nine players. The Referee placed the ball upon the Penalty spot as Aaron Pooke took up his place upon his goal line and began moving his arms around and grimacing at Toby to attempt to put him off from taking his penalty.

Toby took a few steps backwards from the ball for a short run up and then stood waiting for the Referee's whistle.

"Come on Toby!" Shouted Polly from the Cargal House Stand, Toby glanced over to the Referee and then prepared to take the Penalty. The whistle sounded shrill and loud. Toby eyed Aaron Pooke upon his goal line and ran forwards, striking the ball sweetly. Aaron Pooke dived to his right, thinking that a right footed player would most likely place the ball that way, but Toby had struck the ball with his instep and sent the ball hurtling low directly straight down the centre of the goal, sending Aaron Pooke the wrong way. Cheers erupted from the Cargal House Stand; Polly, 'Bella and Carl jumping up and down, scarves waving.

"Toby's scored a Hat Trick!" Squealed Polly.

The Cargal players upon the edge of the Penalty Box ran to greet Toby, hugging him and congratulating him. The Players then took up their positions again as Wombat House kicked off once more. Shortly after this, the Referee gave two short and one long shrill blasts upon his whistle and to the roar of cheers from the Cargal House Stands, The Match came to an end.

"Cargal House Won! YAAAAAY!" Cried 'Bella, jumping up and down with Polly. Bill and Daisy Mudley, John Muggard and Carl Morby were cheering along with the other Cargal Parents. The Wombat Stand was loud with Boos, as their team walked off the pitch and stood by their Manager, Mr Sheldon, who berated them for losing the Match. In the Stands, Tom Taylor was being nudged around by other Wombats, who evidently blamed their loss upon him for getting himself banned from playing in the Match.

The Cargal House Team walked slowly from the pitch with their arms held high above their heads in salute to the Cargal Stand for their support. They reached the touchline where they were greeted by Mr Marden, their Manager.

"Well done guys, well done; great game." Said Mr Marden as the players arrived with him, "Toby what a way to beat the Wombats, especially with Tom Taylor missing from their team." He added.

"You'll get your photo up with your Dad's now, along with the Rugby Cup ones. With the Cricket it makes a Hat-Trick of Cup wins and Winners Medals." Said Keiron to Toby, nudging his arm.

"Yes indeed, Toby, you will see your photo in the corridor in the Cargal House Dorm Wing, as our Grunt's Hat-Trick Hero for this year; So very many congratulations and yes, Keiron, we will also be seeing your Cup winners team photos for the Football and Rugby too; along with your photo for the Cricket, Toby for scoring a Century." Replied Mr Marden.

"Our Grunt's Year Records will be enormous." Said Steve Logan excitedly.

"And don't forget your names upon the team sheets for the Grunt's Cup teams for this and the Trophies for this and the plaque baring Cargal House as Cup Winners for this year engraved upon the Trophies for both the Football and Rugby Cup, to be seen in the School Trophy Cabinet. Each time the Wombats walk past the Cabinet upon their way to Lessons, they will be reminded of the beating which Cargal Grunt's gave to them this year." Said Mr Marden.

Then their attention was directed towards the pitch once more as the Grounds men had bought on a small stage where Parfinkle was standing with two Plinths. The Tanoy boomed out that it was time to hand out the Medals, beginning with the Runners–up. The Wombat Team reluctantly walked from the touch line led by Mr Sheldon up the couple of steps to bring them onto the stage, where they filed past Parfinkle. They each in turn, shook his hand and then accepted their Runners-up medals which Parfinkle hung over their heads and around their necks, before they stepped down from the stage and walked away down the tunnel and back to the Changing Room, not waiting for the following presentation. Now the Tanoy boomed out that it was Cargal House's turn to step up to the stage and receive their rewards. The Cargal House team stepped up onto the stage and one by one, they shook hands with Parfinkle and received their winner's Medals over their heads to hang around their necks upon ribbons.

Then it was Steve Logan's duty as Grunt's Captain for Cargal House, to stand once more in front of the Headmaster and shake his hand, then take hold of the handles as Parfinkle handed it to him. Steve then held the Silver Trophy to his chest. He then turned around to face the Cargal stand and accompanied by a huge roar of cheering , held the Trophy above his head with both hands. Steve Logan then stepped down from the stage and joined the rest of the team where Mr Marden had them pose for a team photo with the Trophy. Then led by Steve Logan holding one Trophy handle and Toby the other, the Cargal House team and Chants of ;

" CARGAL, CARGAL, CARGAL." From the crowd.

The Cargal House Team began to run a 'Lap of Honour' around the pitch. As they did this, it was already rather noticeable that the Wombat House stand had considerably emptied of disappointed and angry, bitter Wombats and their parents. As this was taking place, a lone rather elderly looking figure dressed in a long deep blue Robe adorned with golden motifs of Crescent Moons and Stars, who had been seated at the very top of the Cargal House Stand; apparently unnoticed, turned from the pitch and disappeared in a flash of golden light.

Along with the Grunts, there had been also played the Cardinal's Football Cup Final, won by Wombat House, that Saturday morning and the Weenr's Cup Final, won by Cargal House, following the Grunt's that Saturday afternoon. The Toff's had played their Cup Final, which was won by Hatchell House along with the Seniors, won by Cargal House the day before upon the Friday. The previous weekend had played host to the Athletics, the winning Grunts being;

One Hundred Metres Boys:- Toby Morby, Cargal House.

Four By One Hundred Metres Relay Boys :- Cargal House.

One Hundred Metres Girls:- Tilly Parmenter, Farley House.

Four By One Hundred Metres Relay Girls:- Hatchell House.

Two Hundred Metres Boys:- Colin Finchley, Farley House.

Four By Two Hundred Metres Relay Boys:- Hatchell House.

Two Hundred Metres Girls:- Polly Muggard, Cargal House.

Four By Two Hundred Metres Relay Girls:- Cargal House.

Four Hundred Metres Boys:- Alan Kirk, Hatchell House.

Four By Four Hundred Metres Relay Boys:- Hatchell House.

Four Hundred Metres Girls:- Polly Muggard, Cargal House.

Four By Four Hundred Metres Relay Girls:- Cargal House.

Eight Hundred Metres Boy:- Steve Logan, Cargal House.

Eight Hundred Metres Girls:- Tory Kayle, Hatchell House.

Fifteen Hundred Metres Boys:- Steve Logan, Cargal House.

Fifteen Hundred Metres Girls:- Tory Kayle, Hatchell House.

Shot Put Boys:- Gaynell Eldridge, Wombat House.

Shot Put Girls:- Chantelle Marfon, Hatchell House.

Javelin Boys:- John Pugworth Jr, Farley House.

Javelin Girls:- Virginia Cornett, Wombat House (Disqualified)

High Jump Boys:- Guy Watson, Hatchell House.

High Jump Girls:- Polly Muggard, Cargal House.

Long Jump Boys:- Paul Keeper, Farley House.

Long Jump Girls:- Olivia Hammond, Farley House.

Triple Jump Boys:- Paul Keeper, Farley House.

After the Matches, there was a large feast for the Students and Parents in the Great Hall. In addidtion to the tables for each of the Houses and their years, extra tables had been provided for Parents to join their children. Parfinkle stood and clapped his hand slowly three times; the hub-bub of voices around the hall quietened down for him to speak.

"Good evening Ladies and Gentlemen, Boys and Girls; I wish to thank you all for a great day of sport and celebration for us all, I wish to thank the Parents for their attendants and support of their children taking part in today's events; in fact in all if our events this past week. It just now remains for me to congratulate the winners of the events and to wish you all a happy Holiday, ready to return here a fresh in the next term. After much calculation and rechecking, it gives me much pleasure to read out the Final House Points Totals for this year;

"Farley House :- 267 Points, Well done Farley House," Announced Parfinkle, to a cheering from the Farley House Tables, their Students and Parents.

"Hatchell House :- 345 Points, Well done Hatchell House," Said Parfinkle again over a cheering from the Students and Parents at the Farley House table.

"Wombat House :- 496 Points, Very well done to Wombat House," Announced Parfinkle to more cheers.

"This leaves but one, I am happy to announce, our new and very well deserved Scholl Champions, with 503 Points. The Winners of the School Cup for this year – Cargal House!" Called out Parfinkle over the mounting cheers. The Great Hall erupted in cheers from the Cargal House tables, Students and Parents. Toby, Keiron, Polly and 'Bella were bouncing up and down in their seats with excitement. Mr Thybold walked around the Staff table and was joined by Martin Watchover, the Cargal House Captain, from the Senior's tables, at Parfinkle's Lectern. Parfinkle then handed. The School Cup to Thybold who stood holding the Cup with Martin Watchover while photographs were being taken by the local press and more celebrations from the Cargal House tables sounded throughout the Great Hall. A huge cheer rang out along the tables of the Cargal House Students and their parents. Over upon the Wombat's tables, some Students were booing as Martin Watchover carried the School Cup back to the Seniors table where he retook his seat after showing the other Cargal Students and their Parents the Trophy on his way.

The Celebrations were counted, after the Parents had left, in the Cargal House Wing. Thybold had placed the School Cup in Pride of Place in his Office and had placed the Grunt's Football and Rugby Cup's in the Grunt's Common Room on display. He had also placed the appropriate Trophies which they had won. Of Course, after the Summer Holiday, these Trophies would be placed back into the Trophy Cabinet, all except the School Cup, which would stay in Thybold's Office on display until the Autumn Term.

Thybold had left the Students to their celebrations after toasting the School Cup in his Office. The Students had returned to their year's respective Common Room for their own celebrations. The Cygnets returned to the Grunt's Common Room and sat in their usual place upon the couches in front of the fireplace. The friends were fussing around having photos taken with their awards.

"Come on boys, let's have one of you each with the Football Trophy, then both of you with it," Bossed Polly, arranging them around the Trophy; she took the Photos.

"Now the same with the Rugby Trophy." Asked Polly.

"Right OK," Said Toby, moving to stand with the Rugby Trophy, which his and Keiron's Grunts team had won.

"Just leaves the Athletics awards." Said 'Bella, a little down, as she had not won any.

Toby sat in his place upon the sofa, displaying his Winners Medals for the Football and Rugby Cup Finals, One Hundred Metres, Four By Four Hundred Metres Relay. 'Bella waited for Polly to pose with the Net Ball Cup Trophy, High Jump and Net Ball Cup Winner's Medals and then took another photo. 'Bella then gave the camera to Toby, who took a photo of Polly and 'Bella with the Netball Trophy, both showing their Net Ball Cup Winners Medals hanging upon ribbons around their necks. 'Bella was happier now, that Polly had reminded her about the Netball Medal that she had won as part of the team. Polly then put the camera onto 'Timer' mode and they quickly gathered together all with their School Cup winners medals around their necks, smiled and with a click, the Photo was taken of the Cygnets upon their last evening of being Grunts. Polly sat reading a book while 'Bella was doing some knitting. Toby and Keiron were playing a game of Chess.

"Not reading again, Polly; Ruddy Hell, it's the last evening of the term, we go home tomorrow." Said Keiron, looking up to the ceiling.

"I always read to relax, you know that, Keiron." Replied Polly.

"Concentrate upon the game mate, it's your turn." Said Toby rolling his eyes. Keiron returned to the game of chess, which was won by Toby, evidently, because Keiron allowed himself to become distracted. They played a few more games until they decided to quit for the evening and Polly with 'Bella walked back to their Dorm Rooms with them. They stopped outside their Dorm Room doors.

"So, I've got some last bits of packing to do, so I'll see you two in the morning. Good night and have a good last night as Grunts." Said Polly, holding out her hand for a shake. Keiron made a puzzled face and Toby took Polly's hand and shook it. Then Keiron decided that he might as well join in and shook Polly's hand also. They followed this by shaking 'Bella's hand afterwards.

"Good night Polly, see you in the morning. Can't believe we go home tomorrow, our first year completed!" Said Toby.

"Yes, I know, hard to think it wasn't long ago that we all met." Replied Polly.

"Good night boys, sleep tight." Said 'Bella, happily.

"Good night 'Bella, see you in the Hols, hopefully." Said Keiron.

"Good night 'Bella, sweet dreams." Replied Toby.

They entered their respective Dorm Rooms. Polly and 'Bella finished off their packing and went to bed. Toby and Keiron did the same in their Dorm Rooms. It had dawned upon all four of them that their lives were changing. When they returned from Holiday after the Summer, they would be returning as Weeners, not Grunts. There would be a new year of Grunts starting, which would include Keiron's little Sister, Leonie. So Keiron's older Brother, Tom, would then be starting his Cardinal Year, as a Fourth Year Student, and would mean that there would be three Muddley's attending Toadford. Toby and Keiron slept soundly, after all the effort of the day had tired them out. 'Bella was awake for a short while.

Things were changing, but the Cygnets had no idea how much change there would be in their next year and just how much their lives would really change, never to be the same again. After Breakfast the next morning, the group of friends waited for their Parents to arrive outside in the Car Park, having crossed the bridge to be there.

"Well Gang, here we are, nearly time to say goodbye." Said Keiron.

"Yes, but I hope you will remember to come to see me during the Holidays, you only need to catch a Bus and I have given you all a map for you to find my house." Said Polly.

"Yes we will. Don't forget you're all coming to Pegasus House for a week during the Holiday, Oh yeah, remind Leonie that she's welcome too, please." Said Toby, reminding Keiron about Leonie,

"Yeah, will do Mate, don't worry, we'll be there." Replied Keiron.

"I'll be there too." Said 'Bella.

"Yes, there will be a chance for the whole Cygnet Committee to be together for the first time, including Leonie." Said Polly.

Then it was time for them to look out into the Car Park as first a Silver BMW arrived, with Bill and Daisy in the front seats and a smiling Leonie in the back.

"Hi Guys, great to see you, sorry to hear about your ankle, must have been painful." Said Leonie all smiles.

"Yes it was for a while, but recovering quite well so far." Replied Polly.

"'Bella, meet my little Sister, Leonie, our other Cygnet member," Said Keiron.

"Hi Leonie, I've heard a lot about you and look forwards to you joining us next term." Replied 'Bella.

"Well hopefully you will see us for a week in the Summer, Dad said that if our friends wished to visit more often, then he would put a bunk bed in my room to make Room for 'Bella to sleep upon." Said Leonie excitedly.

"That's great news, so we can see more of each other over the Summer." Said Polly.

"Yes, and I can get to know Leonie." Said 'Bella.

While they were talking, Keiron had been loading his Ruc-Sac and suitcase, with Tom's, into the boot of Bill's car. Then it was time to split up. Keiron joined Leonie and Tom in the back seats of the BMW, while Bill got back into the Driver's seat. Daisy said goodbye from the front passenger seat through the wound down window, Keiron and Leonie called goodbye from the rear seats as the engine roared into life, and Bill pulled away and turned down the driveway out of Toadford School.

Then there was the toot of a car horn as Mr Snoop pulled up.

"Well, I'll see you Guys soon, Text me with the details please." Said 'Bella, who then jumped into passenger seat of her Dad's car, waved out of the window and was whisked away along the Driveway. Polly saw her Dad's car a short distance away and then hugged Toby.

"Let me know when the visits will be and the week at your house and Keiron's, OK, see you Toby." Said Polly, with a tear in her eyes. She kissed Toby upon his right cheek, then walked swiftly over to her Father's car, got into his front Passenger seat and waved to Toby as they drove off along the Driveway. Toby seemed to be in a dream as the Landrover drew up beside him and tooted it's horn.

"Wow Dad, you made me jump!" Said Toby, then he took focus and noticed the front passenger seat.

"Mom! Wow! They let you come home!" Cried Toby, excitedly.

"Yes Dear, but still have a little way to go." Said Rachel. Toby put his Ruc-sac and suitcase into the boot of the car and hopped into the back seat. As they drove away along the Driveway, he reflected upon his first year at Toadford School, the new place he called home, the new place that he belonged.

To Be Continued

Ended December 2015

Copyright R L Sherlock 2015

Made in the USA
Columbia, SC
18 June 2018